NEW YORK REVIEW BOOKS
CLASSICS

KAPO

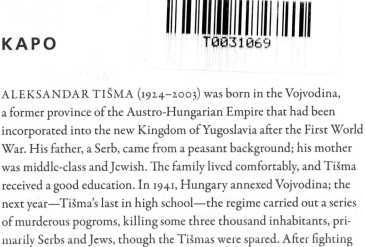

T0031069

ALEKSANDAR TIŠMA (1924–2003) was born in the Vojvodina,
a former province of the Austro-Hungarian Empire that had been
incorporated into the new Kingdom of Yugoslavia after the First World
War. His father, a Serb, came from a peasant background; his mother
was middle-class and Jewish. The family lived comfortably, and Tišma
received a good education. In 1941, Hungary annexed Vojvodina; the
next year—Tišma's last in high school—the regime carried out a series
of murderous pogroms, killing some three thousand inhabitants, pri-
marily Serbs and Jews, though the Tišmas were spared. After fighting
for the Yugoslav partisans, Tišma studied philosophy at Belgrade
University and went into journalism, and in 1949 joined the editorial
staff of a publishing house, where he remained until his retirement in
1980. He published his first story, "Ibika's House," in 1951; it was followed
by the novels *Guilt* and *In Search of the Dark Girl* and a collection of
stories, *Violence*. In the 1970s and '80s, he gained international recognition
with the publication of his Novi Sad trilogy: *The Book of Blam* (1971),
about a survivor of the Hungarian occupation of Novi Sad; *The Use of
Man* (1976), which follows a group of friends through the Second World
War and after; and *Kapo* (1987), the story of a Jew raised as a Catholic
who becomes a guard in a German concentration camp. Tišma moved
to France after the outbreak of war and collapse of Yugoslavia in the early
1990s, but in 1995 he returned to Novi Sad, where he spent his last years.

RICHARD WILLIAMS's translations from the Serbo-Croatian
include the Siniša Kovačević play *Novo je doba* (*Times Have Changed*).

DAVID RIEFF is the author of ten books, including *The Exile: Cuba in
the Heart of Miami*; *Slaughterhouse: Bosnia and the Failure of the West*;
A Bed for the Night: Humanitarianism in Crisis; *Swimming in a Sea of
Death: A Son's Memoir*; and, most recently, *In Praise of Forgetting:
Historical Memory and Its Ironies*.

OTHER BOOKS BY ALEKSANDAR TIŠMA
PUBLISHED BY NEW YORK REVIEW BOOKS

The Book of Blam
Translated by Michael Henry Heim
Introduction by Charles Simic

The Use of Man
Translated by Bernard Johnson
Introduction by Claire Messud

KAPO

ALEKSANDAR TIŠMA

Translated from the Serbo-Croatian by
RICHARD WILLIAMS

Afterword by
DAVID RIEFF

NEW YORK REVIEW BOOKS

New York

THIS IS A NEW YORK REVIEW BOOK
PUBLISHED BY THE NEW YORK REVIEW OF BOOKS
435 Hudson Street, New York, NY 10014
www.nyrb.com

Reprinted by special arrangement with Houghton Mifflin Harcourt Publishing
Company.

The translation of this book was supported
by the Ministry of Culture and Media of
the Republic of Serbia.

Republic of Serbia
Ministry of Culture and Media

Library of Congress Cataloging-in-Publication Data
Names: Tišma, Aleksandar, 1924–2003, author. | Rieff, David, writer of
    afterword. | Williams, Richard, translator.
Title: Kapo / by Aleksandar Tišma ; translated by Richard Williams, afterword
    by David Rieff.
Other titles: Kapo. English
Description: New York : New York Review Books, [2021] | Series: New York
    Review Books classics | Copyright © 1987 by Aleksandar Tišma, translation
    copyright © 1993 by Richard Williams.
Identifiers: LCCN 2019039526 (print) | LCCN 2019039527 (ebook) | ISBN
    9781681374390 (paperback) | ISBN 9781681374406 (ebook)
Subjects: LCSH: World War, 1939–1945—Jews—Fiction. | World War,
    1939–1945—Yugoslavia—Fiction. | Fear—Fiction.
Classification: LCC PG1419.3.I8 K3613 2020 (print) | LCC PG1419.3.I8
    (ebook) | DDC 891.8/2354—dc23
LC record available at https://lccn.loc.gov/2019039526
LC ebook record available at https://lccn.loc.gov/2019039527

ISBN 978-1-68137-439-0
Available as an electronic book; ISBN 978-1-68137-440-6

Printed in the United States of America on acid-free paper.
10 9 8 7 6 5 4 3 2 1

CONTENTS

He had found Helena Lifka. He had recognized her, was sure it was she—unless a whole chain of illusions had conspired to deceive him.

Her emergence from the doorway by the metal plate with the number 16, the number he had been given with the name of the street, the name he had seen at the street corner. Then her appearance, that slight stoop he knew so well, timidity in the hunched shoulders and bowed head, and her legs, those stout, strong columns, the fleshy calves, the knees bent softly inward. The body was changed, a ruin—after all, decades had passed—but not so changed that it didn't bring back memories.

But these thoughts did not form until he was no longer looking at her, not having dared to step into the house after her. While he had her there before him, his mind, everything in him rebelled against recognition, crying out, "It isn't, it can't be!" Perhaps because he could not accept that she had become an old woman, or because he was afraid of what recognition would force him to do: follow her into the house, introduce himself, subject himself to her horror, hatred, even revenge. Revenge least of all, really; he no longer feared her. On the contrary, he wanted to lay himself open before her, to receive her forgiveness.

No, it would be hatred, terror, she would shrink from him as if he were a loathsome thing, a toad or a snake, a creature buried in the unconscious and in dreams, that would, if it surfaced, make her recoil and scream.

He himself had had a similar feeling when he saw her framed in the high, narrow doorway, descending the two steps to the sidewalk. Holding onto the wall as she took the first step, then removing her hand but keeping it raised at chest level, a hand enclosed in a gray cotton glove; raised not to support herself— there was no need of that once she had reached the second step, because the wall was past her shoulder now—but out of habit, as if ready to clutch some kind of support, a proper iron railing, which these stairs did not have. Or perhaps it wasn't out of habit, but in preparation for the future, when such a railing would be indispensable.

He sensed fear in the way she moved; not only in the hand, which remained raised, but in those awkward legs that stepped down without assurance, as if hobbled, bound with cords above the touching knees. Her coat, also gray but lighter than the gloves, bunched above the thighs. A simple coat, cut like a man's, with two rows of buttons and a narrow, snug collar, and it seemed to him that the folds in it were labored and stiff, too, as if they covered ropes.

Against his will, his eyes were drawn to that hinge of the body which is the most important in walking, that center also of femaleness—or, in the male, of maleness—and he thought that if it wasn't ropes (it couldn't be ropes), then it was her underpants, the thick, bulky underpants of an old woman, that were binding her tightly there, piled one atop the other as protection against the cold, though it was only October, because she didn't care how they looked, she wasn't going to show herself to anyone in her underpants. She wasn't, because, beneath them, wrapped in them, there was only old flesh: an old slack belly, graying hairs sparse from rubbing, old flabby pudenda that hung between jellylike thighs which rubbed as she walked, producing moist sores.

Looking at her loins, he felt his own to be old and flabby, so that his hunt for her, his spying from a doorway across the way, seemed indecent, as if the purpose were for these two loins, old as they were, again to come together.

The thought of such a coupling horrified him, made him want to thrust Helena Lifka away, far away, just as horror, an inner shriek of rejection, had been his first impulse when he found her trail again in the truck to Banja Luka, in the newspaper which lay folded under the bench in front of him, discarded, belonging to no one, because the bench was for the moment vacant, empty of passengers.

Yet he had not picked up the paper at first, as if he knew that he shouldn't, that something in it was waiting to attack and bite. Or perhaps he hesitated because the paper wasn't his and he would be violating the law of ownership, but when finally, moved by boredom, he took it from the dirty floor and unfolded it, he read—even before realizing that it was useless to him, printed in a language he didn't understand—the word Szabadka. That was the first word his eyes fell on. He felt revulsion and pain, because it immediately summoned the name Helena Lifka, and Jüdin, which had been written on the same line as that name, along with the number 1925, in the register of new arrivals at Auschwitz.

A foreign newspaper was a natural place for this remembered word, Helena Lifka's birthplace, which had led him to conclude, with relief, when he first saw it in the camp, that the woman came from a country other than his own, probably Hungary, so at least as far as nationality was concerned she was unrelated to him. But now, in the truck, he wondered how a foreign paper found its way to the road between Pobrdje and Banja Luka, where foreigners hardly ever strayed.

It was as if the paper had been planted there, to remind, to threaten. But who would threaten? As the truck bounced along, raising dust, he glanced at the other passengers—two peasant women on the bench behind him, engrossed in a conversation that was raised to a shout because of the noise, and a number of government employees scattered dejectedly in the corners— searching for a possible culprit.

He concluded that it could have been someone else, a third party who on the seat in front of him had dropped the paper under the bench, as bait, and then left. Except he remembered now that when he boarded the truck at Pobrdje, where he had been surveying fields, the paper was already under the bench, and the bench, the entire center of the vehicle, had been empty —which was why he sat there.

He folded the newspaper as he found it, then dropped it back under the seat in front of him as inconspicuously as possible, pushing it farther forward with the tip of his shoe: This isn't mine. But in his thoughts he was unable to ignore it. He asked himself if he had read Szabadka correctly. Perhaps it was another word, one similar to the word he remembered, the same letters but in a different combination. Should he bend over again and pick up the paper, to make sure? He no longer had the courage to do so.

The truck jolted along, making stops. The two women got off, and a new passenger got on, a musician with a tamburitza. The dust from the road poured in under the canvas and settled on the floor and benches and in the lungs, but he kept looking, out of the corner of his eye, at the paper that lay under the seat in front of him, occasionally shifting left, right: there was a danger it might stray into the corner where a bent-over man sat with a hat on his head and a briefcase under his arm, and that he might pick it up and take it with him, to use as wrapping paper if nothing else.

Then he would never find out if he had actually read Helena Lifka's birthplace, nor would he ever know in what kind of paper it had been printed, because in his excitement he had failed to note the name of the paper. So even if he found the courage to make inquiries about Szabadka, in some library in Banja Luka or even in Sarajevo, he would have nothing to go on.

When they arrived at the bus station in Banja Luka and everyone got up, he got up too, but at the opening in the canvas, he stepped back from the pressing crowd, picked up the paper, and shoved it under his coat. His heart pounded: Had this act exposed him? He cast a furtive glance at his fellow passengers as he elbowed his way toward the opening and waited for someone—the man with the briefcase certainly looked like an informer—to thrust a hand into his coat, pull out the paper, and strike him across his face and glasses with it, shouting, "Here's one!"

But nothing of the sort happened. The man with the briefcase got off without looking back, and after him the musician, tamburitza clutched to his chest. Lamian was last, but then it occurred to him that the trap might be set by two: the man with the briefcase would report that Lamian had picked up the paper, and someone else—in uniform perhaps, since it would no longer be necessary to conceal anything—would wait for him right at the opening in the canvas, stand him up straight as he buckled from the jump to the ground, and pull the evidence of guilt from under his coat.

He wanted to put it down again, and looked around for a place, but the driver, who was standing next to the truck, signaled with his hand for him to hurry, so he jumped, clutching his coat just as the tamburitza player had clutched his tamburitza a moment before. Into the dust with a thud, into the small-town bustle outside the station; he straightened his legs, and discovered with relief that the driver's face was no longer turned to him but the ties on the canvas, which he was hastily rethreading through their grommets.

And the uniform? Lamian didn't see a single one, nor did

he see anybody observing him, nearby or from a distance. The square, covered with stalls, counters, and belated shoppers clustered around them, looked as it always did, as if no one was expecting him or lying in wait for him. As if the foreign paper had indeed found its way by chance into the truck that served as a bus to link the remote border villages with Banja Luka. And as if he, Lamian, had by chance sat where some foreigner, perhaps traveling through to the sea, had discarded the paper, had dropped it on the dusty floor.

He went directly home and, locking the door, lowering the blinds, and turning on the lamp, took the paper from beneath his coat and placed it on the table. He unfolded it. Yes, in one of the headlines, the third, halfway down the page, where the bulge of the fold was, Szabadka, in large type on a line with some other words. He tried, with no success, to guess their meaning. Turning the page, he scanned the next sheet spread out before him, looking for the same word, or any word he could understand.

On the third page, he found it again, but not in a headline. It was under a headline, at the beginning of a short news item or report, which began, after the word, with a date written in reverse order: 1947, junius 19. So it was indeed the name of a place, as he had thought, though in the back of his mind, doubt remained, the possibility of a coincidence, for example, what signified a place in the camp register could mean, even though spelled the same, something different in another context: an object, a person's name.

He continued to search for the same word, in the headlines, then lowering his glance to the beginning of each article. He found it seven more times, five of which were on the eighth and last page, where the shortest news items were. From this he concluded that the paper was published in the place that bore that word as its name, or near that place.

He turned back to the front page and started sounding out the huge letters at the top, slanted as if written by hand, and they even had little tails at the end, like those left by the stroke of a pen. The words told him nothing. But directly beneath them he found again, in ordinary type, Szabadka, 1947 junius 20, and then, after a mark which could have only been an equals sign, Subotica, 20. jun 1947. He stared at the words and numbers, at each letter and each number separately, put them together, separated them again, until his eyes blurred.

To clear his eyes, he looked up at the wall, which was cut in half with a shadow cast by the lampshade, and it was as if in that border between light and shadow, he read what now dawned on him: that Szabadka was Subotica in Hungarian, and therefore the paper he had found on the floor of the truck, even though in Hungarian, was printed in Yugoslavia, in the city of Subotica, whose Hungarian name he hadn't known. He had thought that Helena Lifka was a foreigner, at least in her citizenship, a person from beyond a border that he had considered his, though borders had been erased by the war. But in reality she had come if not at that time then certainly now, from within the same borders as he, and possibly lived within those borders, assuming, that is, she still lived.

THE DISCOVERY HAD BEEN SECONDARY, INCIDENTAL, JUST as his relief had been—a relief in reality unfounded—when he read Szabadka in the register of new arrivals.

He had gone to the records office on that autumn morning in 1944 not to establish what country the girl was from but to learn if she was really a Jew, as Lina, the Slovak Blockelteste, had claimed, a claim that had left him astonished and desperate.

With a forced smile, he had got rid of Lina, stuffing into her hands the package of silk underwear he had ready for her. Quivering with impatience, he waited for Riegler to appear so he could ask him for a pass to the office, on the excuse that his count of the Arbeitskommando did not tally. He started toward his destination, stumbled down the rain-soaked path, eyes fixed on the muddy ground in front of his feet, as if it might open up and swallow him, and so almost collided with Scharführer Lang, who gave him such a powerful shove in the ribs that he nearly fell. Then he had to snatch off his cap and report, and suffer a pair of slaps for his inattention, which would have cost him his life if he hadn't had a pass.

The collision seemed such a bad omen, he thought of abandoning his errand. But he knew that if his doubts were not resolved, they would give him no peace, so he continued toward the office, making an effort to walk with more composure.

He went inside, took off his cap, and blurrily established that there were no Germans in the room. Looking for a familiar face among the prisoners bent over their desks, he saw Jelinek, for whom he had wangled a wool vest and some mange medicine from the Kanada supply depot. He went up to him, clicking his heels and reporting loudly, for all to hear, that he had been sent by Kommandoführer Riegler for information about prisoner No. 13698. At the same time, he slipped a cigarette from the split left sleeve of his tunic and laid it among the papers on the desk, so that only Jelinek saw, and Jelinek dropped what he was doing and turned to the tall ledgers on the shelves behind his desk.

Together they found the volume with 11000–16000 on its spine label. Transferring it to the desk, they opened it and began paging through it, reading the numbers under their breath. As they paged, Jelinek felt among his papers for the cigarette, then dropped it into the pocket of his tunic. Finally they found a page with a number at the top that began with 13, and near the bottom, the number 13698, and to the right of that: Helena Lifka, Jüdin, Szabadka 1925.

Lina's claim was thus verified and Lamian's desperation justified, but the name of the place the prisoner came from, by its very unfamiliarity, wove a touch of relief into his distress. Relief, because it lessened the responsibility, it removed the threat of having to confront his victim someday, should both of them survive the camp.

He crossed out the number on his slip of paper, where it was written beside another number, and he forbade Lina to send her to him again, and not just her, but any Jew. With a laugh, Lina promised not to, obviously thinking that he'd been infected with the racial arrogance of the Germans. At the same time, he took care of prisoner No. 13698, from a distance. He asked Lina about her, as if to show there were no hard feelings, or as if to make a joke of the whole thing. Through bribes of a sweater and warm socks, he arranged that the prisoner he had banished from his love life be given a double ration of bread, and before the camp was evacuated, he got Jelinek to move her, in exchange for cigarettes, to a light-duty block.

Only then did he breathe easy, believing he had atoned for his transgression by increasing her chances of staying alive. But he refrained from finding out whether or not she had taken advantage of the opportunity. Without admitting this even to himself, he hoped she hadn't, he hoped she was dead. He never thought that someday he might want to find her. Instead, he drove her from his mind, as he did the other victims of his crimes, crimes committed under duress, crimes committed to ensure his own survival, for which the abuse of his power as Kapo was every bit as necessary as food and clothing.

But the deciphering of Szabadka as another name for the Yugoslav town of Subotica, a town in Upper Bačka, stripped him of his security. It showed him that he had made a mistake, not only in forcing Helena Lifka onto his naked lap and into his bunk, but also in thinking that he could forget about her. She was not a foreigner, she was a Yugoslav Jew, as he was; she had been taken captive in the same German advance, and had returned, if she returned, to the same homeland, the same country. And so she might appear at any time, either looking for him because she learned he was a Yugoslav, or else coming across him by chance while traveling through Banja Luka, on some business or family matter—by chance, like the Hungarian newspaper that carried, at the top of its front page, the Hungarian name for Subotica.

It frightened him, the thought of coming face to face with her, of her reproaches, accusations. He wanted to flee, as if she were already looking for him, as if she had been the traveler who left the Hungarian paper under the bench—not at all by chance, but to warn him of her presence, to torment him before she took her revenge, tomorrow, when her presence would become public condemnation and public shame.

Blinds lowered, he sat sweating in his stuffy mousehole of a rented room, with its creaky, worm-eaten furniture provided by the landlord. It seemed to him, as the warm summer afternoon wore on, that the pursuers Helena Lifka had assembled in the town were closing in, because she had lived here all along, and he never knew it. She had taken her denunciation to the authorities, to the police, the detectives of the security police, the members of the Veterans' Association, National Front, and Party committees, and to all the neighbors, too, going to them when the offices were closed, telling them the true identity of Vilko Lamian, the man they knew as a withdrawn, taciturn lodger in their street, a conscientious employee of the land registry, and a solitary walker on his way to a Sunday or holiday outing in the surrounding hills. She would reveal the beast he was: fiend, torturer, one of Hitler's Kapos, archenemy and archtraitor hidden in his lair in the guise of a meek citizen who kept to himself.

They're coming to spit on me, seize me, hurl me to the ground and trample on me, beat me until I'm half dead, then they'll take off my clothes and wash me, and nurse me back to health so I can be dragged before the court, before the people, exhibited as a monster. Photographed, interrogated, my depravity described in detail, an eternal blot on my race and tribe, my name a symbol of evil until some greater criminal is discovered.

He felt the tightening circle on the skin of his face and hands. The air itself was thick with his capture. They were coming closer; he heard the scrape of their shoes, the rasp of their breath—even as he told himself it was only the sound of evening strollers in the streets, the sound of the landlord Čabrinović and his ailing wife as they sighed and moved about, filling the empty hours with complaints about the neighbors and about him, their tenant, or discussing the next day's marketing list.

Treacherous reassurances; the enemy trying to keep him in this trap. Carefully, to make no noise, he stood up and tiptoed from behind the table to the door and turned out the light. He stood there, deciding how to greet them if they burst in. Grab the nearest chair and flail away until they overpowered him, or thwart them by cutting his own throat? In the drawer he had a pocketknife, one of the first things he had bought in Banja Luka, on impulse, seeing it displayed with other wares at a stall he had passed while shopping for vegetables. Ever since he threw away the Kapo's knife concealed along his calf, he had felt unprotected.

He went to the table, slowly, silently opened the drawer, and felt for the knife, took it out and opened it. They won't take me alive, not again. They'll find the corpse sprawled on the floor, and Helena Lifka's eyes will widen in horror at the spreading pool of blood around me.

He relished the scene: his body on the floor, face up, with a gaping wound in the chest, and his pursuers one after the other edging their way into the circle around him. And she the behind-the-scenes instigator, pushing her way through, putting her tender woman's hand to his chest, pressing in unintentional pantomime of the blade as it entered the flesh between his ribs; she would be speechless, deprived of her revenge, prevented from bringing him to shame.

Hatred welled within him, and he almost wished that this would come to pass. But at the same time he knew that it was mostly play-acting; the woman didn't know his real name or that he was still alive, and it was unlikely that she would find him in this small town in the heart of Bosnia, and more unlikely for her to put a folded newspaper under the bench in front of him, as a warning.

He went over the events of the past few days: all of his movements, to the office and back, the behavior of his colleagues and clients, his trip to Podbrdje, the conversations, the measurements taken and recorded. He could find nothing suspicious in any gesture or glance. He had learned how to look into people's minds, from the littlest signals they gave without knowing it; that was why he had survived.

Again he tiptoed to the door and listened. He could hear a soft, murmuring conversation. Čabrinović and his wife were in the kitchen across the hall, eating their supper early to leave the room free for him. He gripped the knife and cautiously turned the door handle, still ready to plunge the blade into his chest if people rushed in. No one did. He opened the door a crack, peered into the hallway, which was half-lit by the frosted glass of the kitchen door. He looked down the hall, making sure it was empty before he put his hand into his pocket, open knife laid along the palm, and tiptoed out.

In the hallway now, he could hear their conversation—"and tie it with rope" and "you push it through from below." Comprehensible phrases, but strange, of obscure origin, as in the barracks cubicle, when you lifted your head in the middle of the night and the moans and sobs came to you in waves. He sneaked to the front door at the end of the hallway, crouched low, slowly slipped the keyhole cover to one side, and put his eye to the opening. A patch of courtyard in semidarkness, no human shadow anywhere, no elbow or knee. But he still didn't dare go outside. He stood up, went back to the other end of the hallway, the door of the woodshed. Opened it, went inside and down the steps, stopped to listen, then squeezed between the rows of stacked logs, breathing their damp smell of Jasenovac and the forest before going to the window and through its dusty panes observing the rear courtyard.

Slowly, without letting go of the knife, he turned the rusty window lock, opened the window, again listened, then bent down and felt with his free hand for one stump, then another, stacking them, stepping on the top one and climbing onto the sill. Gripping the knife tightly, he dropped into the courtyard, crouched beneath the window, eyes straining to penetrate the darkness.

Bushes; two walnut trees on the left; a path overgrown with weeds. Were they hiding there? He squatted patiently, ears pricked, watching, determined to be more vigilant than any attacker. Only when his knees began to ache (the knees were always the first), did he straighten up.

Carefully he put the knife in his pocket and approached the courtyard wall. Reaching up, he hoisted himself to the top and looked over. The narrow street beyond the wall was deserted, enveloping darkness, lit only by a few kitchen windows in neighboring houses, where people were having supper. Lowering himself to the ground again, he went along the wall to the gate, opened it, walked out. He turned left. The street took him to a small square whose name he didn't know. Here children were playing with hoops taken from a barrel, and several people were passing through on the opposite side, disappearing into a street.

Lamian didn't look at them; by their step he knew they weren't after anyone; they were preoccupied with themselves, harmless. He scanned the windows and doorways to see if someone was hiding there, if he would have to take his hand from his pocket and stab first him, then himself.

From the square he went into the street which the people had entered a moment ago, then turned left, a right angle, to his own street, Teodor Kursula, and his gate. He looked around unobtrusively as he opened it, then went into the courtyard and from there into the hallway. As he reached the door to his room, he heard the kitchen door open and turned to see Čabrinović looking at him, stooped, cap on his head. "Weren't you in, Mr. Lamian?" "I went out for a while, Mr. Čabrinović," Lamian answered casually. "I'll eat now."

He went into his room, turned on the light, took out the knife, closed it, put it back in the drawer, shut the drawer. He waited for Čabrinović and his wife to go shuffling down the hall to their bedroom, then went back down the hallway to the woodshed, down the steps, closed the window, returned to his room.

He took a deep breath, then went to the table and again studied the Hungarian newspaper. Reading the headlines, the columns of fine type that descended to the bottom of the page, he guessed at their meaning, because there was an occasional technical word, international, like "traktorok" for tractor, which somehow gave the gist, though he understood virtually nothing.

He grew tired, then hungry. His agreement with the Čabrinovićes was that he could cook his supper after they went to bed. In the kitchen, he opened the window a crack to let out the smoke from their cooking. Putting a piece of wood on the still-smoldering fire, he took some potatoes from the bin in the pantry, where they were kept with the greens. He cleaned eight large potatoes, dropped them into a pot, covered them with water, and set them on the stove. He sat smoking while he waited. Still unaccustomed to being full, he found every meal a pleasure.

There was no need to improve it with spices, dignify it with plates and cutlery; it was the food itself that mattered, the amount, not the taste, the fact that he could eat as much as he wanted. That was why he preferred to eat alone, and only one hot dish. At midday after work, he couldn't, his hunger didn't allow him to wait for the Čabrinovićes to vacate the kitchen, so he would buy something cold on the way home from work and eat it in his room. But at supper, he let himself go.

As he ate, he thought seriously about running away, preferably now, tonight. Cram his few belongings into a suitcase and leave without a word, perhaps a brief note on the kitchen table, with the rent for the rest of the month.

He'd go straight to the station and get on the first train that pulled out, regardless of its destination. It soothed him to picture the wood-paneled partitions of the coach, enclosing him, separating him from the outside world. To sit there alone, or with a few drowsy travelers, feeling, beyond those strong partitions, the cold created by the movement of the train, but he would be insulated from the cold, and protected from any hand poised to shove its way in and grab him.

I have an identity card in my pocket, not a number tattooed on my forearm, not a red triangle on my tunic and trouser leg, not a pass from Riegler that I must return, but a proper, permanent identity card issued by the police in Banja Luka and bearing the name of Vilko Lamian, born in Bjelovar, nationality Yugoslav, citizenship Yugoslav, civil servant by profession, entitled to disembark from a train anywhere in the country and present himself to the authorities, rent a room, look for work.

Certain documents, yes, would have to be enclosed in his application for employment, but these documents were in a filing cabinet in the Banja Luka City Hall, and copies could be provided at the request of the institution or firm wishing to hire him. He imagined the letter, with its official letterhead, number, date, typed out by some obedient, uninterested typist, not a prisoner, not afraid, but trusting, letting him dictate the official phrases himself, which request "the file of Comrade Vilko Lamian, for the personnel records of our organization," and add, on a separate sheet, a convincing explanation, preferably—indeed, necessarily—in his own hand, to the effect, for example, that the unexpected illness of a close relative forced him to depart without saying good-bye, hence this new job in this new location.

Which would occasion surprise, suspicion, he thought bitterly as he shoved a still-scalding potato into his mouth with his fingers. The resulting burn made his eyes well up with tears. No, that was no good; he had to prepare his departure gradually, planting the reasons, reasons that would sound natural to everyone, so that when he finally left, it would be understood and accepted by all who knew him.

Through the night, he tried to think of the most convincing story, came up with several, with excitement, only to reject them in disappointment. Finally, just before dawn, when he was jumpy with fatigue, he decided on housing problems. The intense desire to have his own apartment, which he hadn't been able to obtain in Banja Luka, having to settle for a furnished room in the house of Čabrinović, a pre-war merchant. True, he had not applied for an independent apartment, as the other newly arrived officials had done, but this reticence would be explained in retrospect, he hoped, by his shyness, familiar enough to everyone by now. There was no contradiction: a shy person, too, could be dissatisfied. With this thought, he fell asleep.

When the alarm clock jolted him awake in the morning, he was dazed and stunned, as during those too-early reveilles in the camp. He jumped out of bed, shoulders hunched and head drawn in, in anticipation of blows. Then he realized where he was and that he was in no immediate danger, that a hearty breakfast awaited him before he set out to the office, where he had a desk and chair and could stretch out his legs or tuck them in as he pleased. Only then did he remember last night's decision, and fell into self-pitying despair. Go away—but where? To which city, which village? Across which border?

How disconcertingly random and arbitrary the choice would be, and he understood that this arbitrariness had crept in only since his freedom, because as long as he was a prisoner and dreamed of escape, he always set some known place as his final goal and haven. The Radaković farm in Prnjavor outside Bjelovar, for example, where after finishing the tenth grade he had been driven by his father in the company car, and where he had entertained himself in the great outdoors with jovial cowherds and stablehands, while his father negotiated with the owner over the repayment of some debt. Or his room at 37 Ilica Street in Zagreb, in the second-floor apartment that belonged to Jančuška, a tailor of women's clothing. He had lived there as a student for two months before moving to 8 Trnska Street and the house of Mrs. Basarabić, a retired teacher. Or the shed in Nevesinje that belonged to Ivanda the railroad switchman, where he had hidden for several nights, a soldier trying to evade capture.

In his thoughts, he had clung to those places, longing for them in all their familiar detail, only to forsake them sadly, one by one, knowing that escape was impossible: he would be caught, beaten, taken to the gallows, and hung on the central parade ground before the ranks of prisoners—as Edeko had been, and Mala, and all the other unsuccessful escapees (they were all unsuccessful). He would be caught long before he had a chance to find out whether those who had once helped him would take him in and hide him.

They probably wouldn't have; it was precisely those people and places that were the least suited for hiding him, because his pursuers, if they hadn't already laid their hands on him in the swamps around Auschwitz, would surely have looked for him among those very people and in those very places.

Now, when he didn't expect pursuit, the old places were no good, because his flight was not from pursuit but from chance, and chance—for the arrival of former prisoner Helena Lifka, the newspaper printed in her city, taken on her trip, and later discarded in the truck, was chance—could intervene anywhere, in any community, large or small, noisy or quiet, on a train or ship, in a theater or at the horse races, in the land registry in Banja Luka, or in any office in any town or any village.

THE BEGINNING OF THIS SECOND LIFE HAD ALSO BEEN marked by chance: that was when he fled during the evacuation of Auschwitz.

Fled in the company of Riegler, his Kommandoführer—Riegler carrying gold, Lamian with only his life, and both with the secret of their alliance. Whether this secret would make them mortal enemies was unknown (he, at least, didn't know) up to the moment they parted. When Riegler came to him in the toolshed that evening after roll call, to tell him a column to Schlossberg was forming in the morning and Riegler would get the two of them into it, this meant either that he wished to save Lamian along with himself, or that he had decided to keep the witness to his plunder in sight, then at some opportune moment eliminate him.

As custodian of the gold, Lamian was no longer needed. Two weeks earlier, in his presence, Riegler had taken the gold bars from their hiding place under the floorboards, examining them one by one in the candlelight. After that, he must have had them with him constantly, sewn into the legs of the boots Lamian had Schmuhle the shoemaker make for him before Schmuhle was killed with phenol. But not all the gold could fit into the boots; the rest was probably fastened around his waist or thighs.

Small and frail as Riegler was, Lamian wanted to seize him by the throat then and there in the abandoned toolshed, tighten his hands and not let go until the burnt-out pipe slipped from the German's cracked lips and the life left his breast. He wanted to split open his head, smash it against the edge of the vise, spill out its corrupt, cunning brain. But Riegler, perhaps himself debating whether or not to eliminate his Kapo here, where the two had concealed their crimes, prudently kept his small wrinkled hand near the holster of his pistol. That precaution aside, Lamian knew that even if he succeeded in overpowering Riegler, without him he would never leave the camp alive; Riegler's Kapo would be the first person the SS would hold responsible for the disappearance of the Arbeitsführer.

When Riegler awakened him—this was the third evening Lamian had sneaked away after roll call to sleep in the toolshed instead of the barracks, on Riegler's advice—he had been surprised by the news but pretended to be groggy, merely nodded in agreement, obedient as always.

As soon as Riegler left, locking the door behind him, Lamian began to get ready. He unscrewed the vise from the workbench, put it on the floor, moved the bench aside, lifted the floorboard, his hiding place—near Riegler's, which was empty now—and took out the clothing he had piled there. Underpants, socks, sweaters, assorted rags. He put the workbench back in place, remounted the vise. Pulled a nail drawer out of the cabinet, and from the hole in the wall behind it took two tins of goulash and two half loaves of bread, all his remaining food, and placed them on the bench. Finally, he pried his knife out of one of the joints in the plank wall behind the anvil—it had been made for him by the inmate Grigorije—and slipped it down his left calf, beneath the felt legging. He opened one tin of goulash, ate it without bread, then stripped and put on all the clothing, stuffing the rags into his tunic along with the remaining tin and the two half loaves of bread. He lay down, waited.

Around him, the camp with its crisscrossing sounds: commands muffled by distance, guards reporting from the watchtowers, the patter of rats in search of refuse and corpses, and the muted raling of the sick, the starved, the sleeping, the dying.

It all merged into one sound which, like the sough of the wind, his ears no longer registered.

Sometimes a shot could be heard, a cry, or a groan cut off. More frequent these last few nights, as the SS men and the stronger inmates killed those who had hidden something from them or those who knew too much. They—someone among them certainly—would have killed him, if Riegler hadn't protected him.

He wondered: Was Riegler really protecting him? Perhaps an executioner had already been dispatched, and any minute now he would unlock the toolshed door with a key obtained from Riegler, and pounce on him and plunge a knife into his chest, making Lamian groan like the one a moment ago. No, Lamian knew that Riegler was too afraid of the final words that would be uttered with the groan, words about gold. So he felt safe, at least until dawn.

It was still dark when the gong sounded. He got up, waited, listened to the commands and the barking and the shuffling of prisoners roused from their bunks. The scrape of a key. But Riegler, or whoever had unlocked the door, did not come in, so for an instant he again thought he would be attacked. He reached for his Kapo's staff, which always rested by the door. But when he moved aside a rag between two slats of the shutter and looked out, in the beam of the searchlight he recognized Riegler, knapsack on his back and wearing a short fur coat he'd never seen before.

Lamian opened the door and went out, keeping the staff down, beside his leg, but Riegler motioned him to leave it. Lamian realized then that he was no longer a Kapo. He was not even the number on his forearm, he was only a piece of flesh being moved along, to be divided and scattered on the roads until there was nothing left.

He tossed away the staff. Riegler locked the door to the

toolshed—as if it would ever be of use to him or anyone else—then shoved him into the column. Lamian found himself surrounded by gaunt faces wrapped in rags, mouths whose breath came out in sputters. He recognized no one, so he ripped the Kapo's insignia from his tunic, threw it in the snow, and stepped on it. They straightened the ranks, the SS men running up and down, but there was no beating. Riegler went to the head of the column near the main gate, where no doubt he had been assigned a place.

When they started, someone at the gate threw a switch, and the entire camp was plunged into darkness. Frost was setting in, and the column stepped briskly, willingly, but Lamian knew it hadn't the strength for a long march and would soon give out. He was right. As day began to break, the ranks slackened, people around him stumbled, and the guards unslung their rifles, to prod the marchers on with the butts. In the rear, the first shots were heard.

Lamian stuck close to the man in front of him, broke into a trot whenever they were ordered to hurry. He saw Riegler again standing at a crossroads where the column turned right along a sunny hillside. He lowered his head so Riegler wouldn't recognize him, but wasn't sure he succeeded.

They didn't stop until evening, when the guards let them lie down in a snow-covered soccer field. He covered his head with the rags he pulled from his tunic, ate one of the breads, then surreptitiously took his knife from under his trousers and opened the last tin of goulash. After he had eaten, he put snow in his mouth, let it melt, swallowed it.

For several hours he lay huddled and blowing into his collar, losing himself from time to time in half dreams. It was still dark when they were ordered to get up and continue the march. Now the ones who by sheer force of will had refused to let themselves fall behind began to drop; they simply sank under the column, into the fog of the road. They had to be stepped around, stepped over, and the shots that then rang out ended all thought of the bodies and directed attention to those still upright.

Daylight came, and it began to snow. The wind blew the flakes into wispy swirls, then died down, and was followed by a transparent, icy emptiness. Mechanically Lamian moved his feet forward, back. Hunger overcame him. He reached into his tunic for the remaining half loaf of bread, ate it in great greedy bites. He kept on walking and breathing with increasing effort, as if he were floating painfully, or were part of some feverish dream, in this column that wavered eerily, people falling less noticeably and the shots in the rear and on the sides less audible though more frequent.

It seemed inconceivable that they wouldn't be given a rest, but they weren't. Everyone stumbled now, Lamian too. Even the Germans stumbled, their caps pulled down over their ears and covered with cobwebs of frost. Not until late in the evening did the soldiers turn them into a woods near the road, crowding them together, posting guards all around.

Riegler was nowhere to be seen; he wasn't among those giving orders or those carrying them out. Lamian, concluding he must have run off with all his gold, made up his mind that he too would escape that night. He watched the sentries as they paced and beat their arms because of the cold, letting their rifles dangle on their chests or propping them against tree trunks. He waited for them to weaken and yield to sleep. Sometimes one did, head dropping, but the others rattled their rifles in warning, and Lamian knew they would be fully alert at the first suspicious movement.

He crawled to the edge of the group, careful to keep trees between him and the soldiers, but when he reached the first tree beyond the ring of guards and was thinking of running for it, a soldier jumped out and pointed his rifle at him. "Where are you going, swine?" the soldier yelled, jabbing him in the neck with the muzzle of the gun. Lamian fell on his side, but managed to shout, "I have to shit!" The suddenness of his cry no doubt prevented the soldier from putting a bullet in him.

As soon as Lamian saw him hesitate, he dropped his trousers and squatted. The soldier turned away in anger and disgust, but Lamian knew the man's vigilance would redouble now. He pulled up his trousers, returned on all fours to the huddle of prisoners, but this time moved closer to the road, where he assumed the ring of guards ended.

He pretended to sleep, but kept an eye on the soldier, who watched him for a long time making sure he was lying quietly; finally the soldier went back behind the same tree. When the guards were relieved by a dozen soldiers from the road, Lamian took advantage of the lapse in attention caused by their brief exchange of words—complaints of hunger and cold—to crawl to his earlier position and again drop his trousers and squat. Then with crouching half steps he slowly made his way to the tree and shuffled around it on his heels until he was hidden by it. He heard the steps of the guard who had replaced the first one, saw his hand appear from the other side, rest on the tree, remain there. Lamian didn't move, face pressed against the trunk, which carried every sound the guard made as he shifted from foot to foot, cleared his throat, grunted, or coughed.

Suddenly Lamian heard a commotion in the huddle of prisoners and a few cries a short distance away, on the road. Clutching his trousers, he rolled deeper into the woods, in a direction parallel to the road. Someone yelled behind him, there was a shot, but Lamian continued rolling and crawling deeper into the woods. He emerged in a clearing, stood up, buttoned his trousers, and began to go around the clearing, when he came upon Riegler.

That is, Riegler jumped him. Lamian caught the movement of an object swinging at him and without thinking ducked and raised an arm to block it. Something hard as iron hit his thumb, but he seized it, gritting his teeth not to scream, and threw himself forward—onto something living, something human. Thrusting out his free hand, he felt a narrowing, a neck, clutched it, then moved his right hand, the one gripping the hard object, to the same spot, and struck with it. Something cracked, something flew, glinting, and fell in front of him. Against the whiteness of the snow he saw a pair of wire-frame glasses and realized that beneath him, suffocating under his weight, was the very person whom two nights earlier he had wanted to strangle: Riegler.

The gold. The gold and his knowledge of it. This unexpected fulfillment of his secret wish seemed too easy, too simple, a blasphemy against fate. To strangle everything by putting an end to Riegler, then face the uncertainty of further flight, was that feasible? Lamian loosened his grip and at the same time, wrenched away the object, which he now saw was a revolver; it fell into the snow. Riegler gasped, "You! I didn't recognize you. Where are my glasses?"

If Riegler had asked for the revolver instead of his glasses, Lamian might have gone on choking him, might have finished him off. As it was, he picked up the glasses—one frame was empty, but the other still gleamed—and set them on Riegler's nose. The revolver, however, he put inside his tunic. Riegler raised an arm, perhaps to grab him, to try to wrest the revolver from him, but no, instead his forefinger stabbed into the white-ness, toward the road.

In place of the earlier noise, silence now came from that direction. And heartbeats, thought Lamian. It was a muffled pounding that traveled through the ground: the echo of distant cannon. Then Riegler's finger shifted to the forest, and the sol-itary circle of the glasses gleamed after it. Lamian understood and slowly rolled off him. Riegler rolled over and, wriggling his bottom, plunged toward the trees on all fours, like a mole. Lamian followed. Making a two-car train, they rapidly moved deeper into the woods. Afraid that soldiers might be resting there, Lamian grabbed Riegler's boot and stopped him. Riegler turned, Lamian shook his head in the direction they were going, but then Riegler shook his, with its single bright lens, and continued on.

They came to a ditch that cut through the forest and led to the road. Riegler scrambled into it, pointed vigorously ahead, and went on. Lamian followed. After a steep rise, the ditch suddenly descended, and they found themselves overlooking a valley in which the rectangles of two houses were outlined against snow. "There," whispered Riegler. "A friend."

Lamian, afraid, shook his head, but Riegler reassured him, spreading his hands, palms blue in the reflected light, up, toward the sky. Lamian believed him even less, and again thought of killing him, strangling him, because he didn't dare shoot him, just as Riegler hadn't dared to shoot before, swinging the revolver instead at Lamian's temple. Lamian could go down to the houses without Riegler, with Riegler's gold as the secret sign, and talk to some man, a Polish peasant he knew nothing about—the idea was so foolhardy, he started laughing to himself, bit back his laughter in hiccups, and shook his head once more: "No, no, you go!" Then shoved Riegler forward in the ditch so that he went flailing downhill and managed to stop only at the very bottom.

Riegler stood up, turned, lifting both arms as if offering a target, as if Lamian would dare shoot in the muffled silence which was all now that concealed them. The revolver suddenly seemed very dangerous to Lamian, proof that he was connected with Riegler's disappearance. So he took it from his tunic and hurled it down the ditch after Riegler. He saw Riegler bend over for it, close his hand around it, pick it up, and stick it in his belt. Then he waved the free hand, and disappeared behind the first house.

IMMEDIATELY HE REGRETTED LETTING HIM LIVE, AND THIS regret would accompany his entire flight, in waves now stronger, now weaker, like the ground he trod.

Take the gold, become fabulously rich. Remain unsuspected of murder, at least outside the boundaries of the camp. Avenge himself, through Riegler, on all Germans and everything Germanic, on the SS, Hitlerites, the Ustaši. Seize this last opportunity to spill, finally, criminal blood, and with it wash away the blood of the innocent. Wipe from the face of the earth the closest witness to his crimes; rid himself of that point on which all his fear was focused, the fear of being denounced and called to answer for his deeds.

His hands itched for the strangling he had not completed and his teeth thirsted for blood as he crawled toward the echoes of cannonfire, avoiding settlements, digging in the frozen earth for potatoes ungathered, roots, anything that could be eaten. At daybreak he regretted not having the gold, when he first dared approach an unknown hamlet and the farmer he found in front of a corncrib drove him away brandishing a pitchfork. With the enticing bait of yellow metal extended on his palm, Lamian was sure he could have got food out of the man, perhaps even shelter. But he blessed his failure to act when he later came across the Russians, who bayed like hounds in the forest as they hunted down the scattered Germans. After nearly killing him, they took him to a transit camp in a factory, where they strip-searched him and barely forgave the knife they found in his legging.

Riegler appeared to him while he lay recuperating in the

straw on the factory floor, a guard pacing back and forth, and whenever he was taken to the office, under guard, to make a statement or expand on a statement he'd made before, he thought he saw the Kommandoführer in a Soviet uniform, in the shadows behind the interrogator, bending down to whisper something in his ear. Or in the interrogator's words Lamian would find information that could only have come from Riegler.

He dreamed of Riegler in the chugging train that took him back to Yugoslavia, Riegler bringing the Russian guard and pointing him out with his finger. "That's him: Furfa, not Lamian, as he claims." In a station along the way, in Czechoslovakia, Lamian asked the reason for the noise and shouting and was told that a Kapo had been recognized and seized in the next car. He was pierced by the conviction that sooner or later, during this endless journey on wobbly rails, the same thing would happen to him. Riegler must be sneaking through the train from car to car, searching, waiting before sticking out his wizened forefinger to denounce.

Even in Yugoslavia there was no relief from Riegler. In Zemun they handed him an identity card with his real name, his undenounced name, and a travel authorization on which he could write his further destination himself and use it without supervision. But instead of going to any place where he was known by that name, Lamian chose for his refuge the town where he had stayed the shortest time, long ago, the most out-of-the-way place of all, surrounded by hills: Banja Luka.

And after he found the Hungarian newspaper, another face appeared beside the wrinkled, snub-nosed face with wire-rimmed glasses: the girlish oval of Helena Lifka. This one came to dominate, taking over the entire stage of his fear, while Riegler sank into the storehouse of retired memories, from then on to be resurrected only when occasion demanded, no longer a threat, merely a curious detail, an old story.

He imagined Riegler living it up in some German city. Not in his village near Munich, of course, where they knew him, but as a stranger among strangers, a newcomer, a rich newcomer if he found the courage and a way to turn his gold bars into money, and the money into a business. Lamian saw him as the owner of some shirt or comb factory, or a wool mill, or perhaps an inn with a few rooms for rent on the second floor and some pretty girls among the help. Riegler as a contractor, gripping the handlebars of a bicycle and puffing on a pipe as he deployed hod carriers and painters on construction sites to repair bomb damage and restore buildings for occupancy. Riegler as a wholesaler, two trucks of his own, traveling here and there with mountains of apples, onions, potatoes. Or leasing slot machines that he emptied every Monday, pouring the change he collected into a capacious sack.

Ridiculous and unimposing though loaded with money, because money couldn't make you taller or fill out your hollow chest or straighten your legs or smooth your complexion; all it did was swell your rump and belly, already protruding, jiggling, and etch greed and sly distrust even more sharply on your face. A small man, Riegler, half a man—even when giving orders to a waitress, unable to keep from squinting at her, front and back, looking for things he hadn't yet exploited. Even drinking a beer at the bar, he measured how much space the foam took up. Half a man while paying, or giving gifts, or lying with Mrs. Riegler in their safe new abode, which he quickly bought for her under an assumed name, or even while inspecting the report cards of his two sons, for whom he had amassed the gold—at least that was the excuse he gave, unable to invent, let alone imagine, any other purpose.

Lamian smiled at him, conversed with him across an unknown distance and in an unknown direction. "Did it pay off, all the conniving, the plundering of the dead, the spoils you clenched in your fist and wouldn't let go of? The cigarettes for medicine, the medicine for sausages, the sausages for boots, the boots for a transfer, the transfer for gold, and gold into bars of gold, gold, gold? How many years have passed—nine? ten?— since the Russians nabbed you at that Polish farmstead, at the bottom of that ditch in the woods, then sent you to Siberia, where you were relieved of your gold-filled boots? Or did the Pole cut your throat that night, when you fell asleep in his bed, and drag you off in secret to a field and bury you boots and all, not knowing about the gold, contenting himself with what he found in your belt?"

For a long time that was the story Lamian preferred, the picture of Riegler packed beneath the clay, where the snow had been cleared and then shoveled back, Riegler buried in his uniform, with belt, revolver, and wallet containing the photographs of wiry, beady-eyed Mrs. Riegler and the two Riegler boys, and buried also with the boots, size 7, so small that the Pole had not kept them to disguise them as civilian boots, knowing he couldn't sell them.

The gold in the ground, hidden for all time, never found by anyone: like its owners, whose jaws it had been pried from before they were burned in the crematorium.

They were in heaven; their gold was in the ground. The separate elements of air and earth. But destined to be rejoined one day, when the ashes floating in the air slowly fell and finally touched the soil, uniting with it after all those years of being borne aloft, seeping now with the raindrops into the narrowest of cracks, down to where Riegler lay in his boots, he already crumbling, flesh and leather alike, but the gold would still be gold, like the pistil of a flower when the petals have fallen off— yellow, gleaming, solid, unbreakable, indissoluble, and united at last with the ashes of those who once wore it.

But no, he would prefer it not to be so: that is he would

prefer for Riegler to be alive. Easier if Lamian knew that both of them had made it out of the swamp of butchery and death. For him to have saved himself and Riegler to have drowned would be too great a favor from chance, too conspicuous, too flaunting a gift of fate. Because they were all dead, every one of them who had seen him clamber over the hill of bones, through the stench of burnt flesh. No, it would be better not to be a unique specimen, an example of a thing that existed nowhere else, a freak.

With Riegler alive, Lamian wouldn't be that freak. And he could testify (impossible to do on his own behalf) that Riegler was no monster, no Satan, but an ordinary person with a single passion, a passion for gold, a passion—and not as deviant as some—which anyone could have without being excluded from the human race. His sin, then, was only human, and if he escaped punishment for that sin, well, such things happened, didn't they? Who knows how many had committed some crime, yet continued to live among people, and lived to die the sort of death that others died! Hundreds of them, now resting peacefully, at one with nature, merged with the earth from which grew the lush, pristine grass and where the roots of lovely, leafy trees drew nourishment, ignorant of the filth that had rotted there. For at a certain point of decay, filth and purity became one, both reduced to their chemical elements, all the peculiarities of their origins stripped away.

With Helena Lifka it was different. Her face, which had appeared beside Riegler's and gradually supplanted it, was the face not of an accomplice but of a victim. It wept. From those large blue eyes, with their widened irises and the whites banished to the corners, eyes open all the way between the broad brown arcs of her brows and the cheekbones of her long smooth white cheeks, flowed copious pear-shaped tears, unstanchable tears, overtaking each other and sliding down her cheeks and across the corners of her mouth, and down her chin and neck, and falling, at equal intervals, one after another, onto her small, languidly upturned breasts. Like the first time she stood before him, naked, she and the doe close beside her. But not, like the other woman, ready to pounce on the food she would receive. Instead, she stood with shoulders hunched, as if fallen in on herself, and with hands crossed over her crotch and pressed between her legs, so that even if she wanted to, she couldn't use a palm or finger to wipe the trickling drops, or smear them over her face.

Probably she didn't think of the tears, too distraught, more distraught than any of the other women prisoners when presented with the temptation of extra food, tasty, abundant food, which ought to have made her grateful and compliant.

She didn't even look at the food, although he was pointing to it with both hands, wanting to pull her, as he had done with the others, from what was hurting her within, pull her from the personal, the individual, and take her by the shortest possible route to the common, the instinctive, which exists in each of us and which ought to be the strongest thing.

"Look what I have for you," he said, using the familiar *du*, following camp custom, but also to emphasize his power of possession and control, even though this was their first meeting; it was only the day before that he had told Blockelteste Lina to send a new prisoner to him in the toolshed, along with the doe. "Look what I have for you," he repeated, pointing to the workbench, which was spread with all the things he'd brought from the SS canteen, and from the sawmill that belonged to Varminsky, a workman from outside, in exchange for lotions and lipstick. "See, bread and butter, ham, a pot of warm milk. Want some?"

She didn't even look at it, didn't even tilt her head so that her eyes, without changing direction, could graze the surface of the workbench. She kept her head low between her shoulders, just as it had been when she came through the hole in the wall and straightened up inside the room, eyes straight ahead, fixed on nothing, wanting not to look but to shed those big tears of hopelessness that slid one after another down her face and body.

AND NOW THAT FACE COULD APPEAR AT ANY MOMENT, demanding vengeance. Not weeping but with an angry fire in those blue eyes, eyes trained on him above the outstretched arm, forefinger first, as stiff as the bayonet on a rifle. A bayonet to stab, to punish the war criminal. He had been prepared for this, at all times, from the moment he began his second, postwar life, but had anticipated a very different kind of accusation: one made by men, who would accuse him of cruelty to the point of murder, of theft to the point of starvation.

The shaming accusation by a woman caught him off guard. It was humiliating. Nor could he confess, defiantly or sorrowfully, justifying what he had done—though he knew there was no justification—by the circumstances that had been thrust upon him. Because the toolshed with the naked bodies of starving, imprisoned women had not been thrust upon him: he had engineered that entirely by himself. So the possibility of being accused by Helena Lifka made him confront, for the first time, his own undeniable guilt. The guilt that was part of his flesh, his blood, part of what made him Vilko Lamian, different in just this way from all other criminals.

The new threat terrified him, it seized him and pushed him toward the abyss from which he had always fled, fled even though he knew, sensed, that at the bottom of that abyss lay the explanation for every evil he had suffered or committed.

The explanation of his differentness, which he had always hidden, been ashamed of, but which had dogged him and created, between him and everything else, uncertainty, unease. People, buildings, streets, shops, marketplaces, the rooms he entered. His parents, his relatives, the fields and parks he walked through with his mother and father or with his classmates. It would appear like an omen, his differentness, whenever he put his trust in someone, or in anything other than himself, and he would awaken from that trust and see it was impossible.

He played with Puba Weinberger and Anita Cohan. Puba the same age as he, son of friends of his parents; Anita a year younger, granddaughter of the landlord. They scampered and chased each other around the cramped concrete square of the courtyard, which the kitchen windows of all three looked out on. They pulled skinny, homely Anita's hair, long and snarled, and took away her doll, one of whose legs was already loose. They kicked a ball, hung and yelled like Tarzan from the rickety frame used for beating carpets, went down to the basement when the ball fell through the basement window, and there groped their way in the dark and felt and tickled each other, the two boys mainly touching invisible Anita, excited by her skin and hair damp with sweat, by her noisy breathing and her shrieks. Outside stretched the endless day, where everything seemed vast and fascinating, but the basement, dank and cold, drew them like a well that aggravates thirst instead of quenching it.

Then voices would begin to call—one, two, three voices, first his mother or Puba's, for dinner, which would be enough to remind the other two mothers busy at their stoves. An end to the mischief; it was back up to the courtyard and from there to their apartments. His on the ground floor, Puba's on the second, and Anita's across from it—the landlord's apartment, the only one with a balcony, from which the booming voice of her father, as he leaned on the railing and smoked a cigarette, his hair bound in black netting, would greet the neighbors early each morning.

Or else Lamian played submarine, alone in bed in his night-shirt, crawling beneath the quilt and making sounds for the pounding of the engines, the gurgling of the water, the blast of an underwater mine—all very quietly, so no one would hear and embarrass him, even though he knew his mother and father were not in the apartment but playing cards at the Weinbergers', a fact that at the same time he tried to put out of his mind, in order not to be overcome by fear at being alone, so he abandoned himself to this submarine danger until his ears caught the scrape of the key in the lock, the squeak of the door. Then he got out from under the quilt, put his head on his pillow, and pretended to sleep, not wanting the faces and words that would swoop down on him if he admitted to being awake.

Or, during summer vacation, he would lie on his stomach in the grass near Plavnica, engrossed in a book by Karl May, galloping bareback next to Winnetoh and ambushing cattle rustlers with Old Shatterhand, when a blow to the ankle would interrupt him and he would look up and see Miša Petarac and Drago Blažetić, barefoot, fishpoles in hand, regarding him curiously.

They noticed no evil; nor did his parents, returning from cards to peek into his room and feel his forehead and tuck the quilt up around his neck. No one noticed any evil, the whole time he was growing up in Bjelovar. He had a secure place there, a place appropriate to his age, with a home and parents who took care of him, and who, in turn, had their own modest place in society. His father, a bookkeeper in a cookie factory, was loved not only by the owner but also by the workers, who came to his home with their shy trust to consult about a promotion, or a job for a relative. His father, with a heartiness that was somewhat boastful, would promise to intercede for them, while his mother, quiet as a mouse, bowed genteelly as she offered them a seat.

His parents were too quiet, too meek. That was what aroused his first feelings of disdain, when he came back from play, from his fantasies, from encounters with other people, other families, came back and saw their anxiously smiling faces.

One evening, returning from a piano lesson, he met Drago Blažetić crying in the street, leaning against a wall by the entrance to The Stag, a cellar tavern. When Lamian went up to him, thinking his friend had lost something, offering to help him find it, Drago punched him in the chest and hissed, with a twisted face, "I'll kill him, I'll cut his throat tonight when he's asleep." Drago blubbered that he had come to get his drunken father and take him home from the tavern, where he was breaking glasses and throwing away money by buying everyone drinks—but his father had thrown him out.

A few months later, on orders from his teacher, Lamian went to see Drago, who was sick, and go over some lessons. In the stuffy room, where the boy lay under a down comforter, Lamian found the father as well: tall, with a mop of glossy hair, vest unbuttoned, very cordial and friendly. As Lamian was leaving, Drago pointed proudly to the rifle hanging by its strap on the wall above the bed. "That's Papa's. For hunting."

Lamian's father not only had no rifle, he never mentioned rifles, not even when talk turned to the war, in which he had also been a bookkeeper, in a supply unit. He loathed that period of his life. In his wants and habits he was as different from Mr. Blažetić as he was similar to Puba's father, Gusti Weinberger, and Anita's father, Ludwig Cohan; similar to all the other people on the first two floors of the building, who were all Jews. But on the third floor, directly above the landlord and next to the bank clerk Arnold Lustig, who was also a Jew, married but childless, there lived a Christian, Ivan Mihovilović, a judge who had a wife and a grown son named Vladimir but called Lacik at home.

At the time, Lamian was unaware of the crucial differences between the majority and minority in the building, and between that same majority and minority in the city. The differences were revealed to him gradually, as through a thin fog that dispersed patch by patch under a slow but steady wind. That wind was scenes and facts which, like the hunting rifle over Drago Blažetić's bed, were insignificant in themselves but took on meaning when related to other scenes and facts, a whole series of interconnected things. The fog meanwhile was preserved by his parents' reluctance to acknowledge the existence of differences.

They had him christened, made him a Catholic, so that the differences would be erased, at least in the future. Not that they stressed it or flaunted it; they themselves remained Jews, considering it too late for them to change, but were unobtrusively Jews, staying away from the Jewish place of worship, not openly observing the Jewish holidays.

Christmas they did celebrate—not by taking little Vilko to Mass, of course, but by trimming a tree and placing it in the dining room. Beneath it, in the glow of lighted candles, they gave gifts to him and to each other. At Easter, he got a new suit and shoes, and his mother supplied him with a bottle of scented water, which on the way home from school the next day he sprayed at the girls in his class. In his first year of high school, he was confirmed, and received a wristwatch from his father in honor of the occasion.

All this, reinforced in school by Catholic religious instruction, which was provided for the majority while the few Orthodox Christians, Protestants, and Jews went into another room, was to convince Lamian that there were no differences, at least not for him. His father told him this explicitly one afternoon, after seeing off two somber, worried-looking men who held their hats in their hands, and to whom he had given a few banknotes. "Refugees from Austria. If we don't help them, who will? But they have nothing to do with you, remember that. You've been christened. You're a Catholic, a Croat. Forget about your origins—mine and your mother's. The only thing Jews can expect is betrayal and persecution."

But Lamian couldn't forget. The two men remained etched in his memory: both middle-aged, respectably dressed in suits and ties, their hats off and clasped to their stomachs. But there was something neglected, askew, in the wrinkles of their well-tailored suits, and something fearful in their bearing, and something secretive in the words they spoke to his father, hissing in a kind of toothless whisper, looking over their shoulders and leaning close to his face, in the hallway, as they left the room. And something obsequious, doglike, grateful and disappointed at the same time, in the bow with which they accepted the banknotes.

They would return, they would appear to him in the darkness as he fell asleep, his thoughts scattering aimlessly: there they would be, in their worn suits and hats, with their darting, suspicious eyes, thieves who robbed him of his peace. He would have to drive them away by concentrating on some other image, some other idea.

But then during the day he recognized them in certain passersby, in his father's friends—not their features or their speech, but that behavior, humble and vigilant at the same time, beseeching and mistrustful, a discordant note wherever they appeared, in whatever street or house. He began to study these people, to classify them according to the traits they shared, and gradually came to identify them with his parents, and then with the other occupants of the building, the Weinbergers, Cohans, Lustigs—everyone except Judge Mihovilović and his family. He concluded finally that all the Jews in Bjelovar were stamped with the same stamp as these exiles and petitioners, these assertive foreigners resigned in advance to defeat. He sensed their weakness, their rootlessness in both the town and the surrounding countryside, their uncertainty because chance had brought them here and made them so timid—and therefore conspicuous and unpleasant.

Yes, unpleasant to him and to the whole community. So Lamian learned to look at them—and at himself among them —from the outside. They were repugnant, they were offensive, and their offensiveness led one to the idea that they should be got rid of. He even heard this voiced out loud, sometimes by his friends—who would abruptly fall silent the moment the words crossed their lips. Silent, he knew, because they suspected, sensed, that he too was different, burdened by his family's difference— and this bothered Lamian more than the sentiment, more than the threat.

He wasn't at all sorry when at the behest of his father, who was determined to make a university man of him, he had to leave Bjelovar, Zagreb being the closest place where this could be accomplished. He chose to study mechanical engineering, though he had no special talent for mathematics or physics, or any interest in manufacturing; his feeling was simply that it was amid the clang of iron that he would most quickly efface all traces of his self-pity and self-directed scorn.

As soon as he was settled in new surroundings, he changed his appearance, following an instinct for mimicry. He had his hair cut short—around the ears, close to the skin—and adopted sporty dress, shunning warm clothing such as scarfs and caps, wearing plus fours and knee socks instead of trousers. He did calisthenics and tried to hold himself as straight as possible, already imitating, with the exaggeration of an impostor, the idols of a generation whose cheers would be for conquest and conquerors.

The trappings of Lamian's desire managed to fool several adherents of this rising tide, among them one prominent battler, a blond, handsome Hercegovinian named Zvonko Gabelić. A fiery orator and participant in brawls with the police, he had been imprisoned for his fanatical Croatian nationalism while still in high school. Gabelić approached Lamian in the assembly hall, and after a few meetings revealed his hopes for an independent Croatia, a Croatia free of alien residues, or foreign matter, as he called it.

Wincing, Lamian nodded, agreed, but when these discourses

led to an invitation to attend a meeting and take a bundle of leaflets for distribution in the neighborhood, he wriggled out of it, fearing that too close an involvement might one day reveal to Gabelić what he of all people shouldn't know.

Lamian didn't even disclose where he lived, giving a vague reply to the question, because although his landlord, a tailor of women's coats and suits, was a Croatian Catholic, the room had been rented by the elder Lamian, who while accompanying his wife to fittings had made the man's acquaintance. Uneasy about this connection, Lamian soon moved out of the room on Ilica Street, explaining to his parents that it was too far from the university. Through an advertisement, he found a place even farther, in Trešnjevka, with a widowed teacher named Basarabić, and there he remained until the completion of his studies. Nevertheless, caution kept him from taking Gabelić there as well.

Mostly he liked to be alone, and since he had to spend a large part of the day with his classmates—at lectures, lab sessions, and in the student restaurant—outside the university he avoided them. He knew where they gathered: in Ilica Street, on Jelačić Square, in the little cafés around the university bookstore, and, in the evening, at Zrinjevac Park. He fell into the habit of going straight home after classes, buying in stores along the way the cold food he would eat for supper. At supper he drank tea made on the retired teacher's stove, which she let him use.

Sometimes he went for a walk, keeping to Trešnjevka, however, whose dark, quiet streets opened onto wide and windy Sava Road, where the trams passed at regular intervals. Workers and tradesmen lived and worked here, people with no interest in advanced learning, and who, it seemed, did not worry about ethnic and religious differences. They went to bed early, the evening's entertainment confined to going to the nearest tavern, where they drank *gemischt*—wine mixed with water—and played billiards.

He didn't go inside the taverns. Alcohol had no appeal for him—in the house of his abstinent father he had never tasted it—and he also was repelled by cigarette smoke, which was against the principles of clean living and exercise he now upheld. He went out only to stretch his legs, looked in only to amuse himself.

Tram stops afforded the best amusement: people gathered there, the men smoking and the women looking past them or else chatting if they happened to meet an acquaintance. Then, when the tram arrived, everyone climbed aboard, one by one, and others, one by one, descended, came out in their place. It was a kind of stage, on which the actors constantly changed, while he, the spectator, did not even have to interrupt his healthy walk.

EARLY ONE EVENING, AS LAMIAN WAS WATCHING THE TRAM passengers, a young woman approached him. A large, shadowy face, lips drawn back in a smile. Strong teeth. When the face came near his, he heard a loud report, like an exploding shell or bursting balloon, followed by a giggle. He jumped. "Did I frighten you?" asked the woman, who had made the sound. She forced herself to stop smiling. "But what else could I do? You were staring at me so hard. I decided to speak to you." The tram rang its bell and slowly moved away from the station; its yellow bulk passed behind her and disappeared down the street. Lamian frowned. "I was staring?" "Yes, and it's about the tenth time. As if you were on duty here. If I didn't know you from the university, I'd think you were a detective."

Explanations followed. She knew him by sight, because they had classes in the same building every day. She was studying engineering. She too lived in the neighborhood, not on Trnska Street but on Gosposvetska, with her parents, who were from Zagreb.

Without thinking about it, they left the tram stop together, and as they crossed the road and entered a side street, she asked him about his daily schedule, his living arrangements, his interests—even why he took those evening walks, always the same route, and always alone. When she left him at the gate of the small single-family house with its wire fence and its garden, he turned and, in a daze, started home, his palm carrying the feel of her warm handshake, his eyes the outline of the long, strong legs he had glimpsed through the fence as she ran up the steps.

This was the first girl to take an interest in him. Usually his reclusiveness repelled girls, and in Bjelovar, where couples were formed only with the approval of the social circle, it had been impossible for him to meet anyone. Branka, however, was free of such constraints; she liked him, chose him personally, and this was highly flattering.

Of course, he sensed immediately that her easy individuality had to derive from some foreignness, and, indeed, the next time they chanced to meet, she said, on why she studied engineering, "I'm Jewish, so I had to choose something practical, something a person can do well with anywhere." Unnerved by this information, he said nothing, certainly not about his own origins. Did the path to intimacy have to lead through the sharing of a curse?

But he couldn't resist the call of that intimacy. Now knowing her schedule, he contrived to leave the university at the same time she did. They would set out for home together. On the way, he would buy what he needed for supper, and she would wait for him in front of the store. And, as they walked, they would talk.

Conversation with Branka flowed smoothly. Her questions, which came in quick succession and followed the line of his own thoughts, were like a pump that drew from him everything he knew and felt. She got him to say things he had never revealed to anyone, things he had never even revealed to himself, which pleased him, for it introduced him to a self he had not known before. He had thought he was a person who arrived slowly and laboriously at conclusions, and who expressed those conclusions uncertainly, but now he found that this was so only because there had been no one to stimulate him and encourage him. With Branka, he was discerning, clever, even eloquent.

Through the eyes of this new cleverness, Lamian began to look around him: at students and professors, his landlord, the salesmen in the shops, and at the books he read and the buildings he passed. It was as if he was constantly preparing for his meetings with Branka: seeing something unusual, interesting, he would immediately think of how to describe it to her, and would be amazed at how original and apt the sentences were that came to him.

So each time he met her, he had a new store of observations and impressions, and poured these out breathlessly, hardly waiting for her to take in one before he delivered another. Early in their acquaintance, she had done most of the talking—asking questions—but now he astounded her with a torrent of brilliant words.

Occasionally, leaving the university with Branka, he ran into Gabelić, who gave a measured nod—to him alone, not Branka —as if disapproving of their friendship. Once, when Lamian was alone, Gabelić passed him coldly, but then stopped and turned to him with his long face and small green eyes. "What's new, Vilko?" he asked mockingly, then said, "Now I see why you don't have time for patriotic service. But did you know that that girl you have on your line is a full-blooded Jew?"

Lamian was struck speechless by the hatred that seethed in this remark.

"Or doesn't that matter to you?" Gabelić went on in the same sneering tone. "Maybe you're a yid yourself, and just know how to hide it better." And he gave him a sharp, probing look.

"No, I'm not," was all Lamian could squeeze from his constricted throat.

"Then you should think about who you're wasting time with when you could be putting it to good use," Gabelić concluded with a mirthless smile and continued on his way.

Lamian was stunned. How dare Gabelić meddle in his private

life? But he was equally shaken by his own cowardly answer. There was a remedy for the first thing, for Gabelić: he could simply stop greeting him. But he sensed that for the second thing, for his lie—or half-truth—there was no remedy.

He decided that from now on he would avoid Gabelić—and Branka too, since it was she who had drawn him, through the spell of their intimacy, into being identified with her. He stopped lingering in front of the university at the hour when she left. The few times he did run into her, he nodded curtly and turned away, though he couldn't help seeing her stop short in astonishment, hands pressed to her chest.

He was sorry for her, but at the same time pleased with his own strength of will and resolve, which he decided to exercise even more strictly. And many opportunities presented themselves, because Branka now appeared in his path even more often—in the assembly hall, in the corridors, outside the lecture rooms as he was leaving, as if she was trying to attract his attention. But the moment he caught sight of her, he would address some hastily contrived question or remark to whatever classmate stood nearby, and remain with that person until Branka went away.

Once he saw her on Sava Road, in a doorway opposite the tram stop where she first spoke to him. He crossed to the other side of the street and walked so quickly, she couldn't catch up. After that, he walked in the area around the railway station.

But one evening, as he stepped onto the square in front of the university, in a moment of absentmindedness that made him careless, he almost bumped into her—just as at their first meeting at the tram stop, face thrust into face. Her face this time recoiled, as if broken into fragments, and she said in a frightened whisper, "Vilko! What's wrong? What did I do?" His heart clenched at the sight of her misery, but he forced himself to turn and run back up the steps to the now empty lecture room. He later left the building by a side door.

For a long time he didn't run into her, but occasionally thought he spotted her: in a distant corner of the university, behind a column or in a deep window casement, furtively watching him.

When he came home one evening, Mrs. Basarabić emerged from her room and after some hesitation handed him a letter in a white envelope. She said that a young woman had brought it, a complete stranger, so at first Mrs. Basarabić had refused to accept it, but relented after the woman pleaded with her, saying she was an acquaintance of his, of Vilko's, a classmate, which Mrs. Basarabić found hard to believe, in view of the woman's rather free behavior. Lamian opened the letter in the presence of his landlady, to allay her suspicions. Even before he saw the signature, he knew that behind the words—written in a large, round, unfamiliar hand—direct, emotional, shocking words, was Branka's yearning face, shattered in its distress.

She wrote that she did not understand why he had rejected her. She had kept nothing from him, not even in her thoughts. But she would not question him; she could see that he did not want to discuss it. Yet she had grown to love him. He was not like the other young men she knew; he was more interesting, more intelligent, more manly. Since her chance meeting with him, he had become an island of salvation in her dreary life among people who didn't understand her. She wanted to continue their friendship, was prepared to continue it under whatever conditions he liked. She begged him to come to her, later that evening when her parents were asleep, preferably around 10:30. He should come right to the house; the gate would be open; she would be waiting for him, would make sure none of the household or neighbors saw him.

He returned the letter to its envelope, feeling the landlady's careful eye on him, and blushed under that eye. But said, "Nothing important," before going to his room. There he sat thinking about the message he had received, finally roused himself and made his supper, then again fell into thought.

In the name of friendship, Branka was offering him everything a woman could offer. This made him proud, but at the same time he was reluctant to accept. There was something excessive, immoderate, about the offer, like Branka herself, her ample body, sallow skin, and careless dress. An appearance that probably deserved the disparaging remarks Mrs. Basarabić had made about her.

Yet a wave of warmth had washed through him as he read Branka's words, and it continued to stir in him, awakening a curiosity to experience that warmth from the flesh as well.

As the evening wore on, and darkness fell outside the window, and the neighborhood voices grew still, and his landlady's footsteps could be heard on the way first to the bathroom, then to the bedroom, this carnal curiosity occupied him more and more. It made his skin burn; it aroused him. When he saw on the clock that the appointed time had come, would soon pass— twenty-five minutes after ten—he jumped up, no longer able to resist temptation. He quietly locked the front door, the gate, telling himself that she would not be there to meet him, and that five or ten minutes from now he would be returning to the solitude of his room, relieved to have missed a mad adventure, with all its messy and unnecessary complications.

But she was waiting for him in the shadows behind her gate, which she had left ajar. She took him by the hand, led him up the steps and across the porch, then into the hallway and from there to her room, where she wrapped her arms around him. He smelled the unfamiliar, suffocating smell of her skin, felt her cheek tighten on his, felt the hot, wet opening of her mouth on his, then he was led across the creaking floor to her bed. Lying down, still embracing him, Branka at the same time began to unbutton his coat, his shirt, with fumbling fingers. She moved her kisses to his chest. Aroused, he took off the rest of his clothes, at which point she simply parted her housecoat—she was naked beneath it—and drew him inside her.

Her body became a runaway machine that jerked and pulled at him and squeezed him, its spasms making the bed clatter as her throat produced sounds that were sometimes sharp, sometimes muffled, like shrieks and moans. The fear that her parents would hear them made his desire subside, and he withdrew, almost angry, but she paid no attention, she continued to kiss him and pull him to her, continued to rotate her hips even without him, until at last she brought them both to cries of ecstasy. Then she was motionless, silent under him, as if suddenly bodiless, like a leaf fallen from a tree.

It was so different from what he had expected, so unlike his previous experiences with the few girls who gave themselves to him after fits of resistance and protracted negotiating. It was so much more exciting and stirring, though unnatural too. He was unable to utter a single word, whether of gratitude or the boasting by which men try, more from instinct than education, to embellish their victory. He merely rolled off her onto the empty half of the bed and took deep breaths until the rhythm of his lungs and heart grew even. Then got up, dressed quietly, and, when she did not stir, murmured good-bye and stole out of the house.

Outside, he looked around to make sure that no one had seen him, and sighed with relief, as if he had escaped a trap. This, he was certain, would be the end of their argument—for that was how he perceived their nocturnal meeting—and although in the days that followed he ran into Branka at the university, he no longer winced at such occasions, now prepared, if she approached him again, to tell her to leave him alone.

She wrote a second letter, again giving it to Mrs. Basarabić. Lamian took it from the landlady without a word and read it in his room. "You left," said the letter, in its now-familiar broad strokes, "without telling me when you'd come again. Come whenever you wish, just give me some sign. Put something in your window that doesn't normally belong there, a vase or a book. I'll go past your house every evening, and when I see it, I'll expect you. Yours, Branka."

He tore the letter into little pieces, threw the pieces in the wastebasket. There was no problem now, because Branka had just said that any future meeting depended entirely on him. And the answer was never.

But the letter kept coming back to him. He remembered its words. An extraordinary letter, a daring letter, a letter of utter abandon, which said he had the right to use her whenever he wanted, like an object. Even her suggestion how he make his wishes known—with a vase or book in the window—was brazen, crude, and so simple, it seemed almost witty and light-hearted.

The idea of mocking her appealed to him: place a textbook in his empty window and make her stand inside her unlocked gate at 10:30, wrapped in nothing but a housecoat and waiting, waiting until eleven, eleven-thirty, twelve. Until morning. He didn't do it, having no reason or wish to take revenge on her, but every evening he thought of the possibility, thought of Branka—the big, warm, bosomy, leggy body at his disposal, which, though repugnant, would be welcome in quelling the youthful needs that tormented him constantly, especially at night.

To drive her from his mind, he approached a classmate in mathematics, a slender blonde he'd long been attracted to. He asked her to the movies, and she accepted. But in the darkness of the theater she would give him only a cold, dry hand; and later, when he saw her home all the way to Upper Town, she refused him a goodnight kiss, saying it was "too soon." He took her out a second time, but when the results were no better, he stopped.

In the next few weeks he went to bars that had dancing, and there tried to get one of the prettier, more attractive women to accept him as a regular partner and allow him to escort her home. He succeeded once or twice, but these women too, sales clerks or apprentices learning some trade, became suspicious when he asked to see them alone. Disappointed, he sought out the math student again, determined to persevere no matter what. He took her to the movies, saw her home, squeezed her hand, but she remained unobliging, indifferent, and as he walked beside her he thought with bitter longing of Branka, of her blazing passion and the submission with which she awaited him. One rainy Saturday evening, when it seemed unthinkable that she would walk down deserted, muddy Trnska Street, he put a book in his window.

It was the same as the first time: she was waiting for him, took him to her room, pulled him onto her in the dark, opened her robe to press her undulating loins against his. But this time he wasn't surprised, wasn't afraid that her parents would wake.

Instead, he coolly accepted her leadership in the game of love, and from a distance watched her jerk and writhe, and listened to her shrieks and moans with a detachment that made them almost comical.

When he left, he didn't swear to himself that this would be the end of it, and to that bitterness was added another: the fact that she had taken him, had chosen and conquered him, and he had submitted, as women usually submit. Tormented by his unmanliness, he turned once more to Zita—that was the math student's name—and in his mind elevated her into a paragon of captivating femininity. He pictured her frail figure, delicate white skin, clear gray eyes, and silky blond hair beside him, beneath him, as he stroked and kneaded and subdued her.

But his dates with her were as unimaginative and barren as before. Zita hardly ever allowed him to kiss her on the lips; showed him her thin, sinewy neck, turned away, each time he bent over her; and when he coaxed and urged and argued, she said he was a nuisance.

The difference between his reveries of seduction and Zita's lack of response, her calling him a nuisance, filled him with rage, and with the suspicion too that behind her reluctance there was nothing at all: no thought, no emotion, only a shallowness of both mind and personality. He longed for the stimulating conversations, the intellectual exaltation and self-analysis that Branka had unlocked. If only it could be Zita, not Branka, that he wordlessly flung onto some bed, wringing yelps of pain and pleasure from her thin, white, flat-chested body! With Branka, on the other hand, he would resume those evening talks that made him interesting even to himself.

But he no longer saw Branka except in bed. Nor did she attempt to see him anywhere else. Once more he was alone in the corridors and assembly hall of the university, and this must have been noticed by the everpresent Gabelić, who again began to greet him amiably, and after a while, as if by mutual agreement, began handing him pamphlets with the terse instruction: "Read it and give it back!"

Opening these pamphlets at home, Lamian found statements that mixed hot and cold, idealism and hatred. Statements about the Croats, those stalwart defenders of Western culture and faith, descendants not of the lazy, stupid Slavs but of the warlike Goths. The Croats, whom the foreign dogs from the East—Orthodox Christianity and Judaism—wanted to drag into the mire of Bolshevism and Freemasonry. Against this, the finest sons of Croatia, in alliance with all the other enlightened peoples of Europe, were mounting a crusade of extermination.

The style, shrill and bombastic, trampled on the rules of taste and even those of basic grammar, just as screaming trampled on thought; but that wasn't why a gloomy Lamian tossed aside the pamphlets. He did it because they spoke of him personally, and revealed a threat that until now he had only suspected. At last it was spelled out, the thing that had set him apart from others, and although this mountain of slander, fabrication, and exaggeration said more about the vile minds of its authors than anything else, he nevertheless saw the grain of truth beneath it.

Yes, he was an alien here. His very attempt to deny that alienness, stopping at neither deceit nor disguise, proved his devious design: to insinuate himself into the lifeblood of a society to which, being of other ancestry, he did not belong. And he and Branka, hadn't their chance meeting in fact been due to an instinctive mutual attraction of kinship? And their unrestrained talk, their critique of social phenomena, hadn't that been an expression of the urge to destroy? And didn't he, in his grasping pursuit of Zita without telling her his race, his true identity, didn't he scheme to worm his way into her confidence like a thief, and then, when she trusted him, to drag her down from the height of her respectable Croatian unbringing, narrow but correct, and into the squalor where he and Branka already wallowed?

He was disgusted with himself, but didn't try to reform, to adopt some Germanic morality, because Gabelić's pamphlets, proclaiming that morality, had convinced him it was a hoax, and besides, there was no room for the likes of him in that hoax, he had been excluded. He was an exile, and now suddenly aware of it.

But he would have nothing to do with his fellow exiles. On the contrary, now that the reason for their exile had become clear to him, the very thought of being identified with them was loathsome. It was reluctantly, therefore, that he went home for the summer vacation, as if he were going to prison. And his parents' home, when he arrived and unpacked his belongings, did seem a prison: dug in, walled off, surrounded by trenches. As a child, he had accepted this difference as natural, a difference whose cause he didn't understand but for which he saw no remedy. The way his parents and all the other Jews crowded together, and their anxious head-shaking—in contrast to Judge Mihovilović and his third-floor apartment, which on summer nights resounded with the songs of Lacik's tipsy friends. But now the difference oppressed Lamian like a sentence to which there was no appeal.

Dejectedly he sat at home, watched his mother move through the rooms with her mouselike haste and vigilance, making their home conform to the taste she had brought with her from the isolation and insularity of her own childhood. His father, coming home from work and burrowing into this hiding place from the world, sighed and sucked his teeth after meals lovingly prepared for him. Proud of the son who had outgrown the hereditary barrier. The son knew better—not only from the pamphlets he'd read, but from the feelings that went with such isolation and confinement—contorting and remaking of oneself in order to escape, and finding that those very contortions marked him and perpetuated his identity.

Outside the town, as it ran smoothly and according to habit, gave him abundant evidence of his exile. Drago Blažetić had become the town clerk. When they ran into each other, Drago, in his hunter's outfit and with a green hat tilted to one side, invited him to have a glass of *gemischt*. Lamian, forcing it down, told anecdotes from Zagreb which he knew would please his friend. The girls who had promenaded as schoolgirls were now young ladies and wives, and on meeting him they took his measure with a cold eye that reminded him of Zita, except that, unlike Zita, they knew who he was. The artisans and minor clerks greeted him as his father's son, but behind their heartiness he sensed envy and malice.

He was glad he had brought his textbooks to help him pass the time, and as soon as he thought his parents had had enough of him, he announced there was a fall exam he had to take, a lie, and returned to Zagreb sooner than planned.

It was in this way that he passed his years at the university, between Zagreb and Bjelovar, with Gabelić, Zita, Branka, and his parents as the four corners of his cell. Corners he was unable to budge, and didn't even try, for fear that if any one of them were displaced, the whole edifice might come crashing down on his head and bury him.

He left everything as it was; patched and plugged cracks only as needed. Returned Gabelić's pamphlets, took new ones, with a guarded look that betrayed nothing. He mustn't be found out as an enemy, but also mustn't be taken for a follower who would be involved in more definite activities, more hazardous associations.

He continued to court Zita, but stopped taking her to the movies after she caught a cold there; he visited her at home instead, where her parents now received him. He would drink tea and chat with Zita's jaundiced father, a senior civil servant, and listen to the cautionary advice of Zita's buxom, overbearing mother. In spite of this sacrifice of his—which actually was no sacrifice, since he liked rubbing elbows with Zita's family, which made him feel he was taking possession of a part of her—he still only squeezed her hand when they were alone, and all his pent-up desires would be discharged into the tempestuous body of Branka Frank, whom he saw only at night, avoiding any contact with her parents as carefully as he was cultivating the acquaintance of Zita's.

When he graduated, he postponed going home. On the pretext that he had to complete some formalities, he remained in Zagreb, until the summons came to report for military service. He stopped at Bjelovar only to say good-bye on his way to Niš. At the artillery base there, his sensibilities were assailed by a crudity greater than he had ever imagined. Obliged to carry out the orders of backwoods noncoms whose bearlike bodies hardly fit into their khaki uniforms, men impervious to the temptation of any civilian ideas, Lamian understood a little of the hatred felt by the authors of Gabelić's pamphlets, the disgust for Balkan coarseness, the longing for things Germanic.

As he counted the months and days until he could take off his uniform, he received letters from his father. These invariably contained, along with a folded banknote, newspaper clippings: advertisements for mechanical engineers. The unspoken suggestion being that it wasn't too soon to begin looking. He applied, and one of his applications, to Banja Luka, received an affirmative reply. And so, except for several days spent eating his fill in Bjelovar, Lamian went directly from the army to his first post, as section chief in a sawmill.

The sawmill was outside the town, and along with his pay he was given a room in the company offices, which were generously heated with wood scraps, a fact of no little importance, since he arrived during the bitter mountain winter. He was greeted by the owners, two brothers by the name of Radić, ex-bricklayers grown rich, and the workers smiled at him good-naturedly on account of his youth. Only seven weeks after arriving at this comfortable outpost, however, he was called away to military exercises in Zvornik, and there, before he had even been assigned a rank, he was caught up like a straw in the whirlwind of the April war.

Pushed and pulled by orders he only half understood, he tugged at the reins of skittish horses, loaded them and himself into cattle cars along with heavy chests filled with cannon parts and ammunition. He endured hunger, lack of sleep, was rained on in the mountains where his battery took up positions, and experienced his first and only bombardment, in which pieces of weapons and the limbs and heads of soldiers flew through the smoke and dust like cigarette butts from a tin ashtray hurled against a wall. He ran here and there and back again to the hysterical commands of young frontline officers left in the lurch by headquarters. With Sergeant Ilija Govorušić and six other soldiers—Montenegrins and Bosnians—he set off through the mountains in search of a regrouped unit they could join. Along the roads and in villages, they came upon scenes of anarchy and devastation. German tanks with swastikas passed unchallenged on roads below them. He and his new companions slept with villagers, shared small amounts of food bought with large sums of money. After Govorušić and the Montenegrins disappeared without warning, Lamian was left with one Bosnian, Veljko

Karišika. Spending his last hundred-dinar note on a bite to eat, he agreed to go with Karišika to his home in Nevesinje, and there stayed with Karišika's brother-in-law, a railroad switchman named Ivanda, when Karišika left to join his wife in the village. When the surrender was announced, the brother-in-law gave Lamian some worn-out civilian clothes and put him on a train for Sarajevo.

The Ustaši were already posted in the train, rifles across their backs, scowls on their tight-lipped, bloodthirsty faces, as if they had stepped from the dog-eared pages of one of Gabelić's books. But Lamian's claim that he had abandoned his shattered unit was accepted without comment as were his military papers which gave his religion, and the guards' mistrust shifted to other passengers. This relatively easy passage, combined with physical weakness and an inability to think of another course of action, led him to continue home by way of Zagreb to Bjelovar. He took connecting trains, showed his military papers at identity checks.

As soon as he arrived, he knew that he had made a mistake. The station resounded with drunken song, the original words replaced by curses and obscenities. He passed through the waiting room, went out onto the front deck with its restaurant, and saw the singers at their tables, civilians wearing Ustaša caps, mouths hanging open; they were interspersed with women who stared dully at half-empty glasses. At one of the tables he recognized Drago Blažetić, and saw that Drago recognized him.

He would have gone back immediately and boarded another train, had he not felt Drago's eyes on him, following him, pinioning him. All he could do now was pretend not to see the danger. Perhaps in that way it would be delayed.

Keeping to the side streets, he made his way home. His mother threw herself around his neck, sobbing. His father, ordinarily collected, had tears running down his face, which he wiped away with the back of his hand, his expression one of childlike bewilderment. As they set out food for Lamian in the kitchen, they told him that they had already been registered as Jews, and that the officials had asked about him, with orders that they notify the municipality the moment they learned of his whereabouts. After feeding their hungry son and sitting with him awhile, elbows on the table, they discussed what should be done. His father insisted that he leave as soon as possible and save himself; his mother, though she made no protest, melted into tears at the thought of parting. They paid no attention to her, talking things over as if she weren't there: what he should take with him, how much money, where to stay—they could come up with nothing better than his student room in Zagreb—and how they would keep each other informed by poste restante.

The time went quickly. Outside, darkness fell and shots could be heard, which was the only reason his father agreed to let him put off his departure until morning. They went to bed, but didn't sleep; Lamian could hear his mother and father fidgeting in the next room, whispering, or sometimes, when they forgot themselves, talking out loud. He heard them going to the toilet, drinking water, peering out the window.

Listening, he suddenly realized that from the moment he arrived they had not said one word about themselves, as if their fate was already sealed. Then he understood that in fact it was, and that they were silently resigning themselves to it. His role in that resignation was also clear: they were resigning themselves because they wanted to save him, their son, and for his sake would do nothing conspicuous or hazardous, as if pushing him forward, ahead of them, out of the flames and toward the possibility of salvation.

He could not accept such a sacrifice, and decided to speak to them, when dawn came, about a different, common course of action. For instance, they could go with him to Zagreb and take the other vacant room at Mrs. Basarabić's, saying they needed medical attention from a specialist. But Lamian knew that wouldn't work; pursuit would follow from Bjelovar; Blažetić, if no one else, would guess where they were—and they would have to register again in Zagreb, this time dragging their son to destruction with them. Slowly he came to the decision to say nothing of this in the morning.

And so it was. They got up, he packed a small bag with essentials, and they parted silently, merely shaking hands and kissing behind the closed door of the entryway, so that he could step over the threshold and into the dawn unburdened by their presence, their proximity, their name, as if he didn't even belong to them.

The Bjelovar station was deserted that morning, and although a guard emerged from the gloom to demand his papers, Lamian felt he had slipped away unnoticed. It was the same on the train, and by the time he reached Zagreb, he breathed a sigh of relief: here he could lose himself in the multitude, a stranger among strangers.

For a moment he was tempted not to go to his former landlady, to look instead for new lodgings, perhaps under an assumed name. He could obtain false papers in exchange for money, a bribe slipped into the pocket of a municipal clerk or some middleman, as he had heard of people doing, the people in trouble who came to his father for help. Yet now that Lamian and his family were the ones in trouble, there had been no talk of false papers when they sat at the table over supper. But that was part of his father's decision not to come into conflict with the law in any way, and thus protect his son.

And so he was deprived of his people's only weapon, deceit, because his father believed that christening had armed him against all evil and that he shouldn't be dragged back into the shame from which he had been delivered! How naive that belief was, yet Lamian couldn't find the strength, nor did he know how, to follow, on his own, and against his father's will, in the path of those mournful shadows. So much his father's son, unprepared for and uninstructed in such dealings, he gave up and headed grimly for Mrs. Basarabić's.

SHE GREETED HIM KINDLY, THOUGH WITHOUT SPECIAL warmth, and invited him to have coffee with her, evidently thinking he was only stopping by in consideration of all the years spent under her roof. After they had finished their coffee and chatted about the events of the recent, short-lived war, he asked whether his old room was available, saying he would like to rent it again. Mrs. Basarabić expressed surprise but assured him it wasn't occupied. She had had only one other student after him, and the student left for home as soon as the war broke out. She had decided then to keep it vacant for the moment, given the uncertainty of the times. However, she said after some hesitation, for Lamian she would make an exception.

He moved in, telling Mrs. Basarabić that he was looking for work, that he had lost his first job when he went off on maneuvers and then to war. After this explanation he himself half-believed that finding work was his real purpose in coming to Zagreb, because the money his father had given him wouldn't last forever. He began buying the newspaper and reading the want ads, studying those especially that asked for experience in engineering.

But few of the ads were directed at educated people, and when he did come across one that suited him, suspicion, like the stench of decay, made him decide not to answer it, a suspicion inspired by the rest of the newspaper, which was filled with threats and condemnations borrowed from the pamphlets he had once leafed through and that were now transformed into laws and decrees. One decree ordered the registration of all Jewish-owned property; another forbade the employment of Jews; another said that Jews had to wear a metal tag with the letter J on their chest to distinguish them from first-class citizens. J's dangled before his eyes, and he saw his parents huddled in their apartment, jobless, vacant-faced; or he saw them in the street when they had to go out to buy necessities and were exposed to the taunts of the mob, perhaps led by Drago Blažetić. When he wrote to them, he cautiously inquired how they were managing. Their answer was that everything, "on the whole," was all right.

And then there was no longer any reason for him to keep his parents separate in his dark broodings; the latest law revoked his right to consider himself a Christian, because of his origins, his unbaptized ancestors. He was thrust back among the Jews. He stopped reading the want ads, and saw that he had done well not to succumb to the few attractive offers they contained: his identity papers, which he would have had to submit, now took away his right to work.

When would his right to breathe, to live, be taken away? That would happen as soon as they discovered who he was, in other words, the moment the Ustaša government became aware of him. He had to postpone that moment, perhaps even avoid it altogether. As long as he was alone, with the credulous Mrs. Basarabić the only person in Zagreb who knew about him, he would be safe. So he continued to live a solitary existence and behaved in such a way that Mrs. Basarabić would think his solitude only a matter of preference. He kept to the daily routine he had followed before the announcement of the anti-Jewish laws: in the morning he bought a newspaper, took it home and rustled its pages, as if reading it, then went out again, as if to apply for jobs, but in fact to walk the streets.

These outings now demanded great composure and self-control, and he prepared for them each time, as an actor studies a role. It was summer, and his plus fours and knee socks, being too warm, were not among the clothes he had brought from

Bjelovar. All that remained of his earlier façade was his short hair. He kept it short, and walked accordingly, with a step that was firm and decisive. But behind that energetic gait his fear flowered, like mold behind a white wall, and his eyes sought barriers, traps, expecting a deranged figure to leap out at him from behind a corner or out of a doorway, and strike him and curse him.

Occasionally Lamian came upon a man or woman with a metal tag on their chest, and he could hardly resist the urge to follow them, to see where they were going and why, and what was happening to them. He worried about running into Branka, she too disfigured by the tag that resembled a dog license. Would he approach her? What would he say to her? But he couldn't approach her; that would draw attention to himself and the fact that he did not wear the symbol of inequality on his chest, because even though ordinarily he lacked the courage to disobey the law, wearing that tag for him would mean parting with his last defense, with the strength that still enabled him to go out; it would mean locking himself in his room, not leaving even to eat, and then Mrs. Basarabić would begin to doubt his story about looking for work, and she would summon armed men to break down his door and unmask him.

Which is what happened, except that he never found out who outwitted him, she or they. Returning home one evening and going quietly to his room, he heard the floor creak and turned to see them coming at him—a man with a reddish, well-trimmed mustache, and Mrs. Basarabić. She was a step behind the man, and her eyes were wide with curiosity and fear. The man grabbed him by the shoulder and asked for his papers. Lamian handed them over. Glancing at the papers, the man asked Lamian if he was the son of the bookkeeper Lamian from Bjelovar. When Lamian said yes, the man ordered him to gather his things and told him he was under arrest. "Why?" Lamian asked, although he knew why. The detective, having no desire or need to explain, said, "You'll see."

Lamian was taken to the fairgrounds and handed over to some soldiers, who shoved him into an unlit hangar where a mass of people lay and sat on the concrete floor. Stepping over bodies, he found a spot for himself, spread his coat on the floor, and sat on it. During the night the iron doors squeaked open and let in new prisoners, individuals, whole families. The room became so packed that the jostling woke the children, who started to cry.

The morning light revealed a multitude of pale, frightened faces poking out of soiled, wrinkled clothing. They were all Jews; he saw this not only by the metal tags on their chests but also by the familiar expression of helplessness and resignation. A few people near him asked him to hold something for them or guard it, but he did not talk to them, though he wanted to ask where they were from. Were they only from Zagreb, or were they from other places as well, perhaps even Bjelovar? Lamian was relieved that he didn't recognize anyone, that there was no one there from Bjelovar to identify him.

Though his connection with Bjelovar was entered in all his documents, he thought of ways to repudiate it. He could claim he was the victim of an error, could say he was a different Lamian, not the one wanted by the police. He weighed the pros and cons of saying this, calculated how much time would be needed to refute it, pondered whether or not it would land him in worse difficulties. These thoughts gave him no peace; they clawed him like feverish fingers as he sat dozing with his head on his knees, or as he went out to relieve himself—in a group, under guard, behind the hangar—or as he received his spoonful of soup and ate it out of a bowl borrowed from a neighbor, a watchmaker, or as he saw the guards entering, carrying out some orders, and feared, each time, that it was his turn.

But no one came for him, no one interrogated him. On the third day, again in the evening, they herded everyone onto a field in front of the hangar, then led them in ranks, down a side street, to railroad tracks some distance from the station. Freight cars were waiting for them there, and the guards loaded them inside. At dawn the train began to move, suddenly stopped, moved again. As it grew light and the day advanced, the cars became closer, sweatier; little air entered through the windows covered with barbed wire; they were given neither water nor food.

The train came to a stop. Evening fell, night, bringing relief from the stuffiness but not from the crowding or hunger or thirst. In the morning there were voices, barking and hostile, then the doors opened and the Jews swarmed out to find themselves at the little station in Jasenovac.

Soldiers rushed at them and hit them with rifle butts until they were lined up by fours. They were made to run down a dirt road with leafy hedges on either side. The beating continued as they ran; some fell, shots were heard, and, with the shots, laughter. The Jews arrived at a wire fence; the gate was open wide, and behind it stood more soldiers, bareheaded, uniforms unbuttoned, cheerful. They, too, began striking, swearing, laughing.

Someone grabbed Lamian and dragged him by his lapel so violently, he could hardly keep on his feet. Then he was at a table where two uniformed men sat, and one of them ordered him to show his papers. As Lamian reached into his pocket, a figure in a tight black uniform and black boots leaped forward. Lamian was nose-to-nose with the narrow face and green eyes of Zvonko Gabelić. "So you're here, you Jewish cur!" he hissed, baring small white teeth. "I knew that's what you were, I could smell it. I was only waiting for you to show yourself." Gabelić took the papers and tore them into little pieces that fluttered to the grass. He pushed Lamian with both hands and, as Lamian staggered, kicked him, a sideways blow with his booted foot, in the hip. "March!" he howled, then said in a calm voice to the soldiers, "Throw him in the tunnel and let him rot there." A hundred hands grasped Lamian, dragged him by the jacket like a doll. His face was soaked with tears of pain and indignation.

BUT THE TEARS THAT FLOWED FROM HELENA LIFKA'S EYES, Jewish tears, he no longer recognized as his own, for by then he was not a Jew, he was a Kapo. He no longer belonged to that corrupt race, he belonged only to himself, to his own body, which strove to vent itself, to burst its chains—in order to live.

Naked, he stood in the toolshed and watched her come near, she and the doe, whom he already knew and immediately motioned into the corner to wait, that he might better examine this new one: her nakedness, her white skin, the round columns of her legs, the small, soft breasts, the short-cropped, light-brown hair, the broad mouth whose thick lips trembled around long, square teeth, and the straight but fleshy nose, and the blue eyes, big as windows, from which tears poured.

She looked a little like a clown, with her inch-long hair, more the hair of a boy than a woman, bristles around ears that lay flat. And her body with its undefined waist, the breasts like those of an aging, pudgy, effeminate man, and her hands joined over her crotch, while her large blue eyes showed no expression, no fear or plea, only gushed big tears that rolled down her face and left glistening tracks on her skin.

He found her more amusing than anything else, and took a playful approach, but not too playful, so as not to reassure her. He restrained his amusement, smoothing it into a kind of mocking politeness.

"Come here," he said, not touching her. Seeing that she did not obey—not in protest, he realized, but out of helplessness, as if her crying were a task that left her neither the strength nor the will to do anything else—he retreated and sat on the bench before the workbench-table. "Look what I have for you. Bread and butter, ham, warm milk . . ." With indulgence he gestured at the delicacies. "If you want to eat, you have to come here and sit with me on the bench and kiss me. For every kiss you get a bite of bread and butter with ham on it, and a sip of warm milk. Want some?"

Prompted by the joke within him, he did not look at her, as if unconcerned whether the appearance and aroma of the food were having their effect; instead, he began to prepare them for her, cutting a broad, crusty slice from the loaf of bread, using the knife to take a whole corner from the half-pound slab of butter and spread it on the bread, and peeling a strip of ham from the heap of ham and laying it on top of the butter. He then cut the slice of bread—through the ham, pink and moist with fat—cut twice down and once across, making six equal bites, and put the knife aside and reached for the pot of milk, which was still giving off vapors of warmth. "Here. Come."

Only then did he look up, but not impatiently, not even questioningly, because he knew she couldn't resist, knew it from experience, from his own hunger, the pit that yawns in the belly, in the whole body, after being without food only a few days. He waited. Still she didn't move, didn't even cast an eye at the workbench, at those delectable morsels that would fill the mouth with bliss and the famished stomach with warm, sweet contentment.

Tears kept falling from her eyes, evenly, neither fast nor slow, as if the faucet behind them had been inadvertently left on and there was no one to shut it off. She herself wouldn't; she wasn't even aware that she was crying, so preoccupied with the reason for her tears, which he didn't know but guessed was something trivial and ludicrous, like the rest of her, ludicrous in relation to the abyss of suffering into which she had fallen.

"You are a virgin," he ventured, and when her lips trembled even more, he knew she was. Which was quite ridiculous, for she was no longer a girl; you could see that by her body—the legs thick and ungainly, the breasts no longer firm, the little wrinkles at the corners of her mouth. The wrinkles could not have been the result of starvation, since her flesh showed that she hadn't been hungry that long, though when delivered to the camp she had probably been plump—one of those marriageable girls who was too choosy and devoted herself more to the pleasures of the stomach than to courtship.

All the more reason why she had to give in: she was pampered, knew what was good, and although she didn't turn her brimming eyes to where he pointed, she could certainly smell the food through the fleshy, nostrils that now quivered in response to his smile. "That doesn't matter," he said, entertained by her maidenly distress. Then suddenly, unexpectedly, he was angry —angry that she could be so stupid, so petty, as to worry about the small membrane between her legs when her very life was threatened, all that she was and all that she possessed.

"Go, then," he said, and looked away from her. They didn't move, either woman. He decided to help her, to take away from her a situation in which she was allowed to hesitate, for hesitation, the illusion of delay, might make her think she was master of her fate. "Go sit in the corner." He waited to hear her move, but heard nothing, so he looked at her again, expecting to find an expression of repentance, submission, but her face remained unchanged, was melted into its soft features, the eyes shining only with tears, as if she didn't comprehend, as if she didn't know the language he spoke.

But these captive women, each one of them, wherever they came from, all understood the few German words required for obedience; they learned them quickly, just as the men did, with their lives at stake. Failure to understand German brought blows about the head and back; it got one tossed into the oven ahead of those who knew the language. No, Lamian saw that that inner resistance was still at work in her, that stubbornness, that fastidiousness acquired by being brought up in some cloistered home where words were carefully chosen and the world's evil, outside the curtained windows, was hushed up.

He stood, stepped over the bench, went up to her, and grabbed both her arms—it was the first time he touched her— and feeling the softness and smoothness of her white skin under his fingers, he turned her around like a large doll on a revolving pedestal. "Move over there, into the corner." She went obediently, walking awkwardly on bare feet that caught on the rough floorboards—not too fast, and not with reluctance, but the way she had entered, completely taken up with her weeping and her misery.

He watched her pale body submerge in the semidarkness beyond the circle of candlelight, where another female shape, a little darker in color, crouched, knees together, head sticking up above the anvil. The other woman's ears, he knew, were pricked for him and his call; her nostrils were dilated to take in as much as possible of the smell that wafted from the workbench, eyes open wide in tension, her mouth drenched with the saliva of her cavernous hunger.

"Come on, you—come here and eat." The crouching body practically leaped up, and he saw the flat face with wide-set brown eyes, which is why he called her the doe. "You, not her." The two bodies changed places, the paler one lowering itself in the corner as the other now moved in his direction on short, slender legs.

He sat down again, watching her stand in place, tense and straight, almost on tiptoe. "Come here." She flitted over to him immediately, brown eyes fixed on the workbench, where the pieces of bread and butter and the pot of warm milk still stood as he had set them out for the clown. The Adam's apple of the doe's slender throat bobbed up and down as she swallowed her saliva. "Sit in my lap." She came to him quickly, slipping between workbench and bench, pushing her knee between his knee and the table, then lowering herself onto his thighs. "Arms around my neck." She raised her arms, bent over slightly, and braced herself on his shoulders. He put a hand on her left breast, put the other one on her waist. "Kiss."

She lifted herself to him, reluctantly took her eyes from the workbench, then closed them and pressed her lips to his. He put his tongue into her mouth, probed the warm, wet cavity, felt his penis rise and touch the flesh between her parted thighs. When he withdrew his tongue, she quickly took her lips from his and opened her eyes. He removed his hand from her breast, reached for some food, offered it to her. She grabbed it with her teeth and began chewing.

Again he put his hand on her breast, kneaded it, then lowered it to her crotch, with its fine brown hairs. His finger sought the moist, sweet opening. When she swallowed the food, he took his hand away, raised the pot, and brought it to her mouth so she could drink. He set the pot back on the table. "Kiss." He repeated this five times, each time caressing her more forcefully, more impatiently as his desire grew, and when she had eaten and drunk enough, he slapped her thigh. "Let's lie down." She got off him, and he followed her, watching the sway of her narrow, undeveloped hips as she went around the workbench. She looked over her shoulder to see what position he wanted; he indicated she should lie on her back. She dropped to the mat, but behind her in the darkness was that other body, which still knelt, head turned toward the corner. Lamian, lying down between the doe's legs, putting his lips to hers and his hands on her breasts, thrust his penis in.

But, thrusting, he kept an eye on the clown, aware that she

was listening, and this filled him with power. He imagined the feel of her small breasts even as he squeezed these pear-shaped, wide breasts, and his testes tightened. Withdrawing, so as not to impregnate the woman, he remained lying on top of her, kissing her cheek, her lips, slowly ridding himself of his desire for her—but not for the clown, whose protruding white ass he now watched. He was within arm's reach of it, could touch it, could gouge his fingers into it and leave painful blue marks; he could climb off the doe and renew his invitation to the clown to come and eat, could continue his efforts to conquer her.

Surely she was regretting her resistance. He could feel what she felt, her stomach contracting with regret now, the discomfort of her crouching position. At first she had thought herself delivered from shame, but now, as she listened to the kisses and the sounds of his lovemaking with the doe, right beside her, she saw that this was nothing dangerous, nothing of great consequence in comparison with the pleasure that could have been hers.

And if he didn't renew the invitation today, but waited until tomorrow, her regret would build in those twenty-four hours. And when she left with the doe, the doe would not be able to resist commenting, in a whispered word or two, on the reward she had secured for herself but which the clown had refused, and this would soften the clown even more. The temptation to take her now, with her resistance still alive, and the prospect of taking her, instead, more easily but with the pleasure deferred and therefore doubled, warred within him like two strong birds beating their wings and robbing him of his breath. He decided to wait. Getting up, he stepped away and said to the two, "You can go."

They both rose, the clown getting caught momentarily on the saws stacked behind the anvil. Lamian went over to the wall at the opposite corner and rapped four times. A board moved, scraping the floor and opening onto a passage that let in light.

A hand appeared, the short, pudgy hand of Lina, in a striped glove, fingers spread. He turned and motioned to the clown and doe to go through. They bent, got down on hands and knees, and squeezed through the hole, first one and then the other. When the light in the hole reappeared, he went over to the nail bin and dug out what he had ready for Lina: six cigarettes, a can of sardines, and a pair of silk stockings, all wrapped in cement-sack paper. He put the bundle into her gloved hand. On the other side of the hole there was a crackling sound, then Lina's head appeared, a yellow silk scarf around her broad red face. "Tomorrow?" she whispered, lips drawn back in a grin of gluttony. "Yes," he replied, taking from the shelf a scrap of paper with the numbers of the two women. He was about to hand it to her when he changed his mind. Tearing it in half to keep the clown's number, he held out the paper. "The new one again, and someone else with her," he said, suddenly determined to magnify his triumph over the clown, because she made him wait for her.

He was impatient for the day to pass, and the night, and a third of the following day, impatient once more to have her naked and in his power. The next day, at Crematorium 3, he picked up two gold teeth for Riegler, pulled by Poldi the corpse bearer from the jaws of a dead prisoner, and he took a new silk corset from the Kanada depot for Lina, hiding both gold and corset in the nail bin the moment he entered the toolshed. Locking the door, he squinted through a crack in the boards nailed over the window, to make sure no one was watching him. Then he went to the workbench, removed the vise, put it on the floor, pulled the mat from the bench beneath and tossed it on the workbench, moved the workbench, and from the hiding place in the floor took the packages of food and the pot. He spread the mat on the floor behind the workbench, then pulled the bench out and set it on the other side. Took three rods and a candle from the lock shelf, stuck the candle in the knothole he had knocked out of the workbench, arranged the rods over the candle, fastened them with hooks. Then unbuttoned his tunic and from his belt took the flask of milk and half-loaf of bread he had obtained from Varminsky, the workman from outside, in exchange for powder and face cream. Poured the milk into the pot, hung the pot on the wire bracket between the rods, took a match from the seam of his glove, lit the candle.

The milk heated slowly, and impatiently he felt the pot several times. Finally he dipped his finger in to see if it was warm. It was, so he went over to the wall that separated the toolshed from the barracks of the women's disciplinary Arbeitskommando. Took the anvil that was leaning against the wall and moved it to the corner behind the workbench. He was sure they were already standing on the other side, in the room of Blockelteste Lina. She brought them from the dormitory, where they were permitted to rest until noon, on the excuse of conserving their strength. He listened and, although he heard nothing, imagined them standing and listening too, with Lina, waiting for the signal.

He tapped with the knuckle of his index finger four times on the panel over the hole, and the panel slowly moved aside, casting light on the floor. Then shadows replaced the light, and two naked women crawled in. First, a dark head shorn to the skin, followed by a bony shoulder, a narrow back, a rump and legs doubled up, lit from the rear. Next, a head with straw-blond hair, a fleshy back with no waist, a flat rump whose globes were divided as if slit with a knife, and round white legs like columns. Finally, Lina's hand holding out a paper with the numbers of both prisoners. He took it, stuffed it in a cubbyhole, turned to look.

The two of them were standing now. The first one was shorter and thinner, with round dark eyes and protruding Negroid lips; the second one was the clown, but he pretended not to know her. His desire grew even as he shifted his glance from Big Lips to that ample white body that was filled with hunger and sobs.

Yes, out of the corner of his eye he saw the tears running down her face, but he decided to let her be until his desire was partially satisfied. "Over there, in the corner," he ordered, motioning with his arm, and summoned Big Lips: "You, come and eat." He took her to the workbench, planted her in his lap, fed her and kissed her, and when she had eaten and drunk her share, told her to get up, took her to the mat behind the workbench, and had intercourse with her. But constantly aware of the other one, watching her as she huddled in the corner hiding her face.

After he ejaculated, he rose and said to Big Lips, "Now you go in the corner." To the other, who hadn't moved, he said, touching her thigh with his finger, "Come and eat." He turned around, not waiting to see if she would obey, but this time certain, feeling slightly lightheaded, that she would. And as he walked around the workbench, he heard her padding footsteps behind him. He sat in front of the candle, cut a piece of bread, smeared it with butter, lay a slice of ham on it, divided it into six equal pieces, moved the pot nearer, and said: "Come."

He looked straight ahead while from the side two feet and two white legs came into his field of vision. Was she still crying? "Sit on my lap." Now it was not only the sight of her but she herself in all her carnality—her touch, her weight, her warmth, her breath, her smell—that descended on him and nestled where he commanded. Still not turning his head, he saw her face. Wet tracks were indeed running down her cheeks, and as he held her and pressed her to him, he felt cold tears on his chest.

"Put your arms around my neck." Her arms rose, drawing the two spongy breasts upward and touching him lightly on the shoulders. "Kiss me." He turned to her, not to see her but to receive her mouth on his. It was soft, warm. He put his tongue out, but it was rebuffed by a wall of teeth. "Open your mouth." Now his tongue had an unobstructed path into that wet chamber. He entered, withdrew, picked up a morsel of food, and put it to her lips. She opened wide, baring long white teeth, which added to the clownish impression. As she ate, he caressed her breasts, belly, the mound covered with hair so light, it was almost white. He gave her some milk and set the pot aside. "Kiss." Again she submitted to his maraudings in her mouth. He gave her a second morsel, then began to instruct her. "When I say 'kiss,' kiss me. Did you ever kiss anyone?" After a short pause, she nodded, her first sign, if not word, to him. "Well kiss, then. Put your tongue in my mouth and twist it." Thinking that might be too much for her knowledge of German, he showed her what he wanted, drawing her close, sucking in her tongue, nibbling it. "I said, twist your tongue." He stuck his own out. Her tongue now moved in his mouth, from tooth to tongue to palate, but aimlessly, following only the letter of his orders, not their purpose.

Again he gave her food, and for the first time looked into her eyes, whose wet irises were a melting blue that left little room for the whites. "Kiss." When she had eaten and drunk enough, he told her to stand, then led her around the workbench. She walked numbly, awkwardly behind him, bumping into the old rusty tools. He pushed her down on the mat. "Spread your legs." She spread them, and he lay on top of her, looking steadily into her eyes, from which tears slowly flowed, as he pushed his way inside her.

It went more easily than he had expected, the initial resistance of the hymen ceasing as soon as he thrust to break it. His strokes were measured, slow, and went on a long time until the rhythm of it finally made him ejaculate, and even then there was more curiosity in this for him than desire. When he got up and motioned to her and Big Lips that they could return to Lina, he

almost regretted that the other one, the one he'd taken his pleasure with first, wasn't staying longer, or that a more provocative
woman had not come with her.

Nevertheless he gave Lina, along with her gift, a slip with
both numbers written on it, and he kept asking for the clown in
the days that followed. After lying with her, he would think with
annoyance that he could have had a better one instead, one
quicker and more obliging, from the multitude of women prisoners at his disposal. But whenever he didn't send for her, his
thoughts would turn to her as he was giving Lina the order for
the next day; to her numbness, to those watery, saucerlike eyes
and long bared teeth that made a good-natured joke of her face.
Once again he would write her number on the slip of paper.

And, the following day, give her food and milk, and take
her in his arms, and observe, with both anger and amusement,
that nothing changed in her behavior, in the passive submission
to him that brought a strange aloofness to the fever of her forced
embraces—and set her apart from the others.

But what truly set her apart was her kinship to him—of
which he was unaware at the time, and which, when he learned
of it, so horrified him that he thrust her from him for good.

BUT WHEN HE SAW THE HUNGARIAN NEWSPAPER, SHE returned in all the horror of her intimacy, giving tangible form to the fear that haunted him: that he would be unmasked.

The next morning, he jumped at the jangling of the alarm clock, threw up his arm to ward off the clubs, the howling litany of the names and the numbers of the people he had killed. He was relieved, waking fully, to see that that moment had been postponed. He left for work, watchful.

In the streets of Banja Luka, men and women went about their business, on their way to shopping or to work, and in their intent faces he saw nothing that had to do with him. Their glances skipped over him; he was not interesting, not important. Yet he continued to expect someone to leap from the crowd, face twisted with rage, grab him by the lapels, and announce to the startled pedestrians, "He killed hundreds of us. Now we will judge him."

Arriving at his desk in the land registry, Lamian felt he had run a gauntlet. Covered with sweat, his back in pain. He buried himself in paperwork, lowering his head to be less noticeable; flinched at every new voice, at the squeaking of the door, at any question directed at him, as if it might be followed by curses and blows.

In the afternoon he went from the battleground of supervised toil to his sublet room, just as in the camp he had gone from the Arbeitskommando to his cubicle in the barracks—with the knowledge, both soothing and horrifying, that one danger had passed but another, even greater, would take its place, because if he had been under everyone's eyes before, now he was alone, and an attacker's will to destroy, if it was kindled, would be concentrated exclusively on him.

He prepared himself for this attacker, this accuser, even as he lay down and rested, as he ate and gathered strength, but knew it was useless to prepare against that single pointed finger, that single memory, the will that was seeking him out and in the end would surely find him.

But the years went by and no one screamed, except in his dreams. No one grabbed him by the lapels. People passed him indifferently, and addressed him only with regard to mundane disputes over property and inheritance. If they spoke to him about the war—and there were many who did, for this was a Serbian area, bloodied by battles and depleted by the deportation of thousands of families, the Radić brothers included—it was only to ingratiate themselves with him and speed up his professional service. "I hear you were at Jasenovac and Auschwitz—terrible!" they would say, and wait for him to talk about it. When he didn't, they dropped history and returned to business.

Seeing that his sullen, abrupt manner restrained their natural inquisitiveness, he became more sullen, more abrupt. But not overly so, for that could inspire doubt, suspicion. Eventually he concluded that the advantages of saying little outweighed the disadvantages: it discouraged questions, while the mistrust it might give rise to would be dangerous only if substantiated by someone's declaration, someone's testimony.

For hours on end he sat on his bed staring into the emptiness of his room, adding up in his memory all those who could speak out against him: guards and prisoners, Kapos, train crews, villagers, residents of the places he had passed through with the column. He summoned up faces—trying to remember in whom he had confided, and how much; to whom he had given his name, nationality, profession in civilian life; and who had seen him in which guise. How he had been dressed, how his beard and hair had been cut, how emaciated and jaundiced he had been, what shoes or boots he had been wearing and how his gait had adjusted to them. Then he ticked off the ways these witnesses had ended. Schmuhle and Kromholz—by injection. Schmaus and Leitner—sent to the front and killed. Varminsky—strangled in a bunker. Lang, Mell—dead in the revolt at Crematorium 2. Morgenstern—bludgeoned to death with a sledgehammer. Novak, Corporal Sommer, Schranke—sent to the front. Poldi—hanged. SS man Platzfig—strangled before the evacuation. Jelinek—dead of typhus. Blockelteste Lina and her barracks chief, Berta—strangled by the SS. Old man Binder—injection. All the workmen, masons, carpenters, tailors, shoemakers—by injection before the evacuation. The doe, the dumpling, Big Lips, and the other girls from the disciplinary Kommando—dead of exhaustion, disease, and starvation. All of them, every last one, dead, except Riegler, and perhaps Helena Lifka—because he had helped her stay alive.

Of the two, Riegler would never track him down and testify against him, because they had done everything together, Riegler the commander and he the executor. Riegler had even ordered Lina to send female prisoners to Lamian in the toolshed, so if Lamian was guilty, Riegler was doubly guilty, and guilty, too, with the gold, which by now he had sold in Germany, waxing rich on the money if he hadn't already lost it. In any case, Riegler would not even want to think about his Kapo Furfa.

And Helena Lifka? But after that jolt of reading the Hungarian newspaper and the fear that she was already here, in Banja Luka, nothing had happened. Time passed, and she didn't appear, so more and more he was inclined to believe that she wasn't looking for him. Perhaps, just as he himself shrank from witnesses not only of his crimes but also of his suffering, Helena Lifka too did not want to go back over it, did not want to be reminded, because no one was wholly untainted. Each of them, in one way or another, in one form or another, had been an accomplice in that degradation and suffering, even if it was only by consenting to endure it in order to live. She as well as he, if not in equal measure then at least in the same way.

No, they would all shrink from one another. He recalled not only his fear but also his revulsion at the very mention of possible meetings with other inmates, even from different camps, his refusal to be introduced to them, to talk with them. It was like refusing to look at food that has poisoned you. All those survivors, each survivor one out of a hundred dead, were hiding from each other and from themselves, in a natural, human attempt to forget, so life could go on.

No, danger would strike only if that improbable scenario, product of his sick imagination, should materialize, or if she or some other surviving witness ran into him in Banja Luka, his hiding place, stopped face-to-face with him in the street, or in the cafeteria, or, looking for a certificate or survey map, in his very office. Recognition, that collision of remembering eyes, the cry "You!" which he could no longer deflect, and which would make everyone present raise his head and ask for the meaning of these gasps of mutual astonishment.

And the witness would keep silent no longer, nor allow herself to be dismissed with hasty lies, and his background would finally come to light: one of their colleagues, Lamian, was a murderer, a Kapo, Kapo Furfa. Accusations and counteraccusations would be exchanged, the public would take notice, idle people eager for a little excitement. Someone would call the police, and he would be arrested and dragged before judges with evidence that could no longer be refuted.

Change his appearance, then?

But he had already done this, instinctively, from the first day of freedom, when he ripped off his prisoner's uniform and replaced it with civilian clothes snatched from an abandoned German house; from the moment he started stuffing himself with food to fatten his body, and shaved regularly, and let his hair grow. In Banja Luka he began wearing eyeglasses, finding that he could not see clearly enough the lines and numerals finely drawn on the yellowed tracing paper of old survey plats. But he asked the optician to grind the lenses in dark glass, saying his eyes were sensitive to the light. Standing now before the mirror, he saw a man entirely different from the prisoner he remembered, a man grown potbellied from starchy food, from too much bread, a man with a bulbous head, hair long and thick, and a sharp nose shortened a little by the dark glasses that hid his squinting eyes.

He noticed that because of the new flesh on his thighs he walked with his legs more apart, walked with a gooselike waddle. This and his whole bearing, the stoop he had acquired in the course of deciphering old documents and avoiding the glances of others, had turned him into the personification of a withdrawn, insignificant civil servant, who would remind no one, not even his victims, of the thin, hard-eyed, brisk Kapo Furfa.

And the neighbors, taking note of his new persona, adjusted accordingly their behavior toward him. Old Čabrinović, who had taken Lamian into his house partly out of pity for a casualty of the war—he himself had lost his only son in the final battles—and partly in order to keep the three-bedroom apartment from being requisitioned, began to invite him for coffee, knocking on his door following the afternoon rest. Not to pursue a friendship, however, but only to speed up certain administrative decisions for friends and relatives. The women in the neighborhood, who had been suspicious and disdainful of his neglected state, began greeting him when they met, and soon were chatting with him and giving him advice on housekeeping, and occasionally even recommended some young woman, hard-working but without means, whom he might marry and thus not have to live alone.

Lamian responded politely but cautiously to these overtures, trying not to reveal any more about himself than he had to, keeping a line of retreat open in case his independence was threatened.

Then one day the land registry, which had hired him on his word as a returnee from the camps, requested his papers for its personnel files. However reluctantly, Lamian had to write to Bjelovar for his baptismal certificate and to Zagreb for his diploma. These documents, instead of being simply attached to his postwar applications and statements, which were stored in the office safe, became the occasion of disagreement between him and the municipal secretary, whose eye they had caught and who wanted to reassign him to the post of technical director of a furniture factory under construction. Lamian put off his decision, then finally turned the job down, afraid of new faces and new chances of being discovered. Three months later, he received a written order transferring him to the railroad as superintendent of the switchyard.

Once there, Lamian decided, after uneasily turning it over in his mind for weeks, that the change was a good one: the staff was small, stable, and through the older, experienced workmen he could manage his subordinates without much direct contact. He felt encouraged, bought some new clothes, took the apartment offered him in the railroad workers' housing project. As he grew accustomed to his new job and gained confidence, he became less timid in his dealings with people.

THE CHANGE IN EMPLOYMENT BROUGHT HIM, FOR THE first time since Bjelovar, Jasenovac, and Auschwitz, into contact with Jews.

He had known of none in Banja Luka—aside from hearing occasionally about some returnee from the camps, or seeing one from a distance, a person nearly always as worn and cheerless as Lamian himself was.

But peacetime gave strength to these former victims, and the creation of the Jewish state in Palestine focused attention on them as a people with the same rights as others. Lamian paid little heed to this event in the news, feeling no connection between himself and the new nation in Asia Minor whose first officials, unknown people, were now appearing in the papers with statements, declarations, and photographs; unreal heirs of the Biblical and Zionist traditions he had heard and read about for so long, traditions that had always seemed like legends to him, the utopian dreams of an exotic race, a myth that was the opposite of the myth he had received from the hand of Zvonko Gabelić.

When Lamian read in the newspaper one morning that war had broken out between Israel and Egypt, he had the sad thought that many who had so narrowly preserved their lives amid the perils of European hatred would now lose them. Not long after, as he was passing through the park and a city official, a Serb from Banja Luka, stopped him and asked, out of the blue, what he thought about the news, Lamian answered, caught off guard, that he believed Israel would win.

The official seemed startled, as if he had not expected such an opinion. It occurred to Lamian then that he had just contradicted the official Yugoslav position, so for the rest of the conversation he tried to reduce what he had said to a calculation based simply on the obvious technical superiority of the immigrants from Europe.

This uncomfortable exchange forced Lamian to reflect. Why had the official asked his opinion about the Middle East war? Could it be because he knew of Lamian's origins, and if so—which was almost certain, since the man, only a passing acquaintance, would not otherwise have approached him on the subject—then how had he found out? In Banja Luka there was no one Lamian knew from Bjelovar, and in all his official papers and elsewhere he had described himself simply as a Yugoslav.

Something about him must betray his race, he thought, and again he considered his appearance. The bulbous head with the thick, brushed-back, graying hair, the sharp, straight nose, the dark glasses which hid his eyes, the ponderousness of his stout body, his quiet and laconic speech: none of it, surely, betrayed anything Semitic, anything foreign or different. But when he began to analyze his behavior, he had to admit that he did not possess the hearty, backslapping manner of the mountain people, who had left their stamp on Banja Luka, those pillars of society who caught one's eye at public meetings, offices, and the marketplace.

He kept a prudent distance from those circles of power and influence, but the ones who naturally belonged to them, for example the official who had recently engaged him in conversation, now and then made him reveal his difference. They asked him for his views—he realized now that lately this had been happening a bit—indeed, even at meetings on technical and business matters, though usually Lamian gave careful answers, answers in harmony with the ignorance and prejudices of these peasants, leaving, with a kind of haughty indifference, the final decision to others.

It was during one such meeting that he made the acquaintance of Isaac Nahmijas, who had recently arrived to serve as circuit court judge in Banja Luka. On hearing the name, Lamian concluded instantly that here was a Jew, and when during roll call he saw a smallish man raise his hand—a thin-faced man with a hook nose and lively dark eyes, eyes that seemed to be drawn in ink—he nodded to himself and felt an uneasy, involuntary kinship.

When the discussion turned to the problems of rail transport, Lamian couldn't resist making a few pointed remarks on the outdated regulations for obtaining spare parts. The judge was so pleased by this that he came up to him afterward, gripped him by the arm as they were walking out together, and showered him with words of support. The next time they met, in the street, the judge spoke to Lamian for quite a while. After a second official meeting, the judge invited him for coffee at his home on a specific afternoon, and with a chaffing tenacity wouldn't take no for an answer.

So Lamian found himself taken almost by force under the wing of a Jewish family, with whom he felt, to his surprise, an immediate intimacy. Nahmijas's wife, a dark-haired woman somewhat larger than her husband, with gentle features and pale skin, a Gymnasium music teacher, withdrew after serving them coffee and candied fruit. The son and daughter, small and lively like their father, came in only to greet the visitor—no one made them show how knowledgeable and smart they were. Peace reigned in the room, and in the waning light of late afternoon the furniture took on soft contours. Though the tempest of the family's move from Sarajevo had taken place only a year ago, the furniture seemed to have stood in that room forever, casually and comfortably arranged for ordinary, everyday use.

In the course of the conversation it came out that Nahmijas was a Bosnian, born in Derventa, that he had been a Communist even before the war, that during the Occupation he joined the Partisans, along with his newlywed wife. They went through the battles together, he as company and battalion commissar, she in the lower echelons. This was strange to Lamian, who would never put himself in harm's way of his own accord, but the strangeness did not bother him, not in this man who spiced his war stories with facetious remarks directed mostly at himself.

Lamian agreed to visit again only after much pressure from his host. He felt he had no right to this friendship, for Nahmijas had opened his life to him like a book, self-mockingly confessing his sins—particularly against his parents, merchants whom as a Communist he had despised, going off to war without so much as saying good-bye and leaving them to the mercy of the Ustaši—while Lamian said virtually nothing about his own life. He told Nahmijas, of course, that he had spent the war in Jasenovac and Auschwitz—that could hardly be avoided—but not how and why he had ended up in each camp, nor what he had done there in order to survive.

Fortunately, Nahmijas did not mind Lamian's silence. Indeed, he needed him more as a listener than as an interlocutor —and not about the past, either, but about the present, that is, the future, since he was full of plans, both national and local.

He merely remarked to his guest in passing, "Where are Lamians from? The name sounds Armenian, or Jewish." The answer—"I'm of Jewish origin but baptized as a Catholic"— was received with no further comment, to Lamian's relief.

Now he saw how free Nahmijas was of prejudice, despite what the man had gone through in life. After their sessions together, spent discussing the measures needed to improve people's lives in Banja Luka and in general, he wondered what Nahmijas would say if he knew that his guest had broken people's heads with a club, forced them into the water to drown, and bought the compliance of starving women prisoners for a slice of bread and a swallow of warm milk. He avoided the judge, but the judge tracked him down, telephoning or simply descending on him in his apartment, for he interpreted Lamian's reluctance to socialize as mere bachelor quirkiness, and the disorder he found in Lamian's rooms only confirmed this.

"Quick, dress yourself, lazybones!" he would command before he was in the door. "Come and get some comfort in a real home instead of this bear's den." He made no secret of the fact that he intended to marry Lamian off, and when his sister-in-law Ella came to visit, this intention triumphantly acquired a definite direction. When Lamian arrived, the judge brought out his wife's younger sister, leading her by the hand like a heifer on a rope. "Look how beautiful she is! My Lydia's beautiful too, I'm not saying she isn't, but if I had known Ella would grow up to be such a Babylonian wonder, I would have waited a few more years. You lucky bachelor."

Ella Cohen was indeed a beauty: dark-haired and white-skinned like her sister, but with ample curves that filled her dress and stockings. She had glistening dark eyes and red lips that smiled a bit crookedly, as if deprecating the ardent sensuality they knew they were creating. Lydia, taking to the woods with her Communist husband, had left Ella in Derventa with the proprietor of a dress shop, a Croatian woman who was to hide her from the persecution, saying she was a relative. From this woman Ella learned the trade, and after the war she set up on her own in Sarajevo, where she married. Now, however, she was divorced, childless, and because after her marriage she had kept only her most loyal customers, she was able to travel, visiting her sister in Banja Luka and her "relative" in Derventa. She took along unfinished dresses and completed them on borrowed sewing machines.

But behind this simple existence a broader life could be sensed: Ella had lived for a time in Israel with some aunts, and in Lyons and Paris while married, having been sent there to study by a Sarajevo clothing factory. In his effusive praise for her, Nahmijas was apparently right when he said that she "knew how to take care of herself."

The offer of such an attractive and capable woman as a marriage partner, even if made with laughter and disconcerting candor, couldn't help but flatter Lamian; in a similarly jesting tone he permitted the Nahmijases to sing his praises to their relative in his presence. But after talking to her alone a few times—he being left to "entertain" her while the host changed clothes and the hostess prepared refreshments—Lamian saw an entirely different person. Free of Nahmijas's jokes and intercessions, Ella was serious, and to Lamian's questions about her travels, which he thought would be the easiest way to begin a conversation, she gave dry, direct answers. It had been hateful at her aunts' in Israel, because everyone there was afflicted with war psychosis, and she had had more than enough of that as a young girl during the Occupation. As for the opulence of Paris and Lyons, she had known none of it, since on the pay sent to her by the firm in Sarajevo she had had barely enough to eat.

She divorced her husband, she said, curling her sensuous mouth, because he became carried away with audacious projects abroad, wanting her to play the role of international fashion designer, which she could never be, and this had humiliated her unnecessarily and made her lose what she valued most: her peace of mind and self-respect. As she spoke, she looked straight at Lamian with her lovely dark eyes, and her look, and the way she moved closer to him so that others couldn't hear, mingling her warm breath with his, made him realize that he could in fact have her as his wife, that he could live with this beautiful, healthy, sensible woman, and have her in bed whenever he wanted, and be fed by her hand, and father her children.

In the same instant, he was aware how far short he fell of such a role, with his secret life and monstrous sins, and the best years of his adult life spent putting on weight and thinking morbid thoughts.

His decision to extricate himself from the Nahmijases was influenced, too, by his long-standing affair with Stanka Bugarin, a clerk at the city hall. As long as they were colleagues, he in the land office, she in the legal section of the municipal government, they merely exchanged greetings and an occasional pleasantry, though they were alike in that both were single and both kept their distance from the noisy familiarity of the civil-servant community. But after Lamian's transfer to the railroad, they were emboldened to establish a regular relationship.

This liaison suited Lamian, for it satisfied his masculine need without burdening him with any obligations he would have been incapable of meeting. Stanka talked to him about the people at work, whom he also knew, making observations that were almost always tinged with mockery; but of her own thoughts and feelings she revealed nothing—except those that concerned her family in a nearby village, whom she loved. Nor did she pry into his heart and mind. It was as if by lying with him on the couch, so unimportant a part of her spinster's furnishings, she was doing something foolish—like jumping into a river from a tippy boat, expecting nothing from it, or if she did, then quickly persuading herself it was only self-delusion.

Their meetings proceeded with a ritual sameness. He would arrive, leave his topcoat or umbrella in the hallway, and sit in one of the two armchairs. She would go into the kitchen to make coffee, then watch him drink it, usually not joining him because she had an acid stomach. She would chatter about the people she had seen, their adventures, misadventures, the ludicrous things said, the nasty things, the tantrums thrown—until, at a wink or gesture from him, the touch of his hand, she would get up, take the bedding from the wardrobe and spread it on the couch while he retreated to a corner to undress. Then she would go to the bathroom to shower, and he would lie down and wait for her. She emerged always the same—naked, thin, her hair tinted a light yellow and tied in a bun—and lay down next to him to receive his caresses.

At the beginning of their affair he had had to promise, each time, not to make her pregnant, but now that she had persuaded herself that he would keep that promise, she accepted his attentions calmly, sedately, showing signs of moderate pleasure but frowning whenever he felt like doing anything out of the ordinary. Not that she was prudish—she displayed her nakedness without shame at the start of every encounter—but anything unusual frightened her, as a possible damage to her health.

When they got up, dressed, and were arranging their next meeting, her facetiousness would return, now directed at him, and was often barbed; she would accuse him of being stingy with his time, proof enough, she would say, that he needed her only to satisfy his desire. He would deny it, would offer to see her the next day, every day, or suggest that she come to him for a change, or that they meet in a public place. To all this she said no, claiming she didn't wish to tire him out, or to expose him to Banja Luka's malicious tongues, and so things remained as they were.

Her sarcasm made him suspect that she wanted him to marry her, or at least to propose. Sometimes he thought of doing that—though it went against his decision not to form permanent attachments, nor did he think that marriage would suit her, since she didn't want children, believing herself too old—she was over thirty-five—and not strong enough for childbirth. But perhaps the banter over arranging their next meeting showed that she herself didn't care to see him that often or for that long, so her anger may have been directed more at herself than at him. She didn't really love him, but this was what bound him to her; had he sensed any love in her, he would have been frightened, unable to reciprocate. Just as he was frightened when he looked into the dark eyes of Ella Cohen.

His avoidance of Ella did not escape the matchmaker's eye of Isaac Nahmijas, or pass without the judge's ironic remarks, which hid his disappointment. The two men grew distant, seeing each other now only by chance, in the street or at meetings, and although Nahmijas occasionally invited Lamian over for coffee, he did not insist, accepting the refusal with an obedient, melancholy wave of his hand.

For Nahmijas there now came bad years. His health began to fail, and he walked the streets contorted with sciatica. His illness brought out the fury and scorn that was in him; he came into conflict with the leading people in the city; accused them of petit-bourgeois indulgence, negligence, corruption. Gradually he became known as a malcontent who wanted to turn back the wheel of history, calling for asceticism in a society where the pleasures of private enterprise were actively flourishing. After one heated outburst at the city hall, where the losses of failing businesses were being forgiven, he was removed from his post as president of the court and transferred to the self-management court, which on paper had the same duties but lacked the authority to impose punishment.

Offended by this demotion, Nahmijas turned down the job and at the same time requested to be pensioned off. This was granted with insulting promptness. Overnight he found himself without work, without a role in society, a fixture of the Banja Luka streets, tottering along and bent over his cane, back twisted, feet dragging, the embodiment of rage. Then discord began to undermine his family, too. His daughter, on whom he doted and who showed a remarkable gift for languages, went off to study in Belgrade and there fell in love with a student of literature. She announced that she wanted to marry him. Nahmijas was opposed; he demanded that she wait until she finished her studies. The next semester, however, she became pregnant and so married against her parents' wishes and with no means of support.

It was time now to forgive and put right what mischief had been done: to find the newlyweds an apartment in Belgrade, to make everything ready for the birth, and above all to supply them with money, which the young man's parents, villagers from the Sandjak, either could not or would not do.

But Nahmijas declared that since his daughter had not seen fit to consult him about her life, he would not assist her in following a path that could only lead to ruin. He refused to go to Belgrade or take any part in ameliorating the young couple's situation. He would not see them or the grandson who had come into the world. His wife had to take over these family obligations.

As she traveled back and forth, he suffered in solitude, and his son was also deserting him little by little, taking refuge in the rock band where he was a drummer. Alone in the empty rooms of his comfortable apartment, Nahmijas ate poorly and went unshaven for days, even when his wife was at home—to rebuke her with his neglected state. One winter morning, when she had left for Belgrade after an argument, he fell ill during breakfast, called an ambulance himself, was taken to the hospital, and died two days later.

WHEN LAMIAN, WHO HAD FOLLOWED FROM AFAR WHAT was happening to his former friend, learned of his death, he was of two minds about going to the funeral. The idea of this obligatory ritual repelled him, who had seen thousands upon thousands of corpses simply thrown into fires and pits. Had seen, and had helped throw them.

Yet something also drew him to Nahmijas, even in death, drew him to this last encounter, as if that encounter, through some sign, might yield an explanation, for something that had been missing, that had left a void, since his forced and senseless rupture with the man and his family.

He went to the cemetery at the appointed time, but when he spotted a cluster of people in front of the chapel, he held back, remained true to his aloofness, and followed the proceedings from a distance. There were several speeches, which reached his ears only in incomprehensible fragments. Then people in uniform stepped away from the group; in their hands and attached to their belts were horns and drums of various sizes, which gleamed in the winter sunlight. Before long, the booming sounds of a march reverberated. Behind the band, the procession formed up, first men dressed in black, pushing the cart with the casket, then a few women in veils—Ella Cohen no doubt the most upright—with men supporting them, then the rest of the assembly, group by little group. To the strains of the march, they walked solemnly out to the middle of the cemetery. There they stopped, a silence descended, then several harsh shouts rang out, the click of metal, echoed, and rifle barrels poked the sky, the sun playing on them as it had on the musicians' instruments before. A deafening salvo. The procession stirred; its ranks loosened; men and women now detached themselves in twos and threes, heading for the exit. Not wanting to be found standing alone by the cemetery fence, Lamian too turned and left.

He was surprised by what he had seen and heard, by that thunderous music, by the people stepping to its beat, and by the shots, the menacing crack of bullets, that had replaced the moment of silent prayer with a challenge to the heavens. Nahmijas had been a Partisan, a commissar, and thus an officer, so his body was saluted in accordance with the brutal pomp of military regulations.

But Lamian could not connect the Nahmijas he had known with the one honored by these rifles. The judge's diminutive form appeared before his eyes, the look that was at once mischievous and melancholy, the limp that Lamian had furtively observed in the last few years. The judge's isolation in a city he had so vainly admonished—and, in the end, his isolation within his own family.

Where in that frustrated curmudgeon was the officer laid to rest to the music of a march? Lamian had the feeling that a trick had been played on him, that Nahmijas had been dressed in the costume and mask of someone else, someone invented. And everyone had gone along with it, even those closest to him, those who loved him. But perhaps only Lamian had known the true Nahmijas. Had known him, yet distanced himself in recent years, resisting the invitations, the pleading looks, the appeals of this sincere and truth-loving man.

A man whose intelligence and experience might have enabled him to understand the most contradictory acts, even monstrous, inhuman acts, if only Lamian had had the courage to talk to him, to place his trust in him. Unaware, he had lived beside a man who could have offered him a hand, a word of compassion—or perhaps of condemnation—in any case that final word which Lamian alone, not confiding, had sought unsuccessfully in his own twisted conscience.

On his way home from the cemetery, he suddenly realized that Nahmijas's death, which had first caused him only mild regret, was a terrible loss—and in the same instant he felt a sharp pain in his stomach.

He had to stop and bend over. The pain gradually subsided, but the moment he tried to straighten, it again cut through him like a sharp knife. He was bathed in sweat, one hand holding his stomach and the other seeking support on the wall of a house.

He was in Vlajko Bogunović Street, which would take him to the Banovina, where he had intended to cross the square and make his way home through the park. People passed by him, a young woman leading a little girl, by the hand, a pair of skates slung over her shoulder. She turned to look, and he met fearful eyes. The child stopped too, but the young woman tugged at her hand, pulling her along with terror-stricken haste.

Lamian managed to lift his head and shoulders. His limbs felt caked with mud, felt foreign to his body, but at least he was not as conspicuous now, standing by the wall, bracing himself with an arm. The coldness of the wall penetrated him and joined the coldness that was building within. His back trembled, his hands shook, and the hand on the wall began to claw, scraping away the loose plaster. His legs shook too, as if the earth were quaking beneath them, but his feet remained planted in the thin layer of fresh snow on the sidewalk.

He shivered and felt that there was nothing between him and the cold, not a stitch of clothing, as if he were standing naked in the street, exposed to the winter wind, like the time Corporal Sommer poured a bucket of water on him and ordered him to stand at attention on the parade ground until evening, because Lamian had taken a sweater from a corpse to keep himself warm.

Now, too, he felt that if he didn't move, the cold would rip him to shreds, and the shreds would be borne by the wind and scattered over the roofs and into the dreary sky. Straining, he moved one stiff, weak leg, then the other, in the direction he was going. Twitching and shivering and holding onto the walls of the houses, he did not cross the square but went around it, and around the entire park, until he finally reached his house and mounted the stairs to his apartment.

Collapsing into an armchair, he continued to tremble. He trembled even though the apartment was warm, the heat on. He could feel the heat, but it had nothing to do with him; a barrier lay between the heat and his body, and the heat could not get through it. He tried to raise himself, to extricate himself from the armchair and stand, but gave up. He was standing in the wind of a raw winter noon, a sunless Silesian noon, in wet clothing, wet rags stiffening in the cold, and Sommer was holding an empty bucket in his hand and laughing, laughing at Lamian standing at attention, a rigid figure coated with ice. And Sommer dropped the bucket in the snow, and around him gathered SS men in overcoats and warm boots, Kommandoführer Riegler and several others Lamian didn't recognize, to see what had caused this merriment, and to join in, because they were eager for laughter, their stomachs full and bodies warm. So Sommer did it again for their benefit, to amuse them, to show them how witty he was, and shook his fist at Lamian, then let it fall, he was laughing so hard. "Don't move until evening, prisoner, or I throw you to the dogs!"

Lamian didn't move. He stood still, even though he was all movement, shivering in every bone and sinew, but he overcame his shivering because it was forbidden; it could be interpreted as an attempt to warm himself secretly, and he was not allowed to warm himself, even if he died, and die he would, whether frozen or torn apart by the dogs, that was what they all wanted, Sommer doubled over with laughter, Riegler watching Lamian intently, the unfamiliar SS men who grew more and more numerous, all out of breath from laughing. There was no one who didn't want his death. He was alone, alone in the wind and snow, in that raw, sunless Silesian noon.

He was alone now too, standing in his apartment by the armchair and shivering. No one saw him, no one suspected that here, in one of the rooms of this three-story building crisscrossed with heating pipes, a man was shivering with cold. On the other side of the wall, people sat in shirtsleeves reading the newspaper or talking; and outside his window, in the street, people were passing by, women leading children by the hand to go skating or shopping. They all had some destination or purpose, and not one of them gave a damn about Lamian and his sins and his need to confess.

But if Nahmijas were alive, Lamian could jerk himself from this spell of ice and go to him, Nahmijas, too, alone and bitter in his room, and throw himself at his feet and through trembling lips dredge up all his cold and loneliness, his suffering and humiliation.

Desperately he yearned for Nahmijas, for his mocking smile and the angry fire of intelligence in his eyes. Before those eyes Lamian could rip from his chest the clothes that so maliciously refused to warm him, and confess everything he had done in order to survive.

He had to find someone to whom he could kneel and unburden himself. How he missed that friendly nook with the comfortable old furniture! Nahmijas would not be there now, only mournful shadows just back from the funeral. Lamian then thought of the most upright among them—Ella, as he had seen her at the cemetery. It was to her that he now wished to crawl, in that apartment where Nahmijas's affection still hovered, and Ella's affection, she whom Nahmijas had intended for him. The warmth of her healthy body as she leaned toward Lamian, the warmth of her moist breath and trusting eyes.

He would ring the doorbell, and she would let him in. He would murmur words of condolence, then ask if the two of them could go to a place where they would be undisturbed, and there he would tell her everything. And she would understand, having occasionally lived with Nahmijas and absorbed some of his acerbity and resistance to generally accepted views, as she once revealed in her ridicule of the international bastions of fashion and wealth.

But even as Lamian conjured up her vibrant figure, the scornful twitch of her full lower lip, he knew that it was too late, that the opportunity had passed. She would no longer lean trustingly toward him; Nahmijas had offered her, and Lamian had refused. Her lip now would curl and pay him back in kind.

She was too healthy, too proud to understand and accept the filth that would come spewing from his mouth; too untainted to be spattered with the blood of the slaughtered, the stench of the terminally ill, the cries and whimpers of the deranged.

One had to live through the squalor and the cold and the threat of death to understand; one had to experience those nights and days of hunger, of listening for danger, of feverish hallucinations; one had to have those stooped figures seared into one's eyeballs, figures dragging themselves through the darkness to the latrine to spill their bloody stool, or to the dispensary for an injection of phenol in the heart. One had to have their desperate whispers in one's ears, their hopeless prayers; and the blows under one's skin, and the paralyzing fear in one's veins. One had to be what he was. What Helena Lifka was.

SUDDENLY HE THOUGHT OF HER: FROM THE FACE OF ELLA Cohen *her* features emerged: the clown's face, the short, straw-like hair, the fleshy white cheeks, the round blue eyes full of tears and staring past him into space, the big wide lips parted over large, long teeth.

A face that had written behind it, like a wax mold of letters into which the metal has been poured for printing, the words he was so eager to say.

Once again he wished for her, for the first time since the camp, wished for her as she had remained in his memory—not to force his way between her legs but to huddle close to her and unburden himself.

He felt in her the tenderness and understanding he had last felt at Nahmijas's house, in conversation with Ella Cohen, but with Helena Lifka there was not the barrier of difference that had hampered him then; there was an openness that warmed his blood, calmed his shivering, relaxed his taut muscles.

He was no longer cold. The trembling abated, until only his hands twitched a little, like treetops when the wind dies, and then they too were still. Because all along he had been wanting her, her alone, but didn't dare admit it to himself.

And still didn't. The next day, after sleeping through the night as if drugged, he denied it. No, if anything, the opposite was true: he could not bear to see her ever again. Hadn't he cast her from his presence as soon as he learned what she was? And then had looked after her only through intermediaries—not to save her for himself, or to save her at all, but simply to alleviate that revulsion he felt at the thought of her; as of some slimy insect he had inadvertently crushed: since he could not undo the injury, at least he could console himself with the thought that the thing, though injured, was still alive. And hadn't he been terrified, horrified, when because of the Hungarian newspaper published in Szabadka he thought he had come upon evidence of her proximity, of the possibility that he could find himself face to face with her?

Again he felt that same hatred and loathing, the need to flee, an irrational, almost mystical impulse that sprang from his constant fear of being discovered, like an arrow from a long-taut bow. He feared her as one might fear a ghost, with her bristled head and brimming eyes, this monument to his deepest shame. And if on his return from Nahmijas's funeral he had begun to shiver, then perhaps he had shivered in fear that his loneliness would lead him to seek a substitute for Nahmijas in her, the ghost who pursued him.

ATTRACTION ALTERNATED WITH HORROR. ONE MINUTE IT seemed that he could not live without Helena Lifka, the next minute that he would die blessed if he never saw her again.

Because when he thought of her now, he also thought of death. This was where the death of Nahmijas had led him, the first natural, private death after the foul public dying Lamian had witnessed so often in the camps.

A natural, private death awaited him as well, who had escaped all those violent, horrible deaths—deaths which for a long time had almost made him smile at the thought of dying in bed. On occasion, when he fell more seriously ill—while working at the railroad, he had had pleurisy, and earlier, at the land registry, infectious hepatitis—he lay in a hospital bed and watched the white coats hovering over him, watched devices being inserted into his body and the behavior of that body as it underwent treatment, sometimes growing stronger, sometimes weaker. He regarded all this as a benign, half-cheerful event. Perhaps he would die; yes, he would, if his body felt like it, if it became incapable of functioning any longer because of some contact with another, infected body, or because one of its parts wore out, a hereditary weakness in some link. The future would be snuffed out, true, but what a comfort to have death be the result of his own weakness, his own will, so to speak, and not the violent shattering of good health, the plunging of a knife into the throat, a sledgehammer blow to the head, the squeals and whoops of the murderer's dance, the snarls of dogs, the bone-breaking solitude of the stand-up cell, and the astonishment, in the final spasm of consciousness, at such overwhelming hatred.

But he saw now that the astonishment was no less when one faced a natural death—because this time the death was real, not imagined as it had been in the hospital, where he believed he would recover. And because it came too early, before that conversation with Nahmijas that would have freed and illuminated. An opportunity lost forever, since Nahmijas was no more.

The absence of Nahmijas now loomed, a forbidding barrier to death, just as that previous barrier, in the camp, had once disheartened the will to live. It turned out that to make one's peace with death, the body's exhaustion was not enough; an inner completeness was also needed, a word at the end, a summing up of what had been lived. And this summing word had to be spoken, and heard, and confirmed—by someone, whose response could be even silence, a look of damnation or forgiveness.

With a stab of pain he thought of his father and mother. In Jasenovac, when he learned which barracks housed the Jewish men of Bjelovar and which camp in Gradiška housed the women, he should have given his parents the chance to say that final word. But he did not seek them out, did not send them a message through some bribable guard, no, he avoided them, telling himself that he was doing the old people a favor, that it would be easier for them to die not knowing that their son was also in mortal danger. Their death was a certainty, so he had not bothered to verify it through official channels.

At Jasenovac he had prayed, not to God but to a nameless power, for them not to suffer, to die as quickly as possible. He did not think of their need to have someone close to them just before dying, that what they said to the one they loved most would give meaning to their suffering. He believed they were old enough, in this circle of hatred and violence, that death would mean liberation, relief. So when he gave his brown climbing boots to Private Jozo, he asked no favor in return, hoping with that instinct of self-preservation that would prove so reliable later in the camp, like a power of prophecy, that this gift would gain him mercy. He did not ask in return to be allowed to see his father or send a note to his mother, that he might hear their final words, if they had any caught in their throats, as his words were now caught in his throat.

He was now much older than they had been then—fourteen years older than his father, nineteen years older than his mother—and yet he still expected something at the end, didn't hurry himself toward death as he had once, in his thoughts, hurried them. He allowed himself time—though did he have the time and strength?—to look for Helena Lifka. Unless he gave up once and for all the idea of meeting her.

The sharp pain that he first felt as he was returning from Nahmijas's funeral later reoccurred at odd intervals. A stomach ulcer? A ravaged liver? Cancer of the pancreas? He felt his body, the belt of flesh that was thinner now, flabbier; he probed his abdomen, his neck—nothing. But in the office, or while getting up in the morning, just as he stuck his feet in his slippers and straightened up, it would come—the knife cutting him in half and bending him to the ground; then the cold, the shivering, would follow and render him helpless.

Sometimes he had to wait an hour for the attack to pass, and sometimes it lasted half a day, which he would spend huddled in bed, fully dressed, buried in the covers and any other fabric that came to hand, shaking from the February cold of Silesia, in the middle of the camp parade ground.

Everything was joined: the parade ground, his illness, the imminence of death, Nahmijas, his parents. Was he condemned, because of his parents, to suffer to the end, mute and unrecognized? Would he sink into the earth without confiding in anyone? Apparently that was how it had to be. He endured the pain when it came, didn't think about it the rest of the time, lived his strict bachelor's routine, which ground and chewed up the days with the food that no longer appealed to him, as if he was sated forever, because that post-camp hunger had finally ended, having held him in its jaws for decades; it had disappeared without his noticing.

He lost weight. His legs and arms grew thin; his shoulders narrowed. In the morning, shaving, he saw that his cheeks were sunken, and his double chin, deflated now to folds of skin, flapped beneath a newly sharpened jaw. Finally even his belly receded and disappeared, so that his suits hung as if the lining had been removed from them overnight.

Stanka saw this, and perhaps others did as well, but they said nothing, no doubt because they were not in the habit of speaking of personal matters with him, in deference to his gruffness. But she began to quiz him, in those afternoons when he visited. "What's wrong with you? Are you ill?" And when he replied, "Why do you ask?" she would shrug and explain with a smile that was not devoid of malice, "You are all pointy and wrinkled somehow, like an old man." "Well, I am an old man," he wanted to say, but refrained—not because he would have been saying something false, but because he had begun to think about her more carefully now that his view of the future had grown tangled. Perhaps, with some effort on his part, and some on hers, she might serve as a substitute for Helena Lifka, whom he never stopped thinking of, though the image of that woman continued to terrify him.

Stanka too was a woman, a woman he had slept with, and for a much longer time than with *her*, though he had long ago stopped sleeping with Stanka. Their afternoon visits, as regular as ever, had become a kind of reminiscence, a return to the scene of the crime, as it were, a postmortem in which there was something both melancholy and self-reproachful. Because in a way he had forced this woman also, taking advantage of her panic at the desolation of spinsterhood, offering her, in her weakest moment, a reward which corresponded more or less to a slice of bread with butter and ham, a cup of warm milk held out to hungry eyes.

Could he hope for forgiveness from Stanka, and for understanding? She too had aged somewhat, though she was twenty years younger and her body, which he now saw only clothed, had not lost that firmness of the childless woman. Her face had dried up and was crisscrossed with tiny wrinkles. Her upper front teeth, now false, had turned a telltale green beside the real ones. Her eyes had sunken and lost their gleam, assuming an expression of myopic distrust. Was she still waiting for some great change that would deliver her from the monotony of growing old alone? Hard to imagine, with her present appearance, her constant fussiness and suspicion, and burdened with this liaison which, though no longer romantic, could not be concealed. He had gone from rescuer to obstacle for her, and the resentment in her remarks about his aging must have concealed impatience: Was he ever going to die?

He decided to break with her, to restore her freedom, though what a mockery this would seem to her, now that she could no longer do anything worthwhile with that freedom. Then he imagined the other extreme: marrying her, giving her, toward the end of her life, the title of married woman, which she no doubt had always desired.

Would this belated step, which she was no longer expecting, draw her closer to him? Or would it lead only to the bitter contemplation of the years lost, the years of full and equal status lost, the years of motherhood lost, and would he find himself with a wife bristling with spite, unable to look at him, much less listen to and understand his secret crimes? But if this was his punishment for what he had done to others, shouldn't he accept it? Didn't marriage offer him just the opportunity he longed for?

While he hesitated, he decided to have himself examined by a doctor. A diagnosis would remove much of his uncertainty. He went to the clinic and told a young woman doctor of his pain and weakness. She began to prescribe pain medicine and vitamins, but he stopped her and asked that she investigate his illness thoroughly.

With a sour face she agreed, and wrote out a whole sheaf of referrals, which in the next few days he took with him as he had his blood tested, brought stool and urine samples to the lab, and stretched out half-naked beneath the x-ray machine. The results were negative, indicating only the minor deteriorations of aging. The doctor glanced ironically at the papers and prescribed the same pills he had originally refused. Was he now a hypochondriac? But while he was still taking the medicine, the familiar attack came upon him, again in the street; the chills, the murky visions of the camp.

He missed his usual meeting with Stanka, and she phoned him and offered, with a certain reluctance in her voice, to come over and help. He said no, afraid that in his weakness he might reveal too much to her; that his condition, and not his own will, might lead him to make the decision he was still agonizing over.

It was only when he felt stronger that he visited her. He described his latest health problem, then said, testing himself more than her, "I should retire. I'm not fit to work anymore. And I want to end this solitary life, get married. That is, if you agree."

"If I agree?" she said, surprised or pretending to be. "And what is it I'm supposed to agree to?"

"Why, to be my wife. That we get married."

She stared at him, then exploded in mirthless laughter. "You and me? What's the point now? You never indicated that anything like that ever crossed your mind."

"You didn't either," he retorted.

"No, I didn't." She threw back her head and drew herself up. "You're not cut out for marriage or any other kind of communal existence. In fact, you're not cut out for anything. You're hardly even a person; more a robot, a machine, I don't know what . . ."

He looked at her in amazement. "Then why did you sleep with me all these years?"

Tossing her head impatiently, she said, "I don't know. Maybe because you were different. Because you're a Jew."

He was astounded. It was the first time anyone had elevated his Jewishness to a virtue. This should have flattered him, but it didn't; instead, it made him feel that he'd been tricked. Throughout their affair, he had believed that Stanka was won over by something they shared, a critical attitude to their surroundings; it turned out now that he had had her all these years only because of the differentness she sensed in him.

Yes, and while he kissed her and probed her naked body as it writhed beneath him, he was making love to a woman who never forgot, not even in those moments that border on delirium, that he was something different. She had tolerated him on top of her precisely for that reason. Tolerated him—just as all of them tolerated him, merely tolerated him, and even that tolerance was possible only now, after the fires of hatred and envy had been extinguished, after the flames had consumed all the fuel, all the Jews. Even he had only begun to tolerate himself as a Jew during this recent period, and for the same reason: the multitude who made that differentness distasteful had disappeared. It was in Jasenovac that reconciliation with the Jews was born, his own and everyone else's; in Jasenovac that his tolerance of his own apartness was born, there and in Auschwitz, in Dachau, in Treblinka, and in hundreds of other camps where for four, five, six years they had arrived one after another, piling up, the human logs that kept the fire going, until the fire devoured them all— except for a few inconspicuous, scorched splinters thrown high by the blaze and swirling in the wind like bits of litter.

He, Helena Lifka. Who else? Other discarded individuals he hadn't known, or if he did know them, he had refused to let them anywhere near him, avoiding that multitude which might give rise to new hatred, a multitude which in fact no longer existed.

All he had left, then, was her, the prisoner he had once thrust from him because he learned she was a Jew, and whom he must now find, because she was a Jew.

HE MADE PREPARATIONS TO GO LOOK FOR HER. AT THE railroad office he submitted a request for retirement. When it was approved—with some difficulty, since they still needed him, unlike the courts and Nahmijas—he withdrew all his savings from the bank, as if not planning ever to return to Banja Luka, and set out for Subotica.

A morning train took him toward her, with the feeling that he was under escort, his own, in irons. It was spring, the beginning of May, but in the hills around Banja Luka there was still a nip in the air; the passengers were bundled up and hunched over in topcoats, their heads buried in the folds of the grimy gray-green curtains. Lamian alone sat among them with all his senses alert, listening to the wheels grinding beneath the coach that was carrying him to compulsion and violence.

Of course, he could turn back halfway. But the thought was painful to the point of nausea: returning to the Banja Luka he had just left, returning to those hills, those streets and houses, his own apartment, which had crumbled, he felt, the moment the door was closed, collapsing into dust from its third story on top of all those people to whom he no longer had anything to say, for everything he had told them was a lie, just as everything he had heard from them was a lie. So he let himself be carried forward, though that direction, too, repelled him.

In Vrpolje he changed to a local train that took him out onto the plain. Here the passengers were jovial, with baskets and string bags set between their feet, taking out food and drink to snack on. They offered refreshments to the driver, who was not partitioned off and sat but a yard away; he chatted with them, and at one point stopped the train to let on an acquaintance with a suitcase who flagged him down from the weeds along the tracks.

The unrestrained earthiness of the scene shattered Lamian's resolve; the coarse words and smells suddenly made his goal unclear, inconceivable even, as if he were standing in broad daylight and poised to plunge into the darkness of a cave simply because he had decided earlier to do so. No longer sure of himself, but feeling that his plan must be carried out, he vacillated at the station in Indjia for an hour and a half before boarding the fast, clean train to Subotica.

This region was new to him, with its silent, subdued people who, like him, all seemed to be headed toward some definite and disagreeable goal. He looked at them, and they at him, but no one said a word in the nearly empty international train. Hungry, Lamian bought cakes and beer from the vendor who came down the corridor with his clattering cart, and a little later a cup of coffee. He lit a cigarette and looked out at the fields, above which a pale, washed-out sun peeked from behind the clouds. Again he had the feeling that he was traveling as a prisoner, though without handcuffs and without the crush of other sweaty, frightened bodies: not under escort, simply dispatched with written orders that were on the same train, in a chest in the baggage car, the elbows of some stern, incorruptible guard resting on the chest.

When the conductor said that Subotica was the next stop, Lamian got up even though the train was still rumbling through fields, and waited in the corridor for it to enter the station. He looked out the nearest window for the first houses, as if impatient to arrive. He was surprised when the clock said only three-thirty; the trip had seemed long and complicated. Even so, little could be accomplished in any government office that day. He wondered why he had not taken an earlier train, why he hadn't planned better.

The suspicion gnawed at him that this carelessness was not as trivial as it appeared. His setting out unprepared on this ill-considered journey would involve him in all kinds of difficulties. Why, for example, hadn't he written first? Although he had no acquaintances in Subotica, he could have made use of official channels, of the railroad office, as a longtime, high-ranking employee. The railroad stood at his disposal with letterhead stationery and seals that would inspire respect and bring swift and accurate replies. Why hadn't he inquired from a distance about Helena Lifka? Did she exist at all, who was she, what was she, how did she behave, what was her position in Subotica society, so high as to be unapproachable, or, on the contrary, so low as to be beneath notice?

The fact that these courses of action occurred to him only now, when it was too late to assess them, added to his indecision as he stepped out into the square in front of the station, amid the few travelers who had got off with him and now dispersed quickly into the nearby streets. He stood alone, his right hand holding a bag that contained shirts, underwear, an extra tie, pajamas, shaving kit, and toothbrush. Ridiculous, to have equipped himself like this, as if for a wedding, his own or someone else's; ridiculous, to be carrying these tokens of bourgeois comfort into the pit that yawned before him. As countless people had taken their valuables with them to the camp.

He started into town, keeping his legs together and stepping cautiously, as if there were mines beneath the asphalt. He went down several streets with stores and cafés, until his bag grew heavy. He stopped, and immediately felt tired, weak in the knees. Glancing around, he picked out an innocuous-looking little man about his own age, whose hands were jammed in the pockets of his overcoat as he walked. Lamian stopped him and asked where he could find a hotel. The man gave a start, then with exaggerated friendliness began to give directions; then changed his mind and said he would show him the way. They walked back, taking the same streets, and finally, very near the station, came to a lone building, multistoried, cube-shaped, almost new. "You're sure to find a room there," said his guide. "Who will ever fill up such a big hotel here in Subotica!"

Ascending the long stairway, Lamian entered a lobby, where some young people were sitting in lounge chairs. He found the reception desk, asked for a room. A thin, uniformed clerk with drooping mustaches and gold-braided jacket registered him and handed him the key to a room on the third floor. Lamian took the elevator up, found his room, opened the door, and no sooner had he thrown down his bag and removed his shoes and coat than he collapsed on the bed. His breathing was rapid, and he wondered if his stomach affliction would strike now, but it didn't, and he fell asleep.

When he woke, the room was suffused with gray light and his body damp. He got up, washed and changed, then went to the window. The street lamps were already lit, making intersecting chains of light below, while the houses arrayed between them were dark, seemed unoccupied. He looked at the clock: six-twenty. He had slept well over an hour. He was hungry, and decided to go out and eat.

The air outside was dove-gray, crisp. It was easy to find the way to the main street, and this put Lamian in a good mood. At last, he thought, he was without obligations. Tomorrow he would inquire about Helena Lifka, and if he ran into any obstacle, anything that would make a meeting with her inadvisable—or even if he himself, independent of any obstacle, decided that such a meeting ought to be avoided—he would turn around and go back to Banja Luka the way he had come.

The weight of compulsion which had accompanied him on his journey lifted from his shoulders. He entered the shopping area, with its bright lights and many people walking; peered into the windows of several cafés; found one of them inviting, and went in. A number of customers sat quietly in front of coffee or drinks. Passing among them, Lamian found the entrance to the dining room, a smaller room, more formal, tables covered with white cloths and most of them occupied. He sat down at a vacant table, and a young, courteous waiter approached. He ordered supper, lit a cigarette, looked around.

The sobriety of the customers surprised him: they sat in two and threes, men for the most part, engrossed in reading the menu or slowly bringing food to their mouths as in some kind of ritual. When his food arrived, he ate slowly too, and drank a glass of wine that tasted better than any wine he had drunk since his stomach trouble began. Then he went back to the hotel to sleep.

But the calm, the confidence he had gained after changing his interview with Helena Lifka from a necessity to a possibility now gave him a feeling of vigor he had not known for a long time. He was reluctant to pick up his key. Young people still sat in the lobby around low, glass-top tables. Music could be heard. Lamian headed toward it, and in an extension of the lobby discovered a bar, dimly lit, with tables like those in the lobby, crowded together. Around the tables were not only young people but also some who were older, and some advanced in years, like himself.

He looked for a place and finally found one, right by the bar. Sat, asked the waiter for a glass of wine, asked more by moving his lips than by talking, which was drowned out by music from a record or tape player. The bartender poured the wine behind the bar, brought it out, set it on the table, and waited to be paid. Lamian paid, and looked around. There were also women among the patrons, mostly young and dressed like men, in pants and sweaters, their hair twisted into tight curls—a style he had seen only on television, for Banja Luka was conservative, and Lamian didn't frequent bars where such modern things might be seen.

This discovery cheered him. It was as if all the old tormenting wounds were erased and a life unburdened by memory, by the past, were presenting itself. A life of the moment. Since he was now retired, he thought, why not move permanently to a town like this one—not Subotica, of course, where he was linked, in a way, to the past, but some other town? There were scores of such towns in Yugoslavia. He could spend the rest of his days there, stretching out the time endlessly, sitting like this and looking on, with nothing to oppress him.

He drank the wine, felt it hum in his head, and thought what it would be like to invite one of these young women for a drink, and then to his room, for that exhilarating release, the way it was when he was young—but better, because he was no longer constrained by youth, with its inner enslavement to sensation. He was no longer constrained by anything; he was beyond time, and all this—Subotica, Helena Lifka—was a figment, unimportant. One died when the time came, or at someone's command, but otherwise one simply lived—ate, drank, smoked, lay with women.

But he did not approach the girls; he lacked the desire to embrace, to couple. He drank, and watched the room gradually empty, the waiter extinguish the muted lighting. Then he rose, a bit unsteady on his feet, and walked to the front desk, took his key from the burly, bald desk clerk now on duty, and went up to his room.

And regretted, in the silence, coming back alone. Even without desire, he should have brought a woman, one of those long-haired, skinny ones in pants, to undress her and lay her on the bed, inhale her youthful fragrance, bury his nose in her hair, caress her small breasts. He regretted the wasted years, his wasted life, and suddenly it seemed that the blame for all the waste was Helena Lifka's. The chill she evoked in him, the horror.

Her naked body appeared to him now, hands crossed over her crotch, the small flabby breasts, close-cropped hair, teary eyes—a grotesque primeval deity, the totem of a tribe to which he had never wanted to belong but which had now subjugated him to its avenging faith. In disgust he threw his clothes off and lay down to sleep. But he tossed and turned, wakeful in the darkness, staring at the figure glowing white, and beyond it the street lights, which he couldn't see from the level of his bed. He tossed and turned, and drunkenly punched the pillow, which was not big enough and kept sliding out from under his head. It was nearly dawn when he finally fell into fitful sleep.

He awoke late, his head and stomach aching. An-gry, he turned over on his pillow, to go back to sleep until he awoke more agreeably, but then he remembered why he was in this strange bed, in Subotica, and forced himself to get up. He shaved, dressed, went down to a breakfast that he barely touched, then out into the street.

It was drizzling; he turned up his coat collar. Now then, Helena Lifka—where do we look for her? He posed the question to himself as if to a thickheaded subordinate: not to obtain an answer—he knew the answer—but because he was in a foul mood. Setting out in the direction of the main street, he stopped the first pedestrian who looked like he had his wits about him and asked where the police station was.

The information Lamian received coincided with his present route, and in no time he saw the place, an old three-story build-ing. Entering the lobby with its teller windows and high writing stands, he found it full of people, who were either standing in line or sitting on the two benches. He located the registration window and got in line. Slowly he moved forward, sweating, surprised at everyone's patience. When his turn came, he told the young clerk with slicked-down hair that he wished to have the address of a person he believed was living in Subotica. He expected this statement to meet with incomprehension—and thus was nervously prepared to explain in detail who he was looking for but, if possible, without mentioning her name or giving reasons for his request. Instead, the clerk calmly directed him to a nearby window, where they would give him the form that had to be filled out in order to obtain the information he wanted.

As simple as that? He was mortified by that simplicity, or, rather, by his own ignorance about how such things were done. The procedure must be the same everywhere, thus he could have familiarized himself with it in advance. Receiving the form, Lamian scanned it quickly. First name, last name of the person sought, just like that, as if the questionnaire had been devised expressly for him and other wartime penitents. Year of birth, previous residence, signature—again he recoiled. Put his real name or a fictitious name? But then what if the clerk asked for his identity card? Again Lamian was furious with himself for being unprepared. He was ready to give up.

He sat down at the end of a bench with the blank form. Was he committing a folly that would land him in jail within the hour, hauled before an investigator who had been waiting for years for him to be brought in? Had Helena Lifka, former camp inmate and since the war a figure of considerable influence, left instructions, like a trap for an animal, that the Subotica Office of Internal Affairs immediately detain anyone inquiring into her whereabouts and question the person thoroughly about his movements from 1941 to 1945? For he could only be a certain Kapo, her one-time tormentor.

Childish fantasies, these, plots from cheap novels, but it was in precisely this way that his instincts had adapted to the threat. Holding the questionnaire loosely, casually, as if to fan himself in the muggy air of the lobby, he began observing the people around him. The woman next to him on the bench, sitting with knees apart; beside her the youth in the windbreaker, who smoked as he studied a form similar to Lamian's; by a pillar, an agitated man of about fifty, who kept jumping up to look over the heads of those in line; a bearded truck driver in blue overalls, who looked dully at the doors as they continually swung open and closed.

Lamian focused on this man. A round, blurry face and a neutral expression. A Wehrmacht man, staying where he's put, no will of his own. Ask him for a cigarette—forbidden to prisoners—and he'll shrink back, but if no superior is around, he might reach into his pocket and drop one in the mud, as if by accident.

Getting up and crooking his leg, Lamian hobbled over to the man, stood next to him, sniffed him out. "I'd like," he began in a mumble, so that he could be heard but still deny what was heard, "I'd like to go outside, some friends are waiting for me, and I thought maybe you could . . . this form for me." He took out his wallet, opened it, slowly peeled off a thousand-dinar bill, and without raising his eyes held it out to the man between red, stiffened fingers. "You understand? Since you're waiting anyway. Just this form." He waved the paper and only now showed his face, slackening his features into a drunken expression. "Stand in line at that window for me—my legs hurt—and just hand them this form." When he saw the man hesitate, he added casually, "Just a second while I fill it out."

The man tried half-heartedly to shake him off, but Lamian took his arm, led him to the counter, and spread out the form. "Your first name, last name?" The man muttered something. Lamian asked him to repeat it. "Address?" Again a mutter, again repeated: the man was from Subotica. Then, at the top, quickly, in block letters, Lamian wrote "Helena Lifka, 1925," and left the rest blank. "There." He put the form into the man's hand, which still held the banknote. "Stand over there—if you're expecting someone, you can see him from the line."

The man began to raise his hand in protest, though it still held obediently the money and the form, but Lamian took him by the elbow and pushed him to the last place on the line. "There you go. Just wait your turn and give that to the clerk. Put the money in your pocket." He bent the man's hand until the other hand finally took the money and buried it in the folds of ample trousers. "That's right. I'll be around here, don't worry." And he moved off to one side.

The truck driver turned to look. Lamian threw a thin smile of apology into his startled eyes, then hobbled off and hid behind a pillar. From there, he watched. The man shuffled his feet, cast glances at the door as he waited in line. Slowly the man neared the window. At last at the window, he stuck first his head and then the questionnaire into the opening, for the clerk. When the clerk left his seat, the man promptly straightened and once again watched the door. Suddenly he was waving his hands and shouting; a young man, also in blue overalls, had walked in, and went over to him. As they talked, both looked around uncertainly. The clerk returned and slid the form back through the window, and the man again stuck his head in, and finally straightened, holding the paper, then left the line and went to the rear of the lobby with his friend.

Lamian emerged from behind the pillar and tapped the truck driver on the back. "All set? Excellent." Taking the form from him, he nodded to both men, then limped his way to the exit. In the street, he turned the first corner and stepped into an open doorway, peering out to see if the two men in blue overalls were following him. They were nowhere to be seen. He lifted the form to his eyes. Yes, it was his, he saw Helena Lifka's name. At the bottom, in the space for the response, was typed: "Moved to Zagreb July 1, 1979, 16 Bogdan Zimonjić Street."

He nodded with relief, as if a weight had been lifted from his shoulders. And so it had: she was gone, moved away, not here. He no longer had to look for her. There was nothing to look for, since Helena Lifka wasn't here, in her Szabadka, which for decades had darkened his vision. To hell with her—he had made this trip in vain, had endured agonies of fear because of it, the fear of seeing her, and for nothing. Well, so be it, he was relieved, not angry.

He folded the form, put it in his pocket, and reentered the street. There was no one around to watch him. He set out for the hotel but in his agitated state took a wrong turn. Unfamiliar buildings in a deserted lane finally awakened him to this. Changing course only led him to other unfamiliar streets. He stopped, sweaty and out of breath. A woman carrying a basket came along, and he bent toward her. "Hotel Patria?" he asked. But she didn't understand him, or didn't hear; she shook her head and narrowed her eyes as if in fright, and continued on her way. He proceeded at random, finally rounding a corner to come face-to-face with a tower he recognized. This led him to the main street and his hotel.

He picked up the key, went to his room, quickly packed. At the desk, the clerk looked at him questioningly. "The bill, please. One night." Impatiently he watched the clerk's fingers, the pencil used to add up the bill. He paid; went straight to the station. At the ticket counter he asked for the shortest route to Banja Luka; didn't catch everything he was told but understood that a train for Novi Sad was leaving in forty minutes. On the platform he bought a newspaper and stared at it without reading. He lit a cigarette, and its bitterness made him realize that he was hungry. Not having the patience to sit down and eat lunch in a restaurant, he ordered two sandwiches and a glass of mineral water at the counter. Ate quickly, drank, went back out on the platform. He paced back and forth, looked at his watch. The train came in. He boarded, tossed his bag on the rack above his head, and, surrounded by the odor of human bodies, closed his eyes.

The train pulled out. Around him, people were talking and eating. What was he doing among these people? He wanted to get home as soon as possible, though he knew that there was no reason to hurry, that nothing awaited him there, only weariness. He should have stayed, he thought. And rested. He should have eaten a proper dinner and got some sleep. And found out for sure whether or not Helena Lifka had left Subotica, because he might have been given the wrong information. But where to find out? The form had given only her new address in Zagreb, not the old one in Subotica, which also had to exist, had to be written down somewhere, because otherwise the young clerk with slicked-down hair wouldn't have found anything in the file.

Only now did it occur to Lamian how incredible it had been for him to find her trail so quickly, so simply, going on facts he had remembered for decades, facts he could easily have misremembered, or they could have been entered incorrectly in the first place, by Jelinek or some other starving prisoner. Or the facts could have changed over the years, especially her last name, because in all that time she could have married, married more than once, or changed her name in some other way. But no, she had remained Helena Lifka, unmarried, or else married and then divorced and reassuming her maiden name, which also happened. He had not even paid that much attention to the facts he had read so hastily over Jelinek's shoulder, looking for only one fact—Jüdin—and yet they had all been correct, those facts, and he had remembered them correctly, every one of them.

He had the feeling that he was the victim of a plot in which he too had taken part, along with the clerk with the slicked-down hair, and the good-natured accomplice in blue overalls, and Jelinek, and perhaps a whole series of invisible conspirators who had seen through him and had been waiting for him to fall into this trap he had made for himself.

But he was glad now to be sitting on the train, no longer in those mysterious Subotica streets sprinkled with a fine rain, where spies were stationed on corners and in the lobbies of the buildings he had to enter—to listen to his inquiries and then send him on, deeper, into the trap.

He had escaped—or had he? He tried to determine this by observing his fellow passengers. If any one of them was there to follow him, they could do nothing now that he had broken free of the trap and its bait, now that he sat in the train like any ordinary traveler, able to tell whoever asked that he was riding through Yugoslavia for pleasure, taking advantage of his retirement. No one could prove otherwise. Even if they searched him, they would find no evidence of his purpose in coming to Subotica, only a train ticket and a hotel bill.

Then he remembered that the form was in the same pocket in which he carried his wallet and ticket. He touched it lightly with his fingertips. He looked around. No, no one was watching. He got up, stepped decisively over the other passengers' legs into the corridor, shoved his way through the people standing at the windows smoking and talking, and reached the toilet. He went inside, took out the form, unfolded it enough to see that he hadn't grabbed some other paper, then tore it into tiny pieces and tossed them into the toilet bowl, pressing his foot on the lever to send a brief, swift cascade of water after them, washing them through the opening onto the ties below.

Now he was finally rid of Helena Lifka, every trace of her. He lingered in the corridor, smoking, delaying his return to the compartment, wanting to spend as much of the trip as possible away from the passengers. He watched the fields slip by, looked at the stations when the train stopped, handed his ticket to the conductor, and listened to the conversations around him until his legs began to ache. Going back to his seat, he shut his eyes and dozed, but not too deeply, lest the train carry him past his station.

At Novi Sad he got off, found his local train and took a seat, unfolded the newspaper he had bought in Subotica, and immersed himself in it. The world was rolling along independent of him, and more battles were being fought. Jews, his kinsmen, the sons and grandsons of his contemporaries, former inmates of the camps, stood in tank turrets and drove, flags waving, through undefended settlements, through human flesh, ripping it apart with machine-gun bullets, rounding up the survivors in camps fenced off with barbed wire.

This revolted him. He laid aside the newspaper. Nations were directed by dark forces, by the need to dominate, to dominate in order to perpetuate themselves, and once they were harnessed to that yoke, there was no escape from it; they had to kill or run the risk of being killed. He was glad he wasn't there, glad he was here in a Europe bled dry and weary, a Europe that had its fill of war and where there were no Jews left to attract hatred. Stanka Bugarin had even chosen him as a lover because he was a Jew. Growing up after the massacre, she saw in his otherness something intriguing, comforting, because he was unlike those whom habit had made odious.

A different generation with different standards, different criteria for attraction and repulsion, so that with his remorse and secrecy he had appeared to her a prehistoric creature, a human mammoth brought back to life from a frozen state to make others reach for their stone axes and flee from his bestial growl. When, instead, he should have sought peace. Peace.

With this thought, he got off the train in Vrpolje and gazed with emotion at the young peasant women with baskets who were patiently waiting beside the tracks. He joined them, and when the train for Bosnia arrived, he hurried with them to the first carriage. But others got there before them, and he had to stand all the way to Banja Luka, bag at his feet, face pressed against the window. He didn't feel sorry for himself: he was rubbish for whom this subordinate position was fitting. Lamian entered the city as one enters a cave. He had only to turn his face to the wall, and he would cease to exist.

HE ARRIVED HOME, WENT TO BED, TURNED HIS FACE TO the wall. Morning found him in the same position. The arm and leg he had been lying on were numb, his forearm wet with saliva that had dribbled out as he breathed through slackened jaws. He felt dizzy; the day ahead seemed too much for him. It was only hunger that finally dragged him out of bed and darkness. He raised the window shades to a bright spring day.

To buy food, he would have to go out; to go out, he would have to dress; and before dressing he would have to wash and shave. He performed these tasks reluctantly, in fits and starts, taking rests in the armchair, staring at the rug, the floor, though there was nothing there of interest. He went out, returned, ate, rested, smoked. Stared into space. Again went out, returned. Slept.

A revolting routine, yet he didn't fail to notice that the trees in the street were budding, the bushes in the park he walked through every day were sending up shoots, and the treetops were fuller, and the sky higher, encircling the rekindled sun with a white ring. And people were bustling, calling to each other, throwing off layer after layer of clothing, freeing their hair to the wind. But this sparrowlike animation, the dust it raised, the noise it made, only suffocated him. He fled from it. He sat in his room, the shades lowered to protect him from the glare, the heat, and the bustle.

He hadn't the strength to air out and clean his apartment. Or to do his laundry. So long as there was clean underwear, he changed it, but then he began, on rising, to take whatever pieces of clothing came to hand, lying on the floor beside the bed or tossed behind the wardrobe the previous night. His rubbish piled up; the kitchen filled with the sour smell of unwashed dishes. He would boil or fry his meals in dirty pans, eat on plates encrusted with food. His body stank. He scratched while sitting in the armchair, legs sprawled. When occasionally he drew a bath and washed, the ring of gray that clung to the white tub refused to be rinsed away.

This stench, this filth, this enveloping debris, he thought, was like the camp, where everything had been polluted, rotten, the food, the clothing, every object. As in the camp, it seemed a miracle to be alive in this pit of decay. But he too, though alive, was decayed: a Mussulman, a walking corpse. He was rot that ate rot only to continue its rotting.

His Kapo's eye could tell decay in the wobbly walk, the stiffened cheeks, the gaping mouth oblivious to its gaping. In the camp, he knew who would stumble tomorrow, and the day after tomorrow lie like a log, to be carried out and stacked on the body cart.

He saw them now advancing with their wooden gait, apparitions in rags, dolls in the shape of human beings but without the substance, the vitality of human beings. They threatened to fill every space, to take up all the air, and he saw himself chasing them away from the feeding pot so they wouldn't disrupt the line, so they wouldn't overturn the pot by crowding forward, reaching with their bony, scabby hands, or so they wouldn't fall suicidally into it. They were condemned to die; that was understood, and no care or nourishment could pluck them from death and return them to life. To hasten their end, therefore, was both compassionate and practical.

It was a relief to see them as corpses—stretched out in the barracks, on their bunks, or in the latrine surrounded by the muck of their bowels, or spread-eagled on the barbed-wire fence, where those whose consciousness still smoldered flung themselves. Death evoked congratulations, applause, like the successful conclusion of an extremely difficult acrobatic act.

And acrobats they were: they walked, they stood in line for rations, they slept in bare cubicles—executing with unsurpassed skill the movements of a life that was no longer in them. Because death was in them.

Lamian searched within himself for the spark of consciousness he needed to leap onto the barbed wire. The method was no problem. As a technician, he knew how: wrap a wire around his wrist, connect it to an outlet in the electric range, turn on the switch. He looked in the cupboard for his tool chest; took out a pair of pliers, a screwdriver, and a piece of wire; removed one of the burners from the stove; stripped the wire and connected it to the outlet; wrapped the rest of the wire around his left wrist, and reached for the knob.

How long would it take for the current to kill him? But that didn't matter; a moment's contact would be enough to knock him senseless, and then he would feel nothing as he lay twitching on the concrete floor, hand dangling from the wire as from a handcuff.

That was how they would find him, after the stench of decay filled the stairwell and drove them to break down the door to his apartment. They would recoil, fingers holding their noses like clothespins, and run to report the suicide of an old pensioner. Reason? None would be found among his belongings: no statement, no confession, not even the form from the Subotica police station, because he had prudently destroyed it on the train. They might speculate—if Stanka or the doctor at the clinic remembered the medical examination that failed to explain his weight loss—that fear of illness had driven him to suicide.

This bothered him: it made him look stupid. Perhaps he ought to leave behind a note. Addressed to whom? To no one, unaddressed: I didn't take my life because of illness. Why, then? He would say nothing else. Nahmijas he could have told, in detail, if Nahmijas were alive. Or Nahmijas's sister-in-law, if only he had got close to her. Who else would understand?

He felt a need to tell someone, felt he had a right to this. Even the Mussulmen, before finally succumbing, would seek out someone to confide in: a neighbor in the cubicle or at roll call, in the latrine or the dispensary, even if the person was only another walking skeleton who appeared to have a shade more strength than they did, a shade better prospect of staying alive. His own ear had received hundreds of such messages: "I can't go on," "I'll die today," "I feel it's the end," "My name is Kraus, from Bydgoszcz. If you ever go there, tell them."

But he had no one to say a final word to, because, leaving the camp behind, he now found himself in a camp of his own, a camp for him alone. He regretted destroying the Subotica form. Picturing it, recalling the information, which he hadn't forgotten, he was once more taken up by the thought of Helena Lifka, her face, her body, this woman who was still with him—only she —in this last camp.

LAMIAN ARRIVED IN ZAGREB ON THE MORNING TRAIN. He stepped down from the carriage in front of a maze of rails jammed with train cars, like obstacles placed intentionally. The long passenger station could be reached only by a cavernous moving stairway, first down, then up, even though the station was near, beckoning with its entrances and exits and passageways and the mob of people that kept emerging on the endless tapeworm of the escalator. The metallic, blaring voice of loudspeakers and the voices from hundreds of mouths whirred like a cloud of bats.

All incredibly, eerily unchanged, enough to make him doubt that forty years had passed since he came and went in this place so many times. Came and went an equal number of times, if you counted the time he left from the spot some distance away, a spot he avoided looking at now, though seeing it nevertheless out of the corner of his eye: the low switchman's shanty at the edge of a woods, where one day at dawn he had been loaded into a cattle car, wrists bound with wire. In which case his arrival at the real, regular human station would change odd to even.

The thought passed through his mind without affecting it, like water through a sieve made of material as unyielding as the goal before him. Head lowered in anger but also to watch his step, he submitted to this up-and-down contraption, this modern, wise, big-city contraption, this boast of a freedom that was still a mockery, because in spite of all the concrete-clad order and regularity there was still the spot beyond the station, forgotten today, out of the way, kept only for animal cargo—but always available for human cargo. Different victims next time, or the same?

He felt the breath of danger, which he had expected and which was why he had resisted this journey. It was a hot wind on the back of his head, a wind of malice, fury, a pressure so familiar, he couldn't imagine being without it. He went to sleep with it, woke up with it, and wore it in public like a hump. It was particularly heavy now, his hump, here at the railway station in Zagreb, and made him short of breath.

Who came here, to this city of half a million people, bastion of the Croats and bastion, too, of the Ustaši, defeated but not destroyed? Some on secret business, for illicit gain, or, like him, in search of a former lover. Perhaps running a risk like his, out of desperation, again like his. Riegler with his business successes built on gold from teeth, Riegler interested in expanding into the Balkans, where labor was so cheap, nostalgically reminiscent of camp labor. Or some other surviving Arbeitsführer, or even Lagerführer, for decades now a captain of industry, of the economic miracle, a man come to rest his faulty heart in the backwaters, less agitated, of Eastern Europe.

Or Gabelić, if he was alive, hiding under another name, behind a newly grown mustache and beard, a clandestine agitator distributing a new kind of pamphlet, printed in Germany, to discontented railroad workers. Or a fellow survivor who owed him a few blows to the head, a few disciplinary pushups, curses, punches; who here in the heart of Croatia was cashing in on his suffering through a pension, disability benefits, and was more than happy to ensure his financial position by whispering to the plainclothes detective at the station exit and pointing a finger at Lamian as he passed on his way out.

The breath, the pressure on Lamian's neck would then condense to a hot, hard fist. "Are you Furfa?" a hoarse voice would say, and though Lamian would deny it, taking out his identity card to prove his name was Lamian, he would be detained, questioned about his movements during the war, and the connection between Furfa and Lamian would emerge, and what he had eluded in sleepy Banja Luka would seize him here in busy Zagreb, all because for one time only—but that is always enough—he had dared, despite his misgivings, to show his face.

A trial, lawyers, handcuffs again, the click of cameras, his bewildered face in newspapers for every reader, every enthralled curiosity-seeker, to see. Here on the threshold of a beginning—or an ending, for who knew what was in store for him?—he would be stopped, stopped just as he was reaching out his hand to find that other hand, to hold it, and, holding it, to explain. Now she would never know that he had tried to find her; that he still lived.

Unless she opened a newspaper and recognized him, averting her eyes in horror from the face that for her was the incarnation of evil, turning the page so as not to see it anymore, crumpling the paper and throwing it into the stove. Or, instead, she might come to the trial, not to testify, of course—shame would prevent her from testifying—but merely to watch from the back row, hidden, taking her revenge as he sweated and squirmed and shrank inside. Rejoicing that his punishment at last had found him, never suspecting that the punishment had found him because he set out to find her, his punishment.

It might not be a bad thing, he thought at the exit as he stepped into the square, squinting like a hunchback at the gray morning. The sun burned his eyes. They grew teary, as if he were crying; he wiped them with his fingers. It might not be a bad thing, because then he wouldn't have to go any farther, and he didn't want to go farther. There were new tracks to cross, streetcar tracks overrun by garlands of people—many more people, it seemed, than before the war, no doubt the result of population growth and the increased tempo of life, the increased mobility.

Despite all those killed for the good of mankind, killed to build an order more encompassing, more subject to control—an order that he, too, with his muscles and his will to serve, had worked to bring about.

That's what he would tell them at the trial. Why not? Yes, I exterminated, I weeded out. Don't you think I was right? Weren't there too many of you? Then they would tear him apart, beat him during the recesses between sessions, strike him right in front of the courthouse as he was being brought in. And the guards would look the other way as the mob cut him up with knives, sprinkling the asphalt with his blood, wringing cries and gasps from his throat as he had seen it done at Gradina.

Those gasps would be his final utterance, and that was how the newspaper reports would bury him: an impenitent whose foulness had been put an end to not according to due process, true, which was to be condemned, but by the will of the people. This would be more dignified than his stammering out excuses —which ones, what kind?—even he could no longer decide, here in this din of people and clanging streetcars and growling automobiles. How he hated these new people, too numerous, whose young strength pushed him, enfeebled, closer to the hospital, the dispensary, the injection in the heart, the flames of the crematorium.

He felt very weak; the trip had tired him. Lying in his apartment all summer behind lowered shades, in the stink and the sweat, had unaccustomed him to exertion. He was no longer able to deal with people and their talk, with the steps that had to be taken to accomplish something, with asking questions and attending to answers, with concealing intentions, feigning indifference, pretending desires.

But he couldn't keep standing here beside streetcars he obviously wasn't using, like a loiterer or childish old man who had forgotten his way. Some self-appointed guardian might peer into his face, shake him, question him, and call an ambulance, and Lamian would be taken to a center for the incapacitated or even to an asylum!

He had to move, and move he did, hopping over tracks in front of a halted streetcar with an agility that surprised him. But he should have first asked the way to Bogdan Zimonjić Street—behind him, in the waiting queue for taxis, he had had his pick of informants, from pensioners who would have been proud that someone turned to them for information, to casual young urban know-it-alls who could not only give him directions but could tell him the exact number of blocks left and right. Now he would have to pick someone on the sidewalk ahead of him, in front of the park, possibly annoying them by intruding on their thoughts.

But what was done was done, and he continued toward the park entrance, as if needing to rest his legs before making up his mind to go on—which wasn't far from the truth. He went down the steps and made for an unoccupied bench, a promise of comfort, but a thin-legged woman in a voluminous coat, a hat on her head and a furled umbrella dangling from her arm, reached it first. With a charitable look, for no doubt she had guessed his purpose, she tucked her coat under her rump and sat down at one end of the bench.

He nodded, to show her that this courtesy was unnecessary, but when he saw her guileless face, with a web of wrinkles around myopic, puckered eyes and a caved-in mouth, he decided to speak to her: "I wonder if I could ask you something. Do you know where Bogdan Zimonjić Street is?"

She was surprised, having expected him to sit down instead. He repeated the question, but it crossed paths with her "Did you want something?" which, uttered at the same time, kept her from hearing. She examined him anxiously from head to foot and tried to guess, "A rooming house? A hotel?" When he stood there uncertainly, she answered her own question. "There are several around here." She rose as briskly as she had sat down, stretched out the hand with the umbrella dangling from its wrist, and pointed into the park, toward the street that went around it, where the Palace Hotel was, she said, one of the best in the city yet not too expensive.

Tipping his hat, he went off rapidly in the indicated direction, to avoid having to explain. But remembered, as he walked, that in fact he needed a hotel. He came out of the park, followed the sidewalk along it, and saw on one of the old buildings the name of the hotel, well known to him from before the war. It was only then that he realized he wasn't carrying any luggage.

He looked down to check. Had he left his bag on the train? He didn't think so, didn't think that there had been anything next to him on the seat or on the rack above. Hadn't he brought it, then? Hadn't he packed at all? All he remembered was his impatience to leave, telephoning for information about the trains—that was probably last night, after the scene in the kitchen with the wire. Then a sleepless night, turning on the light numerous times to look at the clock. His drowsy preparations in the bathroom, his departure for the station in the half-light of dawn, finally boarding the train, and sitting endlessly, nodding in and out of sleep.

There had been no bag catching on anything, no handle that cramped his hand. Was he out of his mind? How would he manage without his things? How would it look when he entered the hotel and asked for a room, carrying nothing in his hands, with only his overcoat and the hat on his head? Who would believe he was a traveler?

But the old woman had assumed he was, directing him to a hotel. Why? Her certainty alarmed him now: it was as if she had known everything about him, as if she had followed him from the train and placed herself in the park like a roadsign. A spy? One of those deployed around the station to watch his every step, even guiding him along, so the noose could be tightened more easily, more securely, when they decided it was time?

He walked by the hotel without going in, without even turning his head—which didn't prevent him from seeing, at the entrance, two tall metal plates on which something was written. To inform, to entice? The ones following him—if he had followers—would be aware now that he'd seen through them and was trying to escape. What new tricks would they come up with? Would they take quicker action, tighten the noose ahead of time, cut off his retreat?

He shuddered. He was in a trap, theirs or his, and didn't have the strength to wriggle free, at least not at the moment, with these colored spots dancing before his eyes, obscuring the shop windows and the people on the street, with whom he nearly collided. He stopped. Everyone was hurrying, going in and out of doorways, store entrances. Only one person looked at him, a young man with a jutting chin who mumbled a quick apology for brushing against him. It all seemed to be an illusion, a chimera. He needed to restore some order to his brain. Also, his bladder was full, was hurting. He hesitated, then submitted to his physical need, which couldn't be dismissed; turning around, he went back to the hotel, passed between the two signs, pushed the glass doors, entered the lobby.

It was quiet and spacious here, but sealed off, like the bottom of a lake. Artificial light, and discreet figures ready to serve but also able to remain silent and motionless. It was like the dressing room of the gas chamber, with the benches along the walls and the numbers above the clothes hangers, and the reassuring instructions not to confuse row and number.

And why not reassure them, if it lasted only a short while, and the ruse was believed until the end? But he had seen the poisoned ones when he served in the Kommando that moved the bodies from the gas chambers to the ovens: naked, clustered in tall heaps, mountaineers who had clambered over each other for the pure air that was running out. Their puffy green faces, their tongues blue and protruding, soiled with the liquid excrement that had leaked out.

How long had that agony lasted? Two minutes, as rumor had it? Or much longer, closer to the half-hour limit, which was how long the doors and window of the chamber stayed bolted? No one knew, except Mell, who liked looking through the window—and the little girl they once found alive at the bottom of the pile. She fluttered her bloodied eyes and vomited rosy pus. Mell killed her with a bullet in the temple, so only he knew how long the cyanide took on humans. Then Mell himself died in the revolt at Crematorium 2, and that circle was closed.

Only Lamian remained, and Riegler, and perhaps a few more he hadn't thought of, to maintain the chain of knowledge, living knowledge, memory—but the law of mortality would ultimately break that chain. And then there would be no uncertainty as to whether a hotel lobby like this one meant a step toward a noose, a bullet, a knife, an iron bar—or, indeed, instead, the civilized comfort promised by the glass walls, the armchairs, and the smoothness of the counter, where a polite young man, a clock on the wall above his head, gave Lamian an understanding, almost tender look.

Lamian muttered "Good afternoon," and the young man said something. Suddenly there was a piece of paper and a pencil in front of Lamian. His identity card wasn't even required; nor was he asked about luggage. The only difficulty was the key, which his stiffened fingers were unable to pick up from the glass counter—and the floor number, which he couldn't remember at first.

"Shall I have the bellboy show you?" the desk clerk suggested, pointing at an area next to the desk, where a pomaded head glistened. Lamian declined, went around some pillars, and found the elevator. Pressing the button, he went up. In the corridor, he walked back and forth, comparing the number on his key with the numbers over the doors, like the numbers in that reassuring dressing room. Numbers—the rules required them. He found his at last, opened the door, entered, and collapsed in an armchair.

The room had two beds. Why two? And two armchairs, a table, and a wardrobe. In the vestibule, a second door led to the bathroom. His bladder was insisting, so he got up, opened first one and then the other door—yes, it was the bathroom, and he urinated with relief. He hadn't urinated since last night. How had he stood the pressure on his bladder while he was filling out the registration form, and while his fingernails chased the slippery key across the glass counter, and while he searched for the door with his key number on it, thinking of the gas chamber—of the warmth of mingled breaths and bodies packed together, the sum of all those whispers of hope and fear, those beseeching, questioning looks he refused to return, as he hurried, pretended to hurry, wanting it to end as soon as possible, without incident, no one discovering the ruse ahead of time, before the doors were closed and bolted, which made the screams inaudible, barely audible, and those anxious families were turned into heaps of poisoned flesh smeared with excrement, ready to be hauled to the ovens?

All this—not only the dressing room—was a ruse, a trap, a trap he himself had created and had fallen into, in his desire for everything to go smoothly, according to regulations, while he slipped through the regulations, got around them, to make it to the next moment, driven by the will to live, always that will. He wanted to live, as did all of them in the dressing room. Even when one fact after another—the confiscation of their baggage, their segregation from the strong and young—told them that they would die, still they sewed valuables into the hems of suits and dresses, or hid them beneath dental bridges; still they obeyed, disrobed, went naked beneath the showers that poured not water but a fog of cyanide. And even then, when death had already engulfed them and torn their lungs, each of them still hoped that he at least would be spared, out of all the rest.

Only one was spared—the girl whose lungs and bloodstream were miraculously resistant. But wasn't that enough, to hope, to obey, to follow the rules?

He was in the same trap, here in this bathroom that also had a shower: high above the tub, arching downward. He looked at the circular rows of holes in the showerhead, just as they had done, expecting warm water—even though they knew they were in a camp, brought in cattle cars that went unopened for days, knew that only the weaker children had been left with them, that all their belongings had been taken away. Expecting, against all reason, warm water, because the will to live commanded them to do so.

That will made them believe in the rules and regulations, in the dressing-room signs that said, in distinct letters, "No pushing, there's room for everyone" or "Entrance to the bathing area." Just as that will prevented him from returning their pleading looks, from telling them with a glance what awaited them, or with a shout, because a shout, he knew, would throw them into a panic, and they would rush to the opposite door, away from the showers, and be mowed down by the machine guns, and he with them. He didn't shout, and left the dressing room as soon as they left it for the shower room, and would see them again only when they were all dead, reentering to disentangle them body by body from the embrace they had climbed into, one atop the other. He would throw them on stretchers and take them by elevator to the doors of the ovens, and use a pliers to remove gold crowns and bridges from their mouths, concealing a piece or two in his secret pocket to exchange for food.

He had survived by his silence; but in his place they would have done the same. Both he and they had kept to the rules, because that was the condition for getting to the next moment, and everyone wanted to get to the next moment: every Kapo, every prisoner, every new arrival, every German. And so they all deluded one another, mutually. No one ever broke through the wall of rules, except to break out of life. Like the rebels of the crematorium Kommando, once they found out they would be killed and replaced by others. Or like those who dug tunnels under the wall—the real wall, not the wall of rules—into the swamp, where the German shepherds sniffed them out and found them. Or like those who flung themselves onto the electric fence, to be killed in an instant.

Only he was alive, because he didn't dig under the wall or throw himself onto it, the camp wall, or the wall in his kitchen when he wrapped the wire around his arm—but he intended, now, to break through it.

THE GRAVITY OF IT: THE MILLIONS OF DEAD. CHILDREN, old people, young women. Those two Jewish brothers, the Starks, both huge, recently delivered to the camp—bankers from Košic, it was said, bachelors, horse lovers. They were forced by Rapportführer Novak to jump into the lime pit while he, Lamian, was forced to wield a club to keep them from swimming out. And old slobbering Zavrazil. Lamian had beaten him with a ladle because Corporal Sommer came upon a fight while the noon meal was being portioned out. And the little Ukrainian boys who spent three weeks kicking a rag ball around in the yard between the barracks, interrupting their game only to ask passing prisoners for bread. Lamian had helped throw them into the crematorium trucks.

And the columns of those who had been selected for him to lead to the dispensary to receive an injection of phenol in the heart. The craftsmen, the last fourteen, who all looked alike, headed by Schmuhle as they walked toward the dispensary, where Riegler herded them. Or the little girl with the doll who stood by the wall in the execution yard as SS man Pfalzig killed her father and mother with a bullet to the back of the head. She waited her turn, and followed Pfalzig's big blue eyes as he stepped toward her and cocked his rifle, and she clutched the doll to her and obediently lowered her head so that the rifle barrel would be at the proper angle to it. And the Russian prisoners, three hundred and sixty of them crowded into a log hut at Brzezinka, the windows sealed with mud so that the effects of cyanide D could be tested on them. And the new arrivals who came at a time when the crematorium was too full. Led into the birch woods one by one, they were killed with a bullet to the head and thrown onto a grate across a fire, where their bodies burned, the fat crackling and the black smoke rising.

And the Serbian peasants, a whole village of them, with carts full of feather quilts and children, and cows tied behind the carts. They were driven to Jasenovac and then, after everything had been taken from them, ferried across the Sava to Gradina for the slaughter. And the ones who died of starvation in the cubicles at night and were found the next morning, their eyes staring at the ceiling. And the ones who died on the parade ground during roll call, upright till the last moment then toppling like posts. And the ones who died beneath clubs. The youth with the albino face Lamian clubbed to death on Sommer's orders because under his tunic he had an apple he took from the worksite. And the stokers of Crematoriums 1, 2, 3, and 4, killed to the last man every two months and replaced with new ones. And the French children, two to five years old, taken from their mothers and locked in Block 19 to die of disease and hunger. And the Gypsies in Section 3c at Jasenovac, fenced off with barbed wire, no roof over their heads and no food. They died feeding on corpses.

Too much for one head, one mind; that was why it rushed forth to be told, to be revealed. But it *had* been revealed, in countless books which, true enough, Lamian never read, though some of them came into his hands. He would read the title, open the book, look at a few photographs of living skeletons, and put it aside. Such books were ashes from the ashheap, he thought, bones from the boneyard. Specimens, exhibits.

Like the exhibits he had heard about, set up around the empty camps as reminders. Or like the films advertised in posters, then appearing on television as well, between the sports report and Drink Coca-Cola. Curiosities among other curiosities, intended to amaze and shock, like the skeletons hanging from ropes in the haunted houses of amusement parks.

No stink of death, no menace in the air, no electrified wire all around, no watchtowers, patrols, and machine guns with their hail of hot lead. No massive, wholesale transformation of living into dead, with death measured by the ton and shaped to the four corners of the fence as if to a mold. Death in bricks of compacted oblivion.

They still lay in the earth, those bricks, pressed deeper into it by feet that failed to recognize them, or they were displayed, some of them, to visitors who came to these famous killing grounds. But what did this prove? That people had been crushed inside them: faces, lungs, hearts, veins, glands? But one knew that from passing through any place of execution, any graveyard. The whole country was a graveyard, and every clod of its soil contained lungs, glands, bones—people. People, and animals, who had also been alive once and then were killed, or died of hunger or old age. And plants that had been trampled, by design or by chance.

Lamian looked again at the shower nozzle, from which nothing came. It was still, and the water behind it was still, blocked in its flow until someone turned on the faucet. A giant faucet had been turned on in Lamian's life, and cyanide had poured from the round, recessed nozzle, and those who were beneath it, herded between windowless walls, fell with their jaws working convulsively for air.

Harvest by spray. After every harvest, a stalk or two remained; the scythe swinging from the left missed it, and the scythe swinging from the right missed it, so it continued to stand in the sun and rain, drawing food through its roots until its ability to renew itself came to an end. Then it fell and was one, belatedly, with the stubble around it.

He was such a belated stalk. It did not matter what he did, he would be one with the stubble. He could travel, remember, regret, question himself; become angry, disgusted; take a wire from a burner on the stove and wrap it around his arm, then disengage himself, postponing, playing. It did not matter.

This whole pilgrimage to Helena Lifka, which was now drawing to an end, to his goal, had been a game, a game of restitution for the things he had failed to do, or for the things he had done but should not have. It did not change the number or arrangement of the bricks that lay regaining their neutrality of earth and air. With his journey or without it, they stayed the same. All the game gained for him was further opportunity to devise and decide. Was it worth it?

He compared standing in the bathroom of a Zagreb hotel with sitting in his apartment in Banja Luka through the sweltering months of last summer, when he hadn't thought, had merely filled and emptied himself according to animal instincts, like a sick animal in its filth, in its lair. Possibly he thought he was dying then; or his body, without his knowledge, was readying to die. He had sweated and tossed in bed until sleep overcame him, had wrinkled his nose at the stench of his body and of the garbage around him, but had done nothing about it, until finally he decided to send the current through his body and end his lethargy, for it had become unbearably tiresome. But this silence now, this safety, seemed no less tiresome, perhaps because he knew there was no real danger, because the giant faucet had not been turned on.

He was safe, at least for the moment. He could go from bathroom to bedroom and close the door behind him, could leave the hotel and take a walk, go into restaurants, shops, buy things, spend money, pass the time until weariness led him back to this rented haven. Was that what he should do, then? Why not? Why? He stood between decision and indecision, weariness and boredom.

A blissful state, really. A return to childhood. With dark corners, true, but even childhood had its dark corners. The oppression of belonging, the shadows thrown by newcomers who, unwanted, unasked, slipped into the picture, burdening it with one more thing to be explained.

And now he was such a shadow, rummaging through other people's corners, bringing doubt and fear. With no justification other than his simple existence, their fate, his fate.

He put on his coat and went downstairs. At the desk stood the same young man who had welcomed him. Taking the key, the man asked Lamian if he was satisfied with his room. Nodding vaguely, Lamian headed for the plate-glass entrance, which was misted over. Outside, it was raining.

He stopped and looked. On the wet, dark sidewalk, people hurried to and fro with umbrellas, or with damp heads tucked into collars. Going out into the rain didn't appeal to him, but neither did returning to the dim lobby, so he stood looking at the little bubbles the raindrops made on the asphalt, bubbles that burst instantly, in glitter. Then the glass darkened and swung open, and the opening admitted an out-of-breath body that tried to get past Lamian.

A man with a coarse, grimy face, leaning against the glass, held it open and let in the smell and sound of the rain. Meanwhile, in the window of a parked car, a second face, a thin one peering from beneath a cap, was looking at Lamian, addressing him with lips moving in words Lamian couldn't make out.

Disconcerted, Lamian yielded to the invitation; he squeezed by the man in the doorway, got a few cold raindrops down his neck, and found himself in front of a car door, which was being opened. An abductor? But in the windshield he saw a bulky, friendly meter box and on the roof the sign TAXI. Relieved, he climbed in. The door clicked shut behind him, and the narrow face beneath the cap asked: "Where?"

Lamian deliberated. He had nowhere to go except in search

of Helena Lifka, but he could not reveal his purpose to anyone. Yet, not knowing the way to her street, he would have to ask. But where? The police station, he nearly said aloud, then remembered that, unlike in Subotica, he now had Helena Lifka's address, and at the police station, or anywhere else for that matter, all he needed to do was ask where it was.

But "anywhere else" might just as well be here in the taxi, so he said: "Do you know where Bogdan Zimonjić Street is?" He waited for an answer, but instead the driver started the car and took off, tires hissing on the wet pavement.

They hummed along past the buildings beyond the hotel, suddenly turned left, grazing a curb, and sped down a wide, deserted street. The driver asked, "What number?" The number was on Lamian's lips, but he checked himself. "I'll have to see. Just stop anywhere." The driver swerved to the left, and the engine sputtered two or three times before the car came to a halt right at the corner of the street.

"This is Zimonjić, both directions." The man waved a thin forefinger. "Sixty-seven," he added. Lamian was about to correct him, but stopped before he revealed that he knew the number. "What? What?" he muttered, and looked in bewilderment at the narrow face until it turned toward him and gave an explanation: "Sixty-seven new dinars. Six thousand seven hundred old."

Relieved, Lamian took out the money, refused the change, and struggled from the taxi. Again he was sprinkled with rain. He turned up his collar and entered the side street, glancing over his shoulder at the corner wall to read the street sign, which, as in a dream, bore the name he had been seeking.

The rain on his neck reminded him to stay close to the wall. Walking beneath the eaves, he reached the first doorway and read number 37. He peered across the street and saw number 22. Next to it was 20 on a door, and the following door had no number. The third building down, its entrance at the top of a flight of steps, displayed number 16, not on the door but on the wall beside it.

He gazed at the house. Small, one story, with its two windows set close together in a smooth wall that seemed to have been recently plastered and painted. The steps from the narrow, recessed doorway fell steeply to the sidewalk. A house built for a single person. It was hard to imagine that with only two windows on the street it would extend much into the backyard.

The other houses were also single-story, except for one farther down the street which had a second floor with a mansard roof. A modest neighborhood, obviously. Lamian had paid no attention on the way, but now that he thought of the route the taxi took, he decided he was beyond Jelačić Square and in Upper Town. An area he had seldom gone to, moving mostly between Zrinjevac Park and Sava Road, with the exception of those evenings when he saw Zita home; but at the time he didn't look around much, what with the strain of watching her and listening to her voice, to the rare and, so far as he could recall, inconsequential words that contained no intimacy, even though he wanted them to be intimate, wanted her suddenly to yield to him, rewarding his perseverance.

Still, he seemed to recognize these houses, their reclusiveness and neglect. On one, the plaster decorations had fallen off; on another, a door was peeling; on a third, the wood of window frames was dark from having gone too long unpainted; several roofs were overgrown with moss. Few passersby, and mostly alone: a woman with a basket, an elderly man with a measured, unhurried step—as if the street was exclusively residential, not intended for traffic, and the people who lived on it left only for short periods and to nearby destinations.

Lamian would be strolling here too, if there had been no war and he had remained captivated by Zita, and he probably would have, even though she never gave in to him, staying always cool and restrained. But didn't that only increase his ardor? Her otherness, too, which actually was his otherness, which he felt when he was with her but she was ignorant of, or so he believed.

Now he was not so sure, not after Stanka Bugarin had exclaimed, "Because you were different! Because you're a Jew!" It had astonished him, brought him to his senses like a slap, a slap that put him in his place as an outsider whom it had pleased her to choose, to allow near her, but never forgetting that he was different.

Zita, too, might have seen him that way, without his suspecting—or had he suspected? He could no longer remember. Perhaps he had hesitated to express his feelings for her more openly, more unequivocally, out of fear that at the moment of such a declaration she, too, would slap him, only this time it would be not the slap of tolerance but the opposite.

Or would she, on the other hand, have agreed to have him despite his difference—for every girl longs to marry, no matter what, and thus a persistent suitor whose presence drives away the rest will almost invariably win. Then, much later, in some quarrel or dispute, the blow would come, the revelation, in his face, that all along he had been considered not a real find but only a consolation prize, a husband to fall back on. Would this kind of slap offend him more than Stanka's, or less? Would it demolish a life he had constructed so meticulously? Or would it leave him indifferent, coming after the fact, Zita being already his, and perhaps bound to him also by a child?

He tried to picture that poor child, the little boy who would hear his mother's cry of hatred and look away furtively, sensing that it involved him, too, because he had come not only from his mother's loins but his father's as well, the father who now turned out to be other, inferior, despised.

Lamian regarded the house that concealed Helena Lifka.

Was it only by chance that it was different, the one smooth facade among those loaded with ornaments, and with those close-set windows and the steps that went so steeply to the street? Didn't this house speak of a different occupant, a different way of life? A solitary life, for Helena Lifka had not changed her surname, had remained unmarried, or, if she married, divorced and returned to her old name, as if washing her hands of the mistake.

And if there had been a marriage, she obviously had no children, otherwise she would have kept her husband's name, which was also theirs. She lived alone.

Was this because of Lamian, the injury he did her, sullying everything male, spoiling for her the touch of love, making it forever an assault on her dignity? Perhaps she had become disturbed, and remained so all her life, revolted by any advance from the opposite sex. Perhaps the mere mention of men would produce in her shudders of loathing, frenzied cries, and she would have to be subdued, locked up in a room without sharp objects, and given sedatives or shock treatment. A cripple, in other words, because of Lamian.

Before he approached her, he needed to find out if this was indeed what she had become. He stood on Bogdan Zimonjić Street, almost directly across the way from her house, but did not move. He was afraid. Of his weakness, his unfitness for this meeting, and of her, of the madness that might be touched off by his appearance and his words.

What would he say? "I'm Furfa, remember?" And would she recognize him through all the changes that had accumulated over the years? She would squint at him, peel away the wrinkles and gray hair, remove the dark lenses of his glasses, and penetrate to the earlier structure of his face, the gauntness etched by starvation and illness. Then her eyes would widen in horror, she would draw back a step, another, and then, with her face contorted and a wail wrung from her chest, she would fling herself to the nearest place of refuge, her house or down the street, arms high, as if fleeing a fire.

How would he catch up with her, reason with her? It would be impossible. Any attempt to stop her would only heighten the terror triggered by his careless approach, the sudden reappearance of Kapo Furfa and the camp. She would rush headlong to the end of the street, the edge of the city, run with her last ounce of strength, as he came bounding into her thoughts like a bogeyman, trying to justify and explain, he the sole culprit of all her woes, the one person she would never be able to confront, who kept her locked away in her solitary house cowering and muttering words of refusal and abhorrence, perhaps to die there, in a corner of some shed in the yard, murdered by the memory of his face.

So she would end, and it would be just as if he had starved her to death in the camp, in that other shed, instead of sending her back to the disciplinary Kommando and arranging for her to get few extra mouthfuls, a few more scraps of warm clothing; and all his efforts on her behalf, which seemed to spring from the premonition that he would need her someday, would have failed.

Need her as a body needs blood, he thought, now that he had found her, only to lose her again, losing strength as well, succumbing to a fit of shivering.

Pain cut across his belly, and he trembled like a straw. The people passing by—a foppish man in a tight black raincoat, head uncovered but dry, because the rain had stopped without Lamian's noticing, then another man, a tradesman or worker, short, wearing a cap, with bristles stippling his broad unshaven face— looked at Lamian with apprehension, reluctant to come near. Finally a man approached wearing a green hat and coat, with a trim graying mustache that bobbed while he explained something, arm extended, pointing down the street. As Lamian turned away in rebuff, he saw that the narrow door of that peculiar house had opened and a woman was coming down the steps, carefully holding out one hand to support herself, a woman who had to be Helena Lifka. He stared at her, trying to overcome his shivering and the pain. With difficulty he straightened, told the man in green to leave him, that he was all right, then drew back farther against the building.

Now she disappeared from view, but when the man in green retreated, looking back with a scowl, and Lamian again stepped from the wall, bracing his legs to keep from falling, he saw her again, now larger and more distinct, wearing a gray coat with two rows of buttons. She walked with a ponderous gait and was bareheaded—the rain really had stopped—and her face was pale as dough, the blue eyes sunk deep into it. Fortunately, she didn't see him, and he pulled back into a doorway to wait for her to pass him with her sacklike form bent forward and with gatherings at the joints, which indicated she dressed too warmly.

Then she walked by, an empty black shopping bag hanging from her arm. She was going shopping, having waited for the sky to clear. Lamian set out after her on shaky legs spread wide, as if on a rolling ship; he followed her slow, ungainly figure with its large head and two large combs, brown and shiny, stuck in the back of her wavy gray hair.

THE COMBS MOVED UP AND DOWN AND THE GRAY COAT
bent stiffly over the heavy rump as her legs plowed forward in
broad shoes with soft low heels. It was evident that movement
didn't come easily to her, that she walked grudgingly, as if she
had had her fill of walking, as if she was fed up, to the crest of
her bowed back and the top of her head pinioned by combs,
with the unvarying motion of her legs—ever since marching in
the Kommando to shouts and threats and curses, guns swinging
from the brawny shoulders of the green-clad guards just as the
empty shopping bag now swung from her hand.

Was she reminded? Was her back stung by the malevolent
eyes, the bullets impatient to whistle into flesh? Were her ears
rent by the curses and insults, the snarls of the guard dogs? Was
her body revisited by the stumbling weakness that resisted the
order to march to the designated field, construction site, or pond,
where there would be bending and lifting and carrying and stacking, with hunger, thirst, sun on the head or ice in the bones, until
impossibly distant evening? Was all this being relived in her now,
as she walked, using the same muscles she used then, to walk?

Or was it like this only today, because of him? Had she
smelled him, had she tossed sleepless in her bed at dawn, sensing
his approach on the train from Banja Luka like a cloud of stinking
sulfur hanging over the blackness of her bedroom? Was that why
she hesitated to go out, making him wait in the doorway across
the street, then went out anyway, convinced he wouldn't leave?

Had she looked neither left nor right because she knew he
was there and didn't want to see him, determined to keep her

back to the fatal bullet so it would finish her off unseen? Because he watched her like a bullet, following at a distance, a bullet ready to fly from its barrel if she took flight. He had dogged prisoners like this countless times, his suspicious eyes fixed on their backs. Yes, he would rush after her, grab her shoulder, and force her to turn around and listen to him. But he knew, even as his blood seethed, that he wouldn't dare, nor would it do any good, because they were equals now, both victims, both alive. Because he had not let her die of hunger and cold like the rest, because he had wanted to possess this equality with her alone.

Except now he did not know how to behave, with her, as an equal. He had been a Kapo, and that was still in the depths of him, perverted depths trained to evil, and he had made it his law. Was there another law? Of humanity? Decency? He walked behind her, and any outside observer would have thought it accidental that they were going in the same direction, the man's gaze on the woman's back. The observer's curiosity might be stirred by the similarity in age between the two, or a resemblance to someone from the past, an old man making comparisons. But no one today would link them to that inhuman, pitiless dance of mutual destruction.

In which who kills whom? If she had had a knife then, or had been able to grab his, stuck in the workbench behind the little pile of food, and if she had had the courage to pay for the murder of a Kapo by standing in the stand-up cell until she died . . . if she had not been weakened by hunger and thus made submissive to him in advance by his gifts of food, then she would have plunged the knife into his chest the moment he first put his arms around her, and he would now be one of those bricks of disintegrating bone and flesh, would not feel this seething or this dizzy indecision, and she, too, would be a brick, would not be afraid, would not remember those moments of ceremonial subjugation, when a single gesture of acquiescence or rebellion would decide her fate in the next moment.

The next moment now was free: she was going shopping. The empty black shopping bag swung not intentionally—she didn't have sufficient will in her for that—but merely with the rhythm of her walking, the movements necessary to advance. Aged, listless motion. Like his, as he followed her. For they were, after all, what the observer took them to be: two old people in the same street, walking in the same direction, to whom nothing fateful would happen in the next moment. Lamian walked behind her, watching, curious to see where she would go, wanting to learn something about her, the more information the better. Perhaps the satisfying of his curiosity would cast off the burden of his fascination with her, a burden that was beginning to exhaust him.

Unless it was illness that exhausted him, the attack which had passed as soon as it appeared but left him with stomach pains and wobbly limbs. He felt a need to stop, to lie down, stretch out, close his eyes. He should turn on his heels and go back to the hotel, to the room which was waiting for him, and get in bed and get some sleep. Then, if his strength returned, he would wash and go down for a change of scenery.

Perhaps by then some young people would be sitting at the tables in the lobby, young women with glasses set between them like little posts, but posts without electrified wire, posts not to divide but to join. He would look at the girls and reflect that their lives had no crucial next moment, no roll call at which you were a living post that in the next moment might be cut down and thrown into the fire. Their lives continued freely to tomorrow morning and beyond, and they were not made to do anything, not forced to march anywhere, not hobbled by hunger or hidden packets of food with which, in the sound of hundreds of thousands who quietly sobbed and cursed and called for their mothers while from the surrounding watchtowers the guards called to each other with their ringing voices, you exchanged power for powerlessness, powerlessness for power, avenging yourself for the shame of your survival by murdering the innocent.

But that did not link the two of them now: she was going shopping, unfettered. At the bottom of her bag or in her coat pocket was a wallet, and she could buy food and drink for many days, for all the days that lay ahead of her. In her house she could stockpile canned goods and biscuits by the ton, if she wished to, and he could do nothing, only watch her.

They were of separate worlds, they who had once been so much a part of one world that they held on to each other, naked, even though they had been pushed into that embrace by two opposing hungers, the wish to obtain food in exchange for submission and the wish to obtain submission in exchange for food. Because there was too little food for all to live, and this presented each with the task of living nevertheless.

Not a task. More the reflex that sprang from the impossibility of that task. The reflex that set them moving, got them up from their wooden cubicles in the predawn darkness, and spewed them out of the barracks door into the star-canopied yard, where the grass snapped with frost and they stood quietly eight abreast until they were counted, their ranks evened out by blows. It drove them, that reflex, like a herd to the trough, shoving and squirming, sticking out their necks, their hands holding pots to grab some warm nothing and pour it inside them and pretend it was something. It arranged them in Kommandos, threw their steps into a march, their voices into a song; it brought them around to meanness and groveling, to enduring humiliation, to violence if necessary, if that made their portion bigger, if that strengthened their prospects for the next moment.

A few ounces of food, that was all they needed, for without those few ounces the muscles would no longer obey, the skin would not remain whole, the heart would not continue to push blood through the vessels, or the kidneys to filter urine, and you became a dying worm pulled by gravity to the cold earth.

A simple trick. It hadn't been necessary to invent it, merely to take a lesson from the tillers of barren fields, who slew each other for the meat of a captured lizard or badger, or from the shantytown unemployed, ready to rob and bludgeon for the price of a bowl of soup. The only new twist was that this poverty was artificially produced, and enclosed by a fence so that it could not be fled. Like disease in a test tube, like pus that had nowhere to drain. A forced crop of decay.

His nose smelled their sweetish odor, his cheeks felt their rotten heat, his ears caught their chatter, at once passive and enraged. Thousands jammed together, starving, staggering, thousands with sores and leaking excrement, thousands going mad, subdued only by clubs, which took the moisture from their flesh, the marrow from their bones, the color from their vision. Thrown into heaps, burned in ovens. But among them, searching, he had found a few unravaged bodies, skin that was untouched, breasts and bottoms that still strutted, that had not yet dried up or lost their pinkness and warmth. How he had sniffed them out! How, in that maze of death and stench and muck, he had discovered the wellspring of health and renewal!

He watched the old woman's body drag itself along the sidewalk ahead of him, swinging the empty shopping bag: a shriveled, hunched body wrapped in thick fabric. He couldn't believe it once stood before him naked, white as snow, and swelling, yielding in his embrace as tears flowed drop by drop from her saucerlike blue eyes and ran down her white cheeks, thick red lips, round chin.

Now she stopped. She appeared to have been forced to do so by a cluster of people on the other side of her, but then he noticed a gleam of glass between them and her. She turned and disappeared. He hurried to catch up with her and found himself at the corner of a building, where there was an entrance to a store and around it people crowding on their way in and out. Casting a glance through the door, he failed to see her, saw only shelves laden with boxes, bottles, jars. A mass of moving overcoats, but not the gray one.

Around the corner was a display window. He looked in,

lowering his head as if intent on the articles arranged at the bottom—boxes, jars, bags, sacks with colorful labels—but keeping his eyes up, hoping that with his dark glasses no one would see that he was looking.

Behind the glass of the window was more glass, a partition, and the double reflection made it difficult to distinguish colors. The coats inside were pressed together as if under orders, or else for safety. Scanning them, and the heads with an occasional hat or cap, Lamian caught sight of two shiny objects: the two combs.

It had to be she beneath them, and indeed, he recognized her coat, though through the double glass it now seemed almost black. She was standing a little to one side—that was why he hadn't seen her from the door—in an area of aisles of packaged goods, where on shelves behind a counter that held a scale the rosy ends of stacked bread could be seen, like children's bare knees. No one was serving behind the counter, but the woman leaned forward, so that her coat rode up stiffly in back; she was sorting through something, stepping left and right, setting objects in front of her. A young salesgirl in a white smock and white cap suddenly materialized. The woman straightened and handed her a full paper bag, which the girl put on the scale and took her time weighing, bending over as she added or removed weights.

Then the salesgirl said something, her lips moving in a serious expression only to fly apart in unexpected laughter that bared her teeth. Throwing back her head and arms, she deftly took a loaf of bread from the shelf and put it on the counter. She bent over, marked something down, then disappeared and returned with several colorful packages. Again she did a calculation, and handed the slip of paper across the counter. The woman picked it up, turning her profile to the window, a flabby white cheek and fleshy nose, and went toward the coats clustered in the middle of the store.

There she stood a long time without moving. New coats and heads both covered and uncovered pressed into the store; some passed her, stopped in front of her, concealing her. Her combs disappeared, reappeared, her profile. Then she was turned in the opposite direction, toward the counter. Her coat sleeves bent, and long-fingered hands emerged to put things from the counter into her shopping bag. Then her coat stopped flexing and moved out of the frame of the display window.

Lamian waited. He went back to the corner. Yes, she was going home, by the same street, with the same listless gait, except now the shopping bag, full and bulging, pulled her down on one side, making her shoulders uneven.

He followed, as if she were a magnet, though it was clear that he would not learn anything more about her. She had simply bought the groceries she needed, and would now make herself lunch. A dish of potatoes or green beans, or perhaps something less common, more refined, like cauliflower or asparagus, to which she would add a veal cutlet or two, tossing them in with the vegetables or broiling them separately. She would move back and forth as she had earlier in the store, cutting, peeling, turning the stove on and off, watching as the ingredients fell apart and changed color; she would breath in their aroma, which would tantalize the membranes of her nose, throat, and stomach, coaxing forth the juices of hunger, and she would surrender completely to the promise of surfeit and pleasure.

Her sole pleasure, perhaps, since the camp, a pleasure that had grown into a passion. The sense of triumph at the moment of fulfillment. She would hum something from her memory while her spoon stirred in the pan, releasing those wonderful smells. And she would continue to murmur the song she had begun while she shoveled the finished meal down her gullet. Or even sing out loud, not thinking of the danger from the morning train that hung over her like a black cloud. If he were to ring the doorbell she was now approaching, interrupt her in her mealtime song, that orgy of pleasure, her mouth would drop open, her voice rise to a shriek, a scream, and crumbs would spray into his face, and half-chewed pieces of food, and spittle and stomach gases.

But that was his hunger, not hers, Lamian decided, at the observation post where he had again stationed himself. After Helena Lifka disappeared into her house, his stomach began to quake, as if a new attack was about to begin. But instead of the pain that cut horizontally across his belly, there was a dull pressure, as if a stone were caught there. His mouth filled with saliva, reminding him that he had eaten nothing since morning, and little the previous day.

He cast a glance in the direction of the corner store, where he could buy food. In other words, leave his post. He would lose nothing by doing so, for he wasn't going to muster the courage to ring or knock at the door, and he had failed to approach Helena Lifka when she was in the street. Which he didn't regret. She would only wail, "You won't let me eat! Even now, you won't let me eat until you've finished torturing me!" He did not want to torture her, but he knew he would, must, if he persisted in his desire to see her.

For the time being, then, he would leave. But he didn't set out immediately; he resisted the call of hunger. It seemed ludicrous, this hunger, his as well as hers; it tickled his gorge into a guffaw that sent hiccuping ripples through his chest. Swallowing chunks from the body of another in order to fill one's own. Like stuffing a bird with straw, a dead bird made to seem otherwise by parting its beak a little and spreading its wings, and putting glass beads with an inimical gleam in place of its lifeless eyes.

He was such a bird, wings spread toward that other, similar bird across the street.

She was preparing her meal, maybe already eating: it was despicable, insulting, and he felt like running to that door and knocking, not to introduce himself and suggest that they thrash over the past together, but to scold her, curse her for an old fool, slave to her stomach, for which she was ready to forget.

He didn't want her to forget. That was why he had come—so that she wouldn't forget. Or was it so that he wouldn't forget? In any case he had to leave this doorway, where there was an unbearable draft (in the gloom behind him were hallways, passageways, perhaps leading to a garden) and where his insides were churning with hunger.

Eat with her? Knock, not to scold or curse but to request a place at her table, sitting at it and watching as she bustled back and forth in front of the stove, peeling and mixing and stirring to that unconscious hum of hers, which he would now accompany with his own hum, making a duet of famished former prisoners.

What an opera! An *opera mundi.* The two of them, gaping mouths agleam with the gold of false teeth, trumpeting their hunger and the joy that it would soon be satisfied. That old familiar duo, Lifka and Lamian, or, since the first letters of their names already matched so well, L&L. Performing at festivals that featured a new kind of singing, in which the notes were subject not to the laws of harmony but to the demands of the body itself. Concerts on every continent, since the need for food was basic and universal. Their itinerary arranged by a team of secretaries, with little flags pinned to a map on the wall; special consideration given to spots with concentrations of former prisoners, who could attend the performances at a reduced rate. Moving encounters, ovations. "Bravo! We couldn't do better at Dachau! Or we at Bergen-Belsen! Auschwitz is still Auschwitz, tops in everything."

"*Im Lager Auschwitz war ich zwar so manchen Monat, so*

manches Jahr," he recalled the tune. But that was a real song, a classic, intended not to mock but reminisce. What jackass thought it up? An inmate from Vienna, according to a camp legend. The kind of song the German guards were partial to, since they, too, felt their stay in the camp was an unerasable part of their lives, and readily grew sentimental over it. *"Kommando, singen!"* the order would resound in the warm May day, a day of white and yellow butterflies, a day whose end would see many of them, butterflies and singers alike, back inside the wires of death; and the prisoners would obediently open their mouths and let the tender notes roll from their throats, adjusting the cadence to their weak, unsteady steps.

Revolting. All that mimicking of life in the non-life inside the wire, all those attempts to preserve a few kernels of humanity. Gathering after supper in the cubicles to drink together a can of denatured alcohol obtained in exchange for cigarettes from the Russians, who siphoned it from the tanks of wrecked planes on the junk heap next to the runway. Christmas, Easter, New Year's—with song again, but this time hushed, quavering song, so the guard wouldn't hear, for it hadn't been ordered. Toys made of scraps of wood and iron scavenged from workshop floors, which handy prisoners would spend weeks carving and trimming into some shape and then, with a smile, present to a Gypsy child or a little Pole hanging around the wire: "Here, go play!"

That need for civility and kindness, which vanished at the first warning from a guard or Kapo, or was cut short by a blow, a swagger stick to the head from which there was no awakening. The honor of trying turned abruptly into nothing. All those diversions of gentleness crumbling into suffering, drowned in suffering, and trampled into the bricks of former bones, former flesh, former blood, former convolutions of the brain. Into nothing.

And so would their song, that cry of hunger and long-awaited pleasure by two who shared the same memories. It would spring from silence only to be replaced by silence. Was that why he had come, instead of keeping silent, silent until the end? To prove, whimpering, sniveling—to prove to whom?—that even in those black dregs he had existed, that something which possessed form and harmony—like those handmade toys—could be extracted from him, even if it was only a song of hunger, a scream of hunger, the wail of a doddering old man who had barely eaten in the last twenty hours and whose legs were weak from standing!

Angrily, he strode down the street to the corner store, but when he looked through the glass door and again saw a curtain of queueing overcoats—new people, no doubt—the will to go in deserted him. What he really needed now, more than food, was to get away to some quiet place, shed his coat and hat and take a breather; a place where he could empty his bladder and wash his hands, settle his bones on a chair at a bar table, and relax.

He turned the corner. Which way was the center of town? He set his course by the recollection of his taxi ride, following it backward. First he went down a quiet street with no shops except for a dry cleaner's, then turned right, into a wider street which ran parallel to Bogdan Zimonjić and was lined with residential buildings. Proceeding from intersection to intersection, he at last found himself amid busier traffic.

Cars, people going in and out of doorways and gates arched with canvas or truncated near the top by raised blinds. He searched among the signs, stopping frequently, until on the third corner he came across what he wanted: three windows of frosted glass, tall swinging doors with SNACKERY written above them, and a separate sign that said SHORT ORDERS AND BEER in smaller letters, jutting from the wall on rods. He pushed open the doors and found himself in a room with tables ranged along the walls to the left and right. In the middle bulged the long semicircle of a massive bar paneled in dark wood. Behind this fortresslike structure stood two waitresses in bright dresses.

On the right all the tables were occupied; on the left, by a

window, sat a single customer. Lamian chose a table near the
bar. Behind it was an empty coatrack, so he first hung up his
coat and hat, then decided, as long as he was still standing, to
look for the men's room. He didn't have far to look: the door
was right by the coatrack, frameless but equipped with a handle.
Inside was a small anteroom with a sink; from there a second
door, open and emitting a pungent odor, led to the toilet. Closing
the door made the room dark, so he opened it again and looked
for the switch. He found it, clicked it on, but no light.

What to do? Leaving the door ajar behind him, he fumbled
in his pockets and found some matches, lit one, then stepped
carefully to the toilet, unbuttoned his trousers, and urinated. By
this time the match had burned out, so he felt for the chain and
found it; but pulling on it produced nothing but a metallic thump
above his head. Lighting another match, he went back out to
the sink and ran water over his hands. He would have washed
more thoroughly, but there was nothing to dry himself with and
he didn't want to be seen in the restaurant with a wet face, so
he merely rubbed his hands, pressed the door handle with his
elbow, and went out.

The table he had chosen was no longer free: a soldier was
sitting there, or, rather, judging by the silver ribbons on his
shoulders, a noncommissioned officer, a handsome blond youth
with close-cropped hair, a grave face, and a glass of beer in front
of him. Since it appeared that Lamian couldn't have a table to
himself, he decided to join this man, who could be expected not
to have companions or to linger too long in the restaurant. Bow-
ing slightly, he asked permission to join him and, when the soldier
nodded indifferently, sat down.

The waitress, a strapping woman who wore a green crown-
shaped band around her brown hair and a wide pleated skirt,
also green, came out from behind the bar and approached not
Lamian but the soldier. She stood over him, putting her hand,

which held a crumpled napkin, on the back of the chair, and said something in a low voice. The soldier threw back his head and laughed, showing large white teeth, but didn't answer, only shrugged slightly. She then mentioned times, a woman's name, the bus, the rain, and went away. The soldier, still smiling, brought his glass to his lips, drained it, took out a cigarette, and lit it.

Lamian also reached for a cigarette and began to smoke. Hunger was burning in his stomach. He looked around for the waitress. She was standing behind the bar now with the other waitress, who was darker and of a somewhat smaller build, but they looked alike because of the same green uniform. He coughed to get her attention, said he wanted something to eat. She turned absently, went over to the next table, without a word took the folded menu from in front of the single customer there, set it before Lamian, and again leaned toward the soldier. Lamian spread the menu out and immediately noted that it was not typed but printed, and therefore fixed. The list of beverages covered the entire left page and half of the right; only at the bottom of the right page, under the heading "Short Orders," did a few dishes appear.

And not a single one of them was familiar; they were merely fancy names, like Wine Stuffing and Minced Appetizer. Only Hunter's Plate near the bottom suggested ordinary food, so that was what he ordered as the waitress was bending toward the soldier. Lamian's glance fell on the half-empty glass in the soldier's large, sunburned hand, and he added, "A beer, too, please" as he closed the menu.

The woman still didn't look at him but did tear herself away from the soldier and went behind the bar, and with a half-smile on her face returned with a glass of beer and a plate of food, which she set in front of Lamian, as an afterthought moving the plate closer to him with a few feminine gestures, then tossing a

"Not much longer" to the soldier as she went back behind the bar.

Lamian looked at the plate: on it lay a bun, and on top of the bun, fastened with a toothpick sticking straight up, a ball of something dark and grainy with a slice of red pepper, oily bright, along the edge. He searched the table for cutlery; there was none. Then he realized that he couldn't use a knife and fork on this multistory dish anyway, so he grabbed the end of the toothpick, lifted it with the ball, turned the ball and sniffed—he could smell onion—before finally taking a cautious bite. It was ground meat, heavily seasoned. He broke off a piece of the bun, put it in his mouth, then hesitantly lifted the pepper with two fingers and bit off the end. The food was not succulent, only hot, spiky dry. But it was food and, washed down with some beer, filled his ravenous stomach. There was too little of it, however; that he could see before he had eaten half the bun and an equal share of the meatball and pepper, so he looked around for the waitress with the intention of renewing his order.

Neither waitress was anywhere to be seen. Lamian noticed a new customer, an older man, approaching from the door, and was surprised to see that the man looked Jewish. Not so much because of something Levantine in the face, which was long and pale, with brown, slightly protuberant, troubled eyes, a broad, prominent nose, thick lips, and a diffident, withdrawn chin—such features were often found in the Balkans—but because of the man's bearing. Lamian unerringly recognized, in the bearing, the sign of that otherness—but to him likeness—which he had always seen as Jewish.

The man wore only a suit, no overcoat or hat, which was at odds with the season, autumn, and at odds, too, with his age. The suit was dark gray, almost black, clean but carried with neither grace nor care, over a shirt that was white but well worn, the top button undone. There was no tie, as if he had thrown on his clothes in haste. A city person, that much was obvious, but lacking the middle-class confidence which comes with position, and becomes more rigid the higher the position. He approached with the gangly walk of an itinerant locksmith or tramp, though the suit said that he was neither. Heading for the table with the lone customer and performing a vague bow that testified to his experience in cafés, he grabbed the back of the nearest chair, pulled it clumsily, weakly, from the table, as far as was necessary, and sat down opposite the man.

Hunched, he turned and raised a white, long-fingered hand unshaped by physical work and waved it as shakily as he had walked. Surprisingly, the waitress, the same one who had served Lamian, appeared out of nowhere—she must have been watching from behind the curtain in back of the bar—and came over. In a raspy voice, the man ordered. Lamian couldn't make out what the order was, but he was sure he didn't hear the name of a single dish that was on the menu. The woman answered with a loud, drawled "Okay," then left with a swish of her pleated skirt. Lamian tried to stop her, to add his order, but it was too late; she had already passed him, playfully touching the soldier's arm on her way.

Lamian quickly finished the Hunter's Plate, only to find that his hunger was greater than before. The way, he remembered, he would gulp down a pot of watery soup and it would be worthless against the gaping void within him, a void like a wound from a murderer's blade. He felt that wound not only in his neck, where he imagined it, but everywhere. He had become one entire wound, a hole of pain, his entrails laid bare, exposed. He had the urge to wrap himself in his arms, for protection, and half expected the new customer to do the same.

It irritated him to see the man instead sitting relaxed in his chair, almost slouching, as if there was no threat and this café really was a place where anyone could enter, sit down, order what he wanted, and wait calmly while the food was being prepared. As if no knife lay in ambush, gleaming suddenly in the hand of the soldier sitting next to Lamian, or the hand of the man who sat across from the newcomer—to be plunged into belly, side, or throat, the newcomer's or Lamian's own.

Slit open, gasping, they would crumple, while the slayer wiped the knife on his clothing and bent down to watch with curiosity, avidly, how the blood spurted, how the severed tendons in the neck released the final puffs of air from the lungs, in little bubbles that grew like balloons and then burst.

Didn't the man know? Or did he have that much faith in his disguise, in that dark gray suit, so ordinary, and in the air of assurance which signified a regular café goer, the bow which implied equality, the very boldness with which he sauntered into the midst of these local customers, acting as if he, too, were local, a neighbor even, from one of the houses nearby, who simply dropped in wearing a suit but no coat, here at the nearest convenient watering hole, this snackery, to have a bite and then leave?

Would they let him leave? The one he'd gone up to, introducing himself and then sitting at his table, would that man go along with the masquerade and not denounce him as an interloper, an unauthorized user of the café's warmth and security? Or would he denounce him and unleash his fury on him?

Lamian waited, staring, as he had waited in the loft at Jasenovac, eye pressed to the hole dug between the bricks, offering a view of the ground in front of the camp headquarters. There beneath a canopy sat Blažuj, the former priest, uniform unbuttoned, cap pushed back on his head. Before Blažuj stood four prisoners, hands tied behind their backs with wire, and two young Ustaša guards, Redžep and Ivo.

The afternoon sun lit up every hair, every fold of skin on their faces and fold of cloth in their clothes. Two of the prisoners had caps; two were bareheaded. The breeze that blew across the yard played with the long, silky blond hair of the one on the right. Lamian's glance returned constantly to that hair, that vestige of gentleness and ease which it was impossible to feel in the narrow loft beneath the roof. He prayed to that gentleness, in the hope that it would triumph and reveal itself to be the only truth, destroying the malevolence that oozed like a muddy spring around the group, the four tied up, the two guarding them, and the one who observed them as he ate.

Blažuj observed them sullenly, his eyes resting on them each time he lifted food to his mouth, which was overhung by the wiry dark mustache he had grown in the camp. The blond hair of the prisoner on the right fluttered in the breeze. The sun gleamed on it, and fell on the canopy as well, on Blažuj's legs and boots beneath the wooden table. It also lit the corner of the table and the tall, round loaf of bread on it, from which Blažuj was cutting large slices and stuffing them in his mouth with bites of meat. The sun glinted on the glasses of rakija they drained and refilled from an uncorked green bottle; it mingled bright and shaded patches on the two guards who, restless in the heat, danced around the prisoners, hitting them in the back, calves, and shins with their hands and feet.

Those blows and the hiss and the curses made Lamian afraid, as did the continuing silence from below, in the chain shop, whose doors were bolted. Otherwise the scene was ruled by the wind, the sun, the swaying of the trees beyond the fence, and the trembling of the sparse grass of the yard. All forces were equalized, and it seemed that things would stay like this forever, vacillating, the men tied up, the man feeding himself, and the guards. But then Blažuj stood, wiped his mouth with the back of his hand, clapped his cap on his head, and left the canopy. He went up to the prisoners, reached for his belt, and took out a knife, whose blade gleamed. Then all at once, frenzied, as if buffeted by a storm, he bent over and began stabbing the four men one after another, in the chest, neck, shoulders, with furious straight thrusts, making them fall on top of each other, because they were tied together, and making them cry and scream until they were nothing but a heap of limbs, heads, and torsos, twisted and torn, Blažuj bending lower and lower over them, almost prone himself, as if he were drinking them in, and the knife, all bloody now, plunged ceaselessly until the last twitch of leg, hand, or head, the last gasp or sigh.

Shaking, Lamian waited to see whether Blažuj would call for new prisoners to be sent, perhaps from the chain shop, which was closest, and perhaps from this very loft, if he sensed that someone was hiding there and peeking out. But that was unlikely, since it was Blažuj himself who had ordered the chain shop locked until he had dealt with the four prisoners, and also since the murdering of them, punishment for some misdeed, had probably satisfied him, and tired him out as well.

But Lamian waited, if not for Blažuj then, as he did the whole time in Jasenovac, for Gabelić: waited for him to emerge from headquarters, where he sat in his immaculate uniform, erect, blond, scrubbed, handsome; waited for him to see the slaughter and be reminded of him, Lamian, and send for him.

That was how it would end, he felt. In one of the convolutions of Gabelić's brain, Lamian stood—fraud, hypocrite, false follower, unmasked heathen, and freak of nature, who deserved the knife and a painful death. So he waited, concealing himself about the camp, reporting for work wherever there was work to report for—on the dike, where exertion and thigh-deep water made legs swell and kidneys rot, or among the gravediggers, panting and staggering as they transported the daily hundreds of killed and threw them into pits. Lamian had been exchanging barracks with the hungriest, the most bribable, in order to get as far away as possible from the places Gabelić might look for him.

He came face to face with him many months after looking through the hole in the loft of the chain shop. This time he was present in the ranks as a pair of Ustaši brought out Sergeant Major Maričić in front of them, then bound him to a tree and withdrew, giving way to Gabelić, erect and pale, who turned to the prisoners and announced that Maričić, though an Ustaša, had lusted after the gold coins the Gypsies hid in their clothing. Maričić had searched them and kept the coins for himself, thus betraying Pavelić and the Croatian state, and for this he would now be punished. Gabelić went up to him, took a knife from his belt, and cut off Maričić's nose and both ears, then ordered him to open his mouth. When Maričić refused, Gabelić cut open the mouth with his knife and thrust the blade inside, at which Maričić slumped down the tree. The two Ustaši untied him and dragged him across the field to finish him off.

A shudder ran down Lamian's spine, because he felt that Gabelić was punishing not Maričić but him, demonstrating the punishment that awaited him. And so one night not long afterward, when called to the hospital as a gravedigger to carry away the body of Antun Frfa, a Communist and a Croat, Lamian lay down in Frfa's place, with the complicity—after much pleading—of Stevan, the nurse. The next day he reported himself recovered and was shortly transported, under the name of Frfa, to Auschwitz.

If it hadn't been for his terror of Gabelić and Gabelić's knife, Lamian would never have dared take that leap among the dead. Instead he would have gone on roaming about the camp, carrying away other dead, seeing off the convoys of future dead across the Sava to Gradina, looking through his secret hole in the loft wall as Blažuj butchered—until his turn came to be butchered.

The terror saved him, and it saved him a second time, in Auschwitz, when drenched with water by Sommer on the parade ground, quaking with cold and the fear that he would freeze, he caught the eye of Alfred Riegler and with a look promised him gold, for which Riegler, as soon as Lamian had recovered, made him the workshop Kapo.

SUDDENLY, LIKE AN APPARITION, THE WAITRESS WAS THERE, carrying a tray. She slipped past the soldier and Lamian, went to the next table, and with a dull clink set down the newcomer's food before him, adding those same feminine touches, which Lamian guessed in the flexing of her bare, pudgy elbows. When she left with the empty tray, the man nodded, reached for the glass of beer, bent down, and took several quick sips. Then he drank from the cup of coffee, grasped the handle and lifted the cup from the saucer, supporting his wrist with his other hand as he slurped. Both hands shook visibly.

Flopping back in his chair, he put his hands in his pockets and took out a box of matches and a pack of cigarettes; set them on the table, sorted for a long time through the pack, which was crumpled and half empty, then selected a cigarette and placed it between slackened lips. After two or three strikes with a match, he lit the cigarette, using his free hand to prop the hand with the match. After a few short puffs he put the matchbox back on the table and with two fingers removed the cigarette from his mouth. He rested the hand with the cigarette on the table, and as it shook, sending the smoke left and right in wavering wisps, he squinted, pursed his lips, and blew out the smoke he had just inhaled, and it rose pallidly to the ceiling.

Lamian looked at him sternly: not a single movement of the newcomer escaped him, not a single twitch of the face. They were the movements of one who sought but was quickly satisfied, who valued the gaining of a thing more than the thing itself. And what he sought was incompatible: beer and coffee, drunk together that way, sip for sip, confounded beer drinker and coffee drinker alike. By ordering them together, the man seemed to want to capture, at one stroke, all the amenities of the café: the abundance of alcohol, the stimulating bitterness of coffee. But as soon as he had sipped and tasted, he sank into an old man's indifference, with no sign of enjoyment.

Because he was a false guest, a trespasser. Because he had come here not to drink beer and smoke a cigarette with his coffee but to compensate for something. Home? Friends? The manner in which he entered, the unsteady gait and inadequate clothing, for autumn, as of someone in the neighborhood merely dropping in, and that practiced bow to his fellow patron, and the mumbled order whose offhandedness said it was always the same, had been for years, and addressed always to the same waitress—all this suggested that the man had home and friends, and that the café and his regular place at one of the tables, and the beer, coffee, and cigarettes were only a supplementary thing, even superfluous, a luxury he could do without, because he led a full and settled life in the vicinity, had a spacious apartment on some broad commercial avenue, where he would call to his wife or daughter, "I'm off to the café," then go out coatless and hatless because they were not quick enough to scold him for his thoughtlessness.

But Lamian saw through him, saw the room in which he truly lived: small, cramped, a former pantry or laundry room at the end of a hallway, next to the toilet used by the whole floor. It was given to him as emergency quarters after the war, when he came back, surfacing like a specter, like a drowning victim who revives only after the water has been pushed from his lungs, or like someone caught in a fire who wanders out of the flames. And in this transient state he remained, unable to find or afford anything better, feeling no need to expand, afraid to, in fact, for that would only reveal how alone he was. So he filled his tiny space with whatever chance led him to acquire, that suit, for instance, whose creases showed that he kept it hanging on a nail in the wall, or spread over the back of a chair.

Yes, the room he came from was a jumble of things strewn over furniture and windowsills, a marketplace confusion of random shapes. He sat on the end of his solitary bed, waiting for the hour when he went to the café, or he lay gripped by sleeplessness in a darkness streaked with the gleam of street lights, streaks that sketched the figures of those he lost in a similar dark confusion, in barracks heaped with rags, where the butchers came with flashlights and lists including the names of his mother, his wife, his daughter, his brother, his son. They were roused with curses, blows to the legs; their hands were tied behind their backs; they were taken out to face the knife, the sledgehammer, the bullet.

And now he was stunned by the fact that he was alive. Alive by virtue of some miracle, the intervention of strength or luck pulling him from death, allowing him once again to be a man in a suit, a man with coins jingling in his pocket, money to spend on whatever he liked, beer, coffee, the warmth of the café.

He sat slouched in his chair, back bent and neck slack, from time to time bringing the cigarette to his lips with a shaking hand that had to be braced with the other hand. Paralysis? A smashed joint or severed muscle? The body was a wonderful mechanism—Lamian knew that from his own—capable of repairing infected wounds and swollen rotting flesh, of closing up tears and cleaning away pus. But the images trapped in the brain could not be cleaned away: they were there even as you sat and smoked amid the hum of the café. It was no longer a café, it was a barracks. Your cigarette wasn't bought in a tobacco shop; you scrounged it by searching the pockets of the dead or in exchange for bread. And it was not just a cigarette before or after lunch, but the last cigarette, always the last, inhaled deeply before an

SS man burst in, before he came toward you along the path between the barracks, carrying your number jotted down for some offense real or imagined, or else with a mental note of your face made when observing your transgression. Or perhaps he simply carried the desire to murder, a rage caused by a letter from home saying that the English bombed the village or his wife wasn't home when his best friend went to call. Your puff on that cigarette would be cut short by a swing of a club, and you'd fall before the cubicle where you had sat smoking that scrounged cigarette, fall on your face in a shallow puddle of blood, and jerk a few times and grow still, or the SS man would still you with a few more blows to the skull, then call the gravediggers, who would strip off your rags, throw you on a stretcher, and take you to the pit or the crematorium.

That's what the newcomer was. If Lamian went up to him now and pulled up the sleeve of his suit, the left sleeve, and the sleeve of his shirt beneath it, he would see under the skin a number in black ink. Skin as pale as the skin on the man's face, or even paler, since the sun never touched it. So deathly pale, bloodless, waxy white, that the number would stand out in all its neat clarity, the only clear thing about him. The truth. The rest of him was all lie and playacting. He lied with the way he sat, with what he ordered, and with the cigarette he brought to his lips, holding one hand with the other so it wouldn't shake. Poor old man, the people would think. An old man who had stolen out of his apartment here in the neighborhood, fooling his family, running off with a few coins in his pocket because he couldn't sit still. He was old but couldn't sit still, the old rascal, still spurred by the swagger of bygone days and probably rambling on about them to himself as he stared into the smoke of his cigarette.

But if they caught sight of the number on his shriveled forearm, they would stop their humorous speculation and suddenly grow serious, and stare at that bookkeeper's mark as if it were a coiled snake. Perhaps they would get up from their chairs and ask for the bill, then quickly leave.

The soldier wouldn't. He'd wait for his sweetheart, since he'd made arrangements with her; he'd stay, sit stonily silent, running a finger over his fogged-up glass of beer. Only on the way to her sublet room where a bed awaited them would he bend to her ear and tell the strange thing he had seen: that number.

But the patron near the man would jump up immediately. A narrow, bony face, small brown eyes, long thin lips, and neatly combed, dark wavy hair. A student, or rather—since he was a bit too old to be bending over textbooks, closer to thirty than twenty—a beginning teacher, or else a civil servant, a law clerk. Yes, a law clerk passing the time in a café between two trials, over a drink that was clear and colorless in its tall glass—probably mineral water with a touch of wine. Young men drank less alcohol now, especially in the cities.

But the soldier was not from Zagreb; he was only serving in the army here, and had found himself a waitress girlfriend, somebody for men in uniform.

Women preferred ones like this civilian. A sure thing. Low rank but high ambitions; clothes neat, necktie knotted beneath the shirt collar. Satisfaction of basic needs guaranteed. His mother's apartment, perhaps, but big enough to accommodate a bride as well, especially if she was working, bringing in money. A future.

Then suddenly those precisely aligned numbers on the withered, pale forearm of an old man. Unnatural, revolting, for numbers to go like that with a living body, that creation of soft flesh, pulsing fluids. A body that barely allowed itself to be constrained by shoes and clothing, the stiffness of leather and cloth, threatening to burst free at any moment. While numbers stood for discipline and computation. How did they originate? Maybe if he read a history of the camps—but no, nowadays you got only articles in the newspaper feature section, side by side with nude models, to which youthful eyes immediately turned, away from the sour, didactic past.

The patron wouldn't believe the numbers. He would bend over, look, perhaps ask for an explanation. And then, when the newcomer hesitated and even pulled down his sleeve, as one hid a wound beneath his clothing, or a syphilitic sore, Lamian would have to take over the role of interpreter, using force if necessary to keep the sleeve rolled up, so that the others could examine what was written on the skin.

There would be a struggle, the newcomer trying to rise to his feet while Lamian pushed him back into the chair. "Be still! I'm Kapo Furfa!" he would yell in the man's face, and slap him maybe into obedience, then explain, as if the forearm were a guinea pig, that what they saw here was something quite ordinary, that thirty years ago it had been done throughout Europe, here in Zagreb as well, certainly in this street and possibly in this very café, if it existed then. That people of the wrong origin and the wrong convictions were caught the way rabid dogs were caught, in nooses, handcuffs, then thrown behind barbed wire with numbers stamped in their flesh to distinguish them, for they no longer had names or addresses. That finally they were killed by hunger and poison, and buried in pits or incinerated in ovens.

So, a new member of the company, with Lifka and Lamian. Another L to add. This time not with music but improvisational theater, a commedia dell'arte of tattoos and history. How would the show be received by its audience? With frowns, protests at this interruption of the enjoyment of their leisure time? Would they ask the waitress to restore order—they were paying customers—even if that meant calling the police? Or would they be delighted by this break in the afternoon tedium of the café, this scene from the sensational past?

Murder and theft were not far beneath the skin, Lamian knew. He felt them in the motionless sitting, in the discreet café pantomime of ordering, paying, sipping beer or mineral water, and making a date with the waitress, her bed waiting.

A very thin, very fragile veneer. Covering intestines and glands. Behind this café shine was the stench of an unlit toilet and a sink without soap or towels; behind this printed menu, on the other side of the bar's plush curtain, were old mounds of ground meat but mostly rice, stale buns, canned peppers. And the waitress, when she untied the apron that cut into her waist, when she took off the white smock and unfastened the pleated skirt that rippled so seductively around her legs, became a flabby village girl who got pregnant every time she had intercourse, because the soldier didn't know how or refused to be safe, so that afterward came the inevitable quarrel: Did he or didn't he, she felt it, but he said he didn't. They would part embittered, each swearing not to see the other again, until desire drove him back to the café where she worked, and once again she yielded to his pleading and persistence. And the civilian sitting across from the newcomer, if he wanted to protect his modest career, he had to be careful not to become involved with a girl who could blackmail him, because his ailing mother at home was strict, had educated him at the cost of great sacrifice after her husband's untimely death. She remembered her family's high position, and all her hopes of restoring it she placed in her son. He couldn't afford to be reckless, but at the same time the pay was low, the work dull; he had wanted to go into something completely different, mathematics, biology, but chose a profession that would most quickly assure a position. The price was now being paid—in discontent, a mask of arrogance, and a boredom he vainly tried to dispel by sitting in taverns like this, between lawsuits he couldn't keep his mind on, wanting only to be left alone with his thoughts, with his overheated imagination, here amid the reek of tobacco and alcohol, at a table with an old man who apparently had fled from his home nearby wearing only a suit: a warning picture of his own future.

Murder was here, ready to spring, in the muscles of hands and jaws. To be someone, to rule. To destroy this lying harmony of straitened means, tedium, obligations—and embark on the turbulent, foamy sea of power. To shoot at living flesh whenever you felt like it, to cut short with a knife, with flame, the crying and sobbing, and sweep away those who did not give you room to breathe.

Gradina. The low, weathered ferry the soldiers pushed him onto with cries of "Go on, gravedigger, we'll need you." And as soon as the ramp was lifted by its clattering chain, he knew that for him there would be no return from this ride, just as there would be no return for the Serbian women and children the soldiers were herding into a pack. He debated whether or not to jump into the Sava, imagined himself swimming, diving beneath the bullets, coming ashore in a willow grove downstream. As the water dripped from him and the shots of his pursuers died away in the distance, he would strike out into the foothills of the Kozara.

The swim across the river, straining toward the far bank as if into an abyss, over the wails of the women and the screams of the children, the lowering sky, the bloody sunset, and his indecision were cut short by a blow to the ribs. "Stay here!" A sign that his plan had been guessed, that nothing would come of it. The horror of imminent death, yet also the calm at the knowledge that death would mean an end to suffering, to hunger and beatings, to the menace of Gabelić. The strokes of the bearded raftsmen with slouch hats brought them closer and closer to the bank, the trees, the fire beyond. Then landfall, and the curses and blows of rifle butts as they were driven off the raft.

An enormous old willow filled with hanging, naked, reeking bodies. Bursting from the bushes, a pack of bearded Gypsies threw themselves on the women, hands as big as spades, dragged them to the fires, where hatless Ustaši, braided coats thrown over their shoulders, jumped to their feet, drunken and boisterous. They dropped their coats and raised their arms, bare to the elbow, showing short, sharklike knives strapped to their wrists with leather thongs.

"Untie them!" they shouted, and the Gypsies tore the wires from the women. "Strip them!" And the Gypsies tore off their dresses, while the women screamed and the children clinging to them screamed. One Ustaša dragged a woman off behind a bush, where he lay on top of her, stabbing her in the side with his knife, opening long, wide wounds.

All the Ustaši pounced on the women. The Gypsies took the children away and held them between their legs or pressed against their chests while the Ustaši plunged their knives into the women, then grabbed the children and stabbed them with even faster strokes. Finally they were all on the ground, and the Ustaši stood up. "Gravediggers!" they shouted, and Lamian, after a kick in the ribs, realized they meant him, so he got to work. He, Danon, Radovan, and a mustached prisoner from Vinkovci grabbed the women's bodies by the hands and feet and carried them to where the Ustaši and Gypsies drove them. To a huge pit, a trench full of naked bodies. Into this they threw the slaughtered women, then another shout, and they returned for more, and after that the children, carried in their arms two at a time, throats cut, skin sticky with blood, or else alive—because occasionally one still twitched. Some Ustaša shouted, "This one's still alive," to which the others answered, "Just throw him in the pit." So they threw them in, carried and threw, then an Ustaša plunged his knife into Radovan's throat, and Danon and the mustached prisoner were led off by two men with pistols in their hands. Lamian heard his name called. Private Jozo came running up, took him by the arm, pulled him toward the bank and the ferry, shoved him on, and whispered, "That's for the climbing boots." Then aloud to the boatman, "Take this one back and hand him over to the guards." And so Lamian was the only prisoner to return from Gradina to Jasenovac.

THE ONLY ONE? THE NEWCOMER—IF HE WAS AT JASE-novac—must have escaped Gradina through some similar bargain. Perhaps he hid in the leather shop where he made boots for officers and handbags for their wives, then took part in a breakout without being cut down by machine gun. Or else he helped Pizilli build the crematorium, then begged a transfer to an easier camp. Or tricked some guard into looking for buried gold together, then gave him the slip.

The two of them would have things to talk about. But any such conversation would soon degenerate into moaning and a tallying of losses: "My mother," "My sister," "My brother." He could feel it, see it on the man's ruined face, a face that had no group picture behind it, no kin. He could see the bare room the man would finally take him to, to show him old letters and photographs found by chance in the neighborhood after his return from the camp. And Lamian would have to look at them, and listen to such explanations as "This was our house," "Here we are in the garden as children," while mounting rage gnawed his stomach.

Rage at letting himself be led like a fool onto the slippery ground of feelings, ties, origins; at being forced to admit their sanctity—as if it hadn't been in the name of those very things that he sank into the arms of murder. The deep ties of blood and language, which had made him shudder as he left the Bjelovar railway station on his solitary way back to his home, when he saw those youths doused in farewell wine, beside sweethearts who shyly, reprovingly stopped the hands that lifted glasses to sad mouths, recruits' mouths, where the sweetness of last night's kisses still melted, mouths now wide open in martial song. Among them he saw the sensitive, tenderly sculpted face of his playmate, Drago Blažetić, pale with envy, shame, and helplessness. Had Lamian obeyed his instincts then, he would have turned and gone back into the station, and taken the first train in any direction, jumping off at the first forest and slipping into it like a wolf. He would have made an ax from a stick and a rock, to hunt wild game, stray cattle, or people, putting anything edible into his mouth, like the prisoners in Section 3c, whom he once watched through the wire as they roasted over a fire the thigh of a dead comrade.

Would he have survived? Would the newcomer have survived? In 3c no one survived, because the only meat came from bodies who had eaten the meat of yesterday's bodies, and the supply had to end sometime; the final body rotted, no one partaking of it. If they were smart, Lamian and the newcomer, they wouldn't sit here so certain of being fed, but instead would jump up and flee before they were fenced off again and kept from food.

But both of them were old, weak, incapable of flight into a forest. The strong ones were all in Israel, with the sons they had fathered there, and those sons now fenced off others with wire, opening the wire only to let in the mercenaries who slaughtered in their stead, just as the Ustaši used the starving Gypsies in Gradina. But Lamian had enough of that endless chain that extended even here, to a Zagreb supposedly domesticated now, to this sleepy café, unreeling its links beneath the tables and chairs, between the legs of the customers and waitresses, who all pretended not to notice it.

Lamian looked carefully at the young man who sat opposite the newcomer and thus had a much better view of him. But not a trace of interest in the newcomer was to be found on the young man's narrow face: the young man was looking past him, at nothing, at his own thoughts, no doubt, woven out of nothing to alleviate the boredom of sitting in a café with a glass of *gemischt* or mineral water, not to mention the boredom of home or work that awaited him afterward.

Nor did the soldier pay any attention to the newcomer. Or to him, Lamian. He drained his beer and twisted his neck to wink at the waitress behind the bar, who was taking off her apron and folding it distractedly.

Closing time? Lamian gave a start. His hunger unsatisfied, he lifted his arm to join the soldier in waving. The waitress nodded, seemingly to both of them, but when she came over, she addressed Lamian alone: "The bill?" A glance at the table, knitted brows. "Hunter's Plate and a beer? Six . . . eight thousand, two hundred." He protested, "But I'm still hungry. Bring me another serving." She shook her head. "The other girl will." "But she's not around," he said, turning to look. "She'll be here in a minute," the waitress replied calmly, and Lamian had no choice but to produce his wallet and pay the bill, fumbling because he had forgot the total, and when she repeated it, he failed to grasp at first that it was in old dinars.

She took the money and went back to the bar, holding the money in one hand and clutching her folded apron with the other. The soldier got up, stretched, took his cap from his belt, put it on his head, and followed her. She first, he following, they disappeared behind the plush curtain.

LAMIAN WAS LEFT ALONE WITH AN EMPTY PLATE AND TWO empty glasses, his and the soldier's. He looked guiltily at the newcomer, as if he had neglected a basic need. "You entertained me," he thought. "The way you gulped things down, the mark of difference you carried." The mark that unsettled and touched, but also angered. The shadowy faces that flickered in the Bjelovar apartment, heralding misfortune. And all the other faces Lamian encountered, which were closer and more real but later disappeared just like those earlier ones, disappeared beneath the same millstone.

His father's face, good-humored and gentle-eyed, brow gleaming down from above, a readiness to understand and to help in his expression, lips parted happily when he was able to slip some worker a secret advance, split wide in a chuckle as he described this at home over dinner. His mother's face, anxious and mistrustful as she punctured his father's loud self-satisfaction, warning him that he'd be overheard, reported, perhaps punished. The faces of the prisoners, trustful and searching, counting on sympathy and help as they turned to him for information about the temperament of some Lagerelteste or Blockführer, or to intercede for them in bartering for food. The faces of the Stark brothers, bankers and bon vivants, firmly confident of their powers of endurance as they pushed the cart across the plank walkway above the lime pit, then astonished at the unprovoked cruelty that pushed them into it. The devoted faces of mothers clutching children who would be taken from them and killed. The exalted faces of the religious, sapped by hunger and madness as they murmured prayers and on sore-ridden legs slogged through the mud to the construction sites. The face of Helena Lifka—yes, that face too, though at the time he didn't know it was Jewish, because he had never seen her clothed, with the yellow insignia, nor had he noticed in the flickering candlelight, as she stood weeping beside the table of food he had prepared for her, the twinkle of the half-star under her tattooed number.

Freaks! Buffoons! No wonder they aroused suspicion and then fury. Not now, of course, now that they appeared one by one, solitary as anchorites from the swamps, so that only by a mockery of chance could two of them come together in the same café. Not now, but then, when herds of them swept through streets, stores, markets, fairgrounds, and theaters, all the places where people gathered for business and pleasure. They had congregated there out of curiosity, from mobility and their footloose lack of obligations, which he had immediately spotted in the newcomer. Their rootlessness, their lack of allegiance to country or language, or an allegiance they changed according to need, contemptuous of all affiliations and borders, disdaining the shackles of history, geography, national colors and symbols.

Marxists, Freudians, Esperantists, femininists, nudists, supporters of every revolution, receptive to every novelty, they scampered here and there like mice, until speared by the claws of the cat, who preferred to lie in the sun.

No wonder they annoyed, with their mouselike scurrying, and were punished for it, beaten. He, too, had beaten them, instructing, "This isn't a marketplace," "This isn't a tavern," "This isn't a synagogue," according to the circumstances—on the parade ground or around the food pot. But also from a personal urge, his desire to rid them of that faith in scheming, or in Jehovah the all-powerful, who wasn't, or to rid them of their blindness to what caused the hatred that snarled at them, the hatred that had horrified him when he read Gabelić's pamphlets, and for which he could not forgive them.

Because it had made him, too, a victim, a foreigner: their existence had prevented others from accepting Lamian as their own. Even his father and mother he could not forgive. In Jasenovac he had hidden from them instead of trying to learn where they were so he could help them out, perhaps, with a few morsels or the news that he was alive. He feared them almost as much as he feared Gabelić, feared not only the sight of their personal suffering, but also the pain it would cause them to find that he too, their son, was among the condemned, that they hadn't helped him in the least by baptizing him and sending him to Mass at the Catholic church, that their ruse—based on faith in deals and scheming, that blind faith—had failed, and he was trampled and destroyed, and in the midst of their own destruction they had not kept him apart and saved him.

It was his parents he beat when he beat the Jews who shirked, trying to slip away and hide when a load of iron was being lifted, or who snatched up scraps of food along the way as they slogged through the clinging mud, or who tried to exchange their bunk for one that was warmer and more secluded, or who robbed a corpse of a crust of bread hidden among its rags, or grasped at some good news, a lie, such as the coming of the Messiah, or feigned illness, and then, when threatened with an injection of phenol, suddenly strutted about on stiffened, sore-ridden legs, puffing out their pigeon breasts, working their jaws and opening their eyes wide, all a trick, a scheme, to look healthy and eager and so survive.

Well, you won't survive, he demonstrated with his Kapo's club, striking them on the back of the head, on flanks, kidneys, temples, and it was the truth, for him as well as them, and he wanted to knock that truth into their heads even at these final moments of their lives, before the death he himself would bring them. It was out of compassion that he wanted to lead them to a quick death, a simple death, by shaking them loose from this faith in deals and schemes, which he himself had inherited from his mother and father, believing he could escape their fate.

And yet he had escaped, he and the newcomer both, thanks to that very faith in deals and schemes, according to which every man has a chance. Unless, on the contrary, he escaped because he had renounced that faith, becoming Kapo Furfa. Giving Private Jozo the pair of boots he admired and asking nothing in return, waiting instead for it to be offered, because the favor might be something more important than permission to see his father in secret or send a message to his mother, it might be his own life, and that, to his parents, would be a much greater boon. Was this the scheming of a Jew, or of a denier of Jews?

He wanted to discuss it with the newcomer, ask him how *he* had been spared, ask what kind of revolution in character shaped by his upbringing had been required for him to save himself. Had he changed himself from battered to batterer, or had he simply directed all his energies into persevering as he was, possessing the strength to outlast all the others?

Lamian looked at him with envy, for he wanted more than anything to have been such a survivor, to have survived without betraying. Had he only been able to live and still slip his parents a piece of bread, put his hand into his mother's cold, emaciated hand, to press and warm it for a moment. Had he only been able not to bludgeon, not to kill, to suffer and stay on the side of suffering, instead of joining those who caused it. Had he only been able to hold out, to endure all those years and have it not matter whether he was the one grain that chanced to be preserved, and not crave food or the pearly flesh that shone voluptuous in the midst of all that decay.

With this lament he muttered to himself and to his burning stomach. Burning with hunger, in its desperation to survive. No, this couldn't be race; it was the beast alone, damned or blessed, that was speaking. And the newcomer was a saint. In the aureole of light from the window Lamian saw him casually reclining in his chair, supremely given over to solitude amid the buzz of the café, to which he had come from the desolation of his room at the end of the corridor, filled with ghosts. One of whom might be he, Lamian. Possibly the newcomer had known him, remembered him, the tormentor. And Lamian had almost gone over to introduce himself and strike up a conversation—instead of getting up the moment he saw him come in and realized what he was, grabbing his coat and slipping out as inconspicuously as possible.

Now Lamian did what he should have done in the first place: he stood up, taking care that his chair didn't scrape, picked up his cigarettes and matches, swayed gingerly over to the coatrack, and put on his coat. Looking neither right nor left, with slow nonchalance that copied the walk of the newcomer when he arrived, Lamian passed him slumped in his chair and staring at the smoke of the fresh cigarette that trembled in his hand as it rested on the table, and left the café.

IT WAS ONLY WHEN HE LAY DOWN IN HIS HOTEL BED THAT he remembered that he hadn't stopped anywhere to eat after leaving the café. But he was no longer hungry; his stomach lay inert at the center of his body. If he fell asleep, perhaps it would have no time to rebel.

Except he had a feeling he wouldn't fall asleep. His eyes remained open, though there was nothing to look at; his attention was heightened, though there was nothing to occupy it. The light fixture on the ceiling: golden yellow, circular, unlit, and around it a white plane. Lower, the armchair with the clothes he had tossed on it, and a window through which the building across the street could be seen. A residential building, because when he had looked out while undressing, he saw, one floor below, in the light of a lamp, an elderly man moving about slowly.

He had noticed him because it was the only window with a light on, yellowish and unnatural in the middle of the day; the windows all around it were dark spaces, blind eyes, which kept him from lying down, because the bed was also in shadows. It was that single lit window that made it possible for him to enter the darkness and lie down.

But lying down, since he wasn't sleepy, had lost its point. Thinking of lighting a cigarette, he looked at the nightstand and saw that he hadn't put his cigarettes there. Should he get up? He hesitated awhile between the need for tobacco and the reluctance to exert the effort needed to get it. He rose finally, made his way to his clothes tossed over the chair, and, as he searched the pockets with practiced movements, he cast an eye at the building across the way. Yes, that single window was still lit, and in it the same man could be seen, only now he wasn't moving, he was sitting at a table, its surface partially visible beneath his folded hands. Large, strong hands. The man was massive, his abundant hair, wavy above the ears, gray.

Lamian took his cigarettes and matches, found an ashtray, and arranged everything on the nightstand. He lay down, propped the pillow up high, and lit a cigarette. He enjoyed his smoke, although in recent years he could tell from the bitterness in his mouth and throat that he was smoking too much. His body could no longer handle the amount of nicotine he took in, a habit acquired following the deprivation of the camps. Now, too, the bitterness spread, but he didn't stop, he merely paused more before bringing the cigarette to his mouth. Finally he put it out, and watched the thin wisps of gray around the fixture and across the ceiling until they disappeared.

So, nothing again. Just like those moments, those hours when he was sure nothing important would happen, where "important" meant the ultimate danger, the ultimate threat: torture, death. It seemed strange that there could be such intervals of peace for camp inmates, but it was true nevertheless, for even in the camps, in places, for some of the people, occasional voids were created by the crudeness and clumsiness of the machinery.

Crouched in the loft of the chain shop in Jasenovac and looking through the hole dug between the bricks as Jeronim Blažuj, former priest, butchered four prisoners. Lamian knew, as he watched quivering in horror, knew to the deepest recess of his instinct that as long as the butchering lasted, as long as Blažuj took the measure of his victims over the mouthful he was chewing and the glass of rakija he was draining, as long as he did not have his fill of roast meat and fresh bread and rakija and did not wish to abandon yet the cool canopy for the lust of slaughter, and for the time it took him to approach the prisoners and draw his knife and then stab until the last of them twitched for the last time—until then, Blažuj's rage and thirst for blood would be directed at no one else, and therefore not at him, Lamian, crouching in the loft and watching through the hole dug between the bricks.

Or returning from Gradina on the ferry, after the slaughter of the Serbian women and children. On the bank he was given to a guard, and while the guard, rifle over his shoulder, escorted him to the barracks along the path that led across the dike, where the tamped-down earth was mixed with the bones of those killed there even as they worked, the path that went past the guard post which opened fire at every suspicious movement, then past Section 3c, where the inmates received neither food nor shelter, then past the fish pond which reeked of the bodies that floated in it with weights on their feet, then to his barracks—he knew that for that time he would be spared a bullet in the head.

Or squatting in the cattle wagon on the way from Jasenovac to a new, unknown camp. He was hungry, thirsty, sweaty from the crush of bodies that sickened him with their stench, and did not know when they would arrive or if they would arrive dead for lack of oxygen and food. But he was certain that as long as the trip lasted, no one would torture him, no one would kill him.

Or carrying corpses, with Otto Kromholz as leader, from the heap behind Block 18 to the crematorium, throwing them two at a time onto the two-wheeled cart. He knew by the size of the heap and the number of carts—six in his team—that he would be left alive until the evening roll call, unless one of the SS escorts or a tower guard went crazy and took aim at him instead of a hare or grouse.

Or lying in quarantine after selection, listening through the plank wall to the shouts and the blows of rifle butts as those who a moment ago were lying beside him got into ranks, then as the voices, echoes of the blows, and clatter of bewildered feet died away. A sigh of happiness escaped his lips, for tonight at least no one was going to drag him from his bunk to the dispensary for an injection in the heart.

The pauses, they were little paradises. The dizziness that came with the easing of terror was like the dizziness that came with the letting of blood. But what good were they, these pauses, since after them came new terror, new danger, images of death multiplying before his eyes until at last their prophecy came true?

Very different from what was now, this life without fences in a hushed hotel, where the pauses went on and on. He would lie here and look at the ceiling, the fixture, or, if that bored him, at the window, beyond which was life, movement, conversations and quarrels. In the waning afternoon people were returning from work or setting off to work, they were handing over duties and responsibilities, exchanging instructions, cautions about some machine or the implementation of some order, or the care of a child or sick person at home.

Lamian was separated from them, separated not only by the walls of the hotel, which ensured him peace and quiet, but also by his differentness. He was something they were not, and he could never be what they were, having lost whatever quality it was that once had bound him to them.

The idea pleased him, for it meant that no one would pay attention to him anymore. The danger was over. He would no longer need to worry about his appearance, about the impression he made. Life would consist of simply hanging on, of monotony enlivened from time to time by the satisfaction of minor needs, cigarettes, food, drink.

Like the man across the street, one floor down. Curiosity again drew Lamian to the window. Had his impression of him been correct? After some hesitation, not wanting to leave the comfort of his bed, he got up and went to the window. The gray man in the lighted window was not at the table; he was up and moving just then, showing Lamian his profile, a curved nose, a brawny, hunched back, a dark suit stretched tightly across it, a tie. A moment later he disappeared.

Lamian moved to the side of the window to get the man back into his field of vision. The man was on the far right, in front of a piece of furniture rather higher than the table. Lamian decided this must be a small wardrobe or a sideboard. The man leaned on it, or leaned over it, looking for something. Then he turned slowly and went ponderously back to the table and sat down. Those large hands again appeared on the table and locked their meaty fingers together, doing nothing, holding nothing.

Which meant he hadn't taken anything from the sideboard. Perhaps, instead, he took something to it. Lamian again moved all the way to the left, to see the sideboard, but on the part visible to him the surface was empty. So, nothing. The man had gone back and forth out of boredom, or for the exercise recommended by his doctor. Or else thinking he needed something from the sideboard and then changing his mind. Now he sat quietly, staring straight ahead. He had small eyes whose expression couldn't be read; they blinked occasionally, that was all.

But this did not go with the man's clean, neat appearance, with the robustness that, despite the bent back, bespoke a person who had everything under control, who lacked for nothing, who was bothered by nothing.

Like Lamian—now. If there had been no Hitler, or if he hadn't been a baptized Jew in Hitler's time, or if he had succeeded in hiding the fact that he was a baptized Jew . . . If he hadn't stopped at Bjelovar after Nevesinje, but instead taken his military papers straight to Zagreb and bought false documents there, or if he had gone to Bjelovar but then lived through Jasenovac and Auschwitz on the strength of his own body, which was no less robust than the body across the street, then he, too, would be sitting in some room, calmly looking straight ahead.

But Lamian wasn't looking straight ahead, he was looking at the gray-haired man, who didn't need to look at anything or for anything, because all that mattered to him was in that lighted room, or in a room adjoining. The man wasn't curious about what was happening in the hotel across the street, expecting no scene there to be of interest to him.

And even if a light were on in Lamian's window instead of his own, the man still wouldn't look—he had made that clear by turning on the light, revealing himself without hesitation to the eyes of others, indifferent to the fact that by turning on the light he couldn't see into their rooms.

Lamian was tempted to verify this: to go to the wall by the door, turn on the light, then stand in the window to see whether or not the gray man would notice him. But Lamian, out of long habit now, hated to draw attention to himself. He couldn't. No, he was not like that gray man. He had been deluding himself, pretending, because of that pause, that respite, wanting it to last forever, as he had tried to make it last forever in Banja Luka a few days earlier, when he thought of running the current of the stove through his body.

Did the gray man ever have such thoughts? For him there was no longer anything to wish, he had everything an old man could want: comfort, enough to eat, an honorable or at least forgotten past. That was what enabled him to show himself in the window of his room, lit up as if on display. And Lamian, had he turned the stove switch before peeling the wire from his hand, would have lain there burnt and black, and people, as they wrapped him and put him in the coffin, would remember him as one about whom nothing unusual was known, apart from his end. And even that end they would explain: he complained of ill health, perhaps he did well to cut short a hopeless situation.

The same situation the gray man was in, only he probably didn't know it. One never knew; not the Mussulmen at Auschwitz, not the elephants at Jasenovac. They didn't know that in a minute or two they would breathe their last. They dragged themselves on swollen, sore feet to the feeding trough, clinking their pots and spoons, or to the latrine, holding on to their bloated stomachs with both hands, though neither stomach nor jaws had the strength to eat, nor did the bowels have anything to expel. Knees stiff, heads bobbing, they simply moved, clutching their rags closer to them, blinking their inflamed eyes, driven forward by an unrest they thought was the unrest of life resisting death, but which was really the unrest of death resisting life.

Now the gray man stood, turned his profile to the window, and moved from the table in the same direction as before. He reached the sideboard, placed his hands on it, removed them, and took a step back, pulling out something dark and rectangular. He looked at this—it was a drawer—rummaged in it briefly with one hand, then did everything in reverse, pushing the drawer back in place, putting his hands on the sideboard again for a moment, returning to the table, sitting down again.

Lamian shivered, because he was only in his underpants and shirt. He reached for his suit. Put on his slacks, socks, shoes, tie, jacket, everything. Now he was the same as the other, could start walking like him, back and forth in the room for no reason, like a hunger that produced no gastric juice, a churning of intestines that had nothing in them, like a Mussulman, an elephant, a body at the end of its strength, circulation gone, mind clouded. For how long? Five minutes? Five years?

He stepped out onto the street. Commotion and crispness, a clear sky. His topcoat was agreeably heavy, because of the chill that did not leave his spine, but his hat bothered him, so he took it off to let the cold air touch his forehead. Where to? Of their own accord, his feet led him in the direction opposite to where he had spent half the day waiting in ambush.

Approaching the railway station, his starting point that morning, he now puzzled over, probed at his decision to come here. It seemed false, a lie, contrary to his nature, which avoided all conflict, all confrontation with unpleasant truths. The traveler who had come for this meeting seemed to be not he but a thing of his imagination.

Even the station—just ahead of him, the straight lines of its broad façade framing the grayish sky, offering to it the plaster carvings along its brow—seemed unreal to him now, like a stage set. And the people leaving it, swarming the sidewalk, were actors pretending to have just arrived, whereas in fact they had gone backstage, unseen, to reappear a moment later in a new role.

He looked toward the park. It seemed odd not to see the thin woman with the umbrella who had directed him to the hotel. Or had her role been so brief, so small, that she was already relaxing at home, nibbling some treat bought with her actor's pay? Which reminded him that he still hadn't eaten a solid meal. But, then, he wasn't hungry. Or tired, for that matter, though he hadn't really got any sleep at the hotel. He felt better, actually, than he had in a long time: light, no pain, no wants, not even fear.

The absence of fear surprised him. He tested this. Two men in conversation were walking toward him, and he tried to imagine that they were only pretending to be in conversation so they could observe him unobserved. He looked at their faces: no suspicion stirred in him. They passed by, and he felt no need to turn and look after them, as he had done so often before, even when he knew it was ridiculous. He stopped and took in the entire square. His eyes did not fasten on anyone, went smoothly over everyone, as if these people were really actors on a stage— and playing the most uninteresting parts. And he could turn his back on them.

Something in him had changed. It was hard to believe that his dream, deeply concealed, had come true, in which he awakened into someone he didn't recognize: a man unafraid, who strode freely along unfamiliar streets, talked to people, and observed the rules of business and personal relations without worrying what plots lay behind those rules.

But this city was not a dream, it was Zagreb, where his downfall had begun, the center of the whirlpool that had sucked him to the bottom, and where the rings from that plunge still rippled: Gabelić, of whose postwar fate he knew nothing; Drago Blažetić, who had probably denounced him, Lamian, from Bjelovar, but had remained unpunished after the war, perhaps even promoted to some position in Zagreb; Private Jozo, whose sense of justice might have driven him to join the partisans and thus kept him alive; and a few nameless Ustaši who might have remembered him and later found out how he had changed from Lamian to Frfa, while Frfa lay buried as Lamian. And Frfa, too, might have had someone, somewhere, who knew him, relatives who could have heard from someone that Lamian had been taken to Auschwitz as Frfa, and was known as Furfa in German, and they could have reported to the Ustaši just who and what Furfa had been at Auschwitz: Kapo Furfa!

And still he wasn't afraid. Someone would put a hand on his shoulder and whisper, "Furfa?" And Lamian would say, "Yes, Furfa," and follow him quietly to the nearest police station, and then to court, to confirm it, to make a statement and sign, and be led handcuffed into a cell, solitary confinement, to live on bread and water. Because he was a Mussulman, he no longer recognized death at his elbow, he tottered after needs that no longer were needs, he paced back and forth in his room with the light on, back and forth from food trough to latrine, paced the streets where he was stalked by specters disguised as newly arrived travelers.

At Sava Road he stopped. The same! Vast, yawning, like a dried-up river bed, with the bridge that engulfed it from above, built of crisscrossing iron like prison bars. Beneath the bridge, bustle and traffic, as in all camps, which had their established paths, the paths of violence, none of which led beyond the bars, but instead choked, clogged, contaminated. The sky, here too dove-gray and cloudless, closed over the bars like suffocating glass. So that freedom of movement was only an illusion. The trams clanged and sped, people waited for them, jumped down from them, caught them, or ran after them. People went into stores, carried packages and string bags, hurried for food or home to sleep, chatted awhile with those they hadn't seen in a long time or with old neighbors.

He, too, had rushed by here hundreds of times, with his books and notebooks, with groceries for his supper, thinking that he was carrying out his plans, nearing his goal, while with every step, unsuspecting, he was nearing something different, a thing planned by others without regard for him or his goal. And their plan proved much more solid and more real than his, right down to the handcuffs the red-haired policeman snapped on his wrists in Mrs. Basarabić's house at 8 Trnska Street.

That was the direction he set out in now, although the prospect of seeing her didn't appeal to him. It repelled him, in fact, even frightened him, despite this absence now of the fear that he himself would be recognized. He would look at her house across the wire fence and flower garden, would be struck not by its appearance, perhaps the same, perhaps changed, but by the prisoner's torpor with which he had approached and entered it that last time, the trap laid for him by the very repetition of approaching and entering, that sequence of steps and of years which had accumulated, drugged him, and led to the handcuffs on his wrists.

But when Lamian came to that street corner, he found that the house was no longer there. The left side was still lined by the familiar little houses with their gardens and wire fences, but the right side, the even-numbered side, had been wiped away, as if by a giant sponge, and in its place rose a multistoried building, monstrous from one corner to the other, gray, with iron balconies and a flat roof. It stood, enormous and rigid, in the place of a whole row of houses like those on the left, houses separated by flower gardens and fruit trees that lifted their thick foliage to the sky in summer, and in winter their white caps and cloaks of snow.

That row of houses no longer existed, among them Mrs. Basarabić's, where he had lived, studied at his desk, and, when his eyes grew tired, looked at the house across the street, which was still standing there, blue, with broad eaves, surrounded by its garden. Mrs. Basarabić's, where he had slept at night, dressed and undressed, read newspapers and novels and the pamphlets forced on him by Gabelić.

Where was Gabelić now? What would he say about this transformation? He had accompanied Lamian home only once, but would certainly remember, if he was alive, the aura of aloofness and individuality given off by each house on the street. What if Gabelić too, today of all days, was stopping in Zagreb, which he ordinarily avoided for fear of being recognized, and had decided to visit the old places, including the street where he once accompanied a classmate whose fashionable appearance had fooled him into trusting him? Then, realizing he had been deceived, he planned to repay him with a dagger in the neck, but the classmate tricked him again and escaped.

Lamian could feel him at his side, breathing. There was no one else in the street, for the residents, both those of the small one-family houses and those of the new apartment building, had retired to their bedrooms, were napping behind the curtains. Even now he felt shame at having deceived Gabelić, who had been striving for something great, for a basic change, not for personal ends or to gratify his own needs, because pleasure meant nothing to him, not even the pleasure of killing. It was only as an example, out of righteous revenge, that Gabelić mutilated Sergeant Major Maričić, letting others finish him off. Just as he would have mutilated Lamian for having deceived him. Gabelić didn't think in terms of individuals but in terms of millions; was inspired by a future in which only people like him would exist, erect, handsome, blond, energetic people devoted to the common good, to progress—once all those who were different were destroyed.

But Lamian, by pretending to embrace such ideals—and a part of him did in fact embrace them—was pursuing another goal, one personal and selfish, namely, to make himself the same as others, and then to use those others. Studying for his engineering degree, he had stolen off to be with Branka in the evenings, to satisfy the sensual part, too, of his ascent. Gabelić was pure, and Lamian was dirty; Gabelić was prepared to sacrifice himself, and Lamian was not. Lamian had followed Gabelić in words alone, submitting to the stronger current of his will but nevertheless trying, in secret, to carry out his own will, which was weaker and directed toward private advantage.

But now they would be on more equal terms, since history had thwarted Gabelić's unselfish will. Or had it? Despite losing the war, he had succeeded in obliterating those he hated, just as the little houses on the right side of Trnska Street had been obliterated. If he were still alive, and here, he could point to the enormous structure that had replaced irrevocably the little houses, and say, "There, now you don't exist either, you who tried to escape us. You, too, have been wiped away forever."

But Lamian would reply, pointing to himself, that he was very much alive, that he existed, that he had wriggled out of the death that had been prepared for him. True, he had wriggled out of it by declaring, a second time, to be on the side of that same will, bludgeoning and murdering in its name, but succeeding, by bludgeoning and murdering, in saving himself.

"We are not all of us dead," Lamian would say, puffing out his chest, "just as not all the houses on this street have been destroyed. See, there they are, people chatting in their yards under the fruit trees, and if these too are destroyed tomorrow, others like them will sprout up elsewhere, little one-family houses with flower gardens and fences, because the human yearning for them, the yearning to be fenced off in the selfishness of the family home, is indestructible."

But even as he said this to himself, as if Gabelić were there, he felt that he was lying, that he was invoking something that wasn't his, for when he had lived here, in a house just like these, he had been no less a stranger than he was living in the concrete high-rise in Banja Luka. Because he hadn't come today to Trnska Street to visit something of his, something close to his heart; he had come to visit a prison, his first prison, the one which with its false domesticity had drawn him into a snare, into handcuffs open wide to receive his wrists.

So perhaps it was the other way around: the little houses were Gabelić's and the high-rise Lamian's. Gabelić was the one who wept over the destruction of native domesticity. Who had stood for the particular, the distinct, and done battle in the name of the indigenous and unique against the universal striving for equality, for blending in, whose advocates were the Jews, and in Yugoslavia the Serbs, hungry to assimilate others. Gabelić was the one who had hated the technological trend of modern times, the worship of inventions, which made everything that was rooted and special disappear. Whose fear and fury were precisely on behalf of these houses with gardens, isolated by their powerful attachment to nothing, despite the buffeting winds of both East and West, but their own affairs. Winds that vanquished this parochial mentality, these narrow affiliations, and planted, like a throne, this monstrous building atop the rubbish heap of prisons and camps, which also had tried to destroy the parochial and narrow. A structure of concrete and iron, identical to every other the world over, cold and practical, mocking all little houses.

He stood and looked at the high-rise and the houses, at the difference, the still-fresh scar of victory—though he wasn't sure whose victory—and Gabelić slipped away. Lamian could still feel him there but no longer heard his breathing, couldn't picture him clearly, his body, the hard features of his face. The wind scattered them, like straw from a scarecrow. No, he didn't understand him, and he had always recoiled from him. He remembered how Gabelić had accompanied him home. Lamian had slowed his pace, ostensibly to be with his companion longer, in fact trying to keep him at the gate while his mind frantically searched his room for any traces of betrayal: the things that would refute the image he had constructed of himself for Gabelić, an object he had not put away—his mother's photograph, for instance, with her oval Oriental face, though he knew perfectly well he didn't have one in Zagreb.

Even then he had felt that the family home in which he rented a room was a trap; that Mrs. Basarabić's good will would last only until she gathered sufficient facts about him to change her mind. Gabelić's entry into the house, and what he might see there, combined with Mrs. Basarabić's suspicions, could close the jaws of the trap around Lamian's neck.

So he had always quaked in fear, had he, though he never admitted it to himself? And even when he sat before his schoolbooks he was becoming a Kapo? He remembered how he had gone secretly, on tiptoe, to Branka's at night, always at night, so no one would see that he was going to a Jewess, whose form, in public, would cast a shadow on his athletic figure. He remembered how in his room, which was filled with invisible shadows and doubts, he had assembled that plaster figure from the shattered pieces of himself, in order to wear it when he went out, then remove it, tear it off, when he embraced her naked body, falling on her with the longing of one who returns from exile.

Like a Kapo! As Kapo, too, he had assembled, collecting gifts "for the Germans": gold nuggets, silk underwear, safety razors, sweaters, medicine, corsets—whatever could be stolen or bartered for in the anterooms of the gas chambers and in the Kanada supply depots, at the risk of being found out, denounced, punished with a bullet in the head. Because it was only with his shirt stuffed with objects of value to everyone among these worthless dregs of humanity, to which he too belonged, that he could stand upright in his slave's rags and inflate himself into a tyrant between four plank walls, in front of starving, naked young women.

So he had the same traits even before history interfered. History had only made available to him the total isolation of the camp, an isolation Trnska Street and Sava Road had merely hinted at, an isolation that prevented his victims from choosing, from eluding, and thus made his power absolute.

Perhaps this was the knowledge he had sought here, the

equation provided by the absence of the house he had lived in before becoming a prisoner and a Kapo; an equation, it seemed to him now, he had foreseen. Yet instinct had kept him away, that defensive instinct, the instinct of self-preservation left over from the time when he still felt fear, guilt, responsibility, unaware that he was not responsible, that he had been born a Kapo and was therefore free of all responsibility.

Cleansed, in other words. Relieved of the burdens of his sins. With a new life ahead of him, as if starting over. As if he were coming to Trnska Street for the first time, in search of an apartment, four walls to shelter him. What door should he knock on? And as he spun on his heels, looking left and right, he really did feel like a new person, a stranger inspecting the area of the city where he intended to settle.

He would approach the blue house with the broad eaves, the one he had looked at so often, long ago, without ever learning who actually lived there, although he saw people going in and out, middle-aged people.

Now he would find out. He would start the conversation by explaining what he needed, a furnished room, and although there might not be one to let in that particular house, he would be invited in out of curiosity, a respectably dressed visitor who had happened by. They would sit him down in a chair and chat as they tried to recall which neighbor was looking for lodgers.

He would find out not only who they were but also who had lived there before them, and who before that, all the way back to the 1940s. If the house had been passed on from generation to generation, they would know everything about the previous residents, and about the residents of the neighboring houses, too, past and present. They might even be able to tell him what had happened to Mrs. Basarabić. Had she managed to live out her life in her own house, or had she been moved into some strange apartment in a newly constructed building?

And how, in one place or the other, had she ended her days?

Illness, no doubt, amid loneliness and bitterness, almost longing for the end, just as the camp inmates had longed for the end, their relatives all having gone up the crematorium chimney. Orphaned, they tottered from food trough to latrine, no longer lifting their eyes beyond the wire.

Lamian walked, and realized that his legs were taking him to the house of another woman, right around the corner, a woman whose fate had not been determined by her years, and who had also left him with mixed feelings: Branka.

BEHIND THE MONSTROUS BUILDING HE EXPECTED TO FIND the tangle of tiny streets he had once walked at night, but found a procession of tall, new structures. He turned around to see whether he had fallen prey to some error, but everything in Trnska Street lay exactly as he had left it, and the direction he had taken was the right one. Which meant that in coming to Trnska Street he had brushed only the edge of the obliteration, that in fact his former street was the border between past and present.

The street at right angles to Trnska was filled in by two high-rises, which blocked the way to Branka's street. Proceeding to the next cross street, he came to another row of high-rises as far as the eye could see. Where was Branka's street, then, even if it had apartment buildings instead of small, single-family homes? He directed his steps down the row, along a narrow sidewalk, and at the end of each building he turned in the direction he remembered, but the buildings were too long, and behind them rose others just like them, so he found himself getting farther and farther from his goal.

He passed between two buildings and came out onto a field where children were playing in sportsuits made of synthetics in bright colors. The center of the field was paved with concrete, and at each end of the concrete stood a post with a basketball hoop. By its location he surmised that here was where Branka had lived: on the site of a modern playground. The children raced back and forth, catching each other, grabbing each other by the sleeves, only to separate again with peals of laughter. Like the tattered little Ukrainians in the narrow space between the barracks, using up the strength of their starved bodies to chase a rag ball kindly made for them and tossed their way in passing by SS man Schranke, who in peacetime had been a tailor. Schranke, only one day later, along with Lamian, would escort the little group to the gas chamber.

He saw Schranke, tall and lean, slightly stooped despite his years of military service; saw his long, yellow teeth stretching a drop of spittle into a thin, glistening thread as his mouth gaped with pleasure while he watched the children. After a moment of hesitation—uncertain whether such a thing was possible in this place where they were starved and beaten—the children pounced on the round object that had come sailing over the wire and made a feeble bounce. And for an instant Lamian saw himself too, passing by the block just then, carrying treasure from the Kanada supply depot inside his shirt.

And once again feeling bitterness in his mouth, because he knew this would be the children's last game, last because it had been given them by an SS man, who also knew it was their last. Lamian had never given anyone the means to play, to forget; not once had tried to obscure the truth. He had hastened to carry out that truth, to carry it out in all its rigor, beating those who didn't obey immediately. Because he, unlike Schranke, believed that to ignore the truth did no good, only harm. Feeding the inner strength, the hope, only prolonged suffering, until strength and hope were inevitably shattered.

And he believed this, probably, when he came here to visit Branka in the middle of the night, for not once had he eased the pain of her great love for him, whether by pretending to reciprocate or by substituting something else—the admission that he needed her, that his manhood needed her body, or the affinity of their ideas, an affinity which had blossomed during the endless talks they had before becoming lovers.

He never even told her he was a Jew, perhaps because he feared that that fact might rouse her hopes, make her think that this could be the basis of something more between them. He offered her not a single prop, not a single toy, not one illusion that would have helped her to meet darkness and ruin with more breath in her chest, more color in her eye. Just as he had offered nothing to his mother, made no effort to send her a message, in exchange for the pair of climbing boots, that he was still alive; nor had he asked permission to see his father and show him that he was still alive.

He had denied his bond to them and his Jewishness, for the two were the same.

If he had been an SS man like Schranke, perhaps he would have acted differently. Perhaps he would have been kind, forced to do evil by his heritage and not by the decision to survive. But had he made that decision in Branka's time, or was it born in the camps, of the gradual acceptance of suffering, his own and that of others, of the ruthlessness that came from suffering? Perhaps it was as he stood on the parade ground drenched with water and freezing in the Silesian wind, or that night in his bare cubicle, as he tried to thaw the cold in his bones, that he realized he must never again leave himself open as he had done by stealing the sweater from the corpse to keep warm, that he must gain the right to confiscate sweaters—that he must become a Kapo. He no longer knew; the past had become hazy. He could no longer see it clearly, just as here on this playground amid tall new buildings he could not find the streets in which his past had been acted out.

Mechanically, he started toward the little one-story houses, toward the place where they once stood, and walked into the playground, among the children. One of them, a small girl, in her frenzied running bumped her shoulder against his thigh, then stopped in surprise and stared at him with round black eyes.

That was how Branka had stared at him, and how his mother had stared at him. A monster appearing where only concord and the frivolity of play was expected. Had they ever looked at him differently? He didn't remember, couldn't bring their faces back to life, saw only the wide open eyes of this startled girl.

The playground had replaced Branka's house, and Branka and his mother had become ashes and clods of earth. There was nothing he could do. He could pat the little girl, and for a moment he thought of doing this, stepping toward her and smiling, making a circular movement with his hand, as if to explain why he had shown up here so suddenly—but he abandoned his intention halfway through.

Branka and his mother had both once been little girls who played rapturously in a neighborhood playground with other children, not knowing that somewhere their death was being decided. Perhaps this little girl's death, too, was being decided, if not at some military headquarters then on an x-ray screen or in a test tube. Such decisions were being made for everyone. And yet the Schrankes of the world made rag balls for children and patted them on the head, even though directly afterward they went off to their military headquarters or to look at x-rays and test tubes containing children's blood. And they called that life, the pats on the head and the decisions intertwined and carried out in lockstep.

Why couldn't he, too, pat her on the head? He followed the girl with his eyes as she moved away. She had noticed his smile and gesture, and for a moment hesitated whether to wait for him. But he'd stopped, so she again looked for her playmates and ran off in their direction. And now he wasn't even sure which one she was, in all the bright clothing, blue, red, yellow, because he couldn't recall which color had been hers.

And couldn't recall, really, Branka and his mother. Both were only feelings, painful and oppressive, shaped by what they had become, inmates of camps for annihilation and murder, ill, shriveled, gray, their bellies swollen, their teeth loose. Yet he saw them in the eyes of that child. Because with them, too, he had failed to complete the gesture of approach. Had never completed it. Had passed the children without looking at them through the wire fence, without thinking of how to amuse them, thinking only of his toolshed with the treasures for the SS men. He was a merchant in lives. A trader. Climbing boots in exchange for his safe return from Gradina; Frfa's corpse for his own body; Frfa's number for his number; the drowning of the Stark brothers for him not to drown. Because they needed a trader, an intermediary; they couldn't do it themselves.

Or could they? He'd never thought about it. Why hadn't they simply slaughtered, straight off? Why, instead of building real slaughterhouses with drains for the blood and grinders for the flesh and bones, had they put up fences around fields, where blood and flesh and bones, mountains of them, would be slowly ground by starvation and exhaustion?

Here was a chink in their resolve, an inconsistency. Why? Had they been divided into bad and good? Hypocritical and honest? Into those who believed that other origins and views should simply be punished, and those who had sworn to drain the blood of all who were different?

Disciplinarians and butchers! He had known both kinds, and a third kind, in which disciplinarian and butcher were combined. Gruppenführer Leitner, who arrived at the head of the rumbling trucks in his open car and stood in front of the barracks, barking commands as he directed the human freight, making sure not an inch of truck bed went unused before he raised his gloved hand and gave the signal for the column to start for the crematorium. And Pfalzig, who killed prisoners by knocking them to the ground, then pressing with the full weight of his body the end of his staff into their mouths and down their windpipes. And Schranke and Riegler, Blažuj and Jozo. He could analyze the types, see what motivated them.

But that was a chink in psychology only, not principle. Perhaps the difference lay, rather, in the variety of circumstances, some camps having room only for a tenth of the people sent to them, while others could accommodate all. However, he never found out why some were sent to one camp and some to another, nor did he read about this in the books that became available just after the war. But the chink existed, and perhaps it had caused the Germans to lose the war. For if they had simply slaughtered, they wouldn't have needed Kapos, and if there had been no Kapos, no one would have softened them up with gifts, gifts that required something in return, some little inequity, a blind eye to the pilfering of food, cigarettes, the lending out of the key to the abandoned toolshed, where hungry young female prisoners could be forced to lie down on the rolled-out mat acquired from the corpse carriers.

One corruption in exchange for another, and this infiltrated their blood, and infiltrated, through them, through the packages sent home, the blood of their loved ones, softening the spine of the German will. Gabelić had correctly assessed the situation when he used his knife on Maričić. Lamian agreed with Gabelić. What the Germans should have done was slaughter, not put up fences. Slaughter, not sap their strength on dikes and construction. Slaughter, not reduce rations. Slaughter, not stand the prisoners in ranks and beat them. Slaughter, only slaughter. Slaughter, slaughter, slaughter.

In the end, the whole earth would be drenched in blood, covered with corpses and ashes. The grass would no longer grow because of all the ashes and blood, nor would grain. Animals and people would have nothing to eat, they would drop in the trenches where they'd been sent, and rot, and their rottenness would pollute the water and poison the air; and the ones sent to bury and burn them would fall on top of them, poisoned, and so would those who came to take their place at tools and arms, and so would those who came as victors to plant their flag over the dead.

Everything would die; this whole sinful world devoted only to itself, bent on impurity. Everything that was murky and deceitful, that succumbed to the temptations of possession, to luxury, the intellect, art, imagination, meditation, discovery, assimilation—everything, in short, the world's Jews had used to dazzle and corrupt.

HE WAS DISTRACTED BY MUSIC AND SONG. IT CAME FROM the playground, where the children had been running a moment before. They now stood transfixed around a hairy, bearded young man in blue jeans and checked shirt; he was plucking a guitar slung across his chest.

The guitar strings twanged loud and lively, while an invisible drum beat out the rhythm to the shivering clang of cymbals, and from the mouth of the young man a deep, pleasant voice joined the instruments and flowed like water in a river. The singer stood straight, and as his hands roamed the strings, his legs jerked, first one and then the other, in time with the drum and the cymbals.

Lamian, noticing objects bobbing behind the young man's thick, curly head of hair and above his shoulders, which were covered with straps, began to circle the playground, where people were now gathering from various directions, and he found himself behind the young man. The bobbing objects were two copper plates on leather thongs and two bells on iron rods. Firmly fixed to the player's waist was a drum that was struck by a small wooden mallet connected to a metal lever and a taut wire, struck every time the musician's right leg jerked back. At a jerk of the left leg, the cymbals came together, and at a shake of the shoulders the bells twitched and jingled. All this noise was embraced and made one by the song the bearded young man sang from deep inside his chest.

At first Lamian found the song incomprehensible, but he soon caught a few English words he had heard before, "love," "heart," "summer," "dreams," and concluded it was English, perhaps American, a cowboy song or else an imitation like those he often heard young people singing on television, young people of various nationalities, even Yugoslav.

This singer, however, was unique, for in addition to his song he provided the accompaniment of an entire band. He was an innovator, a wonder of a man. Lamian continued to circle around him, observed him from the side and from the front, looked at his swarthy face, his short, curved nose and two small eyes buried in late afternoon shadow. An ordinary face, but to Lamian it seemed a mask, a mask that covered something extraordinary. He liked him; he was impressed. And felt, through him, a sense of freedom. The man's own, because he had so obviously succeeded in freeing himself from the trap of usual professions.

Now the singer finished his song, but still ran his fingers over the strings forcefully, rapidly, then rapped the wood of the guitar as the unseen mallet hit the drum and the cymbals clashed. To make all three finishing strokes come as close together as possible, he had to jump into the air and kick back both legs. This amused the crowd, and they laughed. The children imitated him by jumping up and down. For a moment it looked as if the performance would degenerate into individual productions, but then the singer again brought his feet together, straightened, and with a broad, flailing movement of his right hand announced the beginning of a new song.

It was slower, a drawn-out song full of yearning; the bells, shaken by the man's trembling shoulders, imbued it with pathos, while the drum, alternating with the cymbals, played with muted ceremony. Something inconsolably sad was being communicated, filling the space between the uniform multistory buildings with something that concerned them: love not returned, promises broken, hopes lost.

The complaints of a full stomach! But there was no other

kind of song. Even when marching out to work from which many would not return, they sang—at the command of the Arbeitsführer, it was true—the same sort of full-stomach song: about flowers in the meadow, sweethearts waiting back home. Even the camp marching song, *"In Auschwitz war ich so manchen Monat, so manches Jahr,"* composed by a nameless inmate, wasn't free of such sentimentality, since both the slaves and their drivers longed for a home somewhere, for reunion, for someone close, a bond between man and woman. The wire-fenced fields, with which the warriors marked the progress of their conquest, thus degenerated from an emblem of purification by death to an emblem of love-making. The SS officers and noncoms, even the camp commandant, had lovers among the better-fleshed women prisoners, and Blažuj herded the Gypsies into the officers' canteen to play love songs for him before he slaughtered them, so that hundreds of musicians left not only violins and drums on the grounds of the camp—along with their clothing and the gold pieces sewn inside, target of Sergeant Major Maričić's searches—but also the strains of their sobbing songs.

Parallel yearnings: the embrace of both butcher and lover, rule and anarchy, the abandonment to will and tears alike. And this free, late-afternoon singer, this inventor and virtuoso, were he to fall into their hands with his panoply of instruments, they would station him at the camp gate to see off the work teams with a march tempo of drums and cymbals—and afterward would send him, weak from hunger and disease, to get an injection of phenol, and replace him with others, perhaps with a whole orchestra.

They would do it with regret, shaking their heads as they recalled his marvelous artistic feats, the remarkable coordination with which he had used the various parts of his body. What a fellow! What a *Kerl*! A shame he didn't last longer, a shame he didn't have enough food to eat or warm clothing to wear, a shame his strength and resistance were sapped by bloody diarrhea.

But this musician didn't have to worry, because in his pocket he carried a legitimate passport and a permit to perform in public places, in this playground surrounded not by barbed wire but apartment buildings in which yearnings were satisfied within four solid walls, well-heated rooms with full pantries and refrigerators, the family circle. The spanking of children's bottoms, husband-wife quarrels, grumbling about in-laws who take up space and parents who squelch all flights of fancy.

Then Lamian remembered the weedy young man at the café, the one who had sat silently opposite the Jew (if he was a Jew). That man would be capable of rising above the sweetness of this early evening romanticism; he would jam his hands in the pockets of his tight pants, thrust out his narrow chest with the thin, tightly knotted necktie down the center, throw back his bony head, and yell, "Beat it!" And bend down to pick up a rock, and hurl it at the singer, right in the middle of that delirious guitar.

What an uproar then! Would the attacker find any allies? Or would everyone turn on him for spoiling their fun? Perhaps there would be two camps slugging it out while the singer took to his heels. Perhaps he would never again put on those drums and cymbals all hooked up with wires, those bells on metal rods, seeing how extremely foolish he had been to place himself like that in front of strange people, bloodthirsty people.

For the time being, however, he was rocking and shaking, kicking back one foot, the other, rounding his mouth between curly mustache and beard, drawing out the notes then cutting them off with bangs and jingles, all in a passion that seemed to come from fever or pain. As if a hunger deep inside him was rattling its chains, a hunger that had grown dense in its emptiness over the years and now wailed, wailed inside Lamian too, ready to burst from his mouth, so that he had to press his lips together.

The duo of L&L, he thought, recalling Helena Lifka, who for a long time now, for hours, had so magnanimously absented herself from his mind. That branded, bluish face, the lips pressed together in a silence which only hunger, forced hunger, imposed hunger, could open in song.

The two of them would be beaten, he was sure, even without the sour young man from the café. The residents of these new buildings loved too much the comfort they had never known before, the cozy rooms they had forsaken briefly to see and hear the singer up close, rooms to which they would return, where they were mellowed by the proximity of their children, who twined themselves around their legs after safe play. The residents would shrink from the duo, whistle their disapproval, stone them because the singers had violated the pact about songs—that they be free of truth, free of hunger—and this had been observed even in the marching songs composed in the crush of the barracks and the stench of the latrines.

The pact proved stronger than hunger; he saw this in the singer's confident movements, the manipulation of body, wires, and rods, in the dignified strum of fingers over strings, and in the tender song that came from those rounded lips between curly mustache and beard, rising into the free air between the multistory buildings built in place of the homes that had been destroyed. And somewhere up there, near the distant roofs, nightmare presence from the booted kick in Lamian's side to the knife that plunged into the throat of Sergeant Major Maričić, leered Zvonko Gabelić.

On the way back, the memory of the café made him wary of unfamiliar places to eat. It was only in the dining room of his hotel that he finally got a proper meal. Afterward, he sat back and contentedly watched others eat and drink.

They were probably also guests of the hotel, and strangers in Zagreb, for they sat separately, each at his own table, shoveling in the food. Unlike Lamian, no one sat awhile after eating. One couple, perhaps husband and wife, or accountants attending the same convention, left as soon as they paid. For an hour and a half, quite a number of people filed past, many more than the room with its ten or so tables would have indicated at first glance.

In addition to the man and woman who looked like accountants there was a bald, heavyset man of fifty in a dark blue suit. His face grew redder and more worried with each bite; more and more frequently he brought his large hand to his mouth to cover a hiccup or belch. Then he would stop chewing and look at that hand, as if it bore the symptoms of an illness he suspected. There were two young officials who conversed in monosyllables without looking at each other, merely nodding to signal that they had heard and understood. And two women, an aunt and her niece, or a mother and her son's young wife, perhaps on a visit to the son serving in the army. They were reserved, both spinsterishly neat, carefully combed, with handbags on the table, from which they took a tissue, a billfold, a page with writing—a certificate of some sort or maybe a shopping list. There was a blond beauty in a honey-colored dress with a plunging neckline; at once sensual and shy, she had heavy, lashless eyelids that were always lowered. There was a thin girl in blue jeans and a sweater buttoned all the way to her angular chin, her hair tightly curled, almost kinky; she smoked between courses and at intervals asked the waiter for condiments, toothpicks, additional cutlery. There was a well-groomed old man, gray hair slicked down and parted; his movements were slow, and he chewed each mouthful laboriously, reflectively, pushing around the food on his plate more than eating. And a woman in a black suit, with thick dark hair and a face like a full moon, her large teeth protruding. She kept turning toward the door, as if waiting for someone, yet left as soon as she had eaten and paid.

Ordinary people, but he observed them with a dissecting eye. Everything about them interested him, every gesture, every remark, every expression and movement of face, hand, or shoulder. He felt a need to engross himself in them, to follow the way they took in food and with what degree of urgency before washing it down with soothing beverages. Their fullness meant more to him than his own. As if he had come to this restaurant not to eat but to see how others ate. The curiosity of a man long unaccustomed to being among people, or, rather, of a man who has been interested not in people but only in the picture they have of him, for fear he might be discovered.

Now he no longer feared discovery; he was only watching, detached, and this new state of mind pleased him so much that he didn't want to let go of it. He remained sitting even after the diners had thinned out and the only ones left were the old man with the part in the middle and another guest. Short, with reddish hair and restless dark eyes, the man had stormed into the dining room like a cannonball and sat at the first table, by the door, so that Lamian could not hear what he ordered. It was soup—the man used a spoon. He ate quickly, paid, and rushed out at almost the same time that the old man was making a sedate exit.

A little mineral water still sparkled in Lamian's glass, but he did not drink it. He sat on. He no longer had anyone to look at, only the two waiters in the deserted dining room, one older, stooped, leaning on a chair, the other somewhat younger but also tired. They were talking. He watched them with no less interest than when they had danced attendance on the room, gliding from table to table, taking orders or bringing food.

Now the tables were empty. A few still had uncleared plates and silverware, napkins unfolded and abandoned, like scattered white roofs.

Roofs with no one beneath them. It was winter, and the snow had settled on both the roofs and the roads connecting them, and since the animals and people were all dead, the white layer remained untouched. In places, a bulge where the snow covered some forgotten object and copied its shape. The Ukrainian children's ball, which they had not taken with them, surprised by the truck that came for them. The little girl's doll, which she had dropped when the bullet entered her brain and which the corpse bearers had not picked up, knowing it wouldn't buy food or cigarettes, because with the disappearance of the children the doll had become an article without a buyer.

Not a buyer anywhere, just the two corpse bearers dressed in black, talking in a corner, left by accident after the destruction of the camp, forgotten by the SS, who should have liquidated them as unwanted witnesses but hadn't, because the order to withdraw came too suddenly and too late. As at Auschwitz. But not at Jasenovac, where all the witnesses were killed.

Here, however, two were left alive, and they were now discussing what they had seen and done. The loads of corpses they had taken to the crematorium. Multiplying the number of loads by the number of bodies in each. At the beginning they had put fewer on the litter—two, three at the most—but when the turn came for the thinnest among them, the toughest, those who had managed to keep alive even at seventy-five pounds, the number rose to four. How easily we tossed them on top of each other! How light they were, how thin their limbs, so thin you could get thumb and forefinger around them. They wasted away and died silently, as they stood at roll call or sitting with mess tins in their laps, staring with brows furrowed, unable to eat the soup which might have kept them alive.

It was just a dream, his and Riegler's, that in the end only the two of them would be alive, forgotten, left behind with their gold and secret supply of food. That they would relax at last, talk, roar with laughter at the end of the world that had missed them.

The waiters were laughing. The older one was snapping the end of a napkin against the edge of a table, or maybe it was at the shoulders of the younger waiter, who stood beside him, erect, face tight—he had obviously introduced the joke, the occasion for laughter, into the conversation, and knew better than to spoil it by being the first to laugh.

Then they separated, one to the left, the other to the right. At the door the older waiter raised his hand to the switch and turned the lights off, on, and a second time. A signal that Lamian, the last customer, had to go. But Lamian didn't go right away. He wanted to stay, to ask them to pay no attention to him, to turn off the lights and leave. He would remain in the dark, with perhaps a little light from the lobby or street catching the white tablecloths amid the sea of shadows. He would sit and think of what he and Riegler would have done had they been left alone with the gold and hoarded food, around them the dead and half-dead rotting in the barracks. Would the two of them have murdered each other?

But the lights blinked again. Now it was the younger waiter

giving the signal to leave, looking sternly at Lamian and keeping a finger on the switch as if threatening a third flick which would turn loose the German shepherds. Lamian gathered up his things—cigarettes, matches, the glasses case he had absentmindedly taken out—and made his way out of the dining room, stiff and numb from sitting.

THE LOBBY WAS DIM, LIKE THE DIMNESS HE HAD JUST wished for in the dining room. He found a vacant table—a shining plate of glass that floated in a pit of black—and groped for a chair and sat down. He was alone, near a pillar that branched at the top into two arches. In the faint light of the reception desk he could see, at a distant table, the silhouettes of several figures.

He liked the muted lighting in which you could still see people, after the white desolate glare of the searchlight from the watchtower as it slid across the barracks window. You were in your cubicle, hidden, hoping that the beam wasn't hunting you, that the SS would not burst in with their dogs, drag you out and into another barracks, where there was a chair set in the middle of the concrete floor and a nurse in a rubber apron ready to put an injection into your heart.

He remembered sitting like this on some other occasion, in a half-lit room with glassy surfaces and silhouettes huddled around them.

Where had it been? Perhaps the scene came to him only from a story, someone else's, or from a film, it was so vivid and so unusual. But searching deeper in the darkness of his mind, he realized that he had experienced it in the lobby of another hotel, in another city.

When? He went back through the darkness to last summer in Banja Luka, and fastened on Subotica. Which was where he had taken up the trail of Helena Lifka.

He remembered how for a brief moment, at that other table

and in that other gloom, he had allowed himself to hope. And now, too, he was giving shape to that hope—in the softness of the armchair, the human silhouettes, the night owl's atmosphere of cigarette smoke and quiet conversation. His desire to immerse himself in this world. But the thought of going back to Banja Luka sobered him.

Banja Luka had been a mistake from the start, a loathsome place, and not only on his return, which as punishment for being alive had thrust him into the oven of summer headfirst, as he had thrust others into the ovens, and from this he had tried to deliver himself by the wire attached to the stove. It was a pit, with mountains all around, fencing it in with fear. Liberated from one camp, he had chosen another, just as a mole driven from one hole seeks another where the air is equally humid and close.

He had chosen that sleepy town among the mountains as a place to wait, peering out, for the hand of revenge sooner or later to clap down on him. Hiding, pulling into himself, fattening his body to alter his appearance, keeping silent so his voice would not be recognized, squinting behind dark glasses. And he had taken up with a half-woman, a dried-up spinster, panting over her at each meeting but never letting a word out, not from his heart, stomach, or that tight little sausage which did nothing more than pump into her the poison of his pent secrecy and deceit. And he fled from the brave, beautiful Ella Cohen, who had appealed to him to leave those hills, leave behind silence and join her in equality and openness, as young men and women did on nights like this, in the shadows at low tables sparkling with drinks and thick with cigarette smoke, where promises and demands were exchanged in whispers, and no light fell on scenes of affection, doubt, shame, and hate. Here was not the loneliness of old age, whose only road was the distance from table to cupboard in a single room—on the contrary, all here was spa-

cious, wide and deep, still unexplored and unknown, these nocturnal meeting places which filled up and emptied ceaselessly,
always inviting new players into the darkness.

Now he sat in the darkness and enjoyed it. He lit a cigarette
and by the flame of the match saw the glass contours of an
ashtray. Into it he threw the extinguished match, its tip still
glowing, a red point in the sea of ink that spread to the farthest
arch and the table and shapes around it. This was the ink of the
fields beyond the barbed wire, those inconceivable expanses
where people still breathed, moved freely, tramping the roads
and lying in the grass with their faces to the sky, hands clasped
behind their heads, watching the clouds and thinking of what
they would do tomorrow, where they would go, where they
would resettle.

He was sitting in a short, two-wheeled cart, a kind he had
never in his life sat in; it was only as a corpse bearer and gravedigger that he'd pushed a two-wheeler like that, or else had
walked behind it as Kapo, flogging the men to go faster. But
now a horse was harnessed in front, trotting, black in the darkness that hid its color, while he sat and looked at the animal's
rump as it bobbed and gleamed beneath a faint light, perhaps
the distant moon behind clouds. All he had to do was sit, not
even hold the reins, because the horse went by itself at a measured
trot, the cart shaking so gently that it was like a child's cart cut
to the measure of his body and pushed by someone instead of
pulled.

Then he was sitting in a baby carriage, and knew his mother
was pushing it even though he couldn't see her, because he felt
her presence, her scent, something between the smell of risen
dough and bed linen, mild but unmistakable. When he turned
around to make sure it was his mother, the movement hurt his
neck, and the baby carriage tipped so much, he was afraid he
would tumble out. He clutched the sides, and found he was

gripping the soft arms of his chair and that his fingertips were being burned. It was his cigarette, which he quickly moved up between his fingers so it wouldn't slip to the floor. He had fallen asleep.

Amusing, but only to him, because no one else was near. At the neighboring pillar the figures sat leaning toward one another. The cigarette still in his hand, he knocked off the ash and inhaled from it before putting it out.

The two people leaning toward each other now straightened, neck and shoulders first, and as they stood, Lamian saw that they were man and woman, both young. They left the part of the lobby visible to him. Gone to bed, having looked raptly in each other's eyes as they sat together, eyes that gave them the desire to kiss and couple.

And Lamian should go to bed himself, though for the moment he didn't feel tired. But sleep would be welcome after last night's vigil. He got up and walked in the same direction, taking care not to bump into the chairs.

At the reception desk, the clerk—the same one he had dealt with several times that day—bowed with a look of recognition, took the key from the hook in its pigeonhole, and handed it to him without a word. Lamian took the key and started toward the stairs. He heard music. It grew louder as he went forward, and when he reached the stairs, he saw that it was coming not from above, where he was going, but from below. He hadn't noticed before that the stairs also went down, but now, in the evening, they were illuminated, and even more than the stairs leading up.

Stopping to listen to the music, he concluded that it was being played for entertainment, and that possibly the young couple had gone down there. The idea of finding out, or simply doing what they had done—he could not distinguish between the two—appealed to him, so he descended the lighted stairway.

THE STAIRS TURNED ONCE, TWICE, AND THE SOUND swelled more and more powerfully, like water rising from his feet to his head. He came to a wall in which two green plush curtains parted to a reddish gloom and the music. He found himself on the threshold of a low, rectangular room, a band at one end and people sitting along a bar at the other.

Actually, only one man sat at the bar, his naked skull gleaming beneath the red lights; there was no one at the tables which went all the way to the music stand, so that the efforts of the three-piece band—saxophone, piano, drums—could not reduce the sense of desolation.

Lamian was about to turn and leave, when a tall waiter with slickly combed hair detached himself from the darkness by the wall. With a bow and a broad sweep of his arm he invited Lamian to have a seat at whichever table he pleased.

Lamian, not wanting to but acceding to the forceful style of this invitation, went over to the bar, the row of backless stools, and since the sole patron was sitting at the far right, he took one of the stools to the left and climbed carefully onto it. Because there was no back, he had to lean on the bar, and almost bumped heads with the second waiter, a reassuringly wrinkled and weary man, who approached from the rear of the bar and its shelves of bottles.

"What'll you have?" the waiter asked in a growling whisper, leaning forward to wipe the dark surface of the counter that glistened between himself and Lamian. "Something light? Whiskey and soda, a gin fizz?" Lamian muttered that he'd have a fizz.

The waiter nodded slightly and turned to the shelves. Swaying his large behind and the short red tailcoat that hung over it, he located bottles and opened them, filled a glass and shoved it toward Lamian.

Lamian took a swallow and looked around. The tables were still unoccupied, the first waiter nowhere to be seen, and when he turned back to the bar, he saw the same thing, for above the shelves of bottles was a mirror the length of the wall. Like a television screen, it gave him a view of the entire room, and at the same time he could watch the waiter busy in front of him, then going over to the customer on the right and talking to him. But this wide, duplicate scene, unlike the more meager one in the lobby, made Lamian uncomfortable: here he was too much a part of things, practically a participant.

He sensed—sensed only, for this was his first time in a bar, not counting a couple of brief visits to a nightclub, also here in Zagreb, but long ago, before the war, somewhere around Jelačić Square—that demands would be made of him in this place of a subterranean red gloom that resembled hell, but a heavenly hell, where music played and powerful but enticing drinks were served. Where the customer had to conduct himself like a spendthrift, an adventurer. This was alien to Lamian; that was why he fled that nightclub of the past, whose name he no longer remembered, when he was taken there by two students from his class, who revealed to him only after they had entered and sat down at a table, in a darkness similar to this, that they were there to find women of pleasure. At the time he was already torn in his desires between Branka and Zita, so he left the company the moment three garishly made-up women gathered around their table and his companions began introducing themselves and coming to terms.

Out he ran into the chill air of the street, having excused himself with some pressing obligation he just remembered. Even now he could feel the relief that came over him then, recalled it more clearly than anything that had gone before, and he was convinced that he would breathe the same sigh of relief if he got down from this uncomfortable stool, paid for his drink, and left.

But before he could decide to do this—before he even had time to think of it, so intimidated was he by the nature of the place, though he had come alone and of his own volition—he saw in the mirror that a young woman had emerged from the darkness, and when he turned, he saw her directly. She was seating herself on the last stool to the left.

She had brown hair that fell long and wavy onto her shoulders; her breasts and figure were full; and she wore a simple dress with large black and white squares. Then she looked at him, and he saw her face: full and fleshy, with pale cheeks. Her eyes were not large, but clear. Their expression contained no curiosity; they slid over him without lingering, continued to the other side of the bar.

The waiter slowly came over, and Lamian saw him lean toward the woman with the same assured and encouraging manner which had filled him, Lamian, with a feeling of trust when he first sat down. But from the waiter's conduct you could tell that the woman, unlike Lamian, was not a bored hotel guest, nor had she simply wandered in. He clearly recognized her, for he showed no sign of surprise, showed instead a measured solicitude, which could only mean that she too, by a secret understanding, was part of this place.

And she must have come with the knowledge that this place was for adventure and extravagance. Yet, judging by her appearance, she hadn't the means—so the inescapable conclusion was that she expected her foray to bring her those means: in the form of someone else's money. Like those three garish women four decades ago, she was a woman of pleasure, though this was contradicted by her pure, almost chaste face, her modest clothes, her forthright gaze.

The contradiction stirred Lamian's curiosity, gave rise to both lascivious and protective feelings toward the woman, erasing, like the sweep of a hand across the counter, the irritation and mistrust of just a moment ago. Tensely, out of the corner of his eye, he watched the waiter serve her—a brownish-yellow drink in a thin-stemmed glass. At the same time, in the mirror, he noted the entrance of four new customers, one woman and three men. The music wasn't playing then, but when the woman and men sat down at a table, the band struck up a new number, and one of the men went out into the empty space among the tables to dance with the woman, while the others conversed with the waiter who had come from behind the band.

This scene then became the background, blocked by the looming figure of the third man, who had left the table and was making for the bar. He stopped by the stool next to Lamian's, between Lamian and the young woman.

He was thin, hollow-cheeked, with thick black hair combed back, but there were unruly tufts over his low forehead and temples. Going around the stool, he stood close to the bar, so Lamian couldn't see the woman.

Now the waiter came over and looked inquiringly at the man. The man ordered a brandy, and when the waiter brought it, Lamian saw that this was the same thing the woman was drinking, in the same thin-stemmed glass. Perhaps the man had ordered it on purpose, to begin a conversation with the woman. And indeed, he turned to her, showing Lamian the back of his narrow, dark head, which swiveled on his narrow shoulders in their close-fitting dark jacket.

What they said was inaudible to him; he heard only a soft clink of glasses, and from that and the twist of the man's shoulder he concluded that they had toasted each other. This made him angry. Her easy rapport with a strange man all too clearly confirmed his suspicion about the understanding that existed between her and those who came to the bar.

He reached for his glass and took a sip. He felt alone, as if he were sitting in an empty room, one that only reflected images and echoed sounds that came from outside, like a box that contained a camera.

There in the background the man and woman were dancing, flanks and shoulders swaying in imitation of the writhing of love; the musicians bent and straightened ceaselessly; the waiter talked to the customer at the other end of the bar, who nodded as he listened. It all seemed so inconsequential, so unreal.

Lamian's attention shifted to the bony man whose back hid the young woman. He realized that the man had won her, and that it would have been possible for him, Lamian, to have won her. All he needed to have done was recognize that possibility before the bony man appeared and stood alongside her, separating them. He could have done the same thing himself, clinking glasses, opening a conversation. He knew where conversation with such a young woman led, a young woman who came into a nightclub alone, sat down at the bar, and ordered a drink. He would ask if she was alone, if she was free this evening, and the affirmative answer, for it had to be affirmative, would almost demand that he declare his own availability, his own solitude, from which it would follow that they could spend the evening, and the night, together.

He wanted such a conversation for himself, wanted to find out things about her, wanted to establish the easiness of clinking glasses, which had presented itself as a possibility that desolate evening in Subotica, at the Hotel Patria, first in the lobby and then in that dim box which was supposed to resemble a nightclub, a bar, in that little town where none existed. Perhaps the authorities, overly strict, wouldn't issue a permit, or the hotel management didn't dare open a nightclub for fear of public opinion, or wanting to avoid the expense and the unruly crowd it would attract.

It seemed to Lamian that he had foreseen this long ago, that all his unease of recent months came from the need of a nocturnal encounter with a strange young woman who would enter the bar with the same, reciprocal need.

Peering over the bony man's shoulder, he saw part of her cheek, a patch of pale skin, a wave of her hair, and a shadowy fold, either the corner of her lip or the edge of her nose. Stretching his neck, he could see one of her eyes as well, brown and clear, and the eye looked at him. He drew back, but too late, because the bony man had realized, from the direction of her glance or the shadow that fell over her, that something was happening behind his back, and he turned around.

The man's forbidding dark eyes narrowed, bringing the brows above them together, and met his, but Lamian didn't look away. The man interested him almost as much as the woman. Who was he? How old was he? Where had he come from, and what was he looking for in this bar? Lamian would have liked to slip invisible between them, as in childhood he had imagined being able to move unseen among others, in tales of magic rings and cowls. Then he could hear what they said and see what they did, every movement and every wink. And feel every touch and squeeze.

The man seemed to guess this, for he turned his head more to Lamian, but did not show unease or anger; the eyes which were narrowed in suspicion now relaxed, the forehead grew smooth, and the lips parted to expose an uneven thicket of teeth. "Want some company?" A hoarse, tremulous voice, the kind Lamian would have expected from someone much older and less confident in bearing. And in the man's dark eyes, too, there was now a humble expression. Lamian nodded, and in the same moment realized that he had misunderstood the man completely.

Looking him over more calmly now, he noticed how the fabric of his white shirt was slack, the collar ends pilled from rubbing, and his dark suit shiny from many ironings; the man himself, wiry and brisk at first glance, was in fact undernourished and nervous.

He was waving to the waiter now, and that wave was timid, too eager, as if in fear of not being noticed; and when the waiter came over, the bony man said, "The same again? All around?" in a hurried, quavering voice, as if afraid that Lamian might change his mind. Then he slid lightly from his stool, stood behind it, and tugged at the young woman. She looked at him in surprise, then hopped down, high heels clacking on the floor, dress climbing to her thighs before settling back into place and smoothing itself out. The bony man grabbed her arm and moved her to the place he had just vacated. "In the middle, in the middle! Ladies in the middle, that's the rule!" he said, baring his crooked teeth as he sat her on the stool next to Lamian's. "How about introductions!" Their hands crossed paths, fingers jabbing, because the man was too impatient to keep to the order he himself proposed, so that the names, too, Lamian, Karlo, Danica, were barely distinguishable as they tumbled over one another.

Lamian didn't mind: the names were probably false. The bony man was the intermediary, the decoy who helped the young woman strike up profitable acquaintances. This was now confirmed by the waiter, the way he placed their drinks before them—first Lamian's, then the young woman's, then the bony man's. The waiter turned to Lamian with a confidential wink: "On your bill?" Lamian agreed, and was in fact pleased, because by fulfilling their hopes he became a desired and even pampered personage, the center of attention here at the left end of the bar. Male and female alike revolved around him, both making themselves useful. He no longer had to lean over anyone's shoulder to see the young woman; she was looking him right in the face.

He clinked glasses with her, then, as an afterthought, with the bony man. Tilting his glass, he peered with satisfaction along his cheek, watching her arm, her stubby hand which lifted the glass to her lips, lips that parted and arched like two leeches, and he watched the pale skin of her face stretch and gather as she swallowed.

Now it was he filling her—or so he felt—stretching her, parting her lips and pressing them to the rim over which those teasing swallows were made. He was her master, and she the woman on whom his attention focused, and this made him master of the entire bar, of the murky red volcano hole he had dropped into, a shaft full of night, with all its seething, intense sensuality.

Enthroned on his stool, which a moment ago was so uncomfortable but now seemed to have grown, elevating him above the others, he passed inspection on the company under his command: the bony man who helped the young woman by bringing her to patrons who took a fancy to her; the couple dancing in the background and the man at their table, all part of the bony man's retinue; the musicians who played and the waiter who served, and the man, too, at the other end of the bar, because he did not interfere, a loner who already regretted being present at the amusements and celebrations of others, just as Lamian would be regretting it now if the young woman had sat at the right end of the bar instead of the left.

He could imagine how he appeared to the man who sat apart: clinking glasses with the young woman and her escort, haughtily asserting himself as the drinks he paid for were poured down that soft, supple throat. Proud of a conquest that had in fact been handed to him on a platter, on the tray before him which held the empty glasses. But the waiter was already approaching, lids lowered slyly over weary eyes, face indifferent as he muttered through the mustache that spread over his fleshy lips, "Another round?" At which the young woman and the bony man nodded energetically, so another round, of course.

They were getting him drunk, disarming him for some swindle, but he knew that that was one of the conditions, part of the understanding. Just as those two classmates of his, in the nightclub on Jelačić Square, had met this condition—although he didn't ask them about it afterward, pretending not to remember their outing together, which he had got out of just in time. For it was this condition, this swindle, that he had fled that evening, the moment he grasped the purpose of the three fancily dressed women who came up to them with encouraging smiles, like the smile on the bloodless lips of the bony man.

He felt himself sinking, giving in, as he emptied glass after glass, allowing each empty glass to be replaced with a full one, with the young woman and the bony man, allowing the swindle to tighten around him, and the young woman's stubby hand raising the glass on its narrow stem, her lips fitting themselves to the rim, the stretching of the skin of her cheeks awakened in him a feeling of possession, of mastery.

Now everything was smooth and settled, even the conversation that sprang up between them—nothing to do with what he was interested in, nothing about the young woman and her intermediary. What they said was already forgotten in his tipsiness. It was terse, like the words exchanged with the waiter, all gestures and monosyllables, apropos of nothing, for nothing was happening except a repetition of what had already happened, drawing him deeper into acquiescence: permitting what was happening to continue and to be consummated.

In the mirror, meanwhile, he saw a change at the rear: two more couples had arrived, sat down, and they began to dance, so that the space among the tables was now filled with figures bobbing, gliding, bending over, throwing back heads and shoulders, intersecting like crowded type on a page. Then he saw the gleam of a bald head and the glint of eyeglasses in the red gloom, and only after verifying that the man at the right was no longer there did he realize that it was he, the old man he'd ignored, arm now around the waist of a thin, long-nosed woman with a shaggy head of hair, the same woman who came in with the bony man.

They were all in the trap, then, and resistance was futile. Lamian put a hand on the young woman for the first time, on her shoulder. It was soft and full, and the cloth of her dress was warm. You could squeeze it without fear of damaging it, like a good mare or a good piece of machinery or furniture, made of firm stuff, firm and yielding at the same time.

He lay the full weight of his hand on her, and she turned to him and asked, "Do you want to dance?" "But I'm already dancing," he said. He felt heavy, rusty. He had not danced to music since dancing school in Bjelovar, in his second or third year in Gymnasium. After a torturous several months of practicing steps, he was promoted to full-fledged participant in the dances, which he never attended.

Seeing her surprise and puzzlement, he pointed in the mirror, at the bald fat man and the long-nosed brunette. "You know them, I guess. They're your friends, aren't they?" This seemed to unsettle her. She turned to the bony man, who peeked from behind her, smiling as she explained something in his ear. Her shoulder lifted, its heat filling the gap between Lamian's fingers, and now, through her, he was in contact with the bony man, who looked sharply at him, unblinking, his smile frozen. Then the man got down from his stool and went around to Lamian.

"Are you tired?" he whispered. "Ready to turn in?" When Lamian didn't answer, unable to think of a reason why they should suddenly want to get rid of him, the man added, rolling his eyes, "She could go with you." Lamian sighed with relief. So the hard part, the preliminaries, was over; we have reached our goal. He nodded, and the waiter, who was watching carefully, tore a page from a notepad and added up some numbers.

As Lamian paid, the woman also slid from her stool and smoothed her dress with both hands. He got down with a hand from the bony man. All three were now on solid ground, which listed slightly, and they proceeded to leave, accompanied by music as the dancers kept bending and intersecting, the bald man among them, his head on Long Nose's shoulder, his glasses peering from behind her tangled curls.

Now they were outside the entrance, in the light. A solemn silence, as in a waiting room for saying good-byes before a journey. The bony man took the young woman's arm and muttered, "I have to stay. You know, with my friends. But I'll have expenses, know what I mean?" When Lamian failed to comprehend, he slipped his hand inside Lamian's coat, their fingers meeting, and together they took out his wallet, and then, from it, together, two five-hundred dinar notes. The man disappeared, whisked away behind the green plush curtains, leaving the two of them alone to start up the stairs.

Lamian found it comical, the solemnity, this silence after the din, this light after the darkness. He expected some new noise to deluge them and bring them to their senses when they reached the lobby. But there was no one on the landing, and the reception desk was far away, lost in shadow. When he stopped and asked himself if he had to go over to the desk, he was answered by the clink of the key in his coat pocket. He could feel its chain and tag through the cloth. He put his hand in, grasped it with his fingers. The young woman looked upward, and they continued upstairs.

They could have taken the elevator—accessible, he remembered, on every floor—but he felt incapable of making any suggestion, and she probably didn't know there was an elevator, or didn't want to oppose him.

They climbed, meeting no one and without exerting themselves, for their pace was slow, each out of regard for the other, arms bumping against one another. Thus they reached the fourth floor, only slightly out of breath. He pulled the key from his pocket, checked the number and compared it with the number over the door, turned the key in the lock, and only then removed his arm from hers to let her cross the threshold first.

He turned on the light, locked the door, followed her into the bedroom. She had already turned and was waiting for him. "Where's the bathroom?" she asked, separating *bathroom* into distinct syllables, as if he were deaf. When he pointed, she went quickly by him and disappeared. He was left alone.

HE SAT DOWN IN THE ARMCHAIR FACING THE BATHROOM door. That was the way it always was: First take care of physiological needs, so as not to be reminded of them at an inopportune time, and so as not to put any pressure on the lower regions of the body, which will come under another kind of pressure.

He heard running water. In the camp, too, that came first, right after jumping from the cars, and with no shelter other than human. You asked someone to stand there as a screen, because the SS didn't allow the new arrivals to soil this initial assembly point. But that didn't stop them from feasting their eyes, from shouting: What a round, white bottom just popped out of those crusty underpants—makes you feel like tearing into it, like fresh bread. In the dressing room, too, they gawked, lingered there after giving instructions on how to hang up the clothes, and there would be those who pushed some young prisoner, when she was disrobed, into a corner, to give her a good going over while she squealed in terror.

He, too, had gawked—why not?—even though he knew, like the SS men, that in ten minutes they would all be dead. After those living skeletons he looked at day in and day out, it was irresistible to see some lovely body reach unselfconsciously for the clothes rack. And now, too, he could peek through the keyhole or open the door a crack—the young woman hadn't locked it. He knew he'd see a beauty, curvaceous and voluptuous: that much he had been able to assess even through her clothes. And he had held her, squeezed her a little, felt her flesh. But what good would it do him, when he felt no desire. He had felt no desire for the young woman, not once, not even in the bar as she sat next to him with her legs crossed, or when the bony man hid her from view and he thought he had lost her, or when she was restored and offered to him and he lay his hand proprietarily on her shoulder.

All that had evoked only the memory of desire; nothing in him, no part of him had been stirred or tensed, nor was it now, as he sat in the chair facing the bathroom door, listening. His body hung limp. Fatigue? No, surprisingly, he didn't feel tired. He simply drooped all over, like a rag, and felt no need to do anything else. He waited. It was the man's part to wait, the woman's to ready herself, to make herself desirable.

She was certainly readying herself; the rush of water had long since stopped. Perhaps she was drying herself, having no doubt washed, or was standing before the mirror reviewing what she had to offer: face, shoulders, breasts.

Perhaps she had undressed and was lifting each breast with two fingers, checking its firmness, seeing whether it returned quickly to its hanging position, as one checks the firmness and flexibility of the springs in a couch or armchair. Now she was a spring to be lain on, and he was the buyer. The man was always the buyer, for he could earn more than the woman; he made war, he conquered and killed, acquiring those extra goods she needed, goods she wanted to inspire him to continue acquiring in the future.

And the camps were made by men, not women. The SS men brought in the SS women; the male Lagerführer made prostitutes into female Kapos.

Lina, who delivered women to Lamian in the abandoned toolshed, had been a prostitute. Handing over her wards in return for the receipt with their numbers on it, she licked her thin lips, as if lapping up the semen that had spurted onto them, swiveling her fat belly as if straddling a nozzle. Perhaps the barter which brought her silk underwear appealed to her not so much for the underwear itself, which it was unlikely anyone would see on her, as for the exchange of goods and bodies, albeit bodies not her own, and out of obedience to that hard male muscle that demanded obedience.

That stiff member that lifted the riding breeches of the strapping Kommandoführer at the camp entrance, where units passed five abreast on the way to and from work; or on the ramp where the newly arrived women prisoners were unloaded; or on the parade ground, to the tapping of riding crop on boot leg, leather against leather, sinew against sinew, until everything rattled and cracked, just as bones cracked beneath burdens and blows. Gabelić, with legs planted wide in gleaming boots, in front of the headquarters building tapping his whip on his boot leg, the terror of domination, the horror of submission, foreshadowing the fall into blood, the death rattle, one's own mother—docile, smiling timidly, lips already acknowledging her guilt—falling beneath the leering cutthroat, who spreads her legs and penetrates her with his hardened muscle, at the same time using his knife to cut ribbons of flesh from her withered breasts.

It's my own mother I've brought to a hotel room, it's her legs that I'll spread, it's she in the bathroom getting ready, adjusting her submissive smile in the mirror, to please me. A cold sweat engulfed him. But he resisted it. He hadn't tried to help her, in exchange for the gift of climbing boots to Jozo, because he was afraid he'd find her with her legs spread, legs raised around the hairy neck of some Ustaša, and that then he would go mad and attack. In Gradina, as he accompanied the convoy of prisoners across the Sava, he had looked for her face, her submissive face, afraid he would find it, recognize it. He had watched the Ustaši pounce on the women, ripping off their dresses and spreading their legs, and was relieved not to see her there among them, she was somewhere else, safe, out of his sight, and that was why he never again looked for her, nor for his father, contenting himself with the report that Jasenovac had slaughtered all the Jews, every last one, had thrown them in the water or buried them. So wouldn't it be justice for her to appear in this bathroom doorway? Naked before him, as he had never seen her, because she always covered herself in his presence, therefore as only his father had seen her. Lamian had sensed, only sensed, the naked body from which he had issued and in which he still wanted to hide whenever they beat him or forced him to beat others.

Her submissive smile above withered breasts, the gentleness of a woman who knows she must be subjugated, that she must serve instinct, slashing, murdering instinct, even though she doesn't understand it. Or did she understand it, as they all understood it, learned it so quickly, like Lina licking her lips and thrusting out her belly even though no one wanted her, in those silk panties over a bloated spider's belly and drooping bottom? All her wards had understood, eating the bread and butter and ham, drinking the warm milk, and kissing him on the mouth after every bite and every swallow, as he commanded, and allowing his hands to squeeze their breasts and thighs, and lying down on the mat spattered with the slime brought forth by the previous woman.

It was all the same—marriage, the bar, the camp—everywhere the fabric dropped to reveal that crevice from which we all came and to which we all wanted to return, devoting ourselves to that end by blackmailing, buying, knifing.

By now he nearly hated the young woman primping in the bathroom to please him. Yet how much less, how much milder was the force he could use on her. How much better off she was with him, because he would do her no harm, even though he could, locked up with her like this in a room with a bath, in secret, no one knowing of their shared seclusion.

The bony man knew, but he would keep silent, since he, like Blockelteste Lina, was the intermediary who had supplied the victim. What if Lamian were to beat her, gagging her first with some rag so she couldn't scream, what if he whipped her on one of these beds, taking pleasure in his omnipotence and her contortions? What if he tied her up and tortured her all night, her moans through the slaver-soaked gag for him the music of utter submission, then threw her out the next morning, scantily clad, battered, teeth broken? Like a whipped bitch she would drag herself through the lobby past the reception desk, not making a sound, and wouldn't stop until she reached the sublet room she had somewhere, and she would be happy to have been left alive, and too terrified to complain to anyone.

Unless she complained to the bony man, after she recovered, or sooner if he came looking for her, uneasy because she wasn't at the usual places—at a certain table in the lounge of the Palace Hotel, or sitting at the bar for their regular evening rendezvous.

The bony man would be horrified, but would advise her to do nothing until he made inquiries. If he actually did inquire, he would learn nothing from the desk clerk about this thug of a hotel guest, nothing that would encourage him to avenge his partner. For these were prisoners, after all, though they walked in apparent freedom; they were forced—forced by want and weakness, no doubt combined with expensive habits—to stand at attention, at every roll call, before the flag of nocturnal adventure; they were a disciplinary Kommando which regularly returned decimated from its work site, dragging its dead and incapacitated by their arms and legs, always depleted by a tenth, debilitated—and replenished by new arrivals from the trains. They lacked the strength to rebel, to break through their barbed wire fence, for even outside, their dependence was discovered by guards deployed in a ring of watchtowers, and cold, piercing eyes hunted them down and sent them back to work.

She too—Lamian thought, looking at the bathroom door, the gleaming white rectangle behind which the young woman must be bending toward the mirror—she too had gone through the prisoner's training, had learned that obedience pleases, had learned to do what was asked of her even before she was asked, always willing and diligent, showing that destruction of self which pleases the powerful—the Eltesters, Führers, Kapos—and smooths and softens the scowling face, and stays the club-wielding hand raised to strike.

It was as just such a club-wielder that he waited. And the way she appeared—first opening the door a crack, as if afraid she might find him ill disposed toward her, just as the prisoners had been afraid when they stepped over the threshold to leave the barracks. Having checked, she opened the door wide. His attention was not on how she looked undressed, which she was, but whether the signs of submission were there.

He could not see them. She peered out, to see where he was and what he was doing. Then, apparently satisfied to find him sitting so limply with a cigarette between his fingers, she briskly—casually—crossed the room, tossed her shoes on the floor, and dropped her bundle of clothes over the back of an armchair, all in a clump; checked material mingling with the pink, white, and pale violet folds of thinner fabrics. Turning around, she pointed a finger at the bed nearer the armchair and asked, again with exaggerated distinctness, "Here?" When he nodded slightly, she pushed aside the blanket and slowly slid beneath it, thrusting up her hips and curving thighs as she put her head down on the pillow and stretched out her legs.

Custom no doubt dictated that he climb on top of her at once, kissing and pawing wildly, insatiably. Or was it different for older men? He thought of the bald man at the right end of the bar, imagined him sitting here, three steps from this naked woman Lamian had chosen for the night. The bald man would certainly know how to behave in such circumstances, he who had women like this regularly, perhaps two or three a week, or two or three a month, depending on how often he felt desire.

Or: was it possible that he felt no desire for them, only curiosity, and a curiosity directed more at himself than at them, who were merely the objects, the means, for the expression of his mood?

Lamian should draw his chair up to her, lift the blanket, and by the stark light of the lamp look at her shape, her skin, in all its expanse and fullness; the swelling bosom, whose nipples were as flat as coins, or else as plump as cherries, in any case special because they were a woman's, just as there was something special in the absence of hair on her cheeks, and on that pendant at the base of the abdomen, below the triangle of hair which was like a man's.

A mystery one could puzzle over for hours, and from which no lesson followed. It could be touched, if boredom threatened; he could run his fingertips over that smoothness, make it moisten in arousal, breathe in the scent of that moistening.

She was prepared for such senile eccentricities; that could be seen from the way she watched him, out of the corner of her eye, from the pillow, languid but collected. She was expecting what all women expect, after the man has waited and they have stretched themselves out.

But all he felt was curiosity, now that lying in bed had caused individuality to fall away from her, as if it had been concentrated in her clothing, that checked dress which was not typical of bar wear—at least he thought it wasn't, but, then, he was not familiar with the new, postwar fashions. The dress raised questions in him, doubts, the wish to find out more details about her, about the life she led outside the bar, away from the bony man, perhaps in some other, unimaginable role.

Perhaps by day she was a seamstress, and the bony man's wedded wife, with whom she had children; or perhaps she was the former mistress of some fallen mogul. At this moment, however, stretched out in bed and ready to make room for him beside her, she had no connection with any outside, personal life. She was only a body, mute and enigmatic in its repose, a body with a certain shape, a certain degree of warmth, and those sources of moisture. He imagined it tepid to the touch, slow to ignite, casual in coupling—as it had been casual crossing the room. It would need to be shocked by ferocity, cruelty, or perhaps a casualness even more exaggerated than hers, which would rouse and spur her.

All this went through his mind not as something of his own, but as the bald man's way of dealing with her. The bald man would have drawn his chair up to her bed by now, or done something else. Lamian would have liked to watch. He should have made friends with him down there, and when the bony man offered him the young woman, Lamian should have said the bald man was his partner, should have interrupted his dance with the curly-haired woman and invited him to come along.

Or invited the bony man himself. Lamian could have given him two more five-hundred-dinar notes and said: "Come and do with her what I ought to do."

As Riegler had invited Lamian, sensing his desire for the young prisoners escorted by Lina with blows and shouts past the old toolshed on the way to work every morning. He had strutted there in front of him, hands thrust into trouser pockets, pipe between his teeth as around its stem he asked, "Why don't we get a couple of them in the toolshed tomorrow or the day after, and treat them to a nice little snack?" Then reminded him that it was time to go to Morgenstern at the crematorium for the bar of gold.

Was it then that Lamian first decided to enjoy flesh? Or had he had thoughts like that before, widening his eyes and swallowing as Lina's laborers went by in their rags, beneath which you could occasionally see a leg still rounded, or a look that still flashed with animal hunger? The old procurer had taken note.

And now Lamian himself was the old procurer, but with no Kapo to take his place with the naked woman on the bed. And no gold. Instead of gold he had money, which he had given to the bony man. But the bony man or the bald man should give *him* gold in return for the woman he would hand over to them, and along with the gold he would get the right to be present at the enjoying of her. To watch. Riegler hadn't watched; there was no attraction for him in seeing what Lamian did with the women in the toolshed. All he did, when Lamian returned and gave him the key, was sometimes poke him in the ribs and ask, more with the small, squinting eyes behind the lenses of his glasses than in the words he muttered around the stem of his pipe—"*War's gut?*"—and Lamian would say, diffidently, cautiously, that it was good.

Riegler was interested only in gold, which he would take back to his gnarled wife when the war ended. Lamian had seen her once, from a distance, when she came to visit. Gold to dazzle her perhaps, which he couldn't do otherwise. Riegler would put it into her rough hands as she lay in bed waiting for him to join her: one after another of those long ingots, as hard and heavy as swollen penises, cast by old Morgenstern over a kerosene lamp in his cubicle above the crematorium.

Should he, too, thrust money, if not ingots, into the hands of this young woman? She probably expected it, and according to the amount would adjust the warmth of her embrace. But this dependence on her whim bothered him, so he decided to postpone paying. "I'll give you the money later, all right?" he asked around his cigarette, watching for an expression of displeasure on her face. There was none. She only gave a jerk of her bare, rounded shoulder. "As you like . . ." she said, closing her eyes.

His eyes went down her masklike face to her shoulders, which were exposed above the blanket and merged, beneath it, into those unseen white hemispheres with their small red buttons. He could see them if he made the effort of going over and lifting the blanket. He got to his feet, undecided whether to do this now, but straightening sent a stab of pain through his stomach.

Only when he cautiously unbent was he reassured: it wasn't that old pain, it was only the pressure of his bladder. He went to relieve it.

By the bathroom door he turned to look at the woman. She was still lying with her eyes closed. From the bathroom came traces of her vapor, her scent. He turned on the light. Yes, you could smell that someone had washed, though the soap, the towels, everything was in its place.

What luxury! Warm, moist air, cleanliness, oxygen in abundance, and there behind the door, in bed, a naked young woman waiting to be of service, any kind of service. If he had lived as the bald man lived, he could have transformed all his postwar years into evenings like this.

The mirror was slightly fogged. Lamian stood on tiptoe to wipe it off with his forearm. Now he could see himself: an egg-shaped head with pendulous bags of skin on either side of the chin, opaque glasses on a long thin nose, giving him the look of a conspirator or a blind man.

He took off the glasses. His eyes squinted, wary of their own reflection. Not like the bald man's eyes, which had peered genially through their lenses as he hung on the shoulder of the curly-haired woman while they spun and danced. The bald man's thick fingers had played above the cleavage of her bottom, and then, before Lamian's very eyes, the bottom emerged, those two snuggly fitted halves where it was so mortally sad to press a part of your body.

WHEN HE RETURNED TO THE BEDROOM, THE WOMAN WAS still in the bed nearer the window. On her side, facing the chair. Her blanket, however, was rumpled. He saw why only when he went around the bed: the blanket had slipped down her body, baring her bosom.

For a moment he thought she had removed it on purpose, to greet him with her femininity exposed, to encourage him because she saw he was indecisive. He was ready to rebuke her in a mocking way. But then he looked more closely at her face and realized from the way its features and eyes had sunk, and from the oblivious gaping of the mouth, that the woman was asleep.

He leaned over to hear her deep, even breathing: she really was sleeping. But before falling asleep, perhaps thrusting out a leg as she drifted off, she had pushed the blanket away, so that it inched off her, leaving her uncovered above the waist.

In the light of the lamp, the bosom now lay as if on exhibit, and was as he had imagined it—on behalf of the bald man— yet unlike what he had remembered. Since the body was on its side, one of the breasts, the right one, pointed at the sheet just along the lower edge of the pillow, which was flattened like a ball deflated. The other breast, unsupported by anything but rib cage and breastbone, rose like a hummock and then, pulled by its own weight, fell toward the trough which separated it from its mate, nipple pointing in the same direction. Both breasts had lost their enticing fruitlike firmness, their feminine roundness; while the squashed one on the right seemed altogether unrecognizable as breast, the triangular droop of the left recalled the udder of an animal—a cow, a goat, or, most aptly, a giant bitch. It wasn't a breast at all, it was a sack for producing and dispensing milk; all it needed was a puppy or little monkey snuggling closer from below to grab the porous tip in its little jaws, then suck the contents in greedy gulps.

In vain was it white, that breast; in vain was it scribbled with faint and delicate light-blue veins; in vain was it soft, pliant, silky smooth to the touch; and in vain did its tip jut as red as the blood which would fill it instantly at a masculine touch, making it gorged and stiff. For this moment of oblivion and abandonment, which had nothing in common with the task of provoking and seducing, made the breast simply a part of the body, any body.

It did not differ from other breasts in any essential way, except that it had been surprised in sleep, out of its usual waking position, which was more familiar, more attractive.

Everything depended on when breasts were seen, on how they were seen. He might have gone into the room and found the woman sleeping with her breasts uncovered, and this would have aroused him because it was unexpected, or because he had anticipated it so vividly that the actual appearance of the breasts could not annul the welling excitement in him.

Should he cover her up? He decided finally not to, since it wasn't cold in the room, nor did he particularly wish to protect her. He didn't want anything to do with her. Yet the sight of her lying there uncovered did affect him, for it canceled so many of his fantasies and enthusiasms, the surges of the blood brought on by unseen or barely seen breasts, by the imagining of them, because that was not the way they really looked, not when they did not try to please and entice, a wish that perhaps still lived in those emaciated prisoners, or at least the wish not to stop pleasing him.

Yet sooner or later they all bored him, every one of them, and as he returned them to Lina, his carpenter's pencil would cross out their numbers on the slip as a sign that he no longer required them, that a new one, a different one, should be found, abandoning the others to their fate in the Arbeitskommando.

He wasn't sorry that this one or that one would soon die because he no longer wanted her and asked for her, just as now he wasn't sorry that this young woman might catch cold if he didn't cover her. Because he saw in them, as in this one now, nothing but flesh, shape and color, which were transient qualities of a fruit bound to spoil. And he used them for his pleasure until they did spoil, just like apples or lemons, which carry in their meat the imminence of rot, though their destruction is still invisible. They are eaten and sucked in the knowledge that if left untouched, they will soon go bad and be useless.

All the women were fruit condemned to rot, tossed in a heap amid the stench of the camp; but then he would appear, the Kapo of the workshop, to grab the best, the soundest ones before the mold and stench got to them. And sink his teeth into their still-healthy tissue and draw out its juice before throwing them on the rubbish heap for the process of destruction to be completed, which would happen with him or without him.

Lechery? He remembered how he took their measure, fingering them with his eyes as they passed on their way to evening roll call, Lina prodding them with curses and blows of her club to step livelier or sometimes to sing. He assessed them, looking for signs of strength and agility, nothing more. Which was why he failed to see, among the green and black triangles on tunics and trouser legs, the single yellow triangle, the Jewish triangle, mark of special degradation. It went by him, just as the blows and curses raining on the prisoners went by him, and their suffering—unless a blow and the ensuing fall and hasty recovery caused a leg or shoulder to spill out of its rags, revealing itself still further, higher up. Or sometimes a breast, shaken free in falling and then resuming its provocative position, nipple forward.

They didn't seem sacks then, those breasts, even though they were, like the breasts of the young woman asleep now in the bed: because for him, in that darkness and stench, they offered the possibility of arousal and of power, which was the only thing in the camp that could bring him exultation. The other power, the power of the club, though he obediently used it, could not make him exult, because he did not wield it with desire—because he had become Kapo Furfa by freezing beneath the coat of ice which Corporal Sommer had put on him, but beneath that ice, beneath the Kapo's insignia and red triangle, he was really Lamian, a Jew with no yellow star sewn on him, whose heart quaked in fear and horror as he beat those to whom he secretly belonged.

All the other beaters and killers, whether they were called Blockführer, Arbeitsführer, or Kapo, were genuine: cravers of blood and wounds and death. They rose to their positions so that their lust for violence could be given free rein. It excited them to break the bones and crush the skulls of the lower beings who had been handed over to them. Venting their fury on these, they became the supermen they had been promised they would be. Lamian was the only false one among them, Kapo not by conviction or impulse, but merely to save his wretched self. He was the only one who beat with teeth clenched and eyelids squeezed shut, screaming to himself to beat them to death as soon as possible, to make their suffering as brief as possible.

He told Riegler that he could obtain twice as much gold for him if Riegler would order Lina to have female prisoners sent into the old toolshed which was next to her barracks. Or did Riegler suggest it to him, having noticed Lamian's hungry glances as the women's disciplinary Arbeitskommando went by? He no longer remembered; it had all happened amid a tension too great for him to recall it accurately; he had felt the desire too sharply, the desire which would be his last, or so it had seemed, because he expected death as soon as the exhausted slave labor was no longer needed. His foray with Riegler and the toolshed and Lina was more an audacious leap into the unknown, into the abyss, than any consequence of premeditated talk and gifts, although the talk and gifts cleared the way—just as this evening's descent to the bar, the ordering of drinks, and conversing with the bony man had all been steps toward a goal, a goal that had entered his mind only hazily when he sat alone in the lobby after supper, watching the young couple at the table beneath the arch, or before, at supper, or even much earlier, back in Subotica, when he spent a similar evening in a similar hotel during his search for Helena Lifka.

And now the young woman who lay naked in a bed in his room, displayed, delivered up to him, almost like those prisoners. Had he wanted, even if unconsciously, to relive one more time that experience of power amid the darkness of death, the camp that no longer existed replaced by the closeness and gloom of the bar, the mixture of black and red with vapors of alcohol and wisps of tobacco smoke, recalling a scene of hell?

He had succeeded, unerring as a sleepwalker, though he made no special effort, only following his instincts. As he had done then—gold, not calculation, was instrumental, gold transformed now into paper banknotes—peacetime riches. In his bed a woman he didn't know, just as he hadn't known the prisoners. A woman indifferent to him, as they had been, and who, also like them, had a life of her own, to which he, until the moment of coupling, had no access. A life filled with her own wants, bound up with other people and the memories of other people, of whom he wasn't one—and yet the bed she lay in was his.

Looking at the young woman as she slept, at the simple, sunken features of her face, her one breast kneaded into a flat bun and the other hanging like a wolf's udder, he perceived all the senselessness of what he had done. It didn't make death any more bearable or meaningful. Selfishness. The selfishness of the dying?

If he had fed those miserable women, or other ones, by bribing Riegler and using him as shield and intermediary, if he hadn't required anything from them in exchange, or required it not by threat but simply as a man long deprived of women, from women long deprived of men, then nothing would have been lost—although it was doubtful that he could have freed himself of threat, that he would have been understood without it, since it was the universal law of the camp, the camp's very heartblood, the air it breathed.

A madness that could be withstood only by adapting: the SS men, convinced of their duty and right to plunder the living flesh thrust in front of them, thrust before their booted feet and tapping whips. And the Kapos, condemned to death like the rest of that great heap of flesh, but allowed to postpone their death by hastening it for others. It had been he or the Stark brothers. More precisely: he and the Stark brothers together, the brothers together, the brothers first, then he.

If he hadn't obeyed Rapportführer Novak, taking up the rake and then, transfixed by their gaping, wheezing mouths, their rolling eyes, and the grayish water they spat as their bleeding fingers clutched at the clayey bank—used the rake to push away the Starks whenever one of them swam to the edge of the lime pit—if he hadn't obeyed, he would have been pushed into the pit himself, would have been drowned that winter of 1942, but the Starks would have drowned, too, with the assistance of some other prisoner, who as a reward for his proven steadiness of nerve and will would have been taken on as a corpse carrier instead of Lamian. Perhaps he and not Lamian would have stolen the sweater, later, from the corpse and put it on to protect himself from the cold, and because of that Corporal Sommer would have poured a pail of water over him instead of Lamian, and ordered him to stand motionless on the parade ground until evening. And if he had been able to endure standing there frozen for half a winter's day, Riegler would have noticed him and chosen him as Kapo, which would have enabled the prisoner to live a while longer, and if he had been exceptionally lucky and set up a connection for Riegler with Morgenstern in Crematorium 4, then perhaps Riegler would have taken him with the column when the camp was abandoned, so that perhaps this other prisoner would now be standing and bending over a naked young woman as she slept.

Therefore this, both then and now, was the reward for un-flagging vitality, for animal endurance: this unclad woman, sub-ject to his will. A woman who, with her hanging, dog's breast, held no attraction for him.

He stopped looking at her, moved away, turned to the center of the room, but he could still see her as she lay with her mouth half open, her breasts exposed to the light of the lamp.

He went to the light switch, turned it off. Darkness. Would she be awakened by the darkness? He listened but could hear nothing, not even her breathing; no rustle of stirring or turning over. He waited awhile, then again approached her, on tiptoe, trying not to trip on anything, which wasn't difficult, since in the shafts of light from the street the room had quickly begun to reveal its familiar forms.

The street was quietly alive, with a soft, even hum like a distant fountain; the occasional roar of a motorbike passing by; the bell of a streetcar from the direction of the station—or per-haps it was a telephone, since it was too late for streetcars? But no sound came from the woman. Her face, now in shadow, still lay with eyes closed, collapsed into those simple features, while her breasts were not even visible in the deeper shadow behind the mounded blanket.

This stripped the woman of his final shred of interest in her. He was finished with her, even in his thoughts, just as before, in the camp, he would conclude after lying with women in the toolshed that they now bored him. He had only to make this known to Lina, along with some new present—fine linen or a bottle of French perfume—pushing it through the opening in the wall along with the note on which the prisoner's number was written in the Blockelteste's hand, now crossed out by his.

The next day he would wait for a new woman, there in the silence of the toolshed, standing in the darkness as he now stood listening to the street noises. The shout of a male voice, two syllables, like a scream. Lamian went to the window. Beyond it there was also darkness, but darkness nibbled away from below by a row of streetlamps, whose shielded bulbs made a rosy haze up to the third floor of the hotel.

The window across the way was no longer lit, nor were any of the windows near it; the people in the apartments were sleeping, having taken off their shoes and clothes and put them away until the next day, confident they would be getting back into them. They did exactly what he had imagined people doing, during those nights in the camp when he was kept awake by the fear that the SS would come for him with their flashlights and take him away. He had listened to the calls of the guards and tried, in his imagination, to escape beyond their reach, into places that were not camps but villages and towns, into buildings such as the one he was looking at now.

It had been difficult to quell his panic and keep madness at bay; he had had to strain to picture those normal, ordinary houses in normal, ordinary communities not fenced off with barbed wire. It seemed incredible that such houses could exist, and that inside them people lay in their beds, embracing sleep with the knowledge that in the morning they would put on their clothes and shoes and go wherever they needed or wished to go. It seemed fantastic, even more fantastic than the food, which he also imagined when he went to bed as ravenous as a wild beast, and when fear of the SS bursting in did not prevent him from conjuring up various dishes—good, juicy vegetables with big, thick pieces of juicy meat—conjuring so well, his tongue and palate tingled.

Later, when he became a Kapo and did not have to fear flashlights bursting in on him unexpectedly, he began to imagine another nocturnal goal: not sleep followed by a tomorrow where you could get up and dress and go wherever you wanted, but fornicating.

STANDING IN THE MIDDLE OF THE ROOM. HE SHOULD LIE down and sleep, even if only in that second, empty bed. But in order to lie down and sleep he first had to undress, and the ritual of undressing would have reminded him too much of those nocturnal camp fantasies about undressing and going to bed with a guaranteed tomorrow. Fantasies clouded by sins and misdeeds. Binding him, leaving him unprepared to leap out and flee. As if the bed would shackle him.

He considered the armchair. But it repelled him by its nearness to the bed, to the woman in it, whom he had seen and thought about long enough. He went to the other chair, away from the woman, and sat down in it.

Now he was facing the blank wall above the two beds, which was like a dim, yellowish sky on which the reflections of the streetlights flickered in place of stars—because the wind, unseen and imperceptible in here, was rocking the lamps within their protective globes, lifting and dropping them.

Reminding him of the old toolshed, with the angular, pointed, rounded shapes of rusting machines and their parts against the background of plank walls, which despite the boarded-up windows shone a faint yellow. Standing there or sitting on something, tired after lifting the heavy iron with which he hid the space beneath the plank floor hollowed out for Riegler's gold, his reward for a job well done. In shadow and calm, isolated from the chain of killing, invisible and unobserved, abandoned entirely to the senses.

All around him silence, as in this nighttime hotel room, with its echoes from the street—sounds that merged into a uniform hum of thousands of lives crowded together in an enclosed space, the sighing, wheezing, moaning, praying, raling—like a distant waterfall, interrupted from time to time by the calls of the guards in both the inner and outer rings, with their watchtowers and machine guns and searchlights that were on all night, keeping an eye on every inch of the bare, burnt earth trampled by the feet of thousands of prisoners.

The earth was as foul as the feet that trampled it; it reeked of boots soaked with sweat and the fluids of the latrines. Over it flitted plump, furry rats, nourished by the steady harvest of corpses that collected in the cubicles of the prison blocks, around the toilets and behind the barracks, where a nose, ear, or hunk of soft flesh could be bitten off before the gravediggers loaded the cadaver onto the cart like a log and carried it off to the pyres. The whole camp stank of corpses, decay, disease; but Lamian stood or sat there in his hiding place, still alive and listening to the hum of the prisoners who were left alive, the sounds of the guards and the rats, who would scurry in the toolshed as well, if he was still for a moment. Sometimes they scampered over him, thinking he was yet another corpse; they would try to crawl up his pant leg to bite off a chunk of flesh. He would give them a little kick to drive them away, and if they annoyed him by persisting, he would pounce on one of them, onto that firm, living, healthy flesh covered with short, bristly fur, try to catch it and with a single blow smash it against the wall, killing it, punishing it.

But the rats were always quicker, and his fingers would feel only for an instant the dry, bristly fur, and beneath it the warm, living flesh. Like touching something wondrous and awful at the same time, something whose strength, if touched, could imbue him with speed and health, the ability to strike and run, the freedom to slip through all barriers, escape from the camp whenever he wanted to—yet at the same time it was repellent, diseased, it made the hand draw back, the jaws clench, the teeth grit.

In his angry and fearful hands he wanted, too, a piece of woman, also living flesh, covered with hair in the right places, warm and squirming and arousing the urge to squeeze it to death and then drop it in disgust. Amid that desolation and the stink of the dead he wanted to confront his own living opposite, a counterweight to oppose him and affirm him by its opposition; so morning and evening he began to watch Lina's column of prisoners, and when Riegler observed this and let him know he wouldn't stand in his way, the dream conquered shame and created in his mind, scene by scene, a stream of women who came to his embrace.

Lamian began making the dream a reality. He redoubled his pressure on Morgenstern to sell him whatever plundered gold he didn't hand over to Poldi, Eltester of the corpse carriers, and in return he promised a daily ration of forty cigarettes and a bottle of the best wine from the Kanada. He informed Riegler of the imminent increase in the flow of ingots, and at the same time began, in Riegler's presence, to give Lina and her clerk Berta silk underwear and blouses, gold jewelry, and creams from the lavish daily shipments from Hungary. Then, when he brought Riegler's gold to the old toolshed to hide it, he would steal some of the time needed for hiding and use it to clear off the dilapidated old locksmith's workbench, which was covered with scrap iron, a huge rusty vise poking up in its midst. From the wall facing the adjoining barracks he removed a bent anvil and two boxes of worn augers, then put everything back in place, remembering how much time had been necessary. From Poldi he acquired a mat and hid it beneath the workbench. He bought plane fuel from Sergei the Russian and exchanged it for candles with Kromholz at the storehouse. With the aid of a file and pliers he fashioned some bent rods into legs on which to set the tin pot over a candle. In the woodworking shop he bartered antimange ointment obtained from Binder the nurse for some boards cut to measure, then took them to the toolshed and slapped together a bench and some shutters for the windows, nailing them up and plugging the cracks around them with rags. He ran to Varminsky with the agreed-upon roses and boxes of powder that Varminsky bestowed on his daughters and his mistresses in the village, and also promised to have half a quart of milk waiting for him every day, in a bottle hidden behind the door of the blacksmith's shop. With the cook in the SS kitchen he arranged regular deliveries of bread, butter, and ham in return for the morphine Binder would bring him. Then, under the floorboards which he had sawed through and fitted back into place, he dug a spacious cache for the food. Taking a gift to Lina and a separate one for her Stubenelteste, he informed her that he would cut through the wall between the toolshed and her cubicle. For two days he worked on it, carefully removing the bricks from the wall, hiding them among the old tools, and putting boards in their place. With Lina he agreed upon a day and hour when the first two prisoners—two, so he could choose—would be kept behind in the barracks, supposedly to rest. Their clothes taken as security, they would then be moved to her cubicle, where after her signal and his answering knock she would take down the false wall and wait for him to remove the anvil on the other side before sending them over into the toolshed.

Then, finally, he would greet them, also naked; knife stuck in the workbench by the lighted candle which was wedged in a hole he'd made by banging out a knot; the mat spread out in the background. He waited for the signal, answered it, then uncovered the opening and with eager eyes watched first one and then the other prisoner come toward him from the hole on all fours, stripped naked: rats, but the kind that didn't run, because they were human, because they weren't, like animals, ruled by instinct, but by reason, knowledge, experience. So when he grabbed for them, they wouldn't flee helter-skelter with no fear of death, like the rats, to whom death was unknown. These two women knew about death and where it came from. From hunger and disobedience, from the ill temper of those in power, that power which had made them prisoners of this camp, bringing them from measureless distances, from the other end of the continent, in long trains. They had agreed to board the trains, for unlike the rats they possessed reason and subordinated themselves to its explanations, and to the trap conceived by the SS, who scorned the weakness of the non-rats, of reasoning humanity. And now, in that part of the day when all the other prisoners were at work, backs breaking under burdens and blows, in this hiding place behind the boarded-up windows of a long-abandoned toolshed, a trap was being used—by Kapo Furfa.

One by one he pulled them into the light of the candle, then sat them on the bench to place mouthfuls and swallows in their mouths, in return demanding that they kiss him, put their breasts against him, spread their thighs—do everything which is done for a man only willingly. And he didn't care how much that willingness cost them, he exulted in it, this obedience that went against all instinct, just as the SS men exulted when they felt their pulsing violence crush the instincts of the obedient millions beneath them.

But now, remembering those mute hours of rat-catching, he thought about what it had cost them. Pulling in his neck and tightly shutting his eyes, he relived what he had thought and felt then, in the camp, as he beat the prisoners under his command to make them work faster, first the corpse carriers and later the craftsmen in the barracks workshops when they didn't deliver all that Riegler demanded. Their suffering didn't excite him, because his relationship to them was rational: by beating them and taking away part of their food he was only prolonging his own life. But his relationship to the women in the toolshed was mad, just as the SS were mad, delighting in the agony they caused, wallowing in it, falling on their knees before it and worshiping in the darkness of their perverted minds.

He wished now that he hadn't been like that. But he had been, for he remembered the prisoners in the toolshed, not their individual shapes and movements but in general, the ways they were the same, their rigidity, the glassiness of their eyes, the cold sweat on their bodies, the bitter smell that came from their mouths. He felt the chill that spread beneath their skin, into their flesh, their nerves, their minds, as they feverishly calculated gain and loss, obligation and desire, death and life.

And in the depths of their minds he saw himself: naked, thin as a corpse, covered with scars and scabs, terrified eyes, trembling hands, and that swollen member which he shoved up them, proud of its readiness and stiffness, its stiffness sustained by the extra food he purchased at the Kanada with valuables confiscated from Jews who just arrived on the trains and had not yet been taken to the gas chambers. He was also proud that his member was uncircumcised. This meant nothing to them but much to him, because by showing them it was uncircumcised he countered any suspicion that he was a Jew. Because even though he was already Furfa, killer of the Stark brothers and so many other Jews, it was only now, finally, that he no longer flinched as he inflicted pain—in fact, he enjoyed it, and proved his enjoyment by the rising of his unspoiled member.

At that moment of the day he turned into an SS man, not caring what it cost the women who submitted. Because, like the SS men, he considered them only meat which was condemned to spoil—and because the women thought he was an SS man, this lecher whose clutches they had fallen into when pushed from Blockelteste Lina's cubicle through the hole beneath her table and into the abandoned toolshed next door. For no one else, certainly not a prisoner, even a Kapo, had the power to take them off work and have them stripped naked and shoved into the adjoining building. And he spoke German with them, not the prisoners' jargon, though he knew that his skeletal thinness gave him away, along with his shaved head, unwashed odor, the sores and scars all over his skin. He left them to puzzle over this contradiction when they returned to the barracks and examined, alone or together, their improbable experience in the toolshed.

He knew that the experience would stay there, among them, and not spread beyond their immediate circle—which might be dangerous for him—because within that circle a prisoner was isolated more securely than by barbed wire: by the knowledge shared with her masters that she was meat condemned to spoil and die, meat without speech, without a voice, without a name, without a will, without a mind.

He trapped them through their reason and at the same time confirmed his belief that they had none, just as he made them embrace him without acknowledging the embrace, not allowing that it could be anything but extorted, just as the SS believed that their authority could exist only through extortion.

But was that really true? He tried to recall some exception in the procession of faces and bodies, identical, united in their expression; he searched for some sign of reciprocation, collusion, but found none. He wasn't sure. Perhaps he didn't remember because, in his lust, he hadn't paid attention.

But even before the camps, before he even knew the camps existed, when he found himself in bed with Branka Frank, he had stifled her voice, her words, denied her passion, suppressed her quiverings of pleasure—thought them excessive and un-healthy, whereas in fact it had been his instincts which were unhealthy, the instincts of a future Kapo.

He looked at the wall and saw himself naked, his uncircum-cised penis poised as he hopped about on straddling, bent legs, flapping his arms in a kind of war dance—a dance unlike those dances in Bjelovar, which he had taught himself—terrifying women who were already terrified, frozen in terror. In that small private darkness of his, rent by the light of a candle, in a camp that was grinding and crushing him, too, him the all-powerful, he saw himself playing the role of fate, as if the women's fate had not already been decided without him and he were only now deciding it.

All he was deciding was a few days' delay, by agreement with Blockelteste Lina through the intercession of Arbeitsführer Riegler; he was deciding those few extra mouthfuls and swallows, which would prolong their life and thus their torment. Thrusting flesh into flesh a few times, until his penis, pulled from them, spurted between their thighs.

This dance of his penis, performed among the dead, among deaf-mutes, among people gone mad, and women who were nothing but meat doomed to perish. Which he made use of. Feeling nothing for him, not even hate. His dance had banished hate—not theirs, the prisoners' hate, but the hate which sifted in from the darkness surrounding the darkness of the locked toolshed rent by the light of a candle. Sifted in from slogging through icy water, from the hunger, from the barbed wire, from the calling of the guards in watchtowers who protected the darkness within the wires.

Hatred of Gabelić, who stood with legs apart, whip tapping against the leather of his booted calf, and who would recognize him. Hatred of the Ustaši, of the executioners, the SS, his own hatred of himself and his misery, a misery preordained by those childhood shadows who stole into his parents' apartment, into that Jewish house in Bjelovar.

He crushed hatred with hatred, avenged hatred with hatred, avenged himself on these women, knowing that they, too, would stand in line to hate if they knew who he was, not an SS man or even Kapo Furfa, but Lamian the Jew, afraid of the dark.

He drove away his timorous Jewishness by the dance of his erect penis, uncircumcised to warn them against hating. He avenged himself on Zita, who would have seen through him had she granted him her favors, on Branka, who probably saw through him—sensed, during those conversations which flowed between them like a river, that he was a secret member of the same tribe. As he had always been able to sense it when he came across one, like that patron in the café who sat at a nearby table and slouchingly ordered coffee and beer.

They were all his enemies, everyone was his enemy; and so he terrified them and tortured them, as they had done to him; he danced before them naked, covered with scabs and scars, in that tiny section of the camp which he had conquered by bludgeoning and grasping, in that tiny isolation amid the vast isolation of the camp.

But not isolated enough. One morning, Blockelteste Lina asked him with a leer, "How's the little Jewess doing for you?" and his separate darkness collapsed into the greater darkness of the camp, for suddenly it turned out that without knowing it he had terrorized one who was the same as he. Or had he known?

He remembered her tears; they were the only thing he noticed about her, even though others had shed tears, some secretly and some openly, as he made them submit. He remembered a languid white body and a longish head with light, strawlike hair. Blue saucer eyes, from which the tears flowed like water from a spring; the big lips and protruding white teeth that made her resemble a clown. But now, from that face, that figure, emerged another face and figure: he himself, naked, with his egg-shaped head and thin, pointed nose; the even stubble of his cropped head; the bared teeth of the terrorizer, mocking and derisive. A comic imitation of an SS superman, jumping about and waving his arms to frighten.

But in prisoner Helena Lifka fear had already been planted—the fear of her Jewishness, just as it was planted in him that first day when the shadows fell across the threshold of the Jewish house in Bjelovar, shadows like the ones that once fell on her, and never left her, just as his never left him. He had threatened someone who was already threatened, acted out what had already been acted out. The clown wasn't she, as it had seemed to him then, but he.

He squirmed in his chair, raised his hands to his face, to rip off that clown's mask. But his fingers clutched only his own flesh, because the clown was a bowed, aging Jew who once, in a former life, danced in front of Helena Lifka, and perhaps the reason she wept was that she saw he was a clown, this wretch who danced as frightened as she was in the darkness rent by the flame of a candle, separated from the vaster darkness of the camp by wooden shutters and rags stripped from the bodies of dead prisoners.

Had she known? That was all that interested him now, only she. As if she had the answers to all the questions he had asked himself over the years. He sat and tried to recall her face more clearly—not her face as it was now, purplish and puffy, the face forced on him by this morning's encounter, but as it was then, white, with saucerlike blue eyes and close-cropped hair. But the face he was struggling to distill began to melt into other faces, of the women prisoners who had passed through the old tool-shed.

Pointed cheekbones beneath taut, pale skin. Solemn brown eyes whose look carried some intention, a question perhaps. A dark, African-slim face with huge, black, dull eyes, the eyes of a child. A coppery face with black hair, twisted black eyebrows, and sensual lips. A pink face with a long straight nose and ter-rified blue eyes. A childish oval with defiant twitches around the puckered lips. A stern, cadaverous head with an avid expression.

They all mixed together, revolving around him as if on a wheel turned by an invisible hand, making him dizzier and dizzier, until he began to fall and his fingers clutched at some support.

He found it in the soft fabric of the armchair. He sat slumped back, lips and chin wet with drool, the room around him half-visible in the dawn light that was filtering through the windows.

PULLING HIMSELF TOGETHER, HE LOOKED AROUND. A NEW day. As he rubbed his face, his sprouting beard crackled beneath his fingers. Unbuttoning his shirt, he got to his feet, lost his balance, sat down again. Then rose more carefully, steadily, and went over to the window.

The sky above the roofs was gray, either from clouds or the low angle of the sun. But across the way, a little lower down, a window now shone with yellow electric light, that window, but the old man was nowhere to be seen. Perhaps he had turned on the light and gone to wash.

Lamian looked at his watch: ten to seven already. But in October, late October, daylight came late. He turned. The woman he had brought to the room last night was lying on her stomach and wrapped in the blanket, which was a little above her waist, revealing a smooth, flat back in place of those sacklike breasts. The mound of her head was strewn with long hair, a snakelike arm wrapped around it, probably placed there when it began to grow light, to shield her eyes. Strange, that he hadn't heard her move. He may have been asleep for hours.

He went to the bathroom and relieved himself, and washed his hands and face, once more feeling the bristle of whiskers and thinking that he ought to shave. But he had nothing to shave with. He looked at his reflection, made out little white needles sprinkled like flour over the egg-shaped oval: the false, clownish face of a swindler.

Turning away from it, he went back into the bedroom and over to the window again. Stood in front of the glass and looked at the window across the street, one floor below his. The light was still on. He saw the table, part of the chair back, and by moving slightly to the left again saw the cupboard with a few objects on it. The man was nowhere to be seen. Lamian lit a cigarette, taking care to strike the match quietly, and waited.

Now and then from the street the clatter of some vehicle reached his ears, or a door slamming. He felt like opening the window to look out, but refrained, not wanting to disturb the young woman's sleep. Not wanting to face her awake. He didn't know what he would say to her and didn't have the strength to think about it, to think up some line of conversation.

He wanted to leave before she woke up. But wasn't sure he should leave her alone in a room that wasn't hers. She would be disoriented on waking and not know whether to leave or wait for him to return. That wouldn't suit his purposes in the least. Should he leave a note for her? A note and some money?

A whiteness appearing on the next floor down, and moving. It was the gray hair of the old man, who had now seated himself at the table. His head, that broad, fleshy head with its white mantle, settled down in the frame of the window, then ceased to move. Below it, on the table, two hands were clasped in a bulging, faintly violet mound.

Lamian howled within. Anything but that, the Mussulman's repose, the calm before death, the treacherous, unthinking calm of surrender. It assailed him like poison gas seeping from across the way—while inside the room he was threatened by the breathing of the woman, which any moment might turn from sleeping to wakeful breathing and then speech, forcing him to speak as well. To tell her why he hadn't lain with her. To admit his impotence, his lack of interest. Or describe her breasts and how they had been uncovered, hanging like sacks and spoiling her for him. Spoiling all the women he had ever had, spoiling the dances in the old toolshed at Auschwitz, and the memory, too, of Helena

Lifka, who had been reduced to tears by his dance. Who had felt sorry for herself and perhaps—perhaps—even for him.

The abyss was pulling him, this window in front of him, which he could open and hurl himself through before the woman woke and managed to prevent him. Eluding Helena Lifka and her song of hunger, her cries of terror. Her rolling eyes, bulging, recalling the eyes of the Stark brothers as he shoved them beneath the chalky water with his rake, unwilling to throw himself in, too, and be swallowed with them. Just as he didn't want to throw himself in now, but instead to shove in someone else—that gray head, those folded, purplish hands, that Mussulman, whom even in the horror of recognition he had to push into the abyss, because on that depended his own survival to the next moment.

BACK IN BOGDAN ZIMONJIĆ STREET HE SUCCUMBED TO the temptation to seek out the doorway he had tested during yesterday's wait, and from there to continue watching the house with the two close-set windows. But impatience wrenched him out of waiting; he went straight up to the house.

Climbed the first two steps—quite steep, he realized after the suddenness of both the movement and his decision made him stumble slightly, so that he had to brace himself against the wall beneath the shell of the doorbell casing, moving his hand from the wall only to reach for the long, flat handle of tarnished steel. He pressed it, but it turned downward only slightly before resisting firmly. As he had expected, the door was locked.

He felt relieved that the delay he had renounced was nevertheless granted him. But his relief was fleeting; he felt exposed there on top of the stairs, as if he had been tied to a post in punishment.

He forced himself to lift his hand and press the button of the doorbell. No ring could be heard. He waited, doubting that any response would come, now hoping that he'd failed to make the electrical connection, and now preparing himself for the disappointment that would come over him if the bell really did go unheard—until suddenly, without being warned by the sound of anyone approaching, he was startled by the scrape of a key in the lock right in front of his face.

The door began to tremble, as if being separated from its frame for the first time, then it opened slowly, in fits and starts, until finally the light from the street fell on the face of the woman he had observed and followed the previous day.

"Good morning," he began, feeling his heart pound as he lifted his hat. "Excuse me for disturbing you. It's a bit early," he said appeasingly, seeing the reproach in her faded blue eyes framed by glasses—she hadn't worn them yesterday. Then heard her say "Yes?" in a surprisingly high-pitched, childish voice, puzzled.

"My name is Lamian," he said firmly, suppressing his agitation. "And you, I assume, are Helena Lifka?"

She started noticeably at his question, moving her head back a bit, and gave an unexpected answer, "No, I'm not."

"You're not?" he repeated in disbelief. "How can that be?" Shooting a quick glance past the doorbell to the rectangular number plate, which he couldn't possibly have read incorrectly. He confirmed that; no, he hadn't. "Doesn't Helena Lifka live here?"

The woman hesitated, and he had the impression that she was thinking something over, as if it was difficult or forbidden for her to acknowledge the fact he had presented to her.

"She did live here," she said, with the emphasis on *did*, which sounded like an evasion, but not a very decisive one, as if she wanted to gain time.

"Wait," he said, tensing. "It's on account of you that I came to Zagreb. Because I wanted to talk to you, no other reason. I'll explain everything to you."

He shifted his glance from her face to the darkness behind it, hoping to be allowed in. And, once inside, to coax this woman into the frankness she was trying to deny him, because she still did not know who he was.

"May I come in?"

She looked at him without altering her expression of indecision and unease. Her lips were pursed and disapproving; her eyes squinted distrustfully from behind her glasses.

But despite the hostility in her face, the door opened more, to reveal the woman's entire form, in a long dark housedress bulging at the waist with layers of undergarments. She moved back a step or two, then said, reluctantly, "Come in."

Following her inside, he saw a gloomy hallway, at the end of which, above gray double doors, shone a decorative semicircle made of small, multicolored panes of glass. Behind him, the door closed and the key turned in the lock, a sign that he had been irrevocably admitted. He took a step forward.

But the woman said, "Wait," and her long dress fluttered as she went by him and moved farther down the hallway, where Lamian now saw a side door before the door with the glass semicircle above it. She stopped in front of this side door and opened it, and motioned him to follow.

He found himself in a dim room without windows, doors open on both left and right. Through the door on the right he could see heavy dark bedroom furniture, and through the one on the left an oilcloth-covered table beneath a jumble of dishes, and, beyond the table with the dishes, a stove and a window. Leaving the door ajar, the woman turned left and again motioned him to follow. He fell in behind her and entered the crowded, old-fashioned kitchen. An orange-leafed plant outside the window leaned against it like the rusty beard of a giant.

"Sit down," said the woman, pointing to one of two chairs pulled up to the table. Lamian promptly obeyed, laying his hat, which he had taken off, on a stool behind the door.

She herself remained motionless for a moment, watching him take a seat. Then she began transferring the dishes from the table to the stove in front of the window, one dish at a time. He watched her move back and forth, that heavy body in the stiff housedress; it seemed to him that she was dragging things out intentionally while she thought about what approach to take with him now.

When all the dishes had been removed and the table stood empty, she went over to the bulky, white cupboard that stretched from the door to the window. She opened a drawer and took out a cloth which she used to wipe the table, then put it back and returned to the table, standing with her back to the window and hesitating before finally sitting down in the chair across from Lamian.

They looked at each other for a moment, he concentrating on her features, looking for the ones he remembered, she wearing an inscrutable, mistrustful expression. "You knew Helena Lifka?" she was nonetheless first to say, as if her patience had worn thin.

He nodded, and decided to be direct. "Unfortunately, I can't brag about our acquaintance. Or you, either. We know each other from Auschwitz, you and I, that's where." The excitement brought on by his words stifled him, so he paused for breath. "You remember Kapo Furfa?" He peered into her eyes searchingly, desperately. "Kapo of the workshop. Well, that's me."

He expected her to leap up or cry out, but she seemed to have herself under control. She only squinted, as if to see him more distinctly, then sat back in her chair so that the chair creaked. "I wasn't at Auschwitz or any other camp," she stated firmly, determined not to give in to him, "and I've already told you, I'm not Helena Lifka."

He didn't believe a word of it, but was disconcerted by the steadiness of her denial. Apparently she believed she could hold out. "What do you mean, you aren't!" he cried, impatient. "Who are you, then?"

"I'm Julia Milčec," she said calmly, putting her hands together on the table and leaning toward him. "Helena's cousin. Her mother and mine were sisters."

Still he didn't believe her, but he was shaken by her calm. "Where's Helena Lifka, then?" he muttered.

Her gaze dropped to the table, as if the question embarrassed her. Then she looked up, and he saw that her eyes were clouded behind her glasses. "Helena is dead," she said, her voice barely audible. "She died in May of this year."

This statement stunned him. Was the woman in front of him lying? "What do you mean, she died?" He was tongue-tied. "What did she die of?"

"She died of cancer," the woman replied, definite, collected. "Cancer of the liver. She fell ill in March and was laid up for two months. There was nothing they could do. She suffered terribly." She took off her glasses and put them carelessly on the table, so that they lay askew. With one hand she put them right, lenses resting on their frames; with the other she shielded her eyes. But she didn't cry.

Lamian looked at her intently, trying to get behind her defenses. If she was lying, he thought, then it was a gross falsehood; more than gross, illegal, for to lie about death was a matter of fraud, punishable by law and society. Was it possible she was willing to go to such lengths?

"Do you have anything about her death in writing?" He wanted to challenge the deceit, if that's what it was.

She took her hand from her face and looked at him in surprise, large blue eyes widening like saucers, but she answered quite calmly, "Of course I have. I buried her."

They looked at each other steadily, looks crossing like swords. Lamian became conscious of his dark glasses, which gave him the advantage of a shield.

Suddenly the woman stood up and pushed back her chair in seeming impatience. She went around the table, took her glasses from it, and left the kitchen. He heard her banging things, looking through them. He sat facing the window, which was no longer blocked by her head, so that the view of the garden was full, with its trees and shrubs and yellowing leaves.

Finally she came back, glasses on her nose. Going to the head of the table, she gave him a sharp look and unfolded a sheet of paper, which she proceeded to drop, almost throw, so that it fluttered momentarily before coming to rest on the oilcloth.

With a searching hunger he focused his attention on it. Read the name: Helena Lifka. Read the date of death: May 18, 1983. The place of death: Zagreb. The date of birth: February 13, 1925. The place of birth: Subotica. Then he returned to the name and surname. Still the same. He raised his glance to the issuing agency: Socialist Republic of Croatia, Municipality of Zagreb. Then the title of the document: Death Certificate. And he read the date of death once again.

He could find nothing suspicious, nothing dubious. And yet he believed, more now than before, that the woman sitting across the table was lying, that she really was Helena Lifka. Without looking at her, so that even in the shadows behind the dark lenses of his glasses she couldn't see his eyes, he folded the certificate twice but didn't give it back, instead lay his hand on it so that she couldn't take it away. Only then did he look at the woman's face.

The expression that met his glance was surprisingly transparent; and more youthful than a moment before, than especially the previous day, when he had the impression that her real face was hidden behind the crust of old age.

"Do you have any photographs from your youth?" he asked.

This new request—showing continued mistrust—caused a frown that wrinkled the skin between her pale eyebrows and the sharply etched lines by her broad, bluish lips. But she quickly shrugged her shoulders, stood up as she had the first time, went around the table, and disappeared.

This time she took longer rummaging behind him some-where—perhaps, judging by how muffled the sounds were, in that second room with the dark, heavy furniture. She was open-ing drawers and boxes; that much he could follow by ear, care-fully, discreetly, without turning his head to give her any reason to think he was spying. He looked fixedly at the garden, the autumn colors of the vegetation outside the window.

She returned carrying a small bundle. She sat opposite him again, and then laid out photographs of various sizes and unequal clarity, like cards for a game of solitaire, on the oilcloth in front of him, taking care that they were straight, correcting their position.

A faded photograph showing two women and two children, one considerably younger than the other but both with bangs cut to mid-forehead. "This is my mother and her sister Maria, and the two of us here, me ten years old and Helena three," she said, tapping a fingernail on each child's head. A clear photo-graph in half-profile of a pretty girl with long hair, wearing a dark dress with an embroidered white collar: "My graduation picture, 1937." A group snapshot of swimmers, with a lot of mustached men in dark shorts and singlets, some women in long, voluminous bathing suits, and a flock of scantily clad children. She leaned over and tapped two indistinct forms among them: "Lake Palić, well before the war. That's Helena, and me next to her." A photo of two girls hugging each other and laughing, eyes straight at the camera. "Helena and me, here in Zagreb, 1939."

His gaze fastened on this last picture. Yes, that was Helena Lifka, those big eyes, the straight fleshy nose, broad lips open to reveal long, slightly protruding teeth. The other, with her round head, thin lips, and short snub nose, was also familiar, and when he raised his eyes, he found himself before the features of the same girl, now blurred and crisscrossed with wrinkles.

"And this is . . . you?" He pointed doubtfully at the second girl, who was older, more mature than the first.

The woman in front of him looked at the photograph and nodded.

"And this is Helena?"

Again she nodded.

"And she's really dead?"

"Yes!"

"When did she die?"

"In May of this year, I told you. The eighteenth of May."

The eighteenth of May, he calculated to himself. Somewhere around that date he had gone in search of her, traveling to Subotica, perhaps asking for her address at the police station on the very day of her death, or a few days earlier, so that if he had gone straight to Zagreb from Subotica, he might still have found her alive.

This error, this fatal mistake in his quest, the hesitation to go on because he hadn't foreseen that interrupting it or postponing it might cancel it for good, destroying his only chance to confront Helena Lifka while she was still alive—such unbelievable carelessness in so important a matter made him believe for the first time that what the woman said was indeed true: Helena Lifka was dead, and he had come too late.

"Do you believe me now?" the woman across from him spoke up, as if reading his mind.

Looking at her now, he was convinced he had been wrong to link her face, with its yellowish skin, thin lips, and snub nose, to the face of Helena Lifka. He nodded.

"Did you know her well?" she continued to question him. He frowned involuntarily, not wanting to talk any further about his defeat. Yet he owed her an explanation now, since she had given him everything he needed, even though she had never seen him before.

"From the camps, as I said. For a short time in the fall of 1944, at Auschwitz, when tons of valuable things, food, too, started to flood in with the daily shipments of inmates. As an older prisoner and the Arbeitsleiter of some workshops, I was able to give her a few things, that's all."

"She never mentioned you to me," said the woman, peering at him closely, but with no sign of disbelief. "She generally didn't talk about the camps. When I'd ask her—and after we started living together, I would sometimes—she'd always answer, 'It's better if you don't know.' That was her philosophy of life." She shrugged. "Avoid everything that's unpleasant and gloomy. She always tried to emphasize the bright side of things, even when she was younger, even as a little girl."

"Oh?" said Lamian, amazed. Though he had never considered what Helena Lifka's outlook might be like, her tears had given him the opposite impression—that she was prone to despair and hopelessness. "Naturally," he corrected himself, "I couldn't have known that side of her. Everything was so horrible there."

"Were you in the camps long?"

"From the beginning of the war. First in Jasenovac, then after 1942 in Auschwitz." It seemed unavoidable that now he should ask, "And you?" Then he remembered. "Oh, yes, you said you weren't. But how did you get out of it, if you're Helena's cousin . . ."

He didn't finish the sentence, but she did, "You mean, as a Jew?" Then she asked him, "Are you Jewish?"

To this he replied with a shrug, and for the second time in his life answered, as he had once answered Nahmijas, without hesitation, "A baptized Jew, first generation. Which didn't save me from the camps."

"I'm Jewish by birth, like Helena," Julia Milčec informed him. "But I married a Croat, a Catholic, here in Zagreb just before the war, and that saved me. But it drove my poor husband to an early grave, because under the Ustaši he had to hide the fact that I was a Jew, and he was a government official, in the tax office. He was afraid we'd be discovered, so he kept me locked up as if I were in prison, did all the shopping himself, even went to meetings for me whenever I was called, and to medical examinations, claiming I was bedridden and ill and couldn't have any visitors, not even the doctor. He fell apart, went downhill. His heart gave out, and he never recovered; he died before he was even fifty."

"But you survived," added Lamian, though he felt it might be taken as a reproach.

She only nodded pensively. "Yes, maybe I suffered less because I didn't see or hear a thing, sitting locked up within these four walls while he, poor man, had to pretend he supported the regime, and then after the war had to justify his conduct. They barely believed that he had done it all for me, to protect me. We didn't have children, even, so as not to make life any more difficult for us, which meant that after he died, I was all alone. All the rest of my family perished in the camps during the war: Mama, Papa, my sisters and brothers-in-law. Helena was the only one left. She came back, but even with her I only had these three or four years together, after she came from Subotica and moved in with me."

They fell silent. Lamian tried to imagine them, the two women, aged and alone in this solitary house.

"And no one from her family, your cousin's, was left alive?"

The woman shook her head. "No one. Father, mother, brother, aunts, uncles—all taken away and killed." She sighed. "And she never recovered from it, either, even though she tried to forget and talk only about nice things: good books, films, the nice-looking young people she'd see in the street. She never married." She looked at Lamian inquiringly, as if to see whether this information meant anything more to him than a fact. But he shook his head to let her know there was nothing to worry about, and she went on: "She said she didn't want to start a family because she'd never be able to bear losing someone by violence again."

She fell silent. And Lamian asked her nothing further. They seemed to have said everything that might be of interest to each other.

The woman sighed and picked up the photographs from the table, then reached for the death certificate. Lamian removed his hand from it. The bare table seemed to remind her of her duties as hostess, because she asked, "Would you like a cup of coffee?"

He refused, not wanting to put her to any trouble, but her offer made him think of smoking.

"If you don't mind, I'll have a cigarette."

She said amiably, "Go ahead. I'll get an ashtray."

She rose and went out. There was banging in the other room again, and she returned with a glass ashtray as spotless as if it had been just washed. She sat down facing him. He lit up, began to smoke, asked her a few incidental questions about the house—Was it hers? Did she live alone?—to which he received affirmative answers, as expected. When he put out his cigarette, she took the ashtray containing the butt and stood up.

"I ought to go shopping now," she said.

Lamian also stood up and turned to get his hat. Noticing his movement, she went around the table, lifted his hat from the stool, and handed it to him. He took it and remained standing in front of her, with a feeling of disappointment that he had to leave so soon.

"Well," she said, putting out her hand.

He was holding the hat in his right hand, and started to transfer it to the left, but a pain cut across his stomach and he broke into a sweat, lost his balance, dropped the hat, and had to brace himself on the chair, which squeaked under his weight. He began to tremble, to shake uncontrollably, as if he were out in snow and wind.

"Are you ill?" said the woman fearfully, drawing back.

He tried to wave off her question, or answer her, but he was unable to control either hands or tongue.

"Can I get you anything? Should I call a doctor?" she asked. He was unable to answer, or even to make a gesture to refuse her offer, but she seemed to understand him anyway. "Sit down, then," she said, helping him lower himself into the chair. She bent over him. "I'll get my coat."

She straightened up, went out, occupied herself with something behind his back, though he could hardly hear anything over the chattering of his teeth and the rattling of the chair that supported him. Then she reappeared and went around the table in the same gray coat she wore the day before and with a leather shopping bag in her hands, which were clasped under her stomach. "Can you come with me? I'll take you to the clinic. It's right around the corner from here."

He looked at her in the hope of telling her not to hurry him, and again she understood. "All right, then. Stay here until I get back." She looked around. "Would you like to lie down awhile? There's a couch in the bedroom." She pointed behind her, looking at him questioningly. This time he managed to shake his head. "All right, then, I'm going. You rest."

She went out. He could no longer hear her, but he knew that she was leaving and that he could stay, and for the moment that was all that mattered.

The cold made him tremble a few more times, at intervals, then ceased. He sat bathed in sweat, and felt gradually warmer, the warmth starting from his back and spreading down and up at the same time, through his breastbone toward his neck and head.

He slumped back in the chair. Catching sight of his hat on the floor, he picked it up and put it on the table. Then changed his mind and with a great effort stood up and took it and put it on the stool. He straightened; even his stomach no longer hurt.

He took out a cigarette, lit it, and looked around. The doors behind him stood open, and through them he could see furniture, in shadow because the door to the farther room was closed. The woman had no doubt closed it before she left, perhaps even locking it; after all, she had left a strange man in her house; she would at least have secured the room where she kept her money.

Which meant that the farther room was hers, and that the nearer one, windowless and dark, had been Helena Lifka's after she moved in with her cousin, until she died. Though it could have been the other way around, her cousin changing the rooms after her death.

It made little difference. The whole house was neglected; every room in it smelled of old things and the old bodies that had lived among them, lived with their painful memories of terror and violence.

But to him it seemed a paradise, or a part of paradise, because he was able to stay there. For a time. He knew that later he would have to leave, because Helena Lifka's cousin would return from shopping, and when she found him recovered, she would expect him to go. And he would have to obey her, because it was her house, not his.

Yet every part of him cried out to stay. Outside there was horror, desolation, an icy whirlwind that pierced him to the marrow of his bones. Only here was he safe, hidden, even if only for a short time, until the next moment, just as he had been safe in the toolshed at Auschwitz, the windows covered with boards and rags as he listened to the camp's waterfall babble of death rattles and prayers and danced to frighten a prisoner named Helena Lifka.

AFTERWORD

THE AUSTRALIAN WRITER CLIVE JAMES LIKED TO RECOUNT that when he first arrived in Britain, in the 1960s, a feature of conversation among some of the morally serious people he soon came to know was to anguish over the question of what one would have done had one been an inmate in a Nazi concentration camp. For James, always the skeptic, that was tragic, terrifying... and obvious. The truly challenging moral question, he believed, was not what one would have done had one been a prisoner but what one might have done had one had the choices denied to the victims: in other words, what one would have done had one been a guard or, perhaps worse still, a Kapo, that is, one of those prisoners in the camps who in return for supervising and usually atrociously brutalizing their fellow prisoners received all sorts of privileges from the SS men who controlled the camps, first and foremost the greatest privilege in the universe of the Nazi death camps: the chance to survive.

Being a Kapo, no matter how privileged this made one in Auschwitz, Buchenwald, or Jasenovac, offered no guarantees: the German guards could revoke a Kapo's status on the merest and meanest of whims. But while this fate indeed did befall some Kapos, most survived, whereas almost everyone else did not. After that, though, their fates were as varied as their itineraries. Some, notably those who made their way to Palestine in the immediate aftermath of the liberation of the camps, risked being recognized by former prisoners and killed. Predictably, there were also cases of mistaken identity. In one celebrated incident in Tel Aviv in 1946, a man named Asher Berlin was set upon in an alley by a group of men who thought they recognized him as a Jewish collaborator with the Gestapo. In reality, the unfortunate Berlin had not set foot in Europe since immigrating to Mandatory Palestine in 1924. In 1950, the year after the foundation of the state, the Israeli parliament passed the Nazi and Nazi Collaborators Punishment Law that in practical terms—this was eleven years before the kidnapping, trial, and execution of Adolf Eichmann, the only Nazi actually judged under this statute—was aimed at former Kapos and at leaders of the so-called Judenräte, the Jewish Councils that administered the ghettos of Eastern Europe before the Nazis finally deported all their inhabitants to the concentration camps.

These trials went on for twenty-two years. In retrospect, even in the initial two years after the law came into force, former Kapos were judged severely, but with only a few exceptions their actual prison terms rarely exceeded five years, and only one death sentence, to a Kapo called Yehezkel Jungster, was ever meted out, and it was eventually commuted. As the trials continued, the official view softened, and the Israeli judiciary passed from largely assuming the accused were guilty and should have behaved differently through to viewing those who had been Kapos as having had no choice but to act as they did. In this, as the Israeli academic Dan Porat noted in a brilliant account of these trials, the judges' stance, contra Hannah Arendt's severities toward the Kapos and the Judenräte in her book *Eichmann in Jerusalem*, came surprisingly close to that of Primo Levi, who wrote that he believed that "no one is authorized to judge them, not those who lived through the experience of the [camps] and even less those who did not." The great Hungarian novelist Imre Kertész, himself a survivor of Auschwitz and Buchenwald, put the question even more starkly when, in 2002, shortly after winning the Nobel Prize in Literature, he told an interviewer that "Europe's 20th-century totalitarianisms created a completely new type of human being. They forced a person to choose in a way we were never forced to choose before: to become either a victim or a perpetrator."

But it is one thing to follow Levi in feeling that one has no right to judge a Kapo and quite another to try to inhabit a Kapo's mind and heart. And yet this is the project of the Yugoslav writer Aleksandar Tišma's extraordinary novel, titled, quite simply, *Kapo*. As far as I know, with the exception of Bernhard Schlink's 1995 novel *The Reader*, in which one of the two principal protagonists, Hanna Schmitz, had been a German camp guard, *Kapo* is the only major literary novel to have a perpetrator rather than a victim as a main character. But even Schlink's novel is told not from the camp guard's perspective but rather from that of the adolescent German boy who becomes her lover, and later, after she is condemned to a long prison sentence by a postwar German court, her one faithful friend and visitor. When it was published, Schlink's book was widely praised for what admirers of the novel perceived as its attempt to dramatize the process of both confrontation and reconciliation with Germany's atrocious past (in German, this project goes under the ungainly name of *Vergangenheitsbewältigung*, which literally means addressing the past, addressing history). But Schlink was also severely criticized for what one writer, Jeremy Adler, called his "art of generating compassion for murderers." The great Israeli historian Omer Bartov went further, excoriating it for what he asserted was *The Reader*'s implicit message of "Germany as victim." And a German journalist, Willi Winkler, reviewing the novel in the *Süddeutsche Zeitung*, dismissed it as "Holokitsch."

This last charge seems to me unfair, and as a characterization more appropriately applied to *Schindler's List* than to *The Reader*. But in fairness both to Schlink's novel and to Steven Spielberg's film, the ethical imperative of piety that the Holocaust demands of us individually as human beings and collectively as societies has translated badly into evocations of its horror in novels and films, very few of which succeed in keeping kitsch at bay, especially in the sense Milan Kundera put forward when he insisted that kitsch actually "moves us to tears of compassion for ourselves, for the banality of what we think and feel." In contrast, Tišma's Holocaust trilogy, *The Book of Blam*, *The Use of Man*, and *Kapo*, is an antidote to banality and kitsch, not a purveyor of it. Not as well known, at least outside the former Yugoslavia, as Kertész's four Holocaust novels—*Fatelessness, Fiasco, Kaddish for an Unborn Child*, and *Liquidation*—Tišma's novels richly deserve to occupy an adjoining place in any literary Parnassus worthy of the name.

Interestingly, Tišma translated *Fatelessness* into Serbo-Croatian and helped arrange its publication in Yugoslavia, doing this long before Kertész was all that known even within Hungary, let alone internationally. Surely it is not entirely fanciful to speculate that in this, like was crying out to like. Whatever the merits of such speculation, and without falling into the snare of witless rankings, I myself am in no doubt that both sets of novels complement each other. In Kertész, the personal autobiographical dimension is undeniable, even if he always insisted that those who believed his novels were autobiographical were guilty of badly misreading him, and that his "proper place [was] at the writing desk, not in the story." What Kertész meant by this, I think, was that young Gyuri Köves, who undergoes Auschwitz and Buchenwald in *Fatelessness*, and returns home to Hungary to find it under Soviet occupation in *Fiasco*, is an alter ego rather than a simple fictional flag of convenience for himself. Philip Roth made similar arguments about the eponymous main character of his Zuckerman trilogy, and in both Kertész's and Roth's cases, it seems to me that there is simultaneously an element of truth and an element of willful denial in the claim, in short the novelist's resonant admonition: caveat lector. And like the path of Roth's Zuckerman novels, from *The Anatomy Lesson* to *The Counterlife*, Kertész's path from *Fatelessness* to *Liquidation* is one of narrative certainty to an almost literary Heisenbergianism, an insistence on the unreliability of everything.

Tišma's view of his own work was the exact opposite of Kertész's. He believed everything he wrote was autobiographical. And yet it was Kertész who had been a prisoner in Auschwitz and Buchenwald, whereas Tišma, born in 1924 in the Yugoslav province of Vojvodina in the town of Horgoš on the Hungarian border to a Hungarian-speaking

Jewish mother and an ethnic Serbian father, along with his parents, survived the war and even managed to finish his studies in Budapest before the city was taken by the Soviet army in 1944. Tišma and his family only survived because they were saved on several occasions by Gentile neighbors, and because they managed to get out of Vojvodina's capital, Novi Sad, in very early 1942, just before a wholesale massacre of most of the city's Jews on January 20–23, 1942, at least 1,400 of whom were shot and then pushed into the Danube, where those who were still alive drowned. In *The Book of Blam*, the first of Tišma's Holocaust novels, and the book that made his reputation in Yugoslavia as a writer, the eponymous main character, Miroslav Blam, shares Tišma's same lucky escape, though in the book Blam is spared not because he flees Novi Sad in time but rather because he is married to a Christian and has converted to Christianity. In any case, Tišma himself saw neither the Novi Sad massacre nor Auschwitz. As he would later make clear, he had in fact largely repressed his memories of the Holocaust, and these really only were reawakened in him in 1960 after he had visited Auschwitz for the first time at the age of twenty-six, twelve years before he published *The Book of Blam*.

As a novel, *The Book of Blam* is a work of daunting harshness, a kind of retelling of the book of Job set in the midst of the Shoah. Like Job, Miroslav Blam is innocent, a survivor whose punishment for escaping death is the desolate loneliness of a Holocaust survivor lost in its aftermath. Blam is a man utterly possessed by visions of his friends, all of whom the Germans have murdered. Yet paradoxical as it may seem, at least Blam's blamelessness affords the reader a certain moral relief. In Tišma's second Holocaust novel, *The Use of Man*, the canvas is wider. It portrays a group of high school classmates and their destinies after the war begins. The book has its victim, the half-Jewish Vera, who is sent to a concentration camp; it has its hero, Vera's boyfriend, Milinko, who joins Tito's Partisans. It also has its antihero in Sredoje, another of Vera's classmates who becomes a Partisan. And it has its monster, Vera's cousin Sep, who becomes a Nazi. But Tišma does not

make Sep his main focus. To the contrary, if there is a principal protagonist, it is Vera herself. She survives the camps but when she returns
home finds, much like Blam, that she has nothing to return to. Both
characters have cheated death, but, having done so, discover that they
have also in a profound and non-hyperbolic sense spiritually survived
themselves.

Kertész was certainly an Argonaut of desolation, but compared to
Tišma he was almost cheerful. Impossible to imagine Tišma saying,
even in jest, what Kertész had affirmed when he remarked to a dumb-
founded interviewer and, as he then made clear, by no means in jest,
that he felt lucky to have been in Auschwitz. Reading Tišma and Kertész side by side, there is an inescapable sense that where Kertész
stopped, Tišma began. Indeed, it is difficult to think of any other
writer who could deploy the psychological and moral harshness native
to Tišma's literary project. "No man can stare for long at death or the
sun," La Rochefoucauld famously said. But Tišma's work challenges
that conviction in ways that have few equivalents in world literature.
Such unremitting pessimism of the earned rather than the unearned
sort is a rarity in great literature, which is something that perhaps we
as readers should be grateful for. With Tišma, there is nothing ludic;
his is a world beyond pleasure, beyond distraction. And if this highly
reticent writer has a message, it is that even if one manages to escape
through the gates of hell, it is only to discover that another hell awaits
one outside. It is peace as moral anticlimax, and of terrors and sorrows
that peace cannot begin to relieve. Indeed, the only writer of similar
implacable harshness who comes to mind—and the irony is so extreme
as to be morally obscene, even if accurate just the same—is the fascist
Céline, and even then only in his most disgust-laden evocations of the
sordidness and cruelty of abject poverty. And *Kapo* is by far the harsh-
est of Tišma's three Holocaust novels.

In *Kapo*, we are unremittingly in hell's ninth circle. Abandon hope
all ye who enter here? To which Tišma's reply might as well be: Hope?
You might as well be talking about unicorns. Blam in *The Book of*

Blam, Vera in *The Use of Man*—these characters are victims. But as desolate as their lives are, they are not trying to survive at any cost. To the contrary, it is clear in both novels that it is this, in Tišma's eyes, that constitutes their irreducible dignity: They see no great reason to go on, but they go on just the same. In *Kapo*, though, the reader enters a world without any dignity at all. Instead, its focus is on Lamian, a former Kapo who survived the war and returned to his native city of Banja Luka in northern Bosnia, but who lives in terror of having his past as a Kapo revealed. The premise will likely shock and at first alienate any reader who comes to *Kapo* unprepared, much as it would shock and alienate to read a novel about Eichmann in Argentina told exclusively from Eichmann's point of view, however harshly and unsympathetically. *Kapo* is not, in other words, a story of crime and punishment. Tišma is no Dostoyevsky and Lamian is certainly no Raskolnikov. He has not an ounce of guilt or, indeed, of any feeling for anyone except himself. Like Blam and Vera, Lamian is obsessed with the past, or more precisely, seems to find the past more alive than the present. But unlike Blam and Vera—for whom the present is a desolate space filled with ghosts they wish they could bring back to life, even though of course they know that they have no hope of doing so—Lamian's terror of ghosts is rooted in the mortal fear that his past as a Kapo, and as a traitor to the Jews, finally will be revealed.

Lamian has a job but keeps to himself, constantly watchful, consumed by the wish to live and to remain unaccountable for the crimes he committed as a Kapo, the rapes and every imaginable form of brutality about which he reminisces constantly, disgustingly. But as the novel begins, it is clear that Lamian had believed his secret would never be uncovered. Then, completely by happenstance, he discovers that Helena Lifka, one of the women he dragged into his lair, a toolshed in a remote corner of the concentration camp, and raped, had been a Yugoslav Jew just like Lamian himself—something he had not known in the camp. Could she have returned to Banja Luka? Will she denounce him? "She would reveal the beast he was," Lamian thinks, "[a] fiend, torturer, one of Hitler's Kapos, archenemy and archtraitor hidden in his lair in the guise of a meek citizen who kept to himself." And his fate will be terrible: Vengeful survivors, he thinks, will "spit on me, seize me, hurl me to the ground and trample on me, beat me until I'm half dead . . . then . . . they'll nurse me back to health so I can be dragged before the court, before the people, exhibited as a monster . . . my name a symbol of evil"—and here, Tišma's bottomless pessimism finds its way into the mouth of his protagonist—"until some greater criminal is discovered."

At moments, Lamian thinks that he will ask Helena Lifka's forgiveness, but as Tišma portrays Lamian, when his thoughts move in that direction, what he really wants is to forestall her revenge. Then, just as he had feared, Lamian thinks he sees her in the street. She is old, stooped, decrepit, but, he thinks, very much alive. And for the rest of the novel, Tišma takes the reader backward and forward in time: Lamian becoming a Kapo; the women he abuses and rapes; his relationship with Riegler, one of the German guards who has the power over him that Lamian has over the prisoners; and Riegler's and Lamian's escape as Germany's defeat looms. His hysteria mounting, Lamian sets out to track Helena Lifka down, and toward the end of the novel believes he has found her, living in an apartment in Zagreb. Mustering all the courage he has left, Lamian goes to her flat to at last reveal to her his real identity.

But instead of resolution, Lamian finds the bitterest and most unsettling of anticlimaxes. The woman who has opened the door is not Helena Lifka but Julia Milčec, a cousin. Helena Lifka, Julia tells Lamian, had lived in the flat but had died several months earlier—horribly, she adds, of cancer. And Julia herself had never been in Auschwitz or any other camp. At first, he does not believe her. "We know each other from Auschwitz," he insists. "You remember Kapo Furfa? . . . [the] Kapo of the workshop. Well, that's me." But confronted by her steadfast denials, Lamian eventually realizes that Julia is telling him the truth. He is beside himself, and at the same time at the end of his tether, obsessed with the fact that when he had started his quest for Helena Lifka she had still been alive. And yet he finds he can't get up from his chair in what had been Helena Lifka's sitting room, the place where she had lived with the ghosts of her family, every one of whom was killed in the camps, as Julia tells Lamian. Julia sees his distress, and tells him that she must go out but that he can stay for a while, an offer he gratefully accepts. And after she leaves, he finds himself even more rooted to the spot. He knows he will soon be asked to leave, but "every part of him cried out to stay." And then Tišma ends his novel in a few terrifying sentences. "Only here was he safe," Lamian realizes, "just as he had been safe in the toolshed at Auschwitz, the windows covered with boards and rags as he listened to the camp's waterfall babble of death rattles and prayers and danced to frighten a prisoner named Helena Lifka."

I know of no work in European literature that is so unrelenting in its despair. Tišma offers no hope, no consolation. In 1949, on his return from a long exile in the United States to a Germany in ruins, Theodor Adorno said, "To write poetry after Auschwitz is barbaric." Taxed by an interviewer in the early 1960s who pointed out that German poetry had revived and flourished in the intervening years, Adorno replied that yes, it seemed poetry could be written after Auschwitz. But, he added, the question was whether life could be lived after Auschwitz. That is Tišma's question. It should be ours as well.

—DAVID RIEFF

OTHER NEW YORK REVIEW CLASSICS

For a complete list of titles, visit www.nyrb.com.